THE NARROWS

James Brogden

snowbooks

Proudly Published by Snowbooks in 2012

Copyright © 2012 James Brogden

James Brogden asserts the moral right to
be identified as the author of this work.
All rights reserved.

Snowbooks Ltd.
Tel: 0207 837 6482
email: info@snowbooks.com
www.snowbooks.com

British Library Cataloguing in Publication Data
A catalogue record for this book is available from the British
Library.

978-1907777-59-2

*To Mum and Dad, who filled my head with stories,
and my wife and daughters, who inspire them.*

PROLOGUE

PC Andrew 'Rosey' Penrose swung the thirty-five pound cast-iron battering ram nicknamed Big Eddie at the door of 144 Tyler Road. It shuddered but held firm, jarring his arms and rattling his teeth in their sockets, and for precious seconds he did little else except gawp in stupid surprise.

Even fresh out of training, Rosey was not a small man – as his colleagues often observed, he was built like the proverbial brick shit-house – which was why he'd been given the enforcer to wield. An average methods-of-entry officer would get three cracks before handing it over to fresh arms, but Rosey had never taken more than one. Ever.

At the time, those funny rune-like scratches in the paint – the ones that looked a bit like a spoked wheel – couldn't possibly have had anything to do with it. Obviously this door was just a lot more heavily barricaded than anybody had expected.

At the time. Looking back on the nightmare later, he would come to wonder at the world of guilt and recrimination in those three simple words.

Then the DI was screaming at him to get his head out of his arse and open that bloody door *now!* and he swung again. It still wouldn't budge, and with a sick feeling of failure he knew that there was no chance of taking the bastards by surprise;

every second they were at more and more of an advantage. Christ alone knew what they were doing to that poor kid. With a snarl of frustration he gave Big Eddie one more almighty heave, which obliterated the spoked wheel rune completely, and the door smashed open hard enough to bury its latch-box in the wall behind, spraying shards of wood into the dim hallway.

What followed was a barely controlled chaos of shoving uniforms and booted feet thundering into the house. There was crashing and yelling, and the DI actually shouting 'Go! Go! Go!' like he thought he was in a detective show.

Rosey let them go ahead, handing Big Eddie to the last bloke along – it stung his pride, but rules were rules. Three strikes and you're out. He flicked out his baton and went to support the door-opening officers, but he couldn't resist taking a moment to see, as a matter of professional curiosity, what had made the door so hard. He couldn't find anything. No steel plates, no bars, not even, as far as he could see, a simple chain. His Nan could have knocked it down.

He shrugged it off. There was the ever-so-slightly more important business of finding the kid and the perverts who had abducted him, especially before they had the chance to do anything worse, thanks to his balls-up. However, in those few seconds the first rush of uniforms had passed him by, and for a moment he found himself alone in the hall.

Opposite him was a closed door that hadn't been there before.

At least, he didn't think it had; things had been a bit confusing. It wouldn't have been out of place, anyway. The house was a bog-standard two-up-two-down; he'd grown up in one – all of his mates had grown up in them – and he could have mapped the place blindfolded. The door opposite should have led into a small front bedroom with a window overlooking the street.

But in that case, how had everybody else charged straight past and missed it? His colleagues were further in the house and upstairs, storming through the living room and bedrooms.

'Hey!' he yelled forward. 'There's a room here!'

By rights he should have waited for a second body to join him, because rules were rules, but he was buggered if he was going to be yelled at again, and he opened it himself.

Instead of finding himself in a small front room, he was in another hallway. This one stretched *ahead* of him, at right angles to the entry hall and into where the next door should have been, completely against the direction the house should naturally have taken.

He stopped, confused.

The sounds of policemen clumping around in the rest of the house seemed fainter now, as if they were a lot further away than they should have been. The strange hall stretched away, oddly dark in spite of how close the open front door and daylight were, as if the shadows had taken refuge here, lurking in the corners. It was like one of those funfair rooms painted in forced perspective, where at one end you were a dwarf and at the other end a giant, but that was where the similarities with funfairs ended. Wallpaper hung in decaying strips, peeling away from plaster stained with damp and mould.

There was something terribly wrong in this place.

Abruptly, his personal radio squawked into life, making him jump. The reception was fuzzy, punctuated heavily with static: '...enrose... the bloody hell *are* you? ...at once... hear me?'

He snatched it up. 'Sir! I'm downstairs, sir. There's something very odd here. Do you read me, sir? Over.'

Nothing in reply. Just blind, stupid white noise.

And the sound of a small child crying.

Years later, when he tried to describe what really happened – instead of the sanitised version which ended up in his official report – he found that he had little detailed recollection of searching the house, just a hazy and disturbing sense that whatever was there had been too large for the physical confines of the building. A nagging, itching memory of rooms, hallways, staircases, and galleries folding open and around themselves in tortured, impossible geometries.

He understood that this sort of selective amnesia was his mind's way of protecting itself – that if he pushed to remember exactly what the house had been like, he'd be carried off into its own peculiar insanity. Traces of it clung to his senses like the smell of burning on clothes; occasionally if he walked into a strange room he'd still get the sensation that the walls and corners were hiding behind each other and that in the split second before he'd opened the door they'd hurriedly reordered themselves like secretive, grinning children.

He followed the sound of crying through twisted rooms until he came to something like a child's bedroom; it had a scattering of plastic toys, brightly coloured and pathetic against the bare floorboards. The smell of stale incense was pungent in the air, and the amber glow of a nightlight from one corner threw crawling shadows towards him. Hanging from the ceiling was a brass mobile of spoked concentric rings which rotated through each other in a way that hurt his mind more than everything else about the house so far – everything, that was, except for what was happening to the four-year old boy on the bed at the far side of the room.

He was lying face up in the yellow glow, half-naked and spread-eagled on a grubby Transformers duvet, and crying with the dry grizzling sobs of a child near the point of exhaustion. One of his two kidnappers knelt by the side of the bed, his face bathed in fevered light.

It looked for all the world as though he were praying or performing some macabre laying-on of hands, but Rosey never found out for sure, because when he realised where the light was actually coming from he lost it completely. He charged at the kneeling figure, even though it was like running across the deck of a pitching ship, and the other man barely had time to look up in surprise before he had been grabbed by the throat and thrown into the wall.

'Where's your mate?' Rosey shouted into his face. *What the fuck is going on here?*' The kidnapper – or worshipper – was a lanky man wearing an old-fashioned and filthy trenchcoat. Retching for breath, he seemed to be trying to explain something, though all he could do in reply was hold up in one long-fingered hand a cluster of slender needles, as if that were meant to be reassuring.

The boy bristled from the crown of his head to the soles of his feet with a forest of acupuncture needles, and where they pierced his skin it glowed as if from within; what Rosey had taken to be a nightlight was in fact the coalescent radiance of these thousands of pinprick stars. A galaxy of constellations in the flesh, radiating a blast-furnace heat. Appalled, he dropped the trenchcoated man in a boneless heap and moved to start plucking them out.

Trenchcoat clutched at his ankles. 'No!' he wheezed. 'You mustn't! Not the right *way*! …must be done *properly*…' but Rosey paid him no more attention than to plant a police-issue size-ten shoe square in his chest and send him sprawling.

As he pulled out the first of the needles, the boy twitched and cried out, and something like a jolt of electricity shot up Rosey's arm. 'Sweet Leaping Jesus,' he muttered. 'The bastards have wired him up.'

'…disastrous… consequences…' wheezed Trenchcoat.

Rosey, steeling himself for further shocks and sweating profusely in the unnatural heat, ignored him and proceeded to yank out the rest of the needles in great handfuls.

By the time he'd finished, the room was dark and silent except for the exhausted whimpers of the child, the wheezes of a half-throttled man, and his own horrified panting. Whether it was coincidence or because of his actions, the house seemed to drop its defences at that point, and seconds later a small army of uniformed police barged yelling into the room.

PART 1: CITY

1

DEAD NETTLES

Andy Sumner tried to take his mind off the knot of cold panic growing in the pit of his stomach by studying the posters in the travel clinic's waiting room.

Do You Know your Hep A from your Hep B?

We cannot immunise against the desire to wear socks with sandals. That one was actually pretty funny.

Malaria Hot-Spots, a map of the globe on which all of the countries where one could get malaria were coloured a bright, arterial red. Looming over it was a large pop-out mosquito, all spindly legs and grotesquely hunched back, the hungry needle of its mouth-parts ready to plunge into unprotected human flesh.

Nope, not helping. The panic grew bigger, threatening to barrel its way up through his throat and out into the world.

'You okay, hon?' Laura was looking at him with concern darkening her eyes.

'I'm fine, I'm good, I'm good,' he lied and sat back down beside her. He picked up a dog-eared copy of *Boat and Home* and flipped through the pages without reading anything. 'I mean, talk about rubbing it in. Do doctors actually think sick people want to read this stuff?' Without looking up he could tell that she was regarding him with that particular female expression of bemused patience which said that she loved him even though at this moment he was acting worse than a child.

'Is it the needle thing?' she asked.

'Oh, you know, just a bit. But I said I'd be okay, didn't I?'

Just a bit. He was certain that it wasn't a fully fledged phobia; by his understanding a phobia was an irrational overreaction to something, and he wasn't convinced that it was irrational to dislike having sharp bits of metal stuck into you. She'd even helpfully looked it up for him – *belenophobia: fear of pins and needles.* Thanks, darling.

Yes, he'd said that he would be okay, but what he'd actually done was completely fail to realise exactly where it was she'd booked the honeymoon until it was too late, or that a series of jabs was going to be necessary to get him there. Not that he felt he could be blamed very much – as far as weddings went, the received wisdom was to just let Her and Her Mother sort everything out, as long as you were smartly dressed and mostly conscious for the photographs. But Cuba was booked now. Had been for three months. More than just booked, in fact: she'd already bought a new swimsuit, and it was still only November. It was *that* booked. There was absolutely no way he was going to be allowed to back out of this now.

Dear Christ, what was he doing here?

The practice nurse popped her head around the door with a breezy smile and said 'Like to come in?'

Her room was small, with just enough room for a desk, something which looked promisingly to Andy like a minibar fridge, and a narrow hospital-style bed upon which he and Laura perched as she bustled around cheerfully and took their medical histories. Laura knew everything about hers and had even brought certificates to prove it. Andy, for his part, remembered one time when he'd put his hand through the kitchen window and had stitches, but couldn't recall whether or not there had been any injections. As far as he knew he was inoculated against precisely nothing.

'Lovely!' smiled the nurse. 'A clean slate. I'm afraid you're going to be a bit of a pincushion by the end of this, my dear.'

The 'needle thing'. Oh yes, just a bit.

Nurse Barton was friendly and professional, chatting with Laura about the wedding plans and how romantic it was that they were even coming to get their jabs at the same time. She dealt efficiently with the paperwork and turned to remove from the minibar fridge a pair of simple, one-shot, disposable syringes, which, to his surprise, were smaller than biros, rather than the savage medieval instruments of torture he'd imagined.

Didn't matter. He still wasn't going to trust them.

'We'll get the first of your Hep B's out of the way to begin with,' she said, 'and book you in for the second in a month, and then we can get you up to date with your tetanus at the same time.'

'That sounds great,' he said with a tight, wide smile.

'Lovely, then. Let's take care of the bride first while the groom gets his shirt off.'

Laura, as prepared as ever, had dressed in a sleeveless vest top which kept her shoulders bare, whereas Andy had come straight from work in his shop uniform – shirt and tie and name-badge clattering *(Hi! I'm Andrew. Welcome to the Games Barn!)* and he started to untuck himself as Nurse Barton approached Laura with the first syringe.

Laura looked back at him over her shoulder, dark hair tumbling down her back, and tipped him a saucy wink like one of those Vargas girls painted on the noses of World War Two bombers. It might have been that which caught his breath, or it could have been the sight of the needle's tip dimpling her flesh that did it.

'Little scratch…' said Nurse Barton, and the dimple disappeared as the needle broke the skin. A swift, sure plunge of her thumb, a small *squish* noise as the syringe's contents were injected, and that was that. A single ruby-red drop of blood marked the spot, and Nurse Barton taped a wad of cotton-wool over it. Laura had watched the whole thing, fascinated.

Andy suddenly found the room to be hot, stuffy, and claustrophobically cramped. Blood was thumping heavily in his head.

'Next one. You don't have to look if you don't want to.'

'Andy?' said Laura, serious now. 'Just stay looking at me, okay? Seriously, you cannot feel a thing. You're going to be completely fine.'

For a few moments he even managed to convince himself that this was true. It *was* going to be completely fine. How many of these were done across the country, every day? Millions, probably. *Babies* had them, for heaven's sake. It was one of the safest, most routine medical procedures…

'Little scratch…'

…and then all he could see were mosquitoes the size of locusts swarming over his arm, feeding, feeding.

The needle's tip dimpled his shoulder.

Andy's recollection of what happened after that was not one-hundred percent reliable, because although he didn't technically faint, he did, according to one paramedic who attended the scene, 'grey out' for a while. He was aware of a sudden loud bang close by, like a large firecracker going off, and the sudden splash of something hot and wet against his arm.

Plus, of course, the screaming.

Laura was sitting on the other side of him from Nurse Barton and so didn't see exactly what happened to the woman's right hand, nor could she help the police later in figuring out how the syringe had exploded so violently as to tear off most of her thumb and first two fingers. This was only a bit less surprising than the fact that Andy, other than being covered in the woman's blood, remained completely unharmed – not so much as a pinprick from the needle.

Because his memory of this was so fuzzy, Andy kept to himself the impression – which was surely just his imagination, even though it had felt so real – that far from having anything injected into his shoulder, something furious had lashed *out* of it.

***

It was always a relief for Andy to get out of the shop, even if it was on one of Laura's endless list of wedding-related errands.

Birmingham city centre on this particular bright, midwinter lunchtime held an odd kind of stillness. The flat, white, directionless light of winter filled the gaps between each building as the city rested from itself, taking a breather from the summer months when everything was so hot and sweaty and rushed that it all seemed to blur together at the edges. The cold made everything draw tighter into itself, to huddle down into the very essence of its own existence – every bin, lamppost, pigeon, or pedestrian – even the individual bricks and the cracks or straggling weeds between them, so that it seemed a miracle that they didn't just crumble apart, frozen.

The incident at the travel clinic had been such a randomly violent intrusion into Andy and Laura's otherwise ordered and sensible lives that it was simply a lot easier to draw a line under it as one of those bizarre and tragic events which sometimes struck like lightning, and just get on with things. It dampened Laura's enthusiasm over the wedding preparations for almost a week before her sense of urgency renewed itself, and he was sent out on his errand. From his point of view it made more sense to worry about making arrangements for Christmas, never mind next summer, but there it was. A Mission was a Mission.

He could have caught the bus, but walking somehow made everything more real. In fact, there was no reason he couldn't have done this every lunchtime – except that he never did. He wandered out for ten minutes, bought something slathered in mayonnaise from the nearest Pret-a-Manger, went back to the shop-floor and got on with more work – though if anybody happened by he made sure that he was doing something far cooler, like updating his Facebook status or surfing for porn.

He remembered watching one of those *How-Foul-is-Your-Workplace*-style programmes where a small bespectacled Scottish woman had taken swabs from some poor sod's computer keyboard and proceeded to demonstrate the wide variety of spectacularly gut-squittering bacterial flora and fauna where he ate his lunch every day. As if that were the point. What did Andy's head in was the fact that *that was what this guy did,* every single day. Rain or shine. Never even took a break – because what would have been the point? He didn't even smoke.

Ordinarily that was exactly where Andy would have been too, slogging through invoices and emails and playing gastronomic Russian Roulette with his own keyboard – except that today was different. This time he had a reason to get out into the real world. This time he had a Mission.

Marinated vine leaves.

This, as Laura's tone had made clear, was a serious business, and not one to be shirked or taken lightly. A dinner party for their parents – a *proper* dinner party, one which would celebrate their engagement as a transition to a more mature and sophisticated stage of life (*Dear god,* he'd thought, *I think I've just been compared to a pupating caterpillar.*) – required actual food – *dolmades,* to be precise – the preparation of which would at no stage involve reheating anything from the freezer or use of their phone's speed dial. And absolutely no place for anything random.

Lost in such thoughts, he didn't realise how completely blocked the footpath was in front of him until he'd almost walked into a red-and-white striped scaffolding pole.

Workmen were busy in a deep trench which ran the length of a new office development. The sign propped across the pavement, barring his way, requested him politely to use the other side of the road, even though the road in question was a section of the Smallbrook Queensway: three lanes of fast-moving traffic in either direction and a four-foot concrete barrier between.

He briefly considered climbing over the pedestrian railing to his left and skirting the edge of the scaffolding, but the traffic was roaring past so closely that he gave it up as tantamount to suicide. (*Wage slave kills self to avoid embarrassing dinner engagement; body found covered with marinated vine leaves.*) Sighing, he resigned himself to backtracking to the roundabout and taking the underpass, until he noticed the short cut.

Back past the construction site, between it and the corner of the next building, was a scrubby, litter-strewn strip of ground which couldn't even be dignified by calling it an alley. It was only a few feet wide – not at all surprising that he hadn't noticed it before – and he thought it should easily lead him back onto one of those little service streets that ran behind the pubs and nightclubs of John Bright Street. After which it was not much more than a spit and a jump to the Pallasades shopping centre, the Games Barn, and his invoices.

Congratulating himself on having found such a handy short cut, he stepped off the footpath, and the darkness of the alley's mouth swallowed him as if he'd never existed.

The first thing he noticed was that it was much less cold, which he put down to the insulating effect of the buildings on either side. The going was a lot rougher underfoot than he'd thought, too. What had at first seemed to be simply cracked pavement was little more than broken chunks of concrete. The dead, dry-yellow stems of old weeds rattled and hissed as he passed. His shoes were soon badly scuffed and his trouser-cuffs muddy. *And by the way,* said a small voice inside his head, *have you noticed how long this is taking?* Yes, but he told himself that it was because he was being forced to walk much more slowly than normal. He looked back towards the Queensway, thinking that this might not have been such a good idea after all.

Behind, traffic flicked past the alley's narrow entrance. Up ahead, the alley was choked by a screen of dead, black nettles, but beyond that it seemed to be lighter and more open.

That had to be John Bright Street. *Face it, you've still got a big detour if you go back. Plus, your shoes are already buggered anyway.* He pushed past the nettles and out into the street on the other side.

Except there was no street.

A wide expanse of overgrown waste ground stretched ahead of him: mounds of rubble thinly scabbed over with moss and wiry grass. A faint path twisted away into this humpbacked terrain, and far off (much further than he would have believed possible), ran an enclosing rampart of what looked like the corrugated iron roofs of factories or warehouses. He stopped, at a loss.

Alright, so he had miscalculated. Either the buildings between which he was walking weren't quite so wide as he thought, or this city block was bigger than it looked from the street. He wasn't a bloody chartered surveyor; how would he know?

Because something wasn't right here.

For no reason that he could imagine, his right shoulder – the place where Nurse Barton's needle had failed to stick him – suddenly began to throb with pins and needles. Absently, he rubbed it and turned back. No way was he heading out into that wasteland, to be mugged or worse.

The alley seemed darker and more cluttered than before, and there was no longer any glimpses of traffic at the far end. As a matter of fact, he couldn't hear any, either. At all. The blank white noise which sounded so much like the blood whispering in his ears late at night was absent, and in its place fell an absolute silence which was profoundly unsettling.

He checked in his coat pocket, took out the jar of marinated vine leaves and squinted at it, unimpressed. 'These dolmade things better be bloody worth it,' he muttered.

On top of this he now saw the straggling black stalks of dead nettles *ahead* of him, instead of behind, and his reassuring interior monologue died away in utter confusion. Obviously he'd somehow got himself muddled, probably with too much wool-gathering. Trying to ignore the voice in his head which was asking him how exactly one got muddled walking in a straight line from A to B, he carried on past the nettles to make certain, and, instead of the road, found himself facing the waste ground again.

It was much wilder than when he'd last seen it. The piles of rubble were now completely overgrown, some even supporting a scrubby undergrowth of small shrubs, and the roofs in the distance were more rusted and rent with holes.

'Right,' he decided. 'Um…'

He about-faced and marched back in the opposite direction – even though he was no longer entirely sure where that was supposed to lead him – determined at all costs not to run. He might be lost, might even be losing his mind, but he would absolutely not panic.

It was almost more than he could manage, because the alley was now so narrow that the walls scraped against his shoulders on either side and he was forced to shuffle crablike to avoid getting stuck, and when he saw the dead nettles impossibly ahead of him for the *third* time (*deadnettlesdeadnettlesdeadnettles,* his mind sang crazily. *Good name for a band, that.*) the panic burst free, and he ran, even though there was no room for him *to* run, and so he stumbled, tearing the knees out of his trousers and the skin off his palms, picked himself up and ran on until he broke out into the waste land again, wild-eyed and panting.

It was unrecognisable as the same place. The distant warehouses were little more than fire-ravaged ruins, their blackened rafters jutting brokenly at the sullen sky. The faint path which he'd noticed the first time was now a clearly defined and well-trodden track which led away into the undergrowth. Waist-high weeds and grass blanketed the rubble completely, punctuated with small thickets of bushes – their foliage green in defiance of the season. Andy suspected that wherever this was, it treated the seasons with the same casual indifference as it did several other fairly important laws of the universe, and this realisation, though he wouldn't appreciate it until much later, was the start of his acceptance of a wider reality which he had literally only just scratched the surface of. As if to confirm it, he looked back at the alley and saw that it had shrunk to barely a handspan's width.

And the silence. Around, between and under everything, the silence.

'Talk about random,' he said to himself, and he laughed a little, not liking how it sounded. He couldn't go back, because every time he went back it somehow became forward, even though that was plainly impossible. Not only that, it also became wilder – he wanted to say *deeper*, without knowing why. This left him with only one alternative, and he found that he really didn't want to see what was at the end of that trail. There could be anything down there. Anything at all.

He put his hand in his pocket and felt the smooth, sane glass jar of vine leaves. Suddenly, getting this thing back where it belonged became the most important thing in the world. He imagined the kitchen cupboard where he would put it, inside his normal kitchen, inside his normal flat – like that nursery rhyme about the 'dark dark house'. He started slowly forward, his heart thumping, and his eyes scanning every branch and shadow for threats.

After the panic and terror of finding this place, Andy thought that it was all a bit of an anticlimax in the end. The patch of waste ground turned out to be barely more than a few hundred yards wide. Of course, the path was uneven and twisted randomly around the overgrown rubble, but for all that he reached the other side surprisingly quickly. Nevertheless, it was a measure of how tightly strung his nerves were that when he heard traffic murmuring past in the near distance he sobbed aloud with relief. The burnt-out warehouses on either side marched steadily together and met ahead in a ramshackle gate of planks tagged with the inevitable graffiti.

He dragged it open and went out into the street on the other side.

At first glance everything seemed to be gloriously, blissfully normal. Pavement: check. Terraced houses: check. Stray cat being sick in a doorway: check. It was a typical, suburban Birmingham street, with bin-bags on the pavement and a blue and white number seventy-two bus rumbling along under a bright winter sky. His relief was so profound that for a long moment the reality of what he was seeing completely failed to sink in.

He was supposed to be in the city centre. There *were* no streets like this anywhere near where he should have been. There should be skyscrapers all around him, but he peered at the rooftops and couldn't even see the BT Tower.

In spite of the fact that his head felt like it had been screwed on backwards, his watch wasn't lying to him and it said that he'd taken less than five minutes to cross that waste ground. It had only been a few hundred yards across, not much more than a football pitch, and there was no way that he could be anywhere which looked like this. He wasn't at all sure where 'this' was, anyway. The number seventy-two bus coming towards him (Seventy-two? He didn't think he'd ever even *seen* one of those.), read 'Orchard Road to Lowes Hill via Borton Lane' – none of which he'd heard of either.

Andy's stumbling mind was very nearly at the limit of what it could cope with; he couldn't seem to hang on to his thoughts; they kept spiralling off in all directions like blind birds with too many wings. The only reason that the bus stopped for him at all was because he simply walked straight in front of it, dazed. He climbed aboard, paid his fare and sat down like an automaton as his brain twittered and flapped.

It was the maths of it which he couldn't straighten out – the whole distance-time thing. If he could just work it out, the *how* of where he'd gone wrong, everything would be okay. But the small ticking traitor on his wrist wasn't going to have any of it, and by the time he'd got back to work he knew he'd been beaten.

It had taken him two hours and three changes of bus to return from an outward journey of half-an-hour by foot. Somehow, in a way which hurt to think about, that little five-minute, football-pitch-long detour had skipped him five miles across the city, like a stone across a lake.

2
Bex

Bex of the Narrowfolk sat cross-legged on the roof of a derelict tower block and waited for the sun to set. From twelve storeys high, she had an unbroken view across most of Wolverhampton and the Black Country, even as far as the Shropshire countryside, which was a faded golden line at the very limit of sight. At the horizon lay a narrow band of clear sky, which was already beginning to colour in a sunset that didn't touch her, because here the city brooded under an unbroken expanse of ochre and grey.

'You ready to do this?' Dodd stood with his arms folded at the fire-escape door that led back towards the ground.

She shrugged. 'Meh. I think I'll give it a miss. Maybe go back home, let Mum's boyfriend knock me around a bit more.'

'Funny.'

'I'm a funny girl. Everybody says so.' All the same, she got to her feet and shrugged on the small rucksack which contained the entirety of her worldly possessions: a few clothes, her iPod, half a dozen chocolate bars and a huge permanent black marker for tagging her Walk. It was one of the conditions: aside from whatever personal demons you were fleeing, you were leaving behind a world of meaningless acquisition, and if you couldn't fit your life in a bag, there really wasn't much point trying to join the Narrowfolk. She huddled deeper into her coat as a light drizzle began to fall, and she turned back to regard the map one last time.

Spread out at her feet, the entire expanse of the rooftop was a multicoloured tracery of lines and squiggles, rendered in everything from spraypaint to chalk and probably even worse stuff that she didn't want to think about. Some were crisp and fresh, laid down barely days ago, while others had weathered the decades and faded into illegibility. The cumulative effect was almost three-dimensional – garish neon serpents and looped grey intestines twisted around each other in what at first seemed to be a haphazard mess, but which mapped routes through the night-time city taken along forgotten paths, overgrown vacant lots, alleyways, canal towpaths, and patches of wasteland. Punctuating the map like route numbers in a road atlas were the tags of those who had gone before – scribbled graffiti signatures in an alphabet which was taught in no classroom.

Unlike other cities, Birmingham hid its secrets in plain sight. It had neither subway nor skyscrapers – no roofscape to fly up into, no underworld to hide in. For those with nowhere else to go, the only way left to escape was sideways.

'Where do we live?' he asked.

She sighed with exaggerated heaviness. 'Do we really need to do this?'

'Yes we do. Where do we live?'

'I know the whole thing. You *know* I know it.'

'I know. We're going to do it anyway. Where do we live?'
It amazed her how Dodd remained calm in the face of her constant whinging. He was the best scavenger she had ever met, knew the Narrows like the back of his hand, and was the closest thing she had to either a brother or a father. Funny, given that he couldn't have been more than a few years older than she was. The rest of them could go to hell, but Dodd had shown more patience with her than any other human being, and if it meant that much to him, then she could go with that.

'It's just so bloody corny, that's all.' She sighed again. 'Okay. We live in the narrow places.'

'Where do we walk?'

'We walk where the skin of the world is thin.'

'What do we take?'

'Nothing that was not already lost. Blah-de-blah-de-blah. Happy?'

'Ecstatic. So now prove it: cross the city and get home without passing beneath a single lamppost. Tag your Walk; you will be watched, though you won't see those watching. I'll come with you, but I can't help. Make it by midnight, and you will be welcomed as one of the Narrowfolk.'

'Easy peasy, tits-a-squeezy.'

Dodd rubbed his eyes. 'Just sit on the roof, Bex, watch the sun set, and take your leave.'

'Like it says in the song,' she said, 'let's do it.'

So she sat, taking a good look around at the housing estates, the derelict factories and the blind concrete canyons of shopping centres. She felt the echoing weight of a dozen empty floors of burnt-out and pissed-in flats beneath her feet while the map glowed like the tattooed skull of a junkie. She huddled against the drizzle, watching as it faded into a meaningless scribble and the daylight bled from the grey roofs of the estates, and then made her goodbyes.

***

Andy yanked his tie to half-mast as the escalators carried him down from the Pallasades shopping centre to New Street Station. Usually he preferred to take the stairs, since that at least resembled exercise, but tonight it was simply easier to let himself be carried along, conveyer-belt style. Easier to shuffle along tiredly with the shopping-centre herds, through the unmanned ticket barrier (but you always bought one; you never knew), and descend to the platform. More stairs, down into the warm orange-brown smelling fug of diesel fumes and damp humanity.

The platform was crowded with late-night Christmas shoppers, even though it was still only mid-November, so he sat on a footrail, closed his eyes, and filled his lungs with it. The long exhalation felt like dissolving, and was strangely comforting. After the long evening shifts in particular, it was a relief to just let everything go and become another tired corpuscle in the city's old, slow heart. He barely heard when the tannoy announced his train's delay.

What he saw, when he opened his eyes again, was a small piece of graffiti on the polished white tiles of the pillar opposite him, framed between a briefcase and a backside the size of a small East European country.

It nagged at him. It reminded him of the graffiti that he had seen on the gate at today's weird shortcut. Somebody had cleaned it off as best they could, but a faint squiggly pink outline remained, floating just above the glaze of the tile, or perhaps more deeply within it. He supposed he must have seen these things thousands of times before: the tags of street kids on overpasses and the walls of corner shops, but this one almost made sense, as if the swirls and scrawls were coming close to resembling letters spelling out nonsense words he had nevertheless once understood.

Then Buttockistan shifted in front of him, and he decided he was simply zoning out with fatigue.

After a while, passengers began to shuffle and crane their necks like cattle scenting danger. The train screeched and ground its way up to the platform, black fumes roiling into the darkness where the ceiling should have been.

He climbed aboard as late as physically possible, so that when he found himself jammed in with a dozen other passengers in the standing-room-only space by the doors he was at least pressed up to one side rather than surrounded. Leaning his forehead against the curving glass of a door,

27

Andy closed his eyes and waited to be taken home. On the way out of Birmingham city centre, there were five tunnels which he could count with his eyes closed as the train passed through each one and the snarling of the engine altered pitch. Doppleganger effect, or something like that.

Halfway between the fourth and fifth, the train coughed and died, braking to a halt.

Vague exclamations of protest arose from the passengers. The man standing next to him – who was, incredibly, managing to do the Telegraph crossword in this dense crush of bodies – looked up from his paper, sighed, and continued to stare at it. Andy could almost read his thoughts. *No point in raising a fuss; it will sort itself out eventually. Just be patient.* Andy's nerves, on the other hand, were twitching with forced immobility and the sensation of his journey having been disturbed in the process of its predictability and order. He got out his phone and began to text Laura that he was going to be late.

The minutes were dragged kicking and screaming – or, more accurately, muttering vaguely about how they were going to have very firm words with Somebody about This Sort of Thing – into another hour.

***

Bex and Dodd fetched up with a crash against a wooden construction-site hoarding, gasping for breath in the shadows and barely able to stand. On the other side, high-arc security lighting blazed a blue-white nimbus into the drizzling air, but here there was nothing except straggling overgrowth and shadows.

'How can there be… so many… of them…?' wheezed Dodd, his words disappearing into the night like smoke. He slid painfully down the hoarding until he was sitting in the frosty, rubbish-strewn grass, and he groaned.

All Bex could do was toss the shredded mess of her clawed rucksack to the ground and spit a long gluey string of phlegm. Last time she'd run like this had been in PE class; her lungs were on fire, and her mouth felt like it was coated in rust. Then again, she'd never run like this in school – not from things like that.

'Dogs…' she managed. 'They've got fuckin' dogs, man…'

Dodd shook his head and coughed. Almost puked. 'Not dogs. You know what they are. Jesus, my *back*…'

She didn't know exactly when it was that they'd picked up her trail; how it was that she could have been so careless. She'd reached and tagged the checkpoints at Chinn and Roman stations in good time and had dipped into the Narrows to negotiate the city centre, crossing under Broad Street by a semi-collapsed subway which had been abandoned for years due to some typically messed-up piece of urban planning. She'd thought she'd heard something moving behind them at the time and hurried along, dismissing it as a dog or a junkie, and then they were out, and she'd given it no more thought until she'd passed Gas station and was making good time south along the cut of the main Worcester-Birmingham canal. Then she'd turned back and seen at least half a dozen dark shapes following her along the tow path. Less human than any junkie she'd ever known, and more dangerous than any feral dog.

Never once did it occur to her to take refuge in the open lighted spaces of the city. It was nothing to do with the rules of her Walk, just the simple reason that she had long since ceased to consider such places as safe. Having turned from the streetlights and embraced the city's dark and hidden heart, she found it impossible to imagine that her pursuers were more at home here than she. Until was too late.

But they weren't what really scared her, though – this was just nerve-ending stuff, adrenalin rush, fight-or-flight fever. In a weird way she almost liked it. No, what really made her heart stop in her throat was the long, wet smear that Dodd had left on the wood, black in the half-light.

'No way. That's bullshit. They never hunt together. Maybe they were, you know, apes or something. Escaped from the zoo.'

'Course they were, Bex, sure. Giant killer ape-dogs at Dudley Zoo. What were they thinking.' He hissed in pain again and slid sideways until he was lying on the ground.

'Come on, then, let's get you somewhere safer and have a look at you.' She clambered to her feet and got an arm under his shoulders, trying not to notice how slippery and warm they were, and dragged him several yards further along the hoarding until they found a large wooden gate which gave access to the site. It bore warnings of dire retribution to trespassers upon the property of Jerusalem Construction Services, several large safety notices (*Hard-hats Only Beyond This Point!*) and an extremely large padlock which looked as if it had been forged by a medieval blacksmith.

Bex propped Dodd up against the chipboard wall, took from inside her jacket the permanent marker and with quick, economical strokes tagged the gate. For a moment her sigil stood proud and clear against the raw pine, the perfume of evaporating toluene mixing with her steaming breath. Then the padlock opened with a snap and thudded into the damp earth.

She helped him through and dragged the gate shut, but she couldn't do anything about locking it again from this side, so she stumble-carried him across the construction site to its far side, where there were at least some concealing shadows.

The site was huge – not wide, but long, a frozen wasteland of concrete pits and steel beams which framed nothing but darkness. She knew that the other side, facing busy Broad Street, was all one brightly lit billboard, an architect's computer-generated panorama of flawless, gleaming towers inhabited by equally flawless, shining people. A Solution to the Problem of Urban Living in the Twenty-First Century, apparently. Beyond it, Friday evening nightclub crowds jostled and shouted above the thudding of half-a-dozen competing bass beats. Taxis growled, and footsteps click-clacked past on tottering heels barely yards from where Dodd lay, twisting and groaning in a pool of his own blood.

She knelt down beside him as he rolled painfully onto his front. In the patchy oblongs of streetlight, she could see that right between his shoulder blades the battered leather of his biker jacket had been laid open in twin rows of deep parallel slashes, and it was stuck to his flesh with gore from the wound beneath. It looked like he'd been mauled by a tiger. The leather and the cold looked to have staunched the worst of the bleeding, but it was spreading steadily enough for Bex to know that unless they made it to Moon Grove pretty sharpish, Dodd was, medically speaking, fucked.

He seemed to be getting his breath back but was trembling in a way which suggested that shock was getting its teeth more deeply into him than cold, exhaustion, or anything else. She didn't like it at all.

'Well?' he asked.

'It's just a scratch. You'll live.'

'No, man, my jacket. Jesus, get some priorities.'

She grinned. 'I don't know. I think its catwalk days are pretty much over.'

'Shit.'

The main problem was, with all the traffic noise, she couldn't hear a bloody thing. Coming this close to a major carriageway had been a gamble calculated to throw off pursuit, and for the moment it seemed to have worked. For how long – well, that was another question entirely. She might have been optimistic enough to hope that the chase had given up by now, if only there hadn't been so many of them.

Skavags.

A normal hunting pack of two or three was easy enough to avoid if you knew what you were doing, but this time there had been just so many. Dozens. It wasn't natural.

For a second, Bex toyed with the idea of dragging herself and Dodd out from underneath the billboard and trying to attract help, but she knew exactly what would happen: nothing. Nobody would help. No cars would stop, no passers-by would so much as ask them if they were alright, much less offer to help. The most attention they might get would be from the police, who would chalk it up to something gang-related and sling them both into a care home, where you couldn't even run from the things that wanted to eat you.

On the other side of the hoarding, drunken voices laughed, chip-paper rustled, and a half-eaten kebab landed next to them. No. No fucking way.

She stopped and stared at him. 'Just what do you think you're doing?'

He'd struggled up into a sitting position and was taking his jacket off. It came away from his back with a wet peeling sound, and he cried out in pain.

'Put that back on right now. You'll catch your death.'

'Very funny.' He shook his head and held the jacket out to her. 'Take it.'

'Oh please. Spare me the macho bullshit.' She tried to sound scornful and offhand, but it came out a little too much like a plea. 'Please, Dodd, no.' She saw with horror that it was steaming in the night air as his blood froze.

He shook it at her. 'I'm too slow. We both know it. One of us has got to get back and tell Walter there's something seriously messed up going on here. Look, this is a good jacket.'

'Other than the gaping claw holes, naturally.'

He tried to grin, but it just looked more ghastly in the pallor of his face. 'Don't let it go to waste.'

Mutely, she took it. It would have shamed him if she hadn't; the waste of something useful was close to a mortal sin. *Nothing which was not already lost. Oh Dodd, no.*

At the same time they both heard, off in the darkness of the waste ground behind the construction site, the peculiar mewling cries of the things which hunted them. Too many. Far too many.

When Dodd suggested that they split up, she could have objected, offering hollow reassurances that he wouldn't slow her down, that they'd somehow manage together, but it too would have been shaming to both of them. If nothing else, the Narrowfolk had their pride. It formed more of a barrier between them and the strutting nightclubbers than any flimsy wooden hoarding, and it withheld from them the easy comfort of the whitest of lies – even at the very end of things. She simply took the jacket and shrugged it on as he ran in a slow, painful crouch into the darkness.

On a whim she called out: 'Hey Dodd!'

He paused and turned back, nearly invisible. 'What?'

'Watch your back, yeah?'

'Couldn't resist it, could you?' The last she ever saw of Dodd was his middle finger disappearing into the night.

She made her own way, and when she heard the sounds of Dodd's pursuit suddenly escalate into a shrieking frenzy mingled with human screams, she tried not to let her tears blind her so much that she couldn't see where she was going.

It never occurred to her that the ease with which their hunters had found them had a human agency behind it, nor how neatly she and Dodd had been maneuvered. Which was why, when the ambush came, all she had time to feel was a kind of numb surprise.

3

INTERSECTION

Sudden movement flickered in the corner of Andy's vision.

From his position, squashed up against the track-side door, he could see the high embankment on the other side, where a ragged human figure appeared as if out of the very ground itself, tumbling and rolling to land in a heap at the bottom.

Seconds later a wild, pale face smeared up at him at knee-height from the darkness on the other side of the glass, and two small fists began to beat desperately on the door. The face – it seemed to be that of a girl – was shouting something. Yelling, begging, to be let in. Glancing over her shoulder with terrified eyes and then turning back to beat with renewed urgency on the thick glass.

Andy reacted the only way he knew how, the way any self-respecting suburban commuter would react given the circumstances: he stood rooted in shock, gaping down at her like a particularly stupid fish, and did nothing. Open the door? He hesitated, glancing around to see if anybody else was going to do something. Nobody seemed to have noticed the girl at all. She was staring up at him with panic and a kind of hopeless, baffled fury; why wasn't he *doing* anything?

His shoulder – his whole *arm* – began to burn with pins and needles. It was like he'd been dropped in (*dead*) nettles.

Then she reached up with what looked like a large marker pen and scrawled a jagged, looping symbol on the glass. There was a hiss of hydraulics, and the doors popped ajar with a sudden *thunk,* and a thin stream of chill, diesel-heavy air. Pale fingers curled around each door-panel and tried unsuccessfully to prise them apart. Her mouth appeared in the gap, and one eye, bright blue and pleading.

'...please help...' was all he could make out. And to his surprise, he found himself doing just that, ignoring the tinfoil-on-teeth sensations searing down into his fingertips. As he held the doors open so that she could climb inside, he thought he saw something – several somethings, in fact – dart away from the carriage and the sudden light. They moved too fast to be seen clearly, so it must have been his imagination which made them greyish and lumpen. If they were even there at all.

The homeless girl who hauled herself up and into the train was dressed in an almost archaeological layering of clothes, no single one of them intact, full of holes and so deeply begrimed that it was impossible to tell what colour anything had originally been. Short blonde dreads corkscrewed wildly from her head, and constellations of piercings glittered at lip, nose, and ears. Her smell filled the crowded carriage like a living thing as she climbed up right next to him, heaving for breath and clearly exhausted, so close that they were touching. The back of her torn leather jacket left a wet red smear on the inside of the door as it slowly closed again.

The silence in the carriage became deafening. This was clearly too much for Telegraph Man.

'I'm sorry!' he protested, sounding anything but. 'You can't just open the doors and climb on like this!'

Bex looked back down through the door windows and then at him. 'Just did,' she said matter-of-factly.

'Do you even have a ticket?'

She eyed him sidelong, as if considering. 'Tell you what,' she suggested. 'You go and get the guard, or whatever, and he'll call the transport police, and everybody else can enjoy sitting here for even longer in the cold while I'm being arrested so that you can work that chip off your shoulder. How's that sound?'

After a moment's hesitation, he very carefully folded his newspaper away, took out his MP3 player, popped in the earbuds and leaned back with his eyes closed. His fellow passengers were also now doing an impressive job of pretending that she didn't exist. Andy, on the other hand, was simply agog. She was very short, and very very close.

Bex stared back up at him, her nose barely centimetres away from his chin. 'Hi,' she said. 'Got a fag?'

'Uh, hi. No, what? I mean, is that blood? Are you okay?'

'It's alright,' she replied. 'None of it's mine.' And she began to laugh hysterically, in great wracking whoops which sounded too much like sobbing for Andy's liking.

'Oh, hey, look…' He was so completely taken aback that he started searching for a hanky before he realised that he'd never carried one in his entire life, and he cast around desperately for any support, or even any acknowledgement, from just one of the other passengers, but he and the girl seemed to have become both invisible and inaudible. 'I think I should call the driver or something. You look like you need a doctor.'

'Never mind what you think I need, mate.' Then she clocked his badge. '*Andrew*, sorry. I don't need rescuing. All I need is to catch my breath for a bit. Not a sodding conversation.'

'Fair enough.' Andy watched in discomfort as, rather than calming down, she became increasingly more agitated. She stood with her forehead pressed up against the glass, eyes darting to and fro, searching the shadows, tap-tapping a nervous staccato with her marker pen and repeating under her breath a phrase from a song he almost recognised: 'Welcome to paradise… welcome to paradise…' With a cold shock he finally realised the truth: she was a junkie. He was standing next to an honest-to-goodness, down-to-earth, real-life, likely-to-stab-him-in-the-guts-for-another-rock-of-crack-or-whatever-it-was junkie. The best thing to do was to just stand very still, try not to draw attention to himself, and when she pulled a knife, hand over his wallet as manfully as possible.

But as the train finally started up again, she relaxed visibly. The muttering died away, the tapping pen slowed and stopped. Andy began to suspect that he might just survive his journey home after all. Nevertheless, when she turned to him and said 'So, Andrew, where does this train stop?' he jumped as if shot.

'That was an interesting noise,' she observed. 'Again, in human?'

'Five- Five Ways,' he stammered. 'University, Selly Oak, ah, Kings Norton, I think, then…'

'Cheers. Five Ways'll do.' Humming that song to herself again, she started doodling absent-mindedly on the wall next to her. This apparently *was* worth noticing by the other passengers, many of whom sighed, tutted, and snapped their newspapers in disapproval. Bex ignored them and finished tagging her sigil. Escaping onto a railway had been a big mistake, even if it had saved her life, but some habits were impossible to break, even in an alien world.

'Um,' said Andy.

She glared at him. 'What?'

'Well…' he added.

Very deliberately, she reached over and tagged the front of his briefcase, the large strokes gleaming black on its cheap brown leather. The locks popped open and papers slithered onto the floor. 'This?'

He looked down at it, too stunned to be properly angry. Plus, he was a little embarrassed. He didn't know what Telegraph Man carried in his own expensive-looking briefcase but he fancied it was probably more sophisticated than this month's issue of *Empire* magazine and the game cheats to *Homicidal Harlots IV*. Andy was also uncomfortably aware of the intensity of the girl's stare – she had incredible blue-grey eyes, flecked with amber and gold. 'No, I suppose not,' he finished lamely.

'Good.' She got up and opened the door. Cold air blasted in, and he became aware of huge dim shapes rumbling past outside. Brickwork and straggling weeds flashed briefly into existence in the patch of light thrown by the open door, and disappeared just as quickly. They hadn't reached Five Ways yet; did not, in fact, even seem to be slowing down for it. He knew he was going to warn her against jumping, futile though it was. He could feel the words starting up his throat, completely beyond his control, ready to usher him into a whole new world of public embarrassment. It was simply what you did. You helped young mothers with push-chairs down the stairs, put your litter in the bins provided, always washed your hands after flushing, and warned people (including, he supposed, half-crazy and gore-covered junkies who had just vandalised your briefcase) that throwing themselves from a train wasn't a Good Idea.

But by the time all this had flashed through his brain, she'd gone, and his words died in the night-torn air. So he did the only thing he could, which was to gather up his scattered papers.

***

Two slices of darkness in the shape of men stood atop the gravelled railway embankment and watched as the train pulled slowly away, its doors closing on their prey. The taller of the two leaned on a long copper staff as his shorter companion recalled the skavags and tried to calm them; having lost the scent, they were restless and twitchy, snapping at each other in their frustration.

'Carling,' said the man with the staff.

'Yes, boss?'

'She cheated.' The voice was light, as if discussing the weather.

'I don't follow you, boss.'

'The Narrowfolk don't use trains – or planes, or automobiles, for that matter. They barely even use roads. It's against their rules.'

'Yes, boss.'

'So that was really quite naughty of her, wasn't it?'

Carling didn't reply. For one thing, he was still trying to subdue his pack – they definitely were not happy creatures. For another, he never knew half the time how to take his master's moods, so it was often safer to simply stay quiet until he was asked a direct question. Even that was no guarantee. He hoped that this one was rhetorical.

'Carling.'

'Yes, boss?'

'You know how much I hate loose ends, don't you?'

Definitely not rhetorical. 'Yes, boss. Leave it to me.'

***

On the way home from the station, Andy picked up a curry, because it was his turn to cook, and walked the rest of the way in something of a daze. It seemed impossible that his late-shift routine could resume as if nothing had happened. Mr Nawaz at the Sundarbon produced his chicken korma, beef madras and two naan perfectly calmly; further down the street heavy industrial music was thumping from the upstairs window of number forty-seven, and when he elbowed the intercom of his flat because both hands were too full to find his keys, Laura buzzed him up without a word of enquiry because of course who else would it be?

Up the stairs to the third floor landing, where a sorry collection of pot-plants were being communally neglected, he found the door to their flat open. This was, again, nothing at all out of the ordinary, but for some reason this evening he found it profoundly irritating.

'You know you really shouldn't leave this open,' he called, slamming it shut with his heel. He stopped long enough to dump his briefcase in the spare bedroom (graffiti-side down, not that it mattered, he told himself, it was just that he didn't really want to face the interrogation that would inevitably follow). He rustled his steaming carrier-bags down the hall and into the kitchen. Through the doorway opposite, Laura sat on their sofa surrounded by small blue exercise books, ticking them rapidly with a red pen. Her iPod speakers were thumping out Green Day. When he heard which track was playing, a cold shudder of deja-vu ran down his spine, and he switched them off.

'Fine, thanks,' she replied. 'How was yours?'

'I'm serious!' He opened cupboards and rattled plates with more noise than was strictly necessary. 'I could have been anyone!'

She followed him into the kitchen and, as she passed him on her way to the fridge, kissed him lightly on the back of the neck. 'No you couldn't.'

He stared after her. 'I think I should be offended by that.'

'What – that I don't think you're capable of being some kind of sick home-intruder rapist?' She shrugged as she poured them both a glass of wine. 'Be offended if you like, but I think you're probably overreacting.'

He followed her back through into their tiny living room – glass in one hand, plate in the other. 'All I'm saying is that you should be more careful. You can't take things for granted like that.'

'Fine. I'll be paranoid suburban flat-woman creature from now on. I'll demand to see identification from everybody, including the postman. I'll become a recluse, the weird old hermit lady on the third floor surrounded by cats and smelling of wee.'

Andy nodded, chewing. 'Mm-hm. Sounds fair enough.'

'Maybe they'll give me my own episode of "A Life of Grime".'

'And then finally you will have the fame and attention you've always deserved.'

'Eff off, commuter boy.'

They ate watching Millionaire with the sound turned down, sitting on the sofa because the drop-leaf table by the kitchen door was covered in Laura's textbooks, folders, and marking – all of which stood neatly stacked in their appointed piles. It was hard to say whether the work which college set her as part of her teacher training course was any greater than what she was bringing home from her placement school – Andy knew nothing about the job other than what he'd loathed about it at the receiving end – but he was pretty sure the school shouldn't be just dumping work on her like she was actually employed by them. Still, she seemed to be keeping on top of it.

In fact, everything did seem to be so completely normal that he was actually able to forget about the incident on the train for some time, until he was washing up and she'd had to move some of his clutter in the spare room to find…

'What happened to *this*?'

Ah. She leaned into the kitchen, his briefcase dangling off one finger like a dead fish. He glanced at it and resumed scrubbing industriously at a perfectly clean plate. 'Looks like somebody's drawn on it,' he muttered.

'Smartarse. How did it *happen*? Who *did* it?'

'Some kid. Kids.'

'What kids?' She was now enunciating each word as sharply as broken glass, and he knew this one was going to be bad. The briefcase had been a present from her back when he'd been applying for 'proper' jobs, i.e. ones in offices, but he still carried it with him every day despite the fact that all he ever kept in it was movie magazines, comics and game cheats. Sometimes he suspected that she secretly thought he was making fun of her by doing so.

'Druggies. Homeless, it looked like. They, uh, they sort of attacked me on the train.'

'Jesus Christ, Andy!' She was staring at him, aghast. 'Why didn't you *tell* me?'

'Because it was more embarrassing than anything else. Oh, and I'm fine, by the way. Thanks for asking.'

'Don't try to turn this around on me. How did this happen?'

For which, read: How could you *let* this happen? It was his turn to stare. 'What do you mean? You somehow think this is my fault?'

'Well I don't know, do I? You haven't told me a word about what happened. You sit there next to me and eat dinner and then do the washing up and it's been – what? Three hours? And not one single bloody word. Were you even *going* to tell me? And anyway, that's not what I meant.'

'Look. It's simply not worth making that much of a fuss over. There were some kids, they were mucking about, yes it freaked me out a bit but they were just being stupid. I wasn't hurt. And before you say it, no, I am not going to go to the police. It's a stupid piece of minor vandalism, and it's not worth bothering anybody about, okay? Can we just leave it? Please?'

Laura left it. But only, he suspected, in the sense that it had been filed away to be dragged out the next time he did something stupid. For God's sake, he thought with sudden resentment, all he'd try to do was help someone. Except he hadn't, really, had he? It was only after the girl had got the doors open herself that he'd plucked up the courage to help; he'd been more than happy to just leave her to begin with. And leave her to what? What had he even seen?

The song that had been playing through Laura's iPod speakers had been Green Day's classic slacker anthem 'Welcome to Paradise,' the same song that the girl had been humming as she jittered by the door and watched out for whatever was chasing her.

Andy Sumner didn't believe in random. He had long since become used to his life being controlled by such coincidences as this. Except that 'controlled' wasn't really the right word for it. They simply happened to him. Time after time, *all* the time. He'd wake up with a tune in his head and it'd be the first thing he'd hear on the radio that morning – he supposed that was the sort of thing that happened to everybody once in a while, but every morning for a week, without a break? He'd attend a job-centre interview and find himself sitting opposite an old school friend he hadn't seen in years – not only that but the conference room where the interview would be held would have the same name as their old form teacher. That sort of coincidence. All the time. He'd found as a child that that if he allowed these coincidences to inform his decisions life was a lot easier, and often luckier. So he'd buy the album he heard on the radio that morning and maybe find a twenty pound note lying on the shop floor. Or he'd go along to the old school friend's barbecue and meet a gorgeous, bossy, and frighteningly intelligent young woman called Laura Bishop who for some reason known only to the gods actually fancied him enough to go out for a drink with him, and ultimately loved him enough to agree to marry him. He didn't necessarily believe that any of this was pre-ordained or even controlled, but it was pretty clear to him that sequences of events fell into some kind of Pattern, and that if you took advantage of the clues that were dropped in your way, the Pattern would ultimately reward you.

In which case, why did he feel like he was about to throw up? That sick, low-grade swirling sensation he'd been feeling all day thickened somewhere just below his ribcage. It felt like seasickness, like being trapped in the pitch-black cargohold of a ship plowing its way through a storm-swollen ocean: the feeling of being caught up in the movement of something huge and ponderous. He spent the rest of the evening watching the television with unfocussed eyes, seeing instead pale shapes scuttling in the darkness.

Dodd awoke to crawling light and chanting voices.

His mind was like a small flat stone skimming across a nightbound lake. He dipped briefly in and out of consciousness, but even when he closed his eyes, the light still crawled behind his eyelids, and the voices insisted.

Really only one voice, but the echoes picked it up and bounced it around his head. And the echoes' siblings, shadows, breeding cockroaches of light which squirmed under his eyes, over and through his skin. Echoes and shadows of vast concrete buttresses, and the slumbering shapes of heavy machinery standing sentry around the construction site where he was now dying.

Skimming back up again…

Dodd was duct-taped, naked and spreadeagled, to a pair of crossed reinforcing girders at the bottom of a deep pit, smelling oil and steel and the stink of his own flesh burning. None of it had been delerium. He was in actual fact crawling with light. At dozens of points on his anatomy, slender needles transfixed his flesh, and where they did so the skin glowed, searingly painful, like cigarette burns. Motes of light crawled from these needles to coalesce in large multi-floreate patterns at his belly and chest, and to other points elsewhere up and down his body where he couldn't see. It was as if his body were short-circuiting and burning itself up.

'Geburah!' the voice intoned. 'The Fifth Path! Mars, grant us your strength!'

'Grant us your strength…' echoed a chorus of others, from all around him.

A hand reached out of the darkness and planted a needle in the strained flesh where his left shoulder met his torso. New fire took root there and crawled in slow motes toward the flower which burned over his breastbone.

'*Chesed! The Fourth Path! Jupiter, lend us your wisdom!*' Yet another, this time in his right shoulder, burning from inside.

The man in front of him looked for all the world like a businessman, in a dark suit and long winter coat, except for the way it curled and flapped about him in an unfelt wind, like wings, and the lapels, which were ranked with still more needles to come. In one hand he clasped a long metal staff that crawled with static electricity. Other figures stood further off in a loose semi-circle, and beyond them still a retinue of squat creatures kept as far back in the shadows of the pit as possible.

Voices and needles and monsters at his back.

Beneath his feet lay a large, heavily-inscribed stone.

'*Lend us your wisdom…*'

The dark man leaned in closely and favoured Dodd with a conspiratorial smile. 'To tell you the truth, this is all a lot of rubbish,' he whispered. 'But you know how it is. One must keep the congregation happy.' He winked.

'Wha… What are you… ?'

A needle floated free from the jacket of its own accord and impaled itself at the base of his throat. He groaned as heat blossomed there. The dark man seemed to draw sustenance from this, inhaling as if pleased by the aroma of a fine meal.

'I just need to know one little thing. Tiny thing. Hardly worth your trouble. I mean, given that you're dying and everything. You've probably got a bit on your mind. It's just – your girlfriend back there – you wouldn't happen to know where she might have run to, would you?'

Dodd made a noise which might have been *fuck you*.

'Yes,' the needleman sighed. 'Still, I had to ask. Sorry. You carry on, there.' He turned back to the assembled crowd – figures with expensive suits and avid eyes – and declaimed once more. '*Da-ath! The Path which is No Path! Open for us the Abyss…*'

And so it went on, from the soles of his feet to the very crown of his head, until his bristling body was juddering and spasming as its vital energies were channelled into seven swirling vortices down its length, threatening to tear his very fibres apart. He felt as if he were brimming with molten metal. At length the needleman produced a knife, which he flourished high for his congregation, crying: *'The Gates stand ready!'*

'Let them be opened!' came the chorus, ragged and fervent.

The needleman leaned in again. 'This, though,' he whispered, 'this is the real thing. I'm genuinely indebted to you. It's been an honour.'

They opened Dodd then, seven times, emptying his blood onto the inscribed stone at his feet, and beyond the physical torment there was a sensation of voiding, of being *hollowed*, which was almost orgasmic, as though his soul were ejaculating itself into darkness.

He touched water briefly one last time, skipped, and never came back down.

When it was done they lowered him reverently into the pit and waited for the empty vessel of his body to be filled.

4

MOON GROVE

Bex awoke to the smell of baking bread and was immediately, ravenously hungry.

Moon Grove's large dormitory room – nicknamed 'Butlins' because of the chaotic jumble of bunk-beds, hammocks, and random mattresses on the floor – was warm with a drifting mid-afternoon silence.

Everybody would be out scavenging what they could in these last few hectic weeks before Laying Up, except for Ceridwen – known to all as Kerrie the Kook – and her kitchen tarts, who were no doubt baking enough to feed a besieged army, and for much the same reason. The scavengers would be back before night fell and took the temperature with it. Some old faces wouldn't return, and some new ones would appear to take their places – the population of Butlins would replenish itself completely within the weeks as people found other places to stay, moved on, returned, or discovered the Grove for the first time.

Bex thought she had gotten used to this, having been here for six months, but she never imagined that she'd outstay any of the more permanent residents like Dodd. There was a lot about the last twenty-four hours that she hadn't imagined.

As the Moon Grove equivalent of an old-timer, she'd earned a place high up on the third tier of bunks, close enough to the ceiling that her shoulders brushed it every time she rolled over. Last night should have seen her fully accepted as one of the Narrowfolk proper, rather than just another itinerant scavenger, and she'd have earned her own room upstairs, but now everything was messed up all over again.

Memories crowded into the forefront of her mind (doubling back on herself all across the city to throw off pursuit; collapsing over the threshold of the Grove in the early hours of the morning; exhausted explanations; tears, accusations) and she tried to shove them back under the golden silence, but every time she closed her eyes, they jumped at her again.

At a loss for any other way to distract herself, she went in search of breakfast.

She started to shrug some clothes on and discovered that everything everywhere hurt. Overstretched muscles and twisted ligaments complained. Bandages and elastoplast patched her in a dozen places, especially all over her hands – her knuckles and fingertips had been shredded with scrambling over bricks and rubble. Lucky to be alive, she reminded herself.

She couldn't believe that they weren't even going to look for him.

Moon Grove was not so much the name of the building but more properly the short cul-de-sac in which it was situated, but over the decades the neighbouring houses had gradually slipped into decrepitude until the name of the road became synonymous with that of the one house which remained inhabited. It had begun its existence as a large townhouse typical of so many built for the wealthy Victorian middle-class, and so was fairly expansive to begin with, but in the century and a half which followed – during which it was subdivided, partially demolished, and extended numerous times, often without planning permission or indeed much by way of planning at all – it had become a sprawling labyrinth of annexes, porches, attics and wings like a shabby-genteel old fart reclining after the port and cigars.

The kitchen was large enough that she could sneak in without being noticed. Christmas pop music squawked scratchily from an ancient radio as two of the kitchen tart crew were pummelling various incarnations of dough and the third (a man, though he seemed to fit in as one of the girls well enough) was bent down with Kerrie, both of them peering suspiciously into one of the ovens. There was a perpetual haze in the high-ceilinged room – usually of flour, though often as not it was smoke.

The pressure to feed a houseful of thirty or so people each day with the random and often bizarre combinations of ingredients which they scavenged – according to no overall plan or, god forbid, actual menu – attracted a particular sort of volunteer for whom actual cooking skills were much less important than an active imagination and the ability to withstand violent criticism, sometimes of the physical variety. All Bex wanted was some toast. She found half a loaf of bread on one of the wide, cluttered counters, and hacked off a large chunk.

'Oh, so you've finally surfaced, have you?' Kerrie was standing close behind, fists planted on her wide hips, eyes glaring not unkindly below a stormcloud of frizzy ginger hair which was held back in a loose bunch, seemingly by its owner's ferocious willpower alone. 'Should have guessed you'd be helping yourself sooner or later. What do you think this place is – a hotel? The time you come crawling in, looking like death itself.' And she gathered Bex in an iron lung of a hug. 'Are y'alright my love?'

Bex nodded, only slightly crushed. She held herself stiffly; she somehow couldn't bring herself to return the hug. 'Been better, but I'll live.'

'Ah well, you're a strong girl, that's for sure.' Kerrie scrunched floury fingers through Bex's stubby dreads. 'We all loved him. Maybe not so much as you though, eh?'

Bex released herself and gave her a peck on the cheek. 'Thanks.'

Kerrie suddenly became aware that they had an audience. 'And what do you lot think you're gawping at?' she bellowed at the others. 'Get back to work, ye shiftless sods! You think I can't run this place without you? I know people, you know! One phone call – that's all – one phone call!' They sauntered back to their chores with grins and a notable lack of urgency. She swung back to face Bex. 'And for pity's sake, put some jam on that thing. Who do you think you are, Oliver Twist? You'll shame me, you will.'

As Bex was limping away, munching her breakfast, Kerrie added: 'By the way, darling, Walter was asking after you earlier.'

'Was he now?' she grunted and left.

She went back to her bunk and rooted around at the foot of it to find Dodd's jacket, then headed upstairs to the wide first floor landing where his room sat.

Like everywhere else in Moon Grove, the landing was cluttered with the accumulated debris of uncounted years: jumbled piles of boxes and furniture and junk which might potentially have a use and so couldn't possibly be thrown out. The rooms on this floor and the one above were the bedsits belonging to those fully-fledged Narrowfolk who had made Moon Grove their permanent home and who had, more importantly, demonstrated their value to the place through having some particular skill or knowledge.

The topmost floor belonged solely to Walter. It wasn't forbidden or exclusive – had no locks, bars or guards – it was just somewhere you didn't go. It defied easy labelling, like the man himself, who anywhere else would be described as their leader, except that he conspicuously didn't lead. He gave no orders, issued no decrees, pronounced no judgements, but somehow everybody knew what was expected of them. They knew that if you lived in Butlins you earned your bed each day in whatever way you could, and those that couldn't – or wouldn't – left the Grove very quickly.

It was equally clear that no form of crime was tolerated – no hard drugs, violence, or prostitution. From time to time a hardcase would turn up and try to make it his own little empire, or a bunch of junkies would try to scrounge off them, and all Walter would seem to do was have a quiet word with them – maybe while strolling through the allotments behind the house, or by the fireplace in one of the big day-rooms – and the next day they and all their belongings would simply be gone.

Rumour whispered everything from him being a retired stage hypnotist to a serial killer with an underground complex of torture rooms, but Dodd had believed that he just had a knack of convincing some people that this wasn't a place where they wanted to be. It wasn't to say that he was in any way a bad man, just that he seemed to be running the place according to an unspoken law which sympathised with the weaknesses of others but had no place for them.

Rummaging through the pockets of Dodd's leather jacket as she approached the door of his room, she found half a pack of Trebor Extra Strong Mints, no fags at all (despite looking twice and cursing his non-smoking hide), his battered *A-to-Z of Birmingham and the West Midlands*, and (jackpot!) his keys.

She stopped. The padlock hung open on its hasp, and the door was ajar.

Cautiously, she pushed it open. It looked like most of Dodd's things – with the exception of his narrow bed, a Baby Belling stove and some empty MFI shelves – had been packed into boxes and stacked up against one wall. In the middle of the bare floor a tall man was leafing through one of Dodd's books.

'Hello Rebecca,' said Walter, looking up. 'How are you feeling?'

'I'd feel a lot better if I knew what you were doing with Dodd's stuff,' she retorted.

He smiled. 'Sense of youthful indignation still very healthy, I see.'

Inasmuch as it was possible to chew bread with attitude, that was what she did, and glared at him. She realised that she had no idea of his age – he was clean-shaven and dressed simply in jeans and a hoody, but deep lines etched themselves down either side of his mouth when he smiled, and his short thatch of unruly hair was entirely grey. His eyes were very bright, and she was uncomfortably aware of being the sole focus of his full attention. Bex began to wish she hadn't started on him so aggressively. But he was in Dodd's *room*, pawing at his *things*.

'You've got a point though,' he continued, as if reading her mind. 'I imagine we're both here for much the same reasons.' He glanced pointedly at the keys which were still in her hand.

She dropped them back in the pocket of Dodd's – correction, *her* – jacket and continued to chew at him. 'Someone's got to take care of his stuff.'

'Absolutely they do. And of course it has to be you.'

She bridled at that. 'Well, why bloody not? I knew him as well as anyone else. Better, probably.'

Walter threw his hands up in apology. 'Whey, hold up. You misunderstand me. I wasn't being sarcastic. I meant it: of course, it does have to be you.' His tone was conciliatory, but she felt foolish at how easily he'd got a rise out of her. Had he really been mocking her? Her head was still fuzzy and she was almost certainly not thinking straight. 'For what it's worth, he was my friend too.'

'Then why aren't we doing anything?'

Walter's tone was gentle as he sat on the corner of Dodd's bed and laid the book to one side. 'What would you have us do?'

'Send people to go out there and look for him, what do you think?'

'Send people. What an interesting notion. Let us assume for the moment that I am in any way capable of sending anyone to do anything, and just consider a few questions: even if the skavags have left anything of him to find, how are you going to get him back? Who are you going to convince to help you carry a corpse halfway across the city, especially so close to Laying Up? And what would you do when you got him back here? Bury him? How many square feet of ground desperately needed to feed the living will you sacrifice for the dead? Or, if you're thinking of cremating him, how much fuel will you take from the furnace?'

'We should at least tell the police; he must have next of kin. His family deserve to know, surely.'

'And who are they? Do you know? Because I certainly don't.'

'Somebody around here must!'

'Why? What's *your* real name? Forgive me if this sounds a bit harsh but I'll bet my thermal longjohns it isn't Rebecca. Who was she, anyway? A big sister? School friend? Character from your favourite book? Someone as strong as you'd like to be instead of the weak and shameful creature you actually think you are.'

Bex could hardly believe what she was hearing. *A bit harsh?* No question about whether he was trying to get a reaction out of her now, but she found it impossible not to take the bait. 'What's that got to do with anything? Yes, it's my real name, not that it's any of your business!'

'Then why make Dodd yours? He made his decision when he became Narrowfolk, just like you have. Why not let him die as anonymously as he wanted to live?'

'Are you seriously trying to suggest that this is what he would have *wanted*?'

'No, of course not. What I'm suggesting is this: you've got that look in your eye like somebody has to pay for what happened to you and Dodd last night, but you need to keep in mind a few cold truths. One, you're never going to find any trace of him; skavags never abandon a hunt, and they never leave anything behind. You know this. Two, you will never find anybody to blame for what happened, and you can't blame yourself in the absence of that. All other things aside, you did actually manage to complete your Walk – you made it across the city without passing under the light of a single streetlamp…'

'Walk?!' She was incredulous. 'What fucking *Walk*? There was no Walk! Not once we were running for our fucking *lives*! And there *was* somebody there! I saw them!'

'Whatever you saw, or thought you saw, as far as I and the others are concerned, you are Narrowfolk now, and none could be more deservedly so. You've got a place, and a place has become vacant. It's not pretty, but that's how it goes. You said so yourself: somebody has got to take care of his stuff. Well, this is all yours now. Honour his memory by not letting his stuff go to waste – and most importantly, don't waste your own life throwing it away on something you're never going to find. You're more useful to us here and alive than charging off around the city getting yourself killed. I don't know what he would have wanted, but I'll bet he wouldn't have wanted that.'

Bex looked around at the nearly bare room: the narrow, iron-framed foldaway bed, the small bookcase, and the low stack of boxes against the wall. Not much. She wondered how much he'd left from his life before Moon Grove – and then, on the heels of that, what remained of herself. Would her old things still be where she'd left them, or would they too have been packed up into boxes, to be scrapped or sold or given to charity shops? 'Mine, you say?'

Walter nodded.

'Do us a favour, then?'

'Name it.'

'Get out of my room.'

***

The Games Barn was in as plum a position as any manager could hope for when it came to Christmas shopping. The Pallasades Shopping Centre was directly above New Street Station, and even though it had been superceded by that flash upstart of a Bullring Centre, with its light and space and actual architecture, the Pallasades still caught rail travellers from all over the country while they waited for their connections and escalated them up to the waiting shops like a pitcher plant in reverse.

One of the problems with actually working there, as far as Andy was concerned, was that in winter, it led to a virtually nocturnal existence. It would be dark when he set off at the start and returned at the end of each day, the hours in between being spent entirely indoors, even in his lunch hour (what there was of it). After a few weeks of this, he'd begun to feel like some kind of vampire and jumped at any chance to get outside.

No Missions this time, though. No arcane culinary ingredients, and definitely no shortcuts. Just post-its and envelopes.

He was just outside the shopping centre's entrance, on his way down the wide concrete ramp of pavement that descended to New Street, when he saw a young homeless man sitting huddled in a grubby sleeping bag against the wall between McDonalds and the HSBC bank, with two styrofoam cups in front of him.

Predictably, he was being ignored – especially by the businessman who was striding along blithely in the opposite direction, chatting loudly with someone on his hands-free. The only reason Andy noticed him at all was because of the irony: a well-dressed man having a conversation with thin air, waving his arms around and looking more like a street-crazy than the destitute human being right beside him, who he obviously hadn't seen, because he was about to step right on top of him.

A gleaming Italian-leather shoe connected with one of the styrofoam cups, and a brown slop of coffee spilled out of it. Handsfree jerked sideways with a cry of 'Jeezus!' His trouser cuff was dripping. Andy couldn't help smiling.

Handsfree stared in disgust at his ruined shoe and then at the homeless man, whose palms were upraised in the universal gesture of 'Hey man, don't look at me.' He turned back to his invisible friend and said, 'Sorry, Toby, can you hang on a moment?' and took a couple of paces backward. Andy's smile turned sour as he realised that the man was taking a run-up – an actual *run-up*, like he was in some kind of deranged penalty shoot-out.

'Merry fucking Christmas,' said Handsfree with perfect, cut-glass diction, and booted the other white cup as hard as he could.

Coins ricocheted off glass and concrete, spinning and rolling in all directions for yards around. The homeless man leapt up with a cry of outrage and started scrabbling for his change.

'Toby?' continued the other man as if nothing had happened. 'Oh nothing. Just stepped in some shit, that's all,' and carried on straight towards Andy.

Andy wasn't aware that he was going to say anything until it happened. It just sort of slipped out. He'd always been such a polite young man. As the businessman passed him, eyes flicking over his face, unseeing, dismissing, just another wage-slave, Andy leaned in and said, so quickly and quietly that Handsfree might not have been sure he'd said anything at all: 'Dickhead.' Handsfree stiffened, reddened, but being the perfect British man-in-a-crowd ignored him completely and disappeared into the shopping centre.

Andy, along with a few other well-meaning shoppers, stooped to help pick up the scattered change. While he was at it, he dropped in a quid from the petty cash.

Bex tried to find the place where she and Dodd had been attacked, in the futile hope that she might be able to discover some clue to his fate. She couldn't bring herself to start sorting through his belongings until she'd at least satisfied her curiosity on that score. Surely Walter had to understand that.

The problem was, she simply couldn't find it. There were half a dozen construction sites in the single square mile of the city centre alone, and all of them owned by Jerusalem Construction. Typically corrupt big business. Somebody on the Council was obviously getting a nice kick-back, which was lovely for them, and she hoped they enjoyed their nice new soulless shopping malls or whatever, but it made her own task impossible. She'd thought they'd been behind Broad Street, but what if she'd been wrong? There were bars and nightclubs everywhere.

What made it worse was that she couldn't even locate the Narrow where the skavags had first picked up their trail. She wasted the best part of the day making a series of long detours almost all the way back to the tower block, poking and prodding around with increasing frustration, and eventually had to admit that, impossible as it was, the Narrow had simply disappeared.

No. The answer was much simpler than that. She'd fucked up. Somewhere along the line, despite her best efforts and intentions, she'd fucked up her Walk and got Dodd killed.

That night she broke into a house, stole their DVD player, and pawned it at a Cash Converters. The guy who checked it out opened the drawer and removed a Spongebob Squarepants DVD, which he gave to her saying 'That'll be yours then.' She stashed it guiltily in her rucksack, sickened at herself. Still, he gave her enough money to be able to wash away that feeling and most of the next two days with alcopops and Special Brew, so that was okay, and when they ran out she bought a small red craft knife and reopened the safety valves on the underside of her forearm, which had healed up in the months since she'd been with Dodd. Except he was dead now, wasn't he? She slept under a flyover, sheltered in bushes at the base of a concrete buttress, having just enough sense to wrap up in a sheet of plastic so that she didn't die of hypothermia. When her clothes became so filthy and foul-smelling that she nauseated even herself, she raided an Oxfam clothes bin, changing right there in the carpark: a pale, shivering creature, too ill-fed to have anything but a child's body despite her age.

Just like the good old days.

She dreamed of the attack over and over again.

She was trying to pull the train doors open again, staring up at the idiot who couldn't – or wouldn't – help, except now it was Dodd, and he was trying to tell her something. Yelling it at her, but she couldn't hear through the glass. Then the door was suddenly sliding open, and dozens of hands were reaching down to grab at her, pulling her upward by her clothing.

She woke, but the pulling continued. Something man-shaped was leaning over her, stinking of booze and cigarettes and rancid sweat, trying peel her clothes apart.

Bex screamed and thrashed, flailing with all four limbs until her knee connected with something soft, and the shape issued a muffled groan of pain. It receded from her, but she pursued it, lashing out with her boots and an empty bottle which came to hand. It didn't smash like they did in films – just made a series of meaty thuds until the shape stopped moving and it felt like she was beating a wet sponge. She gathered her things from her nest and fled before other manshadows were attracted to the noise.

The following morning she visited the drop-in centre at St Martin's church, where she got a hot meal, her cuts tended, and no questions asked. Walter found her hunched over a bowl of tomato soup with chunks of white bread floating in it like little clouds. He had cup of generic McBrand coffee in each hand and sat down opposite her as if the pause in their conversation had lasted only minutes rather than days.

'So,' he said. 'Finished?'

She looked at the soup, puzzled.

'I meant have you finished punishing yourself?'

She hmphed. 'Stop following me.'

'I was just passing. You're welcome, by the way.'

'I'm serious. Stop following me. I don't need anyone looking out for me.'

'Okay.' He sighed and straightened. 'It's like this. You're smart enough to know that all you can possibly accomplish here is to get yourself arrested and draw attention to the rest of us, and frankly, I can do without the hassle. To be honest, it'd make my life a lot easier if you'd disappeared along with Dodd.'

'Ha. You and me both.'

'But the truth is that you're a resource – a very valuable one, and I can't bear to see a good thing going to waste. We need you, Bex. We need people who know the Narrows, now more than ever. You have a place at Moon Grove for the moment, but you know that it won't last. Think about it. You've got until Laying Up.'

'Will you please. Just. Go. Away.'

She listened to him leave and sat huddled in her jacket as the coffee in front of her grew cold.

***

Bex returned to the Grove just long enough to pack a bag with trades and then took to the Narrows again for over a week, dossing down wherever she could earn space in a squat.

She spent those days revisiting Dodd's friends and contacts, both to share the news of his death and to pick up where he'd left off. She already knew quite a few of them from having followed him around learning the Narrows, and most were happy to carry on trading with the foul-mouthed, corkscrew-haired brat who'd tagged along with him.

As a result she found herself bouncing from one side of the city to another, at each stop indiscriminately taking the first trade that came along. She ended up swapping a dozen cartons of cigarettes in Hockley for a pair of orthopaedic shoes in Quinton for ten kilos of oranges in Brownhills for the services of an unregistered Croatian chiropractor in Moseley. The goods themselves were irrelevant – they just bought her a place to sleep each night. What mattered was that she kept moving, trying to purge her body and mind of their respective poisons with the relentless walking. She found Dodd's A-to-Z invaluable, as it was crammed with tightly scribbled notes of everywhere he'd been in the city and what might be found there. He had also, she discovered over several evenings, been mapping the Narrows – at least, as far as such a thing was possible. Much of what he had scrawled was incomprehensible: weird serpentine routes which seemed to take no account of roads, accompanied by odd symbols and cryptic marginal notations. It didn't matter; it hadn't been enough to stop him getting killed.

The really frightening thing was that they were disappearing at an alarming rate. As the days went by she found that more and more of the Narrows through which she had travelled with him – some as recently as only a few weeks ago – had simply vanished altogether.

The most obvious effect was that in the various squats she visited, preparations for Laying Up took on an edge of frantic urgency. Goods were being hoarded, and as the days went by it became increasingly difficult to find anything to trade. She knew that soon she would have to return to the Grove before everywhere shut their doors.

The other, darker effect of these Closures, as they were called, was that journeys began to take a lot longer and became more dangerous. The strange non-world through which they threaded was not what anybody could call safe at the best of times, but their disappearance was beginning to force the Narrowfolk out onto normal streets, where they were vulnerable to other predators, like gangs and the police.

It seemed that this was already starting to take its toll of victims, because everywhere she went she heard tales of people disappearing. They might have been invisible and untraceable to the police and other authorities, but the Narrowfolk knew each others' pitches and territories: who slept in which doorway, who laid claim to the leavings of which shops and tower blocks. At a time of year when everybody was stocking up on resources against the midwinter darkness, every missed trade and broken deal was noticed, and so were the empty nests of old duvets and cardboard boxes left to be blown away into the night.

Amidst all of this, it was unsurprising that nobody had heard or seen anything of Dodd. Reluctantly, Bex concluded that there was only one remaining avenue of information open to her.

5
FOUNDLING

When Andy and Laura's parents arrived for dinner, she was fretting over the place-settings and he was trying to coax as much space as he could from their flat's tiny living room, but as long as his X-box and some of the more dubious DVDs were well out of sight he supposed it would be fine. She had done something miraculous with shredded lamb, and even the dolmades were, he had to admit, pretty good. He didn't feel it necessary to relate the adventure of how he'd come by the vine leaves – bad enough that he was marrying their daughter at all without being an obvious lunatic too.

There was enough common ground between his own dad's work as a chemical engineer for various multinationals and Gordon Bishop's career in the financial sector for them to have a perfectly amicable conversation about what the government had got wrong with the economy, without having to tread the conversational minefield of politics. There seemed to be a tacit acknowledgement between the two men that things were likely to get tricky enough over the wedding arrangements without making things any worse. Even so, Valerie Bishop was content with how those plans were progressing – there was still half a year to go, after all – to be quite relaxed and chatty, but one anxiety was clearly preying on her mind.

'There's the issue of an announcement,' she said, after the plates had been cleared and Andy had taken care of everybody's drinks.

'Announcement?' asked his dad.

'Yes. A wedding announcement.'

Laura laughed. 'I don't think that's really necessary. This is hardly going to be the social occasion of the season.'

'Possibly not, but it is traditional.'

'Well, Mummy, if it's something you want to do, then please feel free to go ahead. I can't see that it makes a massive difference one way or the other.'

'You may not think so, but there is one thing that I don't think you've considered, which Andrew's parents might have an opinion about, and I thought it only right that they have some say in the matter.'

'Well that's very kind of you,' said his mum, with almost undetectable irony. 'What might that be?' Beth Sumner had spent her life working the sharp edge of welfare counselling and citizens' advice, out of a fiercely keen sense of natural justice. It had been on her suggestion that Andy had dropped out of his accountancy course, despite her husband's insistence that the boy get some kind of career qualification behind him, on the grounds that if he genuinely had no desire for it, then maybe he was better off doing nothing until he knew what he *did* want to do.

Valerie squared herself up in the manner of a person preparing to reluctantly deliver a painful but necessary truth. 'The issue of Andrew's birth mother.'

The room went very quiet. *Oh great,* thought Andy. *Here we go again.*

The nature of his adopted childhood had always held a disproportionately powerful fascination for Laura's mother. It was usually worth a couple of raised eyebrows with people who didn't know him, after which it ceased to be a novelty and just became part of the background static of his life. But for Valerie it was a filter through which she saw everything about him, and which for her provided explanations of every aspect of his personality. Had he dropped out of college? Did he lack apparent career ambition? Did he not like cheese? All of it could be explained by what she plainly thought were the emotionally crippling effects of being an adopted child.

'I'm not quite sure what you're getting at,' his mother replied carefully.

'Simply that, assuming that an announcement is made, we need to consider the implications should she happen to see it.'

'What exactly might those be?' asked his dad, who up to now, he could tell, had heroically resisted the urge to laugh out loud at this. 'Gatecrash the wedding?'

'I hardly think anything quite so melodramatic as that. But it might make things… awkward.' No doubt she was entertaining a Dickensian nightmare scenario of swarms of reality-show-addicted freeloaders with Black Country accents and spray-on tans descending on the reception to loot the gift table.

'Valerie, you really don't need to worry about anything like that happening.'

'Oh? Why not?' She bristled, testy that her concerns should be dismissed so offhandedly.

His father ticked off the reasons on his fingers. 'There's never been any contact from her, and assuming that she's even alive, in this country, and happens to read the announcement, it's not going to mean anything to her for the very simple reason that she won't know what his name is. Andy was what you might call a foundling. He was left with no birth certificate or paperwork of any kind, so he was named after the policeman that found him. You don't have to worry about him being the cause of anything awkward – well, nothing apart from the usual.' He grinned at Andy and tossed back the rest of his beer.

'Thanks for that, Dad.'

Valerie looked at Andy. He shrugged. 'All true, I'm afraid.'

'Well. This is – surprising.'

Yes, thought Andy. Now she could embellish her Catherine Cookson fantasies with images of forlorn young women staggering, heavily pregnant, across windswept moors and leaving their whimpering, newspaper-wrapped bundles in telephone boxes or on railway stations, before ultimately dying picturesquely of consumption, in cobblestoned alleyways.

He smiled and reached over with the bottle. 'Another glass of wine, Valerie?'

***

There was a decided frostiness about Laura in the way she helped him clear up afterwards. Something had obviously pissed her off, but she wasn't going to tell him what it was; presumably it was his job either to work it out for himself by forensically picking apart the whole evening's conversation, or to ask her so that she could tell him what he'd done wrong this time. It was the sort of mind-game that irritated him more than anything else. He stayed up late, until long after she'd gone to bed, playing computer games. At least he knew the rules for those.

Later, he lay as far away as was physically possible on the other side of a rather small double bed, listening to her pretending to be asleep. Through a gap in the curtains, a narrow beam of yellow streetlight fell in a straight line down the middle, lying between them like a prison bar made of gold.

***

Andy dreamt:

...of a house crowded with twisted hallways, which were distorted by random shifts of perspective, where parallel lines always crossed and things got smaller the closer they came.

...of a hundred doorways opening into mute rooms of dust and dead leaves.

...of a great central gallery, dozens of floors high, cathedral-like, surrounded by balconies and gantries, walkways and balustrades, hung with dusty ropes, heavy with mould and warp and rust.

And lost in its labyrinthine darkness a toddler's bedroom: largely unfurnished but at least stable in this nightmare, like an air-pocket in a sinking submarine, or an eye in a cyclone which is trying to rotate in both directions at the same time. Largely unfurnished, that is, but not undecorated, because above the bed, a circular brass ornament turns slowly: a series of concentric, spoked rings rotating within each other, indifferent to the fact that this is impossible – lines and circles sliding past and behind and between each other. Its slow dance fascinates the boy who lies naked on the bare mattress – slightly more than a baby; barely a child – watching bars and crescents of gleaming, yellow-warm metal appear and disappear above him.

But it is not just this which holds him still.

Andy looks down along his body and sees things sticking out of his skin. Things which look like stones, and in another of those twists of perspective which makes his head spin, he sees that they are both tiny, pencil-sized impalements and huge, full-sized standing stones at the same time, and that his body is simultaneously the size of a normal four-year-old boy but also an entire landscape, miles from one shoulder to the other, entire counties from head to toe. All over him, in him, are those needles of stone socketed in his flesh like old, grey teeth, and it is their combined weight which makes it impossible for him to so much as lift a finger, never mind what he wants to do, which is leap off this filthy mattress and run screaming down those twisting corridors...

He awoke so violently that his outflung hand caught the corner of his bedside cabinet. Laura stirred and muttered 'Whuz?' at him, but by the time he'd stopped muttering 'fuckshitfuck' at the pain and mustered enough self-control to say 'It's just me. Sorry, shh, go back to sleep,' she'd already done just that. Doing his best not to rouse her any further, he got out of bed and shuffled painfully into the hall.

The strange-familiar silence of a living-room in the early hours of the morning settled around him, and he wandered here and there, touching the dimly-seen objects of the daytime world. Bunch of keys. TV remote. His Aston Villa mug. Should've washed that up. Bugger. They looked like props from a play that had been interrupted momentarily and were waiting only for the stage-lights to come up so that they could be made real again. He crossed to the window and peered out between the curtains, across the lawn which lay between the block of flats and the garages behind. From three floors up, he could see the ridges of rooftops beyond, outlined in the sodium glow of streetlights, and the shadowed labyrinth of suburban gardens. A heavy frost had fallen, and the blackness glittered.

Blonde dreaded hair and dirty fingertips scrabbling at the train door. Dead nettles and alien graffiti.

'Impossible,' he whispered to the sleeping city. It was only when he turned back to the room that he noticed for the first time how much all the LEDs of their various electronic gadgets looked like eyes staring at him. *Swarm of zombie fireflies.*

'Completely impossible,' he repeated, as he got dressed into a t-shirt, jeans, and two jumpers.

'Really quite fundamentally unfeasible,' as he zipped himself into his coat and laced up his trainers.

But as he eased the door of the flat shut behind him with the barest minimum of key-jingling, he didn't say anything at all. He just shut up and walked. He had no destination in mind, no goal, nothing except the sudden and overwhelming need to get out of his little box and lost in something vast.

6
GRAMMA

He stuck mostly to side-streets and the back alleys behind houses, ignoring the suspicious stares of cats from atop fences and under cars. Past shuttered shops, across dark playgrounds empty even of teenage gangs at this hour (sat on a swing and scared himself half to death with how loudly its unoiled hinges squeaked). He stopped at an all-night service station and bought a curry pasty, microwaved just short of thermonuclear by a surly garage attendant. Other than that he never saw a living human soul.

He watched, entranced, as a fox ran across all four empty lanes of a dual carriageway which was usually choked with traffic during the day. It paused for a second to look at him, its breath steaming. 'Go on, then,' he said, and it disappeared in a flash of orange fur.

He stood for long moments behind the back fences of houses, feeling an uncomfortable, voyeuristic thrill at the thought of families asleep and unaware of his presence, or, when lights were on behind upstairs curtains, trying to imagine what could be happening inside in the early hours. Once, years ago, his Mum had read him Raymond Briggs' *Father Christmas*, and Andy had been fascinated by a huge double-page illustration of the jolly old fat bloke doing his rounds along a row of terraced houses which were shown in meticulously detailed cross-section, with cellars and attics and everything in between. Comfortably tubby people asleep in striped pyjamas; suitcases on tops of wardrobes, and false teeth in glasses beside beds. He'd loved the novelty of being able to see through walls, like having x-ray vision, and despite his better nature, the fascination was still just as strong. Amongst other things, it explained the appeal of burglary and the smugness of cats.

He didn't even realise he was looking for anything until he felt the buzzing in his nerve endings – it wasn't just his shoulder or even his arm by now, but the whole side of his body – and saw the flight of wide, dark steps leading down through a gap in some iron railings. Next to it a large, clean sign had been erected – so new he thought he could almost smell the sap in the wood and the ink on the paper.

This property has been acquired by Jerusalem Construction! it declared brightly.

> *Look out for an exciting new WaterWays Development*
> *of Canalside Cafés and Restaurants*
> *and Deluxe Leisure Cruise Moorings!*

At some point in the past there had been a gate, but it lay twisted to one side and half off its hinges in the weeds and rubbish: empty alcopop bottles and shredded carrier bags. The crumbling concrete post was riddled with strange loops and swirls of graffiti. He stooped to look at it more closely but could make out little detail in the darkness. It was impossible to tell where the steps led beyond the first few yards of scrubby overgrowth and darkness – *down* seemed to be the general idea.

The compulsion to explore this place was almost physical in its intensity. He leaned forward with his hands braced against the gateposts and peered intently into the shadows, turning his head this way and that to get the benefit of his peripheral vision. Somehow it felt right that this – whatever this was – could only be seen sideways. He listened; the traffic noise was muted, just like it had been in that strange shortcut, but he reminded himself that it was the middle of the night. Without the distraction of being freaked out and panicky, he tried to gather as much information about it as possible without actually taking a single step inside, and he came to the grand conclusion that it was dark, cold, and smelly.

Not exactly Narnia, he observed and turned, fully intending to go home. Nevertheless, he found himself on the other side of the gate, surrounded by scrubby bushes. Steps plunged steeply downwards into them, from which the smell of the canal rose; silty and brown.

It was obvious now that the rubbish was the remains of where some homeless person had recently lived; there was a blanket, large panels of soggy, shredded cardboard, and empty tins. As his feet were picking their careful way towards the steps, something metallic and chain-like glinted in the mud – something with a large leather loop at one end which took him a while to recognise as a collar, because it appeared to have broken apart. He told himself that it had simply perished, snapped, and been thrown away when whoever lived here had moved on, taking their mutt with them... but couldn't quite shake the impression that it had been deliberately torn open. And the more he looked around – at the blanket which had clearly been slashed in several places, at the tins (not all of which were actually empty), the more he began to suspect that they had not so much moved on as been driven by someone, or something.

Dead nettles and needles of stone.

For a walk which was supposed to be clearing his head, this was seriously weirding him out. He began to wonder if he wasn't still asleep and dreaming.

He climbed down past the thin trunks of skeletal beech trees to the tow-path and saw the canal gleaming and oily-dark against the orange sky. One thing to be said for the cold: at least the mud had frozen solid.

Some way ahead was moored the squat bulk of a narrow-boat, completely dark except for one red running-light low down by the waterline. A smudge of smoke rose in a straight line from the conical hat of an old-fashioned chimney. *Tourist boat*, he thought. Not so odd to see them at this time of year, but this was a bit out of their way. He'd have expected to see something like this moored closer to the bright lights and fashionable restaurants around Gas Street Basin. Still, whatever; at least the laws of nature seemed to be behaving themselves this time. So, bonus.

Something moved on deck, and a volley of barks shattered the silence.

'Oh, *shit…*'

A light appeared in one of the narrowboat's windows and Andy turned quickly back to the steps, discovering with a weary lack of surprise that they weren't there any more – he was faced with several feet of tow-path which stopped where the canal continued into a pitch-black tunnel. *Can't go back. Going back just makes it worse, makes it – deeper, somehow. Forward, then, bullshit factor ten and damn the torpedoes.*

He put his head down, jammed his hands deep into his jacket pockets and quickened his stride, anxious to get past but equally determined that he wasn't going to run. The barking was punctuated by the clashing jerking thud of a heavy chain straining against bolts sunk deep into wood. It came from an area at the front of the narrowboat which had obviously been converted into a kennel. What were they keeping over there? The Hound of the Baskervilles? 'Hound of the Basket-cases,' he muttered, and strode on. Absolutely not running. Much.

As he passed the front, a woman's broad Black Country voice from belowdecks yelled 'Spike! For Christ's sake, *shut it!*' A door crashed open, and sudden light from behind threw his shadow ahead of him.

'You! What the bloody hell d'you think you're up to?'

Andy kept walking. Whoever she was, she wasn't going to chase him.

'Stop and answer me you little bastid, or I'll set the dog here on you!'

Sigh. This was getting ridiculous. Andy turned around. 'I'm just walking here, lady. Sorry if it woke your dog up, but…' The beam of a powerful torch shone full in his face, and he had to shield his eyes, squinting sideways.

'Walking? At what time in the morning? Pull the other one; it's got bollocks on.'

All he could do was shrug helplessly. 'I didn't touch your boat, if that's what you're worried about. Look, could you just – ?' He gestured into the glare, which dropped fractionally. He had an impression of short, wild-haired age.

'How'd you get in?'

'Look, I already said I didn't…'

'Not the boat, boy. Do I look like a fool? You know what I mean. In.'

In. 'To… what, exactly?'

He seemed to be scrutinised for a long moment before the old woman laughed shortly. 'And there was me thinking you was just playing stupid,' and she turned to go. As she did so, the sweep of torchlight flashed across a rainbow jumble of graffiti covering the whole side of the boat, which he hadn't noticed in the dark.

'Hey!' he blurted. 'Wait a minute! Excuse me, sorry, but what is that?'

'What?'

'That graffiti – all over the side of your boat.'

The old woman made a show of peering closely. 'This? Well glory be, it looks exactly like graffiti. Can't think how I missed it. Thanks for pointing it out; I'll get it cleaned off first thing in the morning.'

He was too excited to be put off by her sarcasm. His heart was suddenly beating high in his throat, his nerves stretched like violin strings through his limbs. 'That's how I got in – I've been following that. I've been seeing it everywhere. It's not just graffiti, though, is it? What does it mean?'

'Well,' she said, bending and pointing to one of the squiggles. 'This one means that it's the middle of the bloody night, and this one means it's cold enough to freeze the tits off the Mona Lisa…' She suddenly sighed, as if the effect of being so relentlessly cantankerous was simply too much. 'Look, I really can't be arsed with all this. Cup of tea?'

'Sorry?'

'You do keep saying that. It's enough to make a body wonder what you've got to be so apologetic about. Bab, you're not a burglar, that's plain. I'm fairly sure you haven't come to murder me in me bed. You'm not 'folk, that goes without saying, though apparently you're thick enough to get yourself lost in the Narrows – even one that has Closed. Either that or you're just very, very unlucky. So do you want a cup of tea before you go off and get yourself killed? Think of it as being a bit like a last cigarette, if it helps.'

'Thanks. I think.'

'Just wipe your feet, that's all,' she humphed.

As he passed the kennel in the narrowboat's bow he could just make out the shape of a large black muzzle lurking below gleaming eyes, and a subterranean growl followed him downstairs after the old woman.

Belowdecks, the interior of the narrowboat looked like a cross between a junk shop and a medieval apothecary. It was lit by paraffin storm-lanterns which swung gently from the low ceiling as the boat shifted, causing shadows to creep back and forth behind wooden chests, small tables piled high with old magazines, shelves crowded with jars, tins, boxes and jute bags, a spidery old sewing machine, and stacks of mildewed paperbacks. Towards the far end of this long, cramped forward cabin, there was a galley space hung with bunches of dried herbs and dominated by a squat, black cast-iron stove.

The old woman drew water for the kettle from a hand-pump, placed it on the hob, and lobbed a few lumps of coal into the stove's belly. A warm, sulphurous smell filled the cabin.

'Pass me that tin,' she ordered, pointing. He passed her down a huge old Ovaltine tin, and she scooped several teaspoons of black and fibrous tea into two chipped mugs.

'Not much electricity in the Narrows, I suppose,' he ventured.

She looked up sharply. 'You use that word like you know what it means. An overdeveloped sense of familiarity is a dangerous thing, lad.' She poured boiling water, frowned into one of the mugs for a moment, extracted something twig-like which she threw away and passed the mug to him. 'Got no sugar. Sets my teeth off. No milk, either. Best you don't ask why,' and she chuckled throatily. 'Still, this'll set you right for home.' She settled into a sagging armchair whose stuffing was metastasising from every seam, and she inspected him over the rim of her mug.

He sipped gingerly. The tea was scalding hot and tasted vaguely of pea-pods. 'They visit you, don't they?' he asked. 'The people who travel through the Narrows. The ones who leave the graffiti.'

She took so long to reply that he thought maybe she had fallen asleep with her eyes open. For a long time here was no sound but the ticking of several clocks and soft clinkering of embers settling in the stove. 'Tell you what,' she replied at last. 'You tell old Gramma here what you think you know, and I'll tell you when you'm wrong.'

'Okay then. They visit you, that's why your boat's covered in their graffiti. It's like signposts or something. Breadcrumbs in the forest. Chalk-marks in a maze.' He was thinking aloud now, working it out as he went along. 'Maybe you're not always here – this is a boat, so maybe you move around, but they visit you anyway for, what, safety? Shelter? Tea?'

He paused, waiting for a response.

Silence.

'I knew it! I *knew* it! And the Narrows. They're – what? Wormholes?'

She snorted in disgust.

Maybe it was the excitement, or the fact that he'd been out walking for miles in the sub-zero early hours, but he felt a sudden and painful pressure on his bladder. 'Um, sorry about this, but would you mind if I used your…'

She waved him to a door on the other side of the galley. 'Be my guest.' As he got up she added. 'It'll be the tea. That's nettles for you.'

At her words he was seized with a sudden dizzying sense of the Pattern coalescing around him, like the moment on a fairground ride when all the forces of motion and gravity cancel each other out and for a breathless second you float, weightless and frozen out of time. When the sensation faded, he found himself in what was surely the smallest of smallest rooms, relieving himself into an ancient vacuum-pump toilet and reading, inches from his nose, the old commandment: *If you sprinkle when you tinkle, please be neat and wipe the seat.*

For the first time he felt as if he might be getting close to some answers. Even if the old woman told him nothing else, her very existence confirmed that at least he wasn't imagining the whole thing. She might very well be as mad as a box of frogs, but that didn't change the essential fact that this was *real*. With a whole constellation – no, *galaxies* of questions orbiting in his head, he pumped the flush and opened the door.

The biggest dog he had ever seen in his entire life sat in the passageway outside. It bared yellow canines at him and unleashed a growl which he felt through the soles of his shoes. Drool spattered between its forepaws.

Behind it, Gramma was dressing herself in a huge coat and a woollen beanie. 'Now don't you go being foolish enough to annoy my Spike, there,' she warned. 'He's not a bad dog, but he's very protective of me, and if you try to move out of there he will make a mess of you. Quite a big one, I should imagine. Don't doubt that for a second.'

'But... I don't...'

She sighed. 'I know. You don't. Neither do I, for what that's worth. You'm not a bad lad if I'm any judge of character, but the plain fact is it's not down to me. Good people are dying – my people – and here you come swanning along all big-eyed and asking questions, and walking where there's no way you *can* walk. Do you understand that? The place where you said you got in, *there is no way in.* It shut weeks ago. So then you'm either lying, or you can do something nobody else has ever been able to do. You're a problem, lad, and I'm not clever enough to sort it out, so I'm taking you to those that are. You just sit tight and don't do anything silly. You mind my Spike. He's not a bad boy.'

She disappeared towards the narrowboat's stern and a few moments later, he heard its diesel engine grumble into life. The boat lurched slightly as it began to move, and he sat down on the toilet seat, feeling utterly confused and helpless. Spike remained rock-solid on his feet – the big muscles in his shoulders and chest working. He was absolutely fucking huge.

Andy couldn't believe he'd just been kidnapped. This was just too surreal. People didn't actually get kidnapped in the real world; they had dinner with their in-laws and arguments with their fiancées and went to work the next morning. Of course, neither did people travel around the city through strange gaps in the world, but somehow that was *so* strange that it was, bizarrely, easier to accept than the prosaic reality of being kidnapped on the loo by a mad old bat in her narrowboat.

Escape: that was people did when they were kidnapped. They tried to escape.

His options were few. There was no window as such, merely a small frosted-glass panel about six inches square. He'd seen a couple of movies where characters defended themselves by setting light to aerosols, but he had no lighter, and all he could see in here was a thick hand-towel, an evil-smelling toilet brush and a tube of haemorrhoid cream. It would be funny if there weren't a dog the size of a small horse staring at him. Spike was a good dog, though, wasn't he? And what did good dogs like to do? Why, good dogs liked to play games, of course. Games like *fetch*.

Andy picked up the toilet brush and waved it playfully. 'Hey boy, wanna play fetch? Wanna chase the stick? Do ya? Yes you do, don't you? Go on boy, good boy, fetch the stick!' He threw it over the dog's head and into the narrow passageway behind.

Spike didn't even follow it with his eyes. If anything, his expression became rather pitying.

'Shit.' There was another game that he knew dogs liked, but it was one which Andy was reluctant to play. It was called *tug of war*. What choice did he have, though?

He reached slowly for the hand-towel which hung by the small sink and wrapped each end around his fists so that it stretched between them like a thick garotte. The dog watched his every movement, growling softly. When Andy stood up, Spike leapt to his feet, the growl rising to a snarl.

'Let's play this, then,' said Andy grimly through his teeth, and took a step forward. 'Come on, boy. Come on then if you think you're – holy *fuck!*'

The dog surged forward and Andy barely got his hands up in time. Its jaws closed around the thick towelling between his fists, but still the momentum of its charge slammed him back against the toilet cistern, then it dragged him forwards, thrashing his head as if worrying at a slipper. Andy was thrown from one side of the doorframe to the other, barely able to keep his grip, let alone his balance. The dog hauled backwards again, dragging him out into the passage, all the while keeping up a steady, clenched snarling. He'd no idea an animal could be so *strong*. He was terrified that it would make a lunge at his throat, but, bred with a bite that could not be broken, it was betrayed by its own instincts and now it couldn't let go of the towel even if it had wanted. Just so long as Andy held on. Another savage thrash. Andy bounced off the passage wall, cracking his skull. The problem was that as soon as he slipped, or let go, or dropped the towel to run, he was dead meat.

He began to give ground (truth to tell, he had very little choice in the matter) and Spike backed up, maintaining a continual loose, rattling snarl very much like the narrowboat's own engine. Into the galley, yanking him from side to side so that he fell against the furniture and was hit by falling objects. It felt like his arms were being twisted from their sockets like chicken legs.

Despite this punishment, a sliver of hope began to grow: if he could keep this up, and the dog continued to back up along the length of the cabin and out the door, back towards its kennel at the front of the boat, he might be able to make a dash for it – leap over the side and possibly make it to the canal bank.

He gave ground again. Yank. Thrash. Snarl. This could actually work.

Then he slipped.

One of Gramma's mismatched rugs rucked up and slid out from underneath his foot. His knee twisted in hot liquid agony and he went down awkwardly, crying out and letting go of the towel.

Suddenly released, the dog fell backwards, and Andy had just enough time to register that this was it, he was going to get mauled and very possibly killed, before it scrambled back onto all fours and threw itself on him. Its jaws fastened on the meaty flesh of his left calf, below where his trouser cuff had ridden up in the fall, and shook him again like a doll. There was no pain at first, just a terrible, bone-deep wrenching sensation and a growing warm wetness in his shoe. Neither was there room for fear amidst the sudden shock. What he felt, as he watched the animal worry at his leg, his blood on its chin, was incredulity and a swiftly growing rage.

Bite *me*? You'd dare bite *me*? For some reason he heard Nurse Barton saying 'Little scratch…'

Power burst from deep in the flesh where Spike's teeth had penetrated. It raved straight into the dog's mouth and illuminated its gullet in red, and for a second Andy fancied he saw it burning from the nostrils and from around the edges of the eyeballs, as if its entire head were filled with fire. The dog jerked like it had been electrocuted and tried to pull away, yowling around its mouthful of his leg, but this time it was held fast by something stronger than its jaws.

Bite this, you mongrel. Andy rammed the power deep into the dog's head with a dark and gleeful savagery. It howled again, and then without warning Andy was looking at himself lying spreadeagled on the floor. There was blood on his teeth and the maddening stench of human terror-sweat in his nostrils, and he knew that somehow he was *inside* Spike's head. He knew too that the dog had simply been obeying his mistress' command, that he bore no conscious animosity towards Andy and was simply trying to be a Good Dog as well as he could. Suddenly sick at himself, Andy let go, and Spike collapsed in a twitching heap.

He dragged himself to his feet and started hobbling forward along the cabin, towards the door.

'What have you *done*? My poor boy, what have you done to him, you monster?' The anguished cry of the old woman came from behind; she'd left the controls at the sounds of fighting and was kneeling aghast over the convulsing body of her pet. 'What have you *done*?' she sobbed.

The narrowboat, unsteered, shuddered into the canal bank and Andy fled, driven by the power of her cries and the horror of what he had done, as much as by what had been done to him. He limped along the towpath into the stagnant emptiness of the Narrows and didn't stop until the sound of her anguish was replaced by the normal murmur of traffic, and the night sky had turned a more comforting shade of orange.

7
TRACES

The Gates stood ready.

Thick swathes of silver-grey duct tape held the girl in a cruciform position between two upright girders. The needleman worked with calm, untheatrical efficiency: dozens of bristling needles damming and redirecting and channelling her *ch'i* into the structure which rose half-built around him, and the glimmer of her dying was reflected in the shining black eyes of the creatures which squatted in the surrounding shadows. It was possible that he may have been humming to himself a little.

'My dear,' he said 'in a little while you're going to want to start screaming. I think that's a very healthy instinct, so you go ahead and scream. As much as you want. Let the world know how much it all hurts, how wrong this all this. This isn't a good way to die, and there's no reason for you to try putting a brave face on it, is there?'

There was no congregation this time, however. No floor show. Those influential men and women were bound to his service as well by one sacrifice as a dozen, and he actually found the whole ceremonial circus – while a tedious political necessity – to be quite distasteful. The pseudo-mystical mumbo jumbo demeaned both her and the cause for which she was dying, though of course it was unreasonable to expect her to believe that he genuinely bore her no malice. So when she spat in his face and cursed him with the foulest of invective, he didn't hold it against her. In the modern parlance, he knew where she was coming from.

He drove the first knife into the base of her spine, where her *muladhara* chakra stood open and energised by the preliminary work that his needles had accomplished, and prepared himself for the upwelling of energy, ready to channel it upwards with the remaining knives as her body incinerated itself from the inside out.

Nothing happened. She simply... died.

'What?'

Her body hung limply from the girders. No longer a gateway. No longer an incandescent, vital conduit for the powers that would ultimately elevate him to godhood. Just dead flesh.

The skavags, sensing his mounting consternation, began to murmur and shift uneasily.

'Carling!'

The younger man snapped out of his open-mouthed shock as if lashed. 'Yes, boss?'

His master didn't deign to reply. For a moment the mask of easy-going bonhomie dropped, and Carling found himself staring into eyes which were as inescapable and pitiless as twin black holes. Something had gone wrong.

Nothing *ever* went wrong.

'I'll find out,' he managed to say.

'Do that.'

***

As Andy struggled up the stairs from the canal, it seemed for a moment that his first few steps away along the pavement were harder than they should have been, as if he were wading through water or being held back by some kind of magnetic force acting on the very iron in his blood. Then he was free and, feeling utterly drained, he retraced his steps home. When he emerged from the row of garages behind their block of flats, he saw that the living room light was on and cursed himself all the way up the stairs and through the front door.

Laura was waiting for him in her dressing-gown, seated at the dining table with her head propped up on one hand and a cold cup of tea untouched in front of her. She raised her eyes to regard him coldly from under a mussed-up fringe.

'Where have you been?' she asked quietly.

'Laura, I – '

'Where have you *been*?' she yelled, slapping her hand on the table with a report loud enough to rattle the cutlery on its hanger. It jingled mindlessly as she glared at him. 'Jesus Christ, Andy, I was worried *sick*!'

'I just went for a walk…'

'A walk? A *walk*?! Andy, look at you! I wake up in the middle of the night to find you gone, and you stagger in at four o'clock in the morning looking like – like -' Lost for words, she got up, stalked into the kitchen and started banging some plates around. He limped to the phone and dialled 999.

She stalked back out again. 'No! I'll tell you what. If this is something to do with the wedding, if this is you getting cold feet and deciding to show me that you're still some kind of free-ranging male spirit thing…'

Then she noticed all the blood.

***

Carling stood on the towpath in the gathering dawn, chucking bits of gravel one at a time at a floating styrofoam cup. He was tired, angry, and his aim was crap, which only made his temper worse.

splish

Shouldn't be here.

He'd been up to the gate and found it re-opened, just as he'd thought. It wasn't a major one, hadn't needed one of those big blood-letting jobs, just your bog-standard iron stake wrapped in copper wire and hammered into the ground. They'd sunk hundreds of the things all over the city. He didn't understand how just one of them going tits up way out here could cause such a failure, but there it was. He just did what he was told.

Nothing seemed to have been tampered with. No new graffiti to show that the Narrowfuckers had been sniffing around again – and yet there it was, wide open and alive.

Shouldn't -*splish*- fucking -*splish*- be here.

'Sink, you bastard thing.'

The skavags suddenly set up a mewling chorus, which told him that they'd finally found something. Running, he found them clustered in a knot far down the tow path. They cowered away as he arrived, their black eight-ball eyes rolling in fear, and when he saw their discovery his heart leapt.

Blood. Tacky, almost dried, but quite definitely a spattering of blood which trailed off along the path. There were lots of ways to track a man, Carling knew – by foot, by rumour – but far and away the best was by his blood. Carling straightened up, put his red-tipped fingers in his mouth, and sucked thoughtfully. With the taste of a man's blood in your mouth, he could never ultimately escape you.

He gave assent to the skavags, who set to the red trail with their long whip-like tongues, licking it clean as they went, and when it petered out they scattered, hooting joyously, looking for more. Hunting for the source. Carling watched them go with something approaching affection.

As he strolled back on his way to deliver the good news, he rolled the salt-gritty taste around his gums and wondered if maybe his line of work wasn't starting to get to him a bit.

8

THE BOLLARD GAME

When the Accident and Emergency doctor started to stitch up his leg, Andy was so dizzy with shock that at first it didn't occur to him to try and stop the man.

'Better make sure you're wearing rubber-soled shoes,' he wanted to joke. He got as far as '...' but the action of raising his head from the pillow to speak caused the big strip-lights over his head to dance in fragmented prisms, and he sank back with a groan. When someone else came in and gave him what he assumed was a tetanus shot, he just let them get on with it. They were professionals – they could look after themselves. Whatever it was that had come out of him seemed to have dissipated for the moment, and nobody suffered any kind of freak electrical attack, so he allowed himself to relax.

In between there were questions, forms, telephone calls.

Throughout the whole process, and including the two-hour wait on hard plastic chairs, he expected Laura to explode at him again. He would have welcomed it, almost. Not that he felt he deserved it, but at least it would have broken the tension. She had dragged on a pair of old sweat-pants and her leather jacket over the nightshirt she'd worn last night – which felt like a million years ago – and he thought she'd never looked more gorgeous. But all she said when he was finally discharged, limping with his jeans-leg rolled up to the knee and his calf swathed in bandages, was 'Come on you, let's get you home.'

'Laura, look, I'm really, *really* sorry,' he started, but she shushed him with a smile.

'It's fine. Honestly. Get your coat on. I'm just glad you're alright.'

Now he knew she was pissed off.

She drove him home in silence through the pre-dawn twilight, along deserted roads. He had to slide the passenger seat right back so that he could prop his injured leg straight out ahead, and so had a good vantage point from which to watch the muscles in her jaw bunching and unbunching themselves as she chewed the inside of her cheek.

She was *really* pissed.

They returned home, and she headed straight to get showered and dressed for school while he changed painfully out of his filthy and bloodstained clothes. By the time he'd made her a conciliatory cup of tea, she'd finished putting her make-up on and was gathering folders into her big shoulder-bag.

'Oh, hon,' she said as she saw him. 'Thanks, but I don't have time. I can just about make it to work if I leave right now. Kate said she'd cover for me, but you know how mad it gets. Really sweet of you, though.' She put a hand gently to his face. 'Plus, you need sleep. When I get home we'll sort all this mess out. You can look after yourself, can't you?' She stole a quick swig of tea and left, closing the door quietly behind her, and he listened to her calm footsteps recede down the stairwell.

Yes indeed, he was a dead man.

Fully intending to make amends by cleaning the entire flat from top to bottom, he crashed out on the sofa and fell instantaneously asleep. This time, there were no dreams. Or if there were, he was able to outrun them.

***

The phone woke him up a little before ten. He stared blearily at the clock, his first panicked thought being that he'd slept right round and into the evening. When he understood that it was still morning and he'd had less than three hours' rest, he couldn't decide which was worse. He limped into the hall and fumbled the phone out of its charge socket.

'Hello?'

'Andy? Nigel.' His boss, having to raise his voice over what sounded like a very full, very busy shop.

'Nigel, hi, yeah. Look, did I call you from the hospital earlier?'

'Yes, you did. How's the leg?'

'I may never play the violin again.'

'Good, good. Listen, I need you to come in.'

'Sorry, can't be done. Doc says no exercise for at least twenty-four hours.'

'I know. You said. But I absolutely must have you in this morning, Andy. It's stock day – I've got dozens of boxes stacked up in the office, full of games I can't sell because I've got no spare hands to check the invoices.'

'Nigel, I'm really, *really* sorry...' and as the same apology came out of his mouth for the second time in a handful of hours he realised how much he hated the sound of it. He felt like he'd been spending half his life apologising for one thing or another. But Nigel was in full flow.

'... know, don't you, that it's only three weeks before Christmas? Your little adventure has gone and played silly buggers with this place, I hope you realise. You know how mad it gets. Still,' he added in aggrieved tones, 'I'm sure you can look after yourself, can't you?'

Laura's words. There it was again: the Pattern unscrolling before him, like a wall of graffiti seen from a train window.

Nigel was wittering on in the background about how stock-checking meant that he could sit down all day and not worry about his leg, but for Andy the decision had already been made. He'd have to leave early and get home before Laura did or there would be hell to pay if she discovered that he'd been disobeying doctors' orders.

'Okay. I'll come in.'

'Thank Christ for that. You've saved my life. Owe you one, buddy.'

***

Andy wasn't above rubbing Nigel's nose in the fact that he was doing him a favour, and so hobbled in wearing jeans and a hoodie – aside from anything else it made it less likely that the boss would change his mind and put him out on the shop floor.

The Games Barn was a seething press of confused-looking parents and hygiene-challenged, adolescent males shuffling amongst the shelves, half-distracted by big plasma screens repeating garish, violent trailers for games, all to a background of seasonal muzak. He managed to avoid it altogether by reaching the shop via the labyrinth of service corridors which ran behind the shopping centre's retail units, dodging large, flat delivery trolleys and piles of crushed cardboard boxes.

Boxes filled every available space in the already cramped office and were stacked to the ceiling in the narrow passage which led to the shop floor. He would have arrived sooner if he hadn't stopped to examine every piece of graffiti he saw on the way. Once or twice he caught delivery workers looking at him oddly, and he hurried on.

His job should have been very simple: open the box, remove the invoice, key titles and quantities into the shop computer, and then yell for somebody who could actually walk to get the contents out on the shelves. One box, however, proved troublesome; try as he might he couldn't square the paperwork with the contents (forty copies of a low-budget, first person shoot-em-up whose charming gimmick involved ripping body parts off your victims and sticking them onto your own character. *Tidings of comfort and joy, everybody*), and so he was forced out to find his good old buddy Nigel and ask him for an executive decision.

As they stood at the till point trying to find a solution, Andy became aware of one customer in particular who was standing very close to him, and very still. He looked up.

Mr Handsfree Dickhead glared back. 'So you work here,' the man observed. 'Imagine my surprise.'

'Ah,' replied Andy. 'Um. Look...' and attempted to back in the direction of the office.

'Not so fast.' Handsfree turned his glare on Nigel. 'Are you the manager?'

'Yes sir. My name is Nigel Clarke. I'm the branch manager. How can I help you?' The oiliness in his voice was betrayed by a sharp sidelong glance which he shot in Andy's direction.

'Excellent. I have a complaint to make about a member of your staff.'

Now both men were staring at him.

'Perhaps, sir, we should discuss this matter in my office?' Nigel suggested, but Handsfree was having none of it.

'Oh no. I'd prefer to discuss this right here, if you don't mind.'

'Of course, sir, I understand that you are angry and upset. It would simply be a lot easier to discuss it somewhere quieter, especially if you wanted to, for example, call our head office and take the matter further with them?'

The prospect of tearing a few strips off Head Office obviously appealed to the businessman more than a bit of light public humiliation, and he agreed readily, preceding them towards the back of the shop. As they went, Nigel hissed 'What in God's name did you do this time?' to which Andy could only shrug.

Handsfree surveyed the tiny office with disdain before rounding on them.

'This little *snot*,' he barked, stabbing a finger at Andy, 'was unbelievably and inexcusably rude to me outside the shopping centre yesterday. The *name* he called me!'

'It wasn't actually all that offensive,' Andy commented. 'I mean, considering. There are worse things you can be called for kicking a homeless guy's money all over the street...'

'That has absolutely nothing to do with...'

'...arrogant, stuck-up, shit-for-brains springs to mind...'

'Mr Clarke, are you *listening* to this?!'

'Now wait a minute,' Nigel interrupted, more assertively than Andy would have believed him capable. 'Are you saying, sir, that this occurred outside the shop?'

'Yes. On the ramp outside the centre.'

'And has nothing to do with selling you any of our products?'

'Well, no, not as such. But see here...'

'And so, properly speaking, would be better described as a quarrel between two private individuals rather than a disciplinary matter regarding the behaviour of one of my sales staff towards a customer.'

Andy could scarcely credit that Nigel was actually defending him here. He wondered if Mrs Clarke had been giving her husband a bit of the old Christmas Cheer recently. But Handsfree wasn't giving up so easily.

'That may be true, but it doesn't change what he called me just a second ago, does it?'

'No,' Nigel sighed heavily. 'No it doesn't, and I desperately wish he hadn't said that. Don't you, Andy? Don't you desperately wish you hadn't said that?'

Andy looked between the two men – the one who wanted him sacked and the other who was unaccountably trying to save his job – then down at the stack of invoices in his hand, and the boxes out in the corridor, and the crowd of shambling idiots out there spending credit they couldn't afford on crap they didn't need, and he felt absolutely sick and tired and fed up with whole thing. He was seized with the sudden conviction that right at this moment there was somewhere else he was supposed to be.

'You know what?' he said, slapping the invoices into Clarke's hands. 'As a wise man once said, I wasn't even supposed to be working today. Thanks for the job. And Merry Christmas, dickhead.'

It must have been a coincidence, but as he limped out of the shop, he found that his leg didn't hurt quite so much any more.

***

On the train home, Andy once again tried to spot the embankment where he'd seen the dread-nettle girl, but it was useless. It all looked the same: dead ground, litter-choked and overgrown with filthy, blighted hawthorns. Still, it was at least a novelty being able to see the homeward journey in daylight. It wasn't even lunch time.

He told himself that he should be feeling more worried about quitting his job, depressed and angry with himself, but all he could feel was a sort of blank weightlessness, as if he'd been walking for days under a great burden which had just been removed. Disturbingly, he found that the voice in his head which told him these things wasn't his at all, but Laura's. He suspected that she was very nearly at the end of her tether; quitting his job less than a month before Christmas might just be enough for it to snap altogether, and he instinctively started rehearsing his apologies and edited explanations of what had happened. But he didn't have the patience for this, either. The strangeness of the last ten days or so was clamouring for more of his attention, like signals on the line warning of a sudden split in the tracks up ahead, hooded lanterns pointing the way to dark, shadow-strewn sidings.

He found that he desperately needed to be off this thing and walking, moving under his own power. Bugger the doctors – his leg barely hurt at all. When the train slowed to a halt at University, he popped out of the doors like a man coming up for air.

'Hello,' said Bex, who was balancing one-legged on a bollard outside the station.

Andy froze. 'Oh my god.'

'Shut up, don't make me lose my… *shit*!' She wobbled, lost it, and jumped down. 'Bollocks. Still, you're here, so it must have worked.' While he was struggling to make his brain operate, she was able to get a proper look at him. He was dark-haired and dark-eyed, probably quite cute if he got a bit of exercise and lost the tendency to go around gaping like an idiot.

'What worked?' he asked finally.

'If I can hold my balance from when the first person comes out to the last person, it means I'm going to get lucky and this is going to be your station.'

'But this isn't my station.'

She threw her hands up in exasperation. 'Which just proves that it works, doesn't it? Duh!'

'You're her, aren't you? You really are.'

She considered this. 'Well, I'm me, if that's what you mean. Ta-daa,' she added helpfully, then looked worried. 'You are Hi I'm Andrew Welcome to the Games Barn, aren't you? I've got a shocking memory for faces. If you're not, then I'm going to have to rethink this whole bollard thing.'

'No, no, it's alright,' he said hurriedly. 'Andy Sumner. Hi.' He stuck out his hand.

'Bex,' she replied and shook it, amused.

'I can't believe this. I was beginning to think I'd imagined the whole thing. Are you okay, you know, after the thing?'

She regarded him soberly for a moment. 'No,' she said. 'Not in the slightest am I okay. I need to talk to you about what happened, but this isn't the place.'

'I suppose you'd better come back to mine, then.'

And she was all smiles again. 'No messing about with you, is there? Chat-up lines like that, I'm surprised the ladies aren't falling all over you.' Following her moods was like trying to chase cloud shadows on a sunny day.

'Sorry, I didn't mean…'

'Walk, Andrew Sumner, walk! Show me to your little concrete box, and there we shall share tales of strangeness and sorrow.'

9
TEA

Andy made tea while Bex hovered nervously, afraid to sit anywhere or touch anything. Everything in the flat looked so *clean*. Even before she'd run away from home she hadn't been used to an especially high standard of living. Not that this place was a mansion, but it didn't look like somebody's boyfriend had sold the television and half the furniture to pay his gambling debts, for instance.

'Here.' He handed her a mug. 'So.'

'So.'

'You stalked me – you first.'

'It wasn't stalking. I just waited at the station for each train until I found the one you came home on. Talk about bor-ring.'

'But that could have taken days! Why didn't you just come and find me at the shop? I know you saw my badge.'

She looked at him searchingly, assessing how much he could cope with, and how much she might need to give away in order to get the answers she needed. Assuming that he knew anything at all. 'Couldn't help notice you limping earlier,' she commented. 'How did you hurt it?'

'I cut myself shaving,' he replied.

'Funny. Wondered if it might have been some sort of urban hiking accident.' When he didn't answer but instead continued to gaze at her over the rim of his mug, she sighed and went over to the window. 'Fair enough. Okay then, have a look out there. Tell me what you see.'

He looked. 'Houses, trees.'

She nodded. 'Uh-huh. And along with them, schools and churches, supermarkets, police stations, shopping centres and all that, yeah?'

'Yes?'

'That's where *you* live. Now, what's behind that?'

'Behind it? I don't know – alleyways?' She nodded encouragement again. *Keep going.* 'Vacant lots, brownfield sites?'

'Not to mention deserted warehouses, factories, demolition sites, junkyards, underpasses, squats, burnt-out pubs, reservoirs, canals… This is where *I* live.'

'I understand. What's your point?'

'Point is, what's behind all of *that*?'

Andy floundered. The common-sense part of him wanted to say *nothing, there's nothing behind that, just more of the same,* except he knew it wasn't true. He didn't know what was true, exactly, and he had no way of articulating it beyond the crudest of clichés, which he was certain she would just laugh at. But she wasn't letting him off the hook so easily.

'Come on, Game Boy, say it, even though you know it's completely mad.'

He threw his hand up – the one that wasn't cradling his precious, normal tea – in despair. 'Okay, it's like some kind of magic,' he admitted and waited for her to ridicule him.

She didn't laugh – didn't even smirk. She didn't call him crazy or foolish or tell him to get his head out of the clouds or even say that she was worried about him. She simply stared back at him very intently with those incredibly blue, amber-flecked eyes, seeming to measure how much he believed what he was saying by how uncomfortable it was making him. He found himself blushing and turned away awkwardly.

'Yes,' she said finally. 'For want of a better word, magic. Behind everything, there are places where the skin of the world is thin, and it is possible to travel to other parts of the city through those places, which is what we do. Some are longer than others. Some only go one way. Some don't go anywhere at all. Some go very deep and take you through places so hellish that even the plants will try to eat you. In a lot of them there are bits and pieces of older parts of the city which have been lost or forgotten about. Birmingham is very old, did you know that?'

She was channelling Dodd now; this was more or less the same speech he'd given her when she first stumbled into the Narrows. She liked the symmetry of telling it to Andy now and warmed to her subject. There was precious little else in her world to warm to.

'It's not as big or as pretty as a lot of other places, and if you read some of the books, it's like nothing existed before the Industrial Revolution. We all love our factories so much. But did you know that there's a Roman fort under the Queen Elizabeth hospital? Or that Brummies made most of the Roundheads' swords in the Civil War? It's not flashy, and it doesn't bring in the big fat American tourist money, but it's there, underneath.' She stopped, somewhat embarrassed at having got carried away.

Chancing what little knowledge he had, Andy ventured: 'You're talking about the Narrows, aren't you?'

She looked up sharply. 'How do you know what they're called? Who have you been talking to? Where did you hear that word?'

A little taken aback by her sudden aggression, he said quickly 'The same place I hurt my leg.' He told her about his expedition to the canal and his run-in with Gramma – most of it, anyway – as well as his strange shortcut from the week before. He didn't tell her anything about the pins and needles, nor what had happened to Spike or Nurse Barton –

not because he felt guilty, but because the mysteries of what was happening inside his own flesh seemed too personal. He hadn't even mentioned any of it to Laura; how was he going to tell this total stranger?

By the time he'd finished, the midwinter afternoon was darkening rapidly over the rooftops and gardens, and several streetlights had already flickered into life. He checked the time nervously; Laura would be home any time soon. Bex was staring at her own darkened reflection in the window, lost in thought.

'It goes without saying that you're telling me probably less than half of what actually happened,' she said, 'but that's fine. The thing is, most people only ever find the Narrows if they've been shown by somebody else. They're not the kind of thing you can just come across by accident. You're simply better off not knowing, trust me. They become your whole life if you're not careful, and this, all of this…' she waved a hand in a gesture which encompassed not just the contents of his living room, but the world outside and everything with which he was familiar '… it all becomes shadows, whether you want it to or not. And if you've somehow found one that's been Closed, well…' She trailed away. Her own knowledge was woefully lacking in this department. She'd expected to have years more to learn from Dodd, but now she'd been thrown into this nightmare alone. Walter would know more, but he'd refused to help look for Dodd, so fuck him.

'It's none of my business. If you ever find Moon Grove, look me up. In the meantime, all I need to know is what you saw from the train.'

This suited Andy fine. 'You running, mostly.'

'That's all?'

Andy shrugged helplessly. 'I don't know. It was dark. I couldn't see properly. Maybe two figures standing on top of the embankment, but I can't be sure.'

Two? Why would there be two? 'Did you see their faces?'

'No – like I said, it was dark; the light was behind them. I barely saw you.'

'Shit. *Shit*!' She slumped against the window, her forehead pressed to the cold glass. 'That's it, then,' she said dully. 'You were my last chance.' Then she sniffed and straightened, making a conscious effort to brighten up. 'Right. Well. Bye then,' she said and headed for the front door.

Andy stared after her in surprise and then limped in pursuit down the short hallway. 'That's it?'

'Yep.' She dragged the door open.

'I got my leg chewed half off because of all this and *that's it*?'

'I thought you said you cut yourself shaving.' She was clumping down the stairwell.

'I don't shave my bloody legs!' he yelled, his voice echoing up and down all three floors for the benefit of his neighbours. As parting shots went, he'd been hoping for better.

10
LACUNA

Andy threw himself onto the sofa and stared gloomily around at the mess, remembering how he'd fully intended to tidy the place up this morning. At the very least he need to wash up the mug that Bex had used, because as hard as it was going to be explaining to Laura how he'd lost his job, that was nothing compared to what would happen if she knew there had been a strange girl in the flat. And she would know. He should also try to air out the room a bit so that it didn't smell quite so much of unwashed, ungrateful homeless psycho-woman…

There was a knock at the door.

Oh great. Just lovely.

'Why darling, you're home early,' he said under his breath as he unlatched the door. The knocking became more of a hammering, and he had half a second to wonder if this was such a good idea before Bex barged past him and back into the flat.

'Two men?' she snapped.

'-?-'

'Two men?'

'Yes, but like I say, I couldn't…'

She strode into the living room, switched off the light and stabbed a finger at the window. 'Something like those two men out there, perhaps?'

Andy and Laura's flat overlooked the back of the block, where there was a small patch of lawn and some shrubbery before the long rectangular line of residents' garages, and a drive lit with security bollards which were just starting to flicker into life in the gathering gloom. Security had been high on Laura's list of priorities for their first place together.

Two men stood in the middle of the lawn, their shadows stretching long towards the building. The taller was dressed in a long coat that curled about his ankles, and in his hand he carried a staff, which gleamed copper-red. As Andy watched, the tall man placed the end of the staff against the ground, and with the heel of his hand pushed its entire length into the earth with apparently no more effort than as if it were a drawing pin.

One by one and without any fuss, the security lights began to go out.

'Yeah,' he said slowly, through a suddenly dry mouth. 'Something like them.' He watched darkness flood across the grass with the fascination of a drowning man watching the tide come in. 'It's a Narrow,' he realised. 'Dear god, he's dropped this whole building into a Narrow.'

'You can't know anything about this,' insisted Bex. 'It's impossible.'

'What – me knowing anything about it or him doing it?'

'Both.'

Bex saw that outside the fading light's periphery, squat creatures prowled and loped. The shorter man, who looked nothing more remarkable than the average skinhead, made a commanding gesture with one arm, and as the final light was extinguished, the skavags boiled towards the building.

The entire block of flats gave a sudden, bone-shuddering lurch which threw them off their feet at the same time as the electricity failed, and the sudden darkness was filled with the creaks and groans of shifting masonry, the crashes of things breaking in distant rooms, and the terrified screams of other residents. For a moment the only light came from Bex's flashing Santa earrings. She fumbled in her rucksack for a torch and snapped it on, picking out Andy's wide eyes and white face with its jittering light.

'What's going on?' he asked, shocked. Plaster dust had drifted in his hair like madness.

She ignored him. 'Ways out of here? Fire escape?'

He shook his head. 'The block's only three storeys – it doesn't have one. Just the stairs.'

They ran to the open front door. The stairwell landing light was swinging crazily and long, deep cracks were opening up in the brickwork. From below came the sound of breaking glass, more screams, and strange ululating cries looping upwards. Bex tried to slam the door, but it had been left open when she'd come barging in, and now its frame was twisted out of true; it wouldn't shut properly, never mind lock.

'What's going on?' he repeated.

'Monsters are eating your neighbours,' she replied harshly. 'You really want to stop asking me that question.'

'Windows!' he shouted, snapping out of his paralysis. 'The bedroom windows are on the side of the building. There's just some bushes and then the fence into next door.'

'But that has to be two storeys, and they'll be down there too. *God* I hate flats.'

'You have a better idea?'

She thought furiously. 'Where's your kettle?'

'You want to make *tea*? Brilliant! Why don't we distract them with some fucking fairy cakes as well!'

'Andy, you're becoming hysterical. Don't make me slap you.'

Bex made it into the kitchen as half a dozen skavags emerged onto the landing. They sniffed around briefly before scrambling into the flat, hooting triumphantly.

Andy slammed the lounge door shut and dragged the settee across it, piled both chairs on top for good measure, and retreated to the kitchen. He attempted to barricade the door there too, but there was nothing anywhere near as heavy and the best he could do was to brace his back against it.

Thuds and crashes reverberated through the flimsy wall; it sounded like his barricade was holding for the moment, but he had a sick feeling that it might not be for very long. Bex had put the kettle on and was tapping a foot impatiently. 'Damn these bloody eco-boil things.'

There was a stupendous noise in the other room, an apocalyptic rending and splintering of wood. It sounded like they were clawing through the very walls. The kitchen door was rammed from the other side, making him lurch to keep his balance.

'Sod it,' Bex said. 'That'll have to do.' She climbed up onto the draining board, kettle in one hand, and booted at the lock of the window above the sink. It crashed open in a blast of frigid air and broken glass and she peered downwards, offering a quick prayer of thanks to the god of cheap double glazing.

Something in the darkness below stared up at her hungrily with flat, shining eyes.

The kitchen door was rammed again, harder this time, and began to open slowly against Andy's weight. His trainers lost their grip and slipped against the linoleum floor. Claw-tipped arms snatched and flailed in the gap.

Bex upended the kettle out of the window and the skavag below gave a bubbling screech, thrashing away into the shrubbery. She turned to grin crazily at Andy, laughed 'Remember, only boil as much as you need!' and dropped out of the window.

He was too busy wondering if she'd injured herself in the two-storey fall to defend himself from the skavag which burst through the door and reared up at him, howling.

Its wrinkled snout lunged at his throat, but he got his hands up in time to grip its head even as it overbore him and drove him against the edge of the sink. Pain flashed in his kidneys. Its flesh felt cold and slick, like old boot-leather, and its mismatched teeth stank of garbage. Claws were opening up his shoulders. More leaping shapes clustered in the doorway, eager to join the bloodletting but frustrated by the confined space.

All he could think to do was squeeze its head as hard as he could and maybe try to gouge out those glittering, obsidian eyes with his thumbs. He imagined his fingers as teeth *(or grey stones, socketed in flesh; where had that come from?)* and pushed inwards as hard as he could, not just physically but with the strength of his terror and rage, until it felt like his fingers had penetrated its very skull, and there was a sense of tremendous pressure building rapidly to such an intensity that things deep inside the creature began to twist and rupture. It immediately tried to escape, keening in agony, but Andy held it fast as its limbs twisted and snapped, thrashing as it died, and finally it slid off him in a misshapen mass.

The creatures in the doorway paused, uncertain. Breathing hard, he climbed backwards up onto the kitchen counter, his eyes riveted on them. *You too,* he promised. *Every single one of you.*

Then his foot caught on the draining board, and he fell backwards out of the window.

***

They clambered over the fence beside the row of garages and into the alley beyond. The darkness behind them was filled with the noise of confusion more than pursuit, but they both knew that the respite was only momentary.

Bex looked left and right, trying to get her bearings.

'Northfield, Northfield, Northfield,' she muttered to herself, and then turned to him: 'How far are you from the Rea?'

'What ray?' he panted.

'The River Rea!' Her voice was heavy with scorn. 'Oh of course, why would you know anything about where you live?' Turning right, but only because it seemed slightly more downhill than the alternative, she trotted away.

'Birmingham doesn't have a river,' he protested, following.

'It has three!' she snapped over her shoulder.

It only took him a dozen paces for him to realise that running was out of the question; the best he could manage was an exaggerated loping limp. He tried to wipe his hands on his jeans as he went. They were covered in filth from the dead skavag.

More dark creatures bounded over the fence behind them, and terror gave new strength to his legs.

They came out of the alley onto a residential street, still in Narrows territory – houses dark, streetlights dead, and a cloud-shredded night sky the only source of illumination. Yet even here the skavags shunned such openness, flitting in the shelter of house porches, leap-frogging over gates and hedges. They began to outflank Bex and Andy easily. The only thing that helped him was the fact that they were heading steadily downhill.

Bex sped ahead, little more than a scrap of shadow. *Not again,* she prayed. *Not this time. Not him too.*

Without warning she dodged left, between two houses. A skavag leapt at her. She ducked on the run and it overshot by inches, claws whickering where the nape of her neck had been, and sprawled in the next driveway along. Andy fled through the gap.

Another back garden, another fence, and suddenly they were plunging down through a narrow belt of trees, then knee-deep in freezing water, and collapsing on the far bank of a stream.

Andy – wide-eyed, with his breath coming in hysterical, hitching gasps -immediately scrambled to his feet to continue running, but Bex grabbed his arm. 'It's okay,' she panted. 'They can't follow us. Look.'

On the other side of the stream, which itself was only ten feet or so wide, the skavags were leaping and keening in their frustrated blood-lust. They would dart at the water and then recoil, stymied and enraged, and turn on their fellows instead.

'It's the water,' she explained. 'Free-flowing water carries a lot of *ch'i* energy. It burns them, I think. They won't even jump it, and they could make this distance easily. They're creatures of decay, the skavags. Entropy on legs.'

'How long until they find another way across?'

'We could always stick around and find out, if you're really that interested.'

It turned out that he wasn't.

***

Carling raged over the contorted remains of his creature. He was barely coherent, screaming his fury at the appalling injuries which had been inflicted on one of his pack and taking it out on the flat's contents. Barber thought he was well on the way to causing more damage than the skavags themselves. It wouldn't have surprised him. The boy had – what did they say these days? *Issues.*

At issue for Barber was a number of disturbing questions. The death of this creature, for a start. It was nothing so very far removed from what Barber himself could do – and had indeed done in the past, when he had been honing his skills – but even so, such damage would properly require hours of work, and this appeared to have been achieved in seconds. For such power to have suddenly arisen in a place as mundane as this – so strongly, so quickly – was unprecedented, verging on the miraculous. It could not be coincidence. There had to be antecedents.

Then there was the fact that his quarry had escaped. He had taken them out of the world and sealed them off so that even if they had somehow contrived to flee the building alive, they should never have been able to get beyond the boundaries of the *lacuna*. And yet they had.

The very nature of who 'they' were, even. He'd assumed that the tampering had been the girl's work, yet Carling's beasts had followed the blood-scent here, and this was most definitely no Narrowfolk squat.

'Carling!' He summoned the boy from his tantrum. 'Make yourself useful. Find out who lives here.' *Or used to*, he added to himself, looking around at the devastation with grim satisfaction. There was no coming back to this place.

11
TO MARKET, TO MARKET

Bex and Andy threaded their slow way through the press of Christmas-shopping crowds on New Street, aimless. In the first chaotic dash to escape the flat, there'd been no thought of where to go except *away*, but Bex had soon hit on the German Market as their destination.

'First thing, we need to get lost,' she'd said, leading him at a punishing pace through the evening rush-hour streets. 'I don't know whether they're following you or me, but we need to mix our trail up with a lot of other people, fast. I'm not leading those things back to Moon Grove. Then we need to get you the price of a bed for the night, because you're sure as hell not sharing with me.'

He didn't know what to make of that last remark but lacked the breath to argue.

The German Market in Birmingham City Centre filled Victoria Square and the upper reaches of New Street like a child's jewellery box crammed to overflowing. It was an artificial Christmas village dazzling with tinsel and lights, arranged in narrow streets through which shoppers meandered shoulder-to-shoulder. They passed small wooden huts offering craftware in an eye-bewildering variety, from brass nativities to woollen jesters' hats, and an even stranger mix of edible goodies: old-fashioned gingerbread, toffee apples, slabs of glassy peanut brittle which needed to be smashed with small hammers before being carried away in crackling paper bags. And then treats with more outlandish names like *gluwein, stollen,* and *lebkuchen,* the very sound of which conjured up images of pine-haunted Bavarian alps and gothic castles.

Even at this early hour of the evening, groups of drinkers were standing around small tables with plastic pints of lager, and lines of bouncing, heavily muffled children were queuing with their parents for the great carousel which gleamed in baroque splendour in front of the Council House.

'Are you hungry?' she asked. He realised that he was ravenous and said so.

They sat on the low fountain wall next to the statue of the River Goddess – which Brummies, with their instinctive appreciation for urban art, had nicknamed The Floozie in the Jacuzzi. A pair of harrassed-looking parents and their three boys were all were working on tipping themselves over the line between fat and clinical obesity by attacking several huge German sausages in hotdog buns. The smallest was whinging that he didn't *like* it, it was too *spicy*, and after some irritated snapping at each other, the family moved on, leaving it behind.

'Grub's up,' she said and helped herself, tearing it apart and offering him one half.

He looked at it. 'You're joking, right?'

Through stuffed cheeks,~ she replied 'Dugh uh luk lukum juhkung?'

'But that's just… unhygienic!'

She swallowed. 'No. What it *is* is hot. Suit yourself – more for me.'

Andy dug out his wallet and went to buy his own. He also searched for a phone booth, but the few that he found were all either vandalised or out of order.

They strolled as they ate, letting the market's light, colour and noise temporarily drive from their minds the shadows of that day's horror. When they finished, she startled him into a near heart-attack by linking her arm with his.

'Come on then, big spender,' she said, waggling her pierced eyebrows. 'Take a girl on the carousel?'

'What? No!' He pulled away. 'I have to go home! Laura will have got back from work by now – Christ alone knows what she'll have found. And what if there are more of those skavag things waiting? I've got to warn her!'

'What if there are?' Bex answered coldly, crossing her arms. 'What exactly do you plan to do? What if there aren't, and they're following you, and you lead them right to her? How stupid are you going to feel then, when your girlfriend's being eaten in front of you?'

'She's actually my…'

'I don't give a toss who she is!' Her sudden anger took him aback. 'The fact of the matter is, Andy, that if you care for her at all, the best place you can be is as far away from her as possible, at least until we figure out what's going on, and the best thing you can do is talk to the people who know about the Narrows. I can help you with both of those – I can get you a safe place to stay and put you in touch with a guy who knows pretty much everything. For god's sake, I'm not trying to have your babies – all I'm asking for is a ride on a frigging merry-go-round!'

He hesitated, indecisive as ever, and hating himself for it. As ever. She hadn't mentioned what to Andy seemed like an even worse alternative: what if nothing happened at all? What if he went back, explained everything to Laura, got his life back on an even keel, and this strange, dangerous, incredible world never touched him again?

'Oh, go on then,' he said at last. She grinned and ran to join the queue.

***

'The thing is,' she said, as they headed away from the market, further down New Street, 'you have to pay your way.'

'Sounds fair enough to me.'

'But you can't use cash, and no, we don't take Visa.'

'Why not?'

She stopped, blowing cigarette smoke at him in irritation. She was smoking a roll-up of what she called 'street-mix,' the collected scraps of tobacco out of a million discarded butts which she kept in a drawstring leather pouch. It smelt absolutely evil. 'Look, if you're going to ask 'why' every time I say something, two things are going to happen. One, I will hit you very hard. And two, you will be sleeping rough tonight. In that order. Okay?'

'Okay,' he mumbled.

'Okay, then.' They resumed their course, heading downhill past gleaming shopfronts towards the Rotunda and the huge Bullring Centre. Shoppers and pedestrians passed, ignoring them, just two more vagrants arguing with each other. The Rotunda was a twenty-storey cylinder of plush, inner-city apartments rising up on their right. 'So we're going to the market to see if we can find you something to trade for your night's kip.'

'But we just came from the market.'

'*That*? It's about as close to being a market as this is to being a Cuban bloody cigar. No, I mean the real markets. The Bullring.'

'But they're closed at night. *I didn't say 'why not'!*' he added in a rush as she turned on him again.

'Yes they are,' she agreed. 'But there's all kinds of closed. What can you do?'

'What do you mean, what can I do?'

'Do you have a trade? Are you skilled in anything? Can you build a wall, fix an engine, plumb in a sink – that sort of thing?'

'Not really.'

'Have you got any professional qualifications? Can you offer legal advice, medical help, private tuition, psychotherapy, etcetera?'

'Nope.'

'Do you know anybody who does, and who'd work for free as a personal favour to you?'

He thought about this. 'No,' he decided.

'Crystal clutcher? Tarot cards? Acupuncture?'

'God, no.'

She blew out her cheeks and carried on walking. 'This is going to be a long night for you, my dear.'

***

When the pressure of too much history squeezes down on a place, sometimes bits of it escape out of the edges. There had been markets in Birmingham's Bullring since the twelfth century, built on the lower southern side of the ridge which ran through the town centre, and almost certainly for many centuries before that.

Successive generations of civic planners had demolished whole streets to make room for them, then torn them all down to be rebuilt not twice, but three times (with a bit of help from the Luftwaffe in between), the dust of each one settling into the bones of its predecessor over almost a thousand years. It was inevitable that some odds and ends would escape the waves of demolition. A piece of building here, a yard of street there; a lamp-post, a horse-trough, an archway. They fell through the gaps and drifted under their own peculiar gravity to collect like beach debris in a short remnant of a long-destroyed road called Spiceal Street.

Andy had never seen anything quite like it. If he'd ever travelled in Eastern Europe or the third world, he would have had some frame of reference to understand the jumbled chaos which Bex lead him through, but his immediate reaction was to wonder how anything remained standing.

He saw the left-hand side of a pub called The Dog, completed on its right by part of a medieval cloister, which sat across a cobbled passageway from market stalls patchworked out of everything from wrought iron to wattle-and-daub. It was crowded and busy with people, brisk and business-like rather than the slow herds further up the road, and most of them had rucksacks like Bex. Some were haggling with the stall-holders over the contents, but most were bartering directly with each other in pairs and small groups.

Bex worked her way from one knot of traders to another, chatting, swapping news, and evidently looking for something or someone in particular. Eventually she called Andy over.

'Andy, I'd like you to meet Aston Stirchley the Third. He's going the same way as us, and he has a job that you can do to earn your bed for tonight.'

The man she introduced him to was at least a head taller than either of them, possessed of a rangy athleticism which was evident even through his layers of brightly patterned woollen clothes. Red-blond hair tumbled out from a pointed, Tibetan-style hat which dangled with bells and pompoms, and he smiled lazily through sleepy eyes and a goatee – he was what Andy imagined Jesus would have looked like if he'd taken up surfing instead of crucifixion.

'Hey,' said Aston Stirchley the Third. 'So you're the mule, yeah? Excellent – I'd've hated to see these things go to waste. Wait right here.' He sauntered off.

Andy turned to Bex. 'Mule?'

'Well, what do you expect? You're good for nothing else, are you?'

Stirchley soon returned, equipped with his own pack and carrying a large burlap sack in his arms, which he dumped at Andy's feet.

'What's in there?'

'Brussells sprouts, man. Food of the gods. Twenty kilograms of stinky green gold.'

'And I'm supposed to do what – carry them?'

Stirchley laughed – an easy, friendly sound. 'Well what do you expect them to do – fly themselves there? Of course carry them! Can't have Christmas without brussels, now can you? Let's get going, yeah? I'm freezing my tassles off here.'

***

You're good for nothing else, are you? It stung but he couldn't deny that she had a point.

Andy trudged along behind them, hefting his sack of sprouts and reflecting on the frightening speed with which his life had fallen apart to this degree. He was just starting to get an idea of how fundamentally ill-equipped he was to survive in any sense that mattered.

Being able to defend himself against physical attack had been a matter of simple knee-jerk reaction; he'd had no more control over it or idea of what he was doing than if he'd swatted at a stinging wasp, just on a slightly larger scale. He was more acutely aware of the layers of safety net which had lain between him and where he was now – not that this was rock bottom, but he guessed it was pretty close. With his job gone, there'd been social security to fall back on, maybe, but what if he was refused it for having quit rather than being sacked? He knew that Laura would support him, galling though it was to his pride, but if they split over this, what then? Back home? That too was only temporary inasmuch as his Mum and Dad weren't going to live forever. Nothing he could consider held the promise of security or permanence.

In an oddly comforting way it felt like he'd simply cut to the chase, dropped right to the very heart of the matter without having time to build up his hopes as each intermediate safety net frayed and broke beneath him. He shifted the sack and decided that if this *was* all he was good for, then he was going to be bloody good at it. Better this than whatever waited at the bottom.

Bex and Stirchley had stopped and were arguing.

'It was open last time I came by here,' he protested.

'Well it's closed now, isn't it?' she shot back, flipping through Dodd's A-to-Z. Now more than ever she wished she knew what his funny little squiggles and symbols meant. *What were you doing, Dodd? What were you looking for?* 'I want to check this out, just while we're passing.'

'Whatever, Little Bee. We're not going to get to the Grove much before midnight at this rate, so I guess a few more minutes aren't going to make a world of difference.'

Andy dumped the sack, glad of the rest. 'What are you looking for?'

'There should be a Narrow here. Not a big one, just shallow enough to shave off half a mile or so. But it's closed. A lot of them have been closing recently. I want to see if there's any sign of how or why.'

'Don't you think that might be dangerous?'

She gave him a look.

'Fair enough,' he said.

Using her torch, she peered to and fro on the ground and in the bushes on either side of the lane in which they were standing, but the shadows which its light threw obscured more than it revealed. She had no realistic expectation of them finding anything; it had just seemed like too good an opportunity to pass up. On the map Dodd had marked this spot with something that looked like a cross bisected with an arrow. It meant nothing to her, but he must have found *something* here.

Andy sat and caught his breath while Stirchley busied himself rolling a cigarette. Pages from a discarded local newspaper flapped at him close by, muddy and torn, catching his casual glance. He couldn't quite read it properly in the darkness, but what he thought he saw paralysed his breath with the sensation of the Pattern spinning itself around him in the darkness like a spider's web, or a net slowly closing.

'Stirchley,' he said, trying to keep his voice steady. 'Do you mind if I borrow your lighter for a second?'

'Sure,' he replied, and tossed it over. Andy used its flame to read the pages that just happened to have flapped open right next to him.

Community announcements. Church news. Births and Deaths.

Weddings.

'It's here!' he yelled, jumping to his feet.

Bex spun around in alarm. 'What? What's here?'

'Whatever you're looking for. It's here. I know it.'

'That's rubbish. How can you just know it?'

'How do I know *anything* about this? Look, just trust me, okay, it's here. Keep looking.'

He helped, sweeping the lighter flame close to the earth, and it didn't take long to find. 'What about this?'

She found him crouched a little way further on, having scraped mud and leaves away from a pale, circular patch of ground just to the side of the pavement. Closer, she saw that it was concrete, a plug of it buried in the earth for no obvious reason. From its centre protruded several inches of a thick metal bar.

'It looks like when they cut away iron railings, like in front of buildings,' he said. 'You know, when they needed metal for the war?'

'Yeah, but this isn't part of a railing. One bar?' She took hold of the sawn-off end and gave it an experimental tug. 'Nope. It's in there pretty solid.' She straightened up. 'I don't think this is anything. Probably just coincidence.'

'Exactly,' he said grimly and tried it for himself. Smoothly, and without apparent effort, he pulled a three-foot-long iron spike from its anchoring concrete. As its gleaming tip cleared the ground, a massive explosion of pins and needles crashed through him, causing him to yelp and drop the bar with a clang. The three of them were so startled that it took them a few moments to realise that a gap had opened up in the bushes and that the sky was no longer its customary shade of sulphur orange.

Stirchley was staring at it wide-eyed, with an unlit roll-up dangling from his lower lip. 'Now that's cool,' he said slowly. 'Does this mean it's open again?'

'I have no idea what any of this means,' replied Bex, looking at Andy with a strange expression. He thought it might have been respect. 'But apparently there *is* something you're good at. Come on. Better bring that thing with you. Walter's going to want to see it.'

'No way. I'm not touching that bloody thing again.'

'You broke it, you pay for it,' she said, shouldering her rucksack and heading cautiously into the Narrow.

'Whatever that means,' he muttered, glaring at the spike as if it might leap up and strike him. He prodded it with his toe. Nothing happened. He gritted his teeth and gingerly picked it up by the very end using only thumb and forefinger. Still nothing. Hefting it more confidently and reclaiming his sprouts, he set off after her.

'Hey, you know what this means?' said Stirchley, loping along beside him.

'Enlighten me.'

'It means you're King, man!'

'King? King of what? How'd you figure that?'

'Surely you've heard the prophecy? Whomsoever draweth the pointy, metally thing from the concrete block shall be crowned rightwise king over all the scutters!' They both laughed, and if there was anything nearby in the darkness to hear the sound, it did not disturb them.

PART 2: HOUSE

1
Taken In

The dining room of Moon Grove was dominated by a huge, oak refectory table, braced and bracketed with iron, which looked massive enough to provide the raw material for another entire building all on its own. People crowded around, on, and in some cases under it; sitting, chatting, occasionally eating. Things seemed even more chaotic on the other side of the serving hatch from which people were taking their meals, each one accompanied by a blast of steam and a din of clattering and shouting.

A sign above the kitchen door read 'Strictly Kitchen Tarts Only. Trespassers Will Be Dinner'. Andy didn't think it was an idle threat, either.

Bex waved him to an empty space at the table. 'Wait there,' she said. 'I'll get us some food,' and bypassed the queue to go straight through the door, leaving him to perch somewhat anxiously.

Stirchley had taken his sprouts – and, almost as an afterthought, tipped Andy for his hard work with a spliff – before ambling over to the other side of the room where one wall was completely dominated by a blackboard the size of a railway station departures board. It was covered with job rotas, to-do lists, and a calendar; oddly, nine days between December sixteenth and the twenty-fifth were completely blank, without even the dates, just the words 'Laying Up' written across them.

Around this were chalked a host of other more cryptic messages, which read somewhere between shopping list, car-boot sale, freight manifest and labour exchange:

Stechford Arch: bag spuds for 2 gal. red diesel

Spire Oak: bed & board for plumber

Happy chickens (good layers) for 80W UV bulbs. Will accept dancing pole.

Everything imaginable was being offered by someone, somewhere. Cigarettes, booze, drugs by a hundred names, flour, legal representation, joinery, reiki healing, turnips, pasta, solar panels, dildos, pickled onions… and every so often one of the squatters would check the board, scribble something down on a scrap of paper or the back of a hand, and leave; or else a new arrival would come up, still bundled against the outside cold, and either erase something or make an addition before setting to a bowl of stew at the great table. He wondered how many other Moon Groves there were across the city to support such a tortuously complex network of barter and favour-trading. It could in no way be described as organised, but it obviously worked.

Bex came back with a tray bearing two bowls of stew and a can of Vimto each, and great doorstop slices of bread. The stew was rich and delicious, but, as he was finding with most things recently, not in the conventional sense. The thing which he had just fished off his spoon, for example, could have been sweetcorn or a lemon-flavoured Skittle. It was hard to tell. Bex was obviously feeling more relaxed now that they were safely indoors, and he felt safer about pressing the questions which he'd been biting back during their journey.

'Most of the people who come through here are just ordinary old homeless folks,' she said. 'Squatters. They earn a meal and a bed for the night by bringing in something we need – it's usually food – and then they move on. Next night they might be in a hostel, or kipping on a friend's floor, or sleeping rough. Most can't bring enough to afford more than two or three nights at a stretch, but lots of them come back. Take Laying Up, for example. Our doors are shut for nine days, which is a lot longer than it sounds, and this place will be heaving to begin with, but by the end most of them will have moved on and just us Narrowfolk will be left.'

'And you are?'

'Oh we're the hard-core crazies,' she grinned. 'We *choose* to live this way. We're off-grid, underground, between the cracks. If there was a safety net, we didn't fall through – we jumped.'

'Why on earth would anyone choose this?'

'Lots of different reasons,' was all she replied, without looking at him. 'When you've slept rough for a few weeks, you'll be entitled to ask that question.' She tore off a chunk of bread and munched darkly.

Sensing that he was treading on dangerous ground, Andy tried changing the subject. 'So who decides how long someone can stay?'

'Walter has the last say. He's got this big list of all the stuff we need, except it changes day by day, so one week someone will bring, say, a bag of limes worth three days and the week after that the same bag of limes will be worth nothing because we've had a glut. Plus we'll have been eating Thai chicken curry for a week.'

'That doesn't seem very fair.'

'No, it's okay, I quite like Thai food.'

He threw a crust at her. 'I mean it doesn't seem very fair, because how's he supposed to know it's worth nothing?'

'Fair doesn't enter into it. It's not the London Stock Exchange. You check the board, you scavenge what you can, sometimes you get lucky, and sometimes you don't.'

'It just seems a bit haphazard, that's all.'

She flourished her spoon. 'Ta-daa!'

'Hello, Bex,' said Walter and sat down next to her with a bowl of stew, ignoring her startled reaction. 'And Andy, very glad to meet you. I'm Walter Lyttleton. Welcome to Moon Grove. Do you know you smell of sprouts?'

Andy struggled for a response which didn't involve opening and closing his mouth like a goldfish. 'You know who I am?'

'In a manner of speaking. I've just had a very interesting conversation with a young man called Aston Stirchley the Third, about, amongst other things, the opening of closed Narrows. Admittedly he doesn't strike me as having a particularly strong grip on reality, but I am intrigued, to say the least.'

This was not the Fagin-esque figure Andy had imagined. Walter Lyttleton had a long, good-humoured face and a slightly distracted manner, as if while he was talking to you, the other half of his mind was somewhere else, making connections and associations to a vast body of obscure knowledge acquired over decades of ranging the streets and the spaces in between. For Andy, who'd never been terribly good at reading other people, it was the most frighteningly clear first impression of another human being he'd ever had. He was seized with the impossible, and equally unshakable, conviction that he'd met this man somewhere before.

'Of course, your first question,' Walter continued, 'is "What are the Narrows?" Unfortunately, as is the way with first questions, the answer is neither simple nor short. I hope you are sitting comfortably.

'You are aware, I assume, of the existence of such things as leys – or as they are more commonly known, ley *lines*? A silly tautology, like pin number or scuba gear, but be that as it may. Good. These are imagined as a network of channels which carry and regulate the earth's life energy, in exactly the same way as the *lung mei* meridians of acupuncture circulate a person's *ch'i*.

'From the dawn of humanity, the earliest neolithic traders and herdsmen instinctively followed leys, like birds navigating by the earth's magnetic field, and later the Romans appropriated many of these ancient ways into their road-building programmes. Two intersect in Birmingham as a matter of fact, and there was a fort at Metchley to keep peace between the squabbling tribes of Britons hereabouts, though there never was a Roman town as such. But, leys. And the Narrows. Imagine, if you will, a ley as a smooth but swiftly flowing river. A river of life energy, yes?'

Andy nodded.

'Now imagine that someone takes several large tipper trucks loaded with boulders, and dumps those boulders into the river. What happens?'

'The water flows around them, I suppose.'

'Ah, no, not the water – the river. They are two very different things.'

'I don't follow you.'

'The water doesn't change. It gets where it's going just the same – reaches the sea, evaporates, precipitates and so on. Circle of life. Hakuna matata.'

'Gesundheit,' said Bex.

'But on the way there, the river is distorted completely beyond recognition. It fragments into a hundred smaller streams, forms eddies, back-currents, whirlpools, rapids and doldrums. It might crest over one boulder in a great standing wave and dive below another, undermining the stream-bed and scouring down through the land's old bones.

'What do you think happens when a ley, running unimpeded for hundreds of miles across open countryside, hits a city, with its hundreds of huge tower blocks of reinforced concrete rooted deep in the body of the earth?'

'It fragments.'

'Exactly. It splits, it flows apart, going in countless contradictory directions, diving and resurfacing, but always taking the path of least resistance.'

'And that's what the Narrows are!' he said, excited, finally getting it. 'Turbulence!'

'Yes.'

Andy was only half-listening however, and his excitement was half unease. Walter's description of buildings rooted in the earth's flesh had stirred memories of the nightmare which had driven him from the flat and onto Gramma's narrowboat. Coincidence. The air felt thick with Pattern. Suddenly it was difficult to breathe.

'The leys still exist in fragments, though very few people recognise them for what they are. Most cities have them, whether they're called twittens, ginnels, snickleways, whatever. They're the places where middle-aged office workers walk their dogs on Sunday mornings, where teenagers drink alcopops and snog each other on Friday nights. They're also the Green Roads where off-road bog racers drive their huge four-by-fours and churn fields into muddy, lunar landscapes, and the holloways where farmers lose their sheep. Sometimes the roads follow the leys, and sometimes the earth's *ch'i* flows into where our centuries of footsteps have worn through the skin of the world, because we are the land and the land is us.'

Bex was singing sarcastically under her breath: 'We are the world, we are the children…' but both men ignored her.

'And you use the graffiti to navigate.'

'To navigate, yes, because the Narrows drift. As buildings rise and fall, streets are demolished and shopping malls grow like tumors in the suburbs, the Narrows twist away from their established courses and we have to keep track of them.'

'I get it.'

Walter smiled patiently. It was a smile which said *No you don't. You don't remotely get it.*

'Here's where it gets complicated.'

'It's been simple so far?'

'Relatively. The next question is: when you're travelling through a Narrow, where exactly are you?' He fished a pickled onion out of his stew and sliced it open on the table across its width. 'Consider reality as structured basically very much like an onion. It's not a particularly new idea. Everybody from the ancient Egyptians through to the great Renaissance thinkers have modelled the cosmos as a concentric layering of heavens, hells, electron orbits, you name it. Everything in the world as you understand it inhabits just one of these layers. Now imagine somebody getting a pin and sticking it at a shallow angle through the skin of the onion, piercing several layers, and coming out on the other side. That, in effect, is what you do when you travel through one of the Narrows.'

'Sort of like a parallel world thing.'

'Almost, but 'parallel' implies something made out of straight lines running alongside each other and never meeting except at infinity. We are talking about circles here, which might seem like geometrical nit-picking, but it's important because the shorter the cut, the deeper you go.'

'Yes! The first time I went into one I tried to go back but I just kept getting deeper and deeper.'

'You tried to go against the flow. You got yourself caught in an undertow, so to speak.'

An undertow. That was exactly what it had felt like.

'And your next question is…?'

'What's at the centre?'

Walter threw his hands wide. 'I have no idea. No-one does. Some believe that it holds the source of all Creation. Others, that there's nothing except an absolute crushing depth, like a black hole. Do you want to know what I think?'

Andy nodded, even though his head was starting to feel uncomfortably full.

'The Narrows are a land of husks and rinds, the destination of all that is broken, lost or worn-out in our world. Nothing exists there except crumbling fragments of the city from previous centuries, preserved in the backwater eddies of contorted ley-lines, forever sifting downwards like ocean debris falling from the riot of life and colour in the warm, bright upper shallows and down into unfathomable darkness, where the only living things are pale, blind creatures. I suspect that if you could get to the centre of it all, the only thing you'd find would be a frozen singularity which would crush your soul instantaneously and absolutely.'

People had paused in their conversations and meals to listen to him, and when he stopped talking, the room was filled with a tense, expectant silence.

'You'd better show him,' said Bex to Andy.

Reluctantly, as if it were some kind of admission, Andy brought out the iron stake from under the table and laid it on the table in front of Walter. 'I think somebody is deliberately interfering with the Narrows,' he ventured. 'I've seen them twice now. We both have,' he added, with a nod towards Bex.

Walter stared at the stake as it lay gleaming on the table, and Andy could feel the man's dismay radiating from him in chilly waves.

'Wha-at?' Andy enquired slowly. 'What have I done now?' The feeling that somehow, somewhere he'd messed up again began to grow like a hollow stone in his throat.

'Andy,' replied Walter, 'just out of curiosity – just to humour an old man – please tell me: was it your idea to pull this from the ground?'

Bex bristled. 'Of course it bloody was!' she retorted. 'And I know exactly what you're on about, so why don't you drop the act and speak to me straight?'

'Very well then.' Walter turned the full face of his regard upon her, and she raised her chin defiantly. 'I congratulate you. You've proven yourself right. There is some unknown agency out there deliberately interfering with the Narrows. I was wrong.' He sounded far from apologetic, however.

'Well. Uh. Good!' she said, trying to be self-righteous and succeeding only at sounding petulant. 'That's good, then.'

'Clearly, whoever can do this is extremely dangerous, possessed of abilities we cannot understand and using them for purposes of which we remain ignorant.'

'Exactly! That's what I've been trying to tell you! The disappearances, the closures – they're all linked. We've got to do something!'

'Something, yes. Something like, perhaps, alerting this person to the fact that not only are we aware of his existence, but that we also,' and here he pointed directly at Andy, 'have the ability to undo his work?'

Andy gulped. 'Hang on a minute,' he protested. 'We? Who we? I'm not part of this.'

'You are now, boy. You became part of it the moment you took this wretched thing,' and he prodded the stake with disgust. 'Whoever put it there knows for certain now that his activities have been discovered and that they can be countered. He's going to come after you with everything he has. Your only bit of good luck, Andy, is that he probably doesn't know who you are, but the consequence of *that* is he's going to come after the rest of us with everything he has instead. He'll assume that you're one of the Narrowfolk. It will never occur to him that you're nothing more than an ignorant suburbanite who lacks the basic wit to avoid meddling with things he doesn't understand.'

'Hey, I…'

'Quiet, boy. Your lot has been thrown in with ours, whether you like it or not. You're one of the Narrowfolk now, and you're in my house, so stop wittering and start learning to deal with the consequences of your actions.

'As for you,' he rounded back on Bex. 'Do you think me blind, girl? Do you think that I cannot keep this place and my people safe for more years than you have existed without knowing something of what passes in my city? Do you think I and those close to me have not heard the same rumours that you have and tried to uncover as much of the truth as we can? And do you not think, *Bex*,' as she tried to interrupt, 'that we might be just a bit better at it than you are?'

He glared at them both and rose to leave. 'Laying Up will commence at first light,' he announced curtly to the whole room. 'I appreciate that this is several days early and doesn't leave you as much time as you'd like – nevertheless, make what arrangements you can.'

He left, and the wave of dumbstruck silence collapsed into roaring breakers of consternation as everybody began to talk at once.

***

Moon Grove did not have a telephone landline, but after dinner Andy was introduced to Phil the Phone, a grinning man of indeterminate east-European origin who had earned a permanent place at the Grove by his ability to provide free, untraceable phone calls and internet access, very discreet and no questions asked.

'You call international, long distance, or local?'

'It's just a local call. Just a quick one.'

'You need email? Text? Video maybe?'

'No – just a straightforward phone call. You know.'

'Okay.' Phil the Phone rummaged through the various pockets of a huge, multicoloured puffer jacket, examining and discarding half a dozen handsets – some of which were so old they actually had aerials – before settling on one and handing it to Andy with a toothy grin. Whatever the economic deficiencies of the emergent post-Soviet democracies, they apparently had some shit-hot dentists. 'This one is good for you, I think.'

'Why this one in particular?'

'It has screensaver of naked lady.'

'What's *that* got to do with anything?'

'You phone fiancée, yes?'

'Oh, and by the way, how is it exactly that everybody seems to know everything about me already?'

'She tell me,' Phil the Phone waved to Bex, who was suddenly very busy testing the bulbs on a string of fairy lights. 'You phone fiancée to say you lose your job and not coming home tonight; you have dirty picture to cheer you up while she chews off your balls.'

'That's not what I was… oh never mind, just give me the bloody thing.' The assumption was alarming. Regardless of what Walter had said about his lot being thrown in with theirs, he had no intention of staying here any longer than a few hours.

He tried the flat first, not expecting anything, and was unsurprised to hear the long whine of a disconnected signal. He called her mobile and found that it was switched off. He tried his own mobile – he could visualise it clearly, in the inside pocket of his thick walking jacket which was hanging pointlessly on the back of the front door – and was a little worried to find that disconnected too. He supposed it must have fallen out in the chaos and been broken. Finally, feeling like he'd been putting off an unpleasant chore, he called Laura's parents. If she weren't there, she would certainly have contacted them. The phone rang longer than it should have done before the answering machine kicked in, and he tried to feel disappointed but all he could manage was a kind of guilty relief.

'Face it, my friend,' drawled Aston Stirchley the Third, drifting past in a cloud of sweet-smelling smoke, 'tonight you're going nowhere fast, just like the rest of us. Be where you are and try to enjoy it for what it is.'

Bex linked her arm with his, and this time he didn't protest. 'Come on, misery-guts,' she said. 'You're going to help us with the decorations.'

***

They gave him some drawing pins and a big cardboard box full of holly sprigs and set him to pinning one above each of the windows. Afterwards – as he and Stirchley enjoyed an after-dinner spliff which, all told, he felt was thoroughly deserved – he asked about it.

'What's with the holly over the windows? I thought it was supposed to be mistletoe.'

'Ah,' said Stirchley, as if Andy had just made a highly cogent point in a complex argument. '*That* is to keep out the fairies.'

Andy thought carefully about this – which in itself was a measure of just how stoned he was becoming. 'But wouldn't you want the fairies to come in?' he said eventually. 'Aren't they supposed to do favours and odd-jobs for people – like mending shoes and stuff?'

'You're thinking of elves. No – fairies, we definitely do not want.'

'But why?'

'Okay. You know fairies are basically tied to nature, yes? Forest glades, running streams, that sort of thing?'

'Ye-es…'

'So. Do you have any idea what a couple hundred years of living in an urban industrialised environment does to a fairy? All the toxins, the chemicals – not to mention the etheric pollution of all that frustrated, claustrophobic humanity jammed together generation after generation?' He shook his head and took a long toke, continuing nasally: 'You know how polar bears get after they've been in the zoo too long?' He shook his head again and expelled a long stream of smoke. 'Urban fairies. Fuckin' psychos, man.'

They were sitting in a high-ceilinged living room full of slumbering sofas, listening to the small tribe of Moon Grove children being told a bedtime story in front of a huge open fire. It was a tale he'd never heard before: the story of the Holly King and the Oak King and of their competition to win the love of the White Lady of the Woods who held the Forest Crown as her prize.

It was evident that this was one in a long series of tales because the children already knew the names of the characters and their catch-phrases, joining in so loudly and exuberantly that he couldn't imagine these kids hunched in front of games consoles or school desks. The Oak King transformed himself into a wren, and the Holly King turned into a robin, and they chased and tricked each other through the forest in their quest for a magical eight-pointed egg.

'Eggs don't have points,' objected one sceptical seven-year old. This was greeted with a chorus of general objection, and in order to save face, he added 'Well what kind of bird lays an eight-pointed egg, then?'

The storyteller – a slender young woman who herself looked rather birdlike – replied gravely: 'One with a very sore bottom,' whereupon story time degenerated into wild shrieks and giggles. The children were packed off to one of the upstairs dorms and the storyteller – who was introduced to Andy as Lark – settled herself back with the adults.

'That was a great story,' he said.

'Thanks. It helps them understand what this time of year is all about, but without stuffing it down their throats.'

'You mean Christmas?'

Lark smiled. 'Sort of. The solstice – midwinter. It's a very old tale, much older than the Nativity. Do you know why we Lay Up for the solstice?'

'To be honest, I was afraid to ask. It's not going to have anything to do with the uttermost depths of existence, is it?'

She laughed easily. 'Not really. The Oak King is summer, and the Holly King is winter. Their fight is the year-long battle between the two. As the days get shorter and colder the power of the Holly King grows until it reaches its strongest on the midwinter solstice – but at that moment he is defeated by the Oak King who gradually grows in power until midsummer, when the Holly King defeats him in turn and so on. It's a metaphor for the eternal cycle, the round of the seasons.

'The midwinter solstice is a dangerous time for the Narrowfolk to be abroad. The leys are supercharged with energy, and the Narrows become dangerously unpredictable. Anybody unwise enough to travel at this time of year risks terrible consequences. Some get lost, sucked in too deep to ever find their way back to the surface world. Others claim to have seen strange things spewed out of the depths – terrible things that make skavags look like kittens.

'So we lay up food, water and fuel against the Holly King's strength, and hide for nine days and nine nights – four either side of the solstice. Just long enough to let things calm down again. We cut ourselves out of the circles of the world for a little while, singing songs and telling tales, and come out the other side on Christmas Day.'

'Strung out and starving,' added Stirchley with a nasal giggle.

'Not to mention stinky,' chimed in Bex.

'Fat,' contributed someone else.

'*Bloated* more like.'

'Stir crazy and completely fed up with the sight of each other.'

'Just like any ordinary family Christmas, then,' Andy concluded.

Their laughter broke Lark's story-spell, but in its place grew a looser, warmer enchantment of simple fellowship which carried Andy through to the early hours, when they made their goodnights. When Bex had told him that she lived in a squat, his imagination had conjured up a vision of splintered floorboards, overflowing bin-bags, and gaunt, grey smack addicts heating tins of baked beans over naked candle-flames. In no way had it prepared him for the warmth, noise, and homely chaos which had enveloped him over the last few hours.

Bex found him a pillow and a blanket, and he crashed out on a sofa in the last light of the dying fire. He lay for some time, listening to the wind, and found it very easy to imagine as the rising malice of the Holly King, beating restlessly around the house, searching for a way in.

2
ROSEY

Andrew 'Rosey' Penrose was making a Christmas wreath in the woods on Wychbury Hill when Pete Sumner called and told him that his son had disappeared off the face of the earth.

The sound of his phone startled him so much that the pain in his back – which normally didn't bother him at all when he came up the hill – flared with savage agony, and the familiar feeling like broken glass grinding between the fused vertebrae of his lower spine made him bite back a curse. It startled him because there was no phone signal up here. In all the times he had come here, there never had been.

He laid down the holly-woven hoop of willow which he'd been working on and took out his phone, examining it suspiciously. The signal-strength showed no bars. There was even a little symbol of a crossed-out phone on the display, and the words 'Limited Service' where it normally read 'Vodaphone'.

And yet still it rang.

He knew that if he moved barely five yards in any direction, he would get a full signal clear as day. Wychbury Hill was only just on the outskirts of town – one of a low range which nestled to the southwest of Halesowen and the Black Country – so coverage was never normally a problem. The fact was,

Rosey liked being out of contact with the world. He'd spent the last couple of hours relaxing in the peace of this place, letting his hands make something, and for another preciously short span of time enjoying the fact that here, for whatever quirk of nature, his crippled back didn't hurt. It was one of those things about the world which Rosey, for the sake of his sanity, never thought about too hard or questioned.

The phone's screen now said *Caller ID: Sumner*, even though he'd had no contact with the family for years. How had Peter even found his number? *Go away,* he begged it silently. *Leave me alone. It was sixteen years ago.*

Mercifully, it stopped ringing as his answerphone cut in.

The physiotherapists who had cajoled, bullied, and tortured him back into mobility had tried to suggest swimming as the best thing for his spine, but his first and only trip to the swimming baths at Halesowen Leisure Centre had left him with serious doubts about the therapeutic benefits of chlorine-induced blindness, and he'd taken to walking instead. He'd rambled over the Lickeys, the Clent Hills, and even as far as the lonely height of the Wrekin, discovering that a man built for full-contact sports could still enjoy an energetic lifestyle even if his rugby-playing days were over – and discovering too a previously unsuspected joy in making things out of the raw materials of field and hedgerow.

Wychbury Hill was an Iron Age fort with a dark history of having been ransacked and burned by the Romans, and an even darker reputation for modern witchcraft and pagan worship. What interested his policeman's instincts – which no amount of early retirement was ever going to blunt – were the tales of smaller, human darkness. Like the mysterious Bella, found murdered in a hollow wych-hazel in 1943, whose death was never solved. Or the fact that in 2002, when the oldest yew tree was burnt down by either pagans or vandals, people left flowers and messages of affection by its remains. What kind of people left flowers for a dead tree, he wanted to know?

There was something about this particular spot, though. He called it a 'quirk of nature' to himself; the fact that here, and only here, the back pain which the doctors had told him was chronic, inoperable, and untreatable – except by the kinds of drugs which would make him a junkie for life – simply disappeared completely. The irony was that while it afforded him some relief from physical pain, his discomfort about the place ran altogether deeper. It stemmed, he suspected from having been mixed up in the Sumner business all those years ago. Yes, he'd promised to look out for the boy, but sixteen years?

His phone began to ring again.

Limited Service. Caller ID: Sumner

Rosey wondered if he would even have found this spot if the business at Tyler Road hadn't happened. Maybe it had sensitised him, somehow, to more subtle energies in nature, whatever they were. Maybe he owed the boy that.

With great reluctance, he pressed the connect button and raised the phone to his ear.

***

'We'll have to be quick,' said DS Fallon as he led Rosey past a couple of uniforms and through the barrier of incident tape in front of the ruined block of flats. 'This thing is a fucking jurisdictional nightmare, you know. Environmental Health say it's a dangerous structure and nobody can go in until it's been properly shored up, and the anti-terrorist mob won't let anybody in because they don't want a bunch of council workmen bollocksing up the forensics. I ask you. War on terror? Don't make me laugh.'

'What's Counter Terrorism got to do with this?' asked Rosey, surprised.

'See all that glass?' Fallon pointed out the glittering debris on the ground surrounding the flats. Every single window that

Rosey could see on three floors had smashed. 'They're saying it's a bomb factory that went tits-up.'

'I don't think so. Anything big enough to take out all of those windows would throw stuff for miles. This looks like it's just fallen out.'

'Don't tell me, mate,' the other man grumbled. 'I just bloody work here.' He stopped before the entrance lobby, where the security light was dangling by its wires and the door hung twisted on one hinge, and turned back to Rosey. 'I don't know what kind of favours you called in to get here, but just don't go touching anything and costing me my job, alright?'

'Don't worry.'

Fallon grunted sceptically as they edged their way into the lobby. 'Upstairs,' he said. 'Number six.'

Rosey's back started to shout at him as he climbed, not helped by the unreliable state of the stairs. They were cracked and covered in rubble, and some kind of support seemed to have gone on one side, because every step sloped sideways towards the stairwell's echoing throat.

'Me,' said Fallon, 'I'm going with earthquake.'

Rosey couldn't help uttering a short laugh of disbelief.

'No, seriously. Earthquake. We're on a fault-line here, you know. I mean don't get me wrong, it's not a big one, we're not going to have the earth opening up and lava and Tommy Lee Jones running around waving his arms in the air like they do in California. But we've got a decent, honest-to-goodness geological fault line running right across the middle of the city, and every so often it gives a little shrug.'

'Every so often.'

'Case in point: September two-thousand and two. One o'clock in the morning, measured four point eight on the Richter scale. The epicentre was in Dudley – your neck of the woods. They felt it in bloody *Carlisle*.'

'I remember that – I thought somebody had driven a truck through the back garden.'

They reached the landing; it was twisted, as if a giant pair of hands had tried to tear it in half like a phone book.

'There you go then. I tell you, you don't need bloody bombs to make people desert their homes. If it'd been me having my tea when this happened I'd have buggered off myself. Mark my words, in a few days' time all the residents that we can't account for will turn up kipping on their mates' floors or staying with relatives. Here we are: number six.'

They picked their way into the flat, around patches of fallen ceiling plaster in the hall. Dim light from the rooms on either side (box-room, bedroom, bathroom) filtered in, dusty and cold. It had a queer smell – not just broken, but broken and *old*. In the lounge he found a cracked Aston Villa mug with a mat of green mould in the bottom. He showed Fallon, who wasn't impressed.

'Young people these days – I don't know.'

'Can't you smell it though? This place feels like it's been abandoned for weeks, not just a day or so.'

'Look, the point is that the young lady who lives here – a very smart-looking and, it has to be said, quite fit bit of skirt by the name of *Muzz* Laura Bishop – reported to the officers at the scene that her fiancé was nowhere to be found. She'd checked his work, they'd said he'd clocked off early, he hadn't called and she had no idea where he was. He'll turn up either tomorrow or the day after with a hangover and a nice little collection of love-bites.'

Rosey had found a photo album at the bottom of a bookcase which had spilled most of its contents on the floor. He flipped through the pages – photographs of a young couple who could have been anyone: eating pizza with friends, standing in snow somewhere Welsh-looking, covered in silly string at a party. The boy – young man, he corrected himself – looked cheerfully and utterly nondescript. Brown hair, brown eyes, clean shaven. Was this what he looked like, all these years later? It could have been anyone. Rosey was struck with a sudden and overwhelming sense of the absurdity of what he was doing. *Get a grip on yourself, old man.*

Fallon was already bored. 'Well look, you have a nice mooch around up here, and I'll be waiting downstairs. Just don't go looting anything, alright? I know the pension's shit but please, don't make me arrest you.'

Left alone, Rosey wandered through the wreckage of the flat, trying to get some sense of the life which the boy had lived here – and more importantly some clue to his present whereabouts. He failed miserably on both counts. He puzzled over the strange gouges in the kitchen door but couldn't be sure that they weren't anything more suspicious than earthquake damage – if Fallon was to be believed. Without the presence of another human being, the shadows were darker, and the silence acquired a watchful malevolence.

Back when this sort of thing had been part of his job, he'd invariably felt like something of a trespasser, picking through the jumbled pieces of other people's lives. Crime scenes especially. Even when searching suspects' homes there'd been that sense of broken continuity, of lives on pause: things dropped, to be taken up again after he was gone. But here... here everything felt simply abandoned. No, worse than that – dead, used up, sucked dry. In the wardrobe, clothes hung dusty and moth-eaten. Food in the fridge had rotted and then dried to a crust. He was walking through a brittle honeycomb which only carried the shape of what it used to be, and if he poked it hard enough, it would collapse in on itself.

Whatever had happened here might well have occurred yesterday afternoon at a little after half past four, but it looked like the effects had lasted for weeks. Something had aged the place, and it carried that brooding weight badly. There had only ever been one other time in his life when he'd felt something like this.

Suddenly, he couldn't get out of the flat fast enough.

***

If Tony Fallon thought that there was anything odd about Jerusalem Construction's head office, he didn't say anything. He just waited quietly while Mr Barber read the dossier which Tony had compiled for him.

In his admittedly limited experience of such things, he'd have expected the head office of a multi-million pound construction and development company to be a bit more flash. Something with a bit of chrome and glass, and maybe a big old piece of corporate sculpture that looked like a pile of spanners and cost more than a hospital. Not, as in this case, King Edward House on New Street, the top floor of which seemed to have escaped any kind of development since the Second World War. It looked and smelled like an old school library. Honest to God, the light switches were actually bakelite.

But he didn't say anything. Mr Barber didn't seem to like what he was reading, and that made Tony extremely nervous. Still, there was one extra tiny piece of information which wasn't in the file – nothing, really – and the only thing worse than telling Mr Barber something he didn't like was not telling him something important. Problem being that it was impossible to guess what the man thought important at any given time.

Tony had seen what happened to people who disappointed Mr Barber. So yeah, fuck it, he was nervous.

He cleared his throat.

Barber looked up. 'Something else, Detective Sergeant?'

'Well, yes sir, sort of. It's probably nothing more than a coincidence.'

'Do I look to you like a man who believes in coincidences, Detective?'

'No sir.' What he looked like was the kind of man who, if the rumours were true, could fuck your career in the arse so badly that you wouldn't even be able to get a job as a lollipop lady. 'If you'll refer to document 4, you'll see it's a police report from a PC Andrew Penrose, written in 1993.'

Barber regarded him, waiting. Fallon felt his upper lip starting to sweat.

'It's just that yesterday afternoon I gave Penrose a guided tour of Sumner's flat. Apparently he knew somebody who knew somebody who owed a favour, and he wanted to check the place out. No idea why.'

'I take it you haven't read the rest of this, then,' said Barber, indicating the dossier. Police statements. Child protection reports. Fostering and adoption papers. All attempts at papering over the gaps in a life broken almost as soon as it had begun.

'Not in great detail, no.'

'That may very well be for the best, at least as far as you're concerned. Thank you, Detective – you may go.'

Barber watched the other man scurry from his office. His favourite stripe of police officer: discreet, reasonably priced and essentially spineless. Nevertheless, he had done an effective job at putting together a lot of information at short notice. It was not comprehensive – not even in the ordinary sense – but there was enough for Barber to confirm his suspicions about whom he was dealing with.

Andrew Sumner, was that what they'd named him? The stolen boy. Destined for such greatness and denied it by an act of stupid, ill-considered conscience. Barber had written him off as a lost cause nearly two decades ago and moved on with his work, but it seemed that something had awoken in the boy at last. He wondered whether it was it too little, too late. Even the hero-cop had come out to play, too. And all of it now, right now, just when his own preparations were so nearly complete.

No, it couldn't possibly be coincidence.

Barber moved to the window and looked down at the street six floors below – the early evening crowds milling around under strands of garish Christmas lights, oblivious of anything but the bright, empty *now* of their lives.

The past was not a different country, and they did not do things differently there. It was all around, all the time, hiding in plain sight just on the other side of awareness, on street-corners and in the alleyways of people's minds. It was in the dust under their feet and the rain which fell on their heads. He'd stood here and watched the skyline of this city burn under German bombs, and then as bulldozers levelled what slums were left to make space for tower blocks and ringroads, and now again as these were being pulled down by his own hand to make room for the future. A clean slate from which to create anew. The key to successful urban development, in his opinion, was knowing which bits of the past to preserve, and which to obliterate utterly.

There were a lot of old names in that dossier; Fallon had done his job well. Barber took out his phone and called Carling.

The next few days were going to be extremely busy.

3
FAULT

Andy was woken by a confusion of running and panicked voices.

'He's doing it!'

'Is he doing it?'

'Where's my stuff? Shit!'

'Swear to god, he's doing it *right now*.'

'But there's a load of people still out!'

'Where's my sodding *stuff*?'

Figures were running back and forth through the room – and all over the house by the sounds of it. Feeling unwashed and generally scuzzy, he dragged the blanket around his shoulders and wandered in the direction of where the majority of Narrowfolk were hastening towards the back door. He wondered if there was any chance of scrounging a cup of tea for breakfast.

He found a nervous crowd muttering uneasily to themselves just outside, as if they were afraid to venture any further. Nobody took any notice of him. Their attention was fixed on the figure of Walter, who was engaged in spray-painting the most intricate graffito Andy had yet seen on the fence at the bottom of Moon Grove's expansive allotment-garden.

It was circular in design and took up most of the six-foot-high larch-lap panel, resembling an impossibly intricate Celtic knot, and after the manner of Narrowfolk sigils, it seemed to float simultaneously just in front of and just behind the surface. Evidently the work required great concentration because Walter was completely oblivious to the agitated crowd growing at a cautious distance.

He looked terrible. His clothes were mud-smeared and torn in several places, and there were dark half-moons of exhaustion under his eyes. He looked as if he'd spent the entire night since his sudden departure hiking back and forth across the city. In fact, his rucksack lay flung to one side as if he hadn't even bothered to stop since he got back, but had marched straight through the house and begun painting this bizarre mural.

In the cold light of morning, Andy realised something which should have been obvious to him last night: Walter was completely off his trolley.

His words over dinner now seemed ridiculous and impossibly melodramatic, and Andy was suddenly angry – with the old tramp for trying to put the frighteners on him, but mostly at himself for coming close to believing any of it.

'Holly King my arse,' he muttered scornfully, turning away from the assembly and heading back through the house towards the front door. The building which had glowed with a welcoming warmth while he was tired and vulnerable was, he now saw, in reality a semi-derelict ruin; roof-tiles were missing, plasterwork was crumbling, and the woodwork was warped with damp.

'Skavags. Laying Up. Narrows. Cosmic bloody onions.' Walter was as mad as a box of frogs, and he'd taken the rest of them with him.

Moon Grove was chaotic with people hurrying up and down stairs, stuffing bags and rucksacks with their belongings, and doing last-minute swaps and trades in the corridors before Walter completed his sigils and took them out of the circles of the world ('Bollocks,' said Andy to no-one and everyone.

'Total bollocks.') He shoved through them, out the front door and marched up the cul-de-sac towards where it joined the main road. Others were ahead of him; lone, grey individuals scurrying to be gone as quickly as possible.

'Bye then.' Bex was lounging against the graffiti-tagged wall of the off-licence on the corner, eating an apple. A few feet beyond her was the pavement, busy with bus-stops, two-for-one offers and all the grimy sanity of the real world. He craved it and the ignorance it enjoyed, as an insomniac craves sleep.

Nevertheless, he stopped.

'I'm sorry,' he said fiercely. 'But I can't do this.'

She shrugged. 'Okay.'

'None of this makes any sense. Surely you can see that?'

'Mm-hm.'

'I've got to get back to some kind of normality. This is all getting just way out of hand.'

She waved him on with her apple. Relieved that this hadn't turned into a scene, he made to pass her.

'Yep, that's probably right,' she said, 'but what are *you* going to say to *her*?'

'What do you mean?'

'"I'm sorry but I can't do this",' she recited. '"None of this makes sense surely you can see that I've got to get back to some kind of normality." That's most likely what she'll say alright. Your darling fee-yon-say.'

He sighed. It was going to be a scene. 'That's not funny.'

'It wasn't meant to be. Have you got your story worked out, then?'

'I don't need a story.'

She laughed in his face. 'Oh, right. So you're going to tell her the truth, are you? I can see that working. Good luck with it. Andy, there's nothing you can tell her that she will either believe or understand. They'll lock you up and throw away the key. Keen to marry a nutjob, is she?'

'Fine then. I'll tell her I've been staying with friends. Lie, in other words.'

'Ouch. That one stung. You're getting good at this.'

'Sod off.'

'Actually, I meant the story that you're going to have to tell her when you've settled back all nice and comfortable in suburbanland and the dark men finally find you and send every monster in the world through your front door. That is, assuming you're able to tell her anything once the screaming begins.'

'That's not going to happen,' he said, trying to sound convinced.

'Why not?' she scoffed.

'Because none of this is real. It can't be. It doesn't make *sense.*'

She slapped him. She did it so hard and fast that at first he didn't realise what had happened; like a razor cut, the pain came after a long moment of dull shock. Then she tore off her jacket and threw it at him. 'What do you think made those holes?' she yelled, 'Fucking *moths?*' He was astounded to see that she was suddenly crying. 'People are *dead*, you insensitive shit! People I love! We're fighting for our lives, and you come swanning in with some kind of miraculous ability which nobody understands, and you could help us, but oh no, *none of this is real*, is it?'

She stormed away back to Moon Grove, leaving Andy standing at the very edge of the street.

He would leave it up to the Pattern, he decided. That at least was something you could rely on. He had absolutely nothing: no money, no phone, no way of contacting anyone or travelling anywhere except by his own two feet. Nothing felt right, so the only direction remaining to him was to turn left. Which he did. Why not? He had no reliable way of making decisions except on the most spurious, random grounds.

This is how it works: find the tell-tale hints and flicker-glimpses which show how the grain of the universe runs. Head down, don't look up, don't see how far you're walking, don't plan ahead so much as a footstep because planning falls into the Narrows too. Scuff one toe, so scuff the other to balance it up. Count every car coming towards you as a plus and every car going away as a minus and see if an answer comes to you when they balance out at zero. Read the licence plates for significant dates or initials. Catch music from shop doorways and listen for messages in the lyrics. Focus on the middle distance, a point in empty mid-air several feet ahead. Assign a number to every letter in Laura's name, total it up to seventy-seven and compare that to…

… a phone booth next to him rang, precisely once, and fell silent again.

He stared at it. It was derelict, its glass panes smashed, and there were weeds growing all around the base – including one tall, straggling, dead black nettle.

He entered. The interior was worse: stinking and vandalised beyond repair. He lifted the handset, expecting it to be dead too, but wasn't really surprised when the small rectangular LCD display lit up with the message *Out of order. Please report Fault #77.* The handset was purring with a quietly patient dial tone.

Andy felt the Pattern threading itself within his flesh, strands of pins and needles coursing up and down his limbs and torso before shimmering out of his fingertips and into the telephone receiver where he grasped it.

He punched in the number of Laura's mobile.

'Hi, Laura, it's me.'

There was a pause – a little too long for comfort – before she replied: 'Andy. I was wondering when you'd call.' Not the gushing exclamation of love and concern – or even anger – he'd been expecting.

'I tried calling last night. You were out.'

'I spent most of the evening at a police station. Amongst other things, I was filling out a missing persons report. Andy, where have you *been*?'

'I've been staying with... friends. I just wanted you to know that I'm alright. To not be worried. Are you okay? What did the police say?'

'Never mind them. Where *were* you? Were you there when it happened? Why didn't you wait for me?'

'I was there,' he said carefully. 'It all happened very suddenly. I suppose I was sort of in shock afterwards, not thinking straight. Are you at your parents'?'

She sighed as if suddenly very tired. 'Yes. No, the police were good. There were quite a few of us there – people from the flats, I mean. You know old Mrs Taylor from downstairs?'

'Sure.' They fed her cats when she went to visit her grandchildren in Coventry.

'She heard me talking with the policewoman about the missing persons report and she said she'd been out doing her shopping and seen you walking home from the station in the middle of the afternoon, if that helped.' An ice-age of silence stretched out after her words. Andy hadn't even noticed the old dear. 'She also said that you were with a girl. I said yes, thank you, that really helped a lot.

'Who is she, Andy?'

There was that feeling again, of being both present and absent at the same time, of being a thousand miles away inside his own head, hearing himself talk without the conscious act of speech.

'There's nothing I can tell you that you would believe or understand,' he found himself saying.

'Oh I don't know. Quite a few things are starting to make a lot of sense now. How about you try telling the truth for once?' She was angry and close to tears now, but unlike Bex, who wept out of rage and frustration, this was just plain fear – fear of being left alone, fear of a love's death – and he suddenly felt both desperately sorry for her and more appallingly impotent than ever in his life. 'Andy, are you having some kind of…' she couldn't bring herself to say it, so whispered: '…breakdown?'

The truth? If he had a clue, he just might. His hollow laugh echoed in the shabby phonebooth. 'No, I'm not going mad.'

It was almost funny – he'd called with the intention of trying to patch things up but, as ever, events were forcing him into almost precisely the opposite course of action. If he told her the truth she would think he was losing his mind, which might lay to rest her fear that he was cheating on her, but the flip-side was that she would then be forever living with the false hope that he would one day get 'better', and that was a lie which he wouldn't inflict on her. Better that she hate him for being a shit than pine for him as a lunatic. 'What's happening is weird, but it's real.'

'Well then, I'm sorry,' she said fiercely, 'but I can't do this.'

'Okay.' Even though it was everything but okay.

'I've got to get back to some kind of normality. This is all getting…'

'…just way out of hand. I know.'

'Goodbye, Andy.'

'Goodbye, Laura.'

He hung up the phone and walked back to Moon Grove, where Bex was waiting for him.

***

By the time that Andy returned, Walter was finishing the last of his sigils in multicoloured spraypaint on the surface of the road outside Moon Grove. It was the last of four, each set at the cardinal compass points in a circle around the house, and its intricate knotted design was fully nine feet wide.

Those inside the circle saw hazy wisps of white mist begin to seep out of the ground around its circumference. They drifted in a slow clockwise rotation, gradually thickening like strands of candy-floss as the diverted ley energy precipitated water vapour out of the damp air, and hardening in opacity until a blank white wall surrounded everything: the house, the vegetable gardens, chicken coops, greenhouses, toolsheds, and a curving slice of tarmac at the front.

The Narrowfolk children ooh-ed and aah-ed, and immediately wanted to run off and play hide-and-seek in it. Their parents held them tightly, warning them again, as they so often had, that if you strayed out, you would never find your way back in.

The adults regarded the blank white wall with a mixture of relief and dread. On the one hand they would now be safe while the earth-*ch'i* was in spate over the midwinter solstice, and the malice of the Holly King raged. On the other, it seemed to only accentuate the danger of the outside world, now that it could not be seen.

Anybody standing outside the circle when Walter completed his sigils would not have noticed anything quite so dramatic. It would have seemed like a trick of the eye, or the product of an overtired brain, because one second the house and its grounds were there, and the next second it simply wasn't.

4
LAURA

When the front doorbell rang, Laura was sitting at her mother's glossy ten-seater dining table with a drift of paperwork arrayed before her like the world's biggest game of solitaire.

She was appraising, prioritising, planning. School had let her end the term early – it was only Christmas word games and DVDs at this time of year, anyway, which anybody could cover – but after a morning of drifting aimlessly through the immaculately vacuumed expanse of her parents' home, being made endless cups of tea and enduring the terrible sympathy of a woman who had never really believed that her daughter was capable of making her own decisions (but, heaven forbid, would never actually say so) – well, being busy was what kept Laura going.

The insurance claim forms were a lifeline, and the police reports helped her sleep at night. Strangely, working through the minutiae of detail about the incident with the flat helped her to keep at bay the truth of what had really happened.

It definitely helped her to stop thinking about Andy.

Her father was at the office, and her mother was at a charity lunch, or possibly a satanic black mass, so she answered the door herself, despite the fact that company was the last thing she wanted. She could no more disobey the manners that had been bred into her than she could change the colour of her eyes.

'Excuse me, miss, but are you Laura Bishop?' The man was large, fortysomething, with thinning, close-cropped hair and a politely neutral expression.

'Yes? Are you from the police?'

'In a roundabout sort of way, yes, I suppose so. My name is Penrose; I'm working with Detective Sergeant Fallon. I was wondering actually if I might have a word with Andrew Sumner, if he's in?'

She looked at him. 'You have got to be joking.'

'I'm sorry?'

'You're not, are you?' Laura was incredulous. 'Are you people really this incompetent? Last night I spent an hour having a nice police-woman explain to me very patiently how they can't file a missing person's report unless he's been gone for a week, and have I tried ringing around his friends and relatives? Well I tried that – it didn't take very long, as it happens – and no, they haven't seen him, and now you're here asking the same stupid questions! Who are you, Mr Penrose, and what do you want?'

Deciding to take a risk, he asked 'How much has Andy told you about his childhood?'

It would have been so easy to just shut the door in his face. Far easier to accept the simple and painful truth that Andy no longer loved her, had cheated on her, and left. Andy had always said that he had no interest in his birth parents, and as far as she knew had never made any attempts to find them, saying that he was the child of Beth and Pete Sumner, and everything else was just an accident of genetics. She was inclined to hold him to that, to the responsibility for his actions as a grown-up, and childhood influences be damned. She believed in actions, not excuses – but that was her mother talking.

'I think you should probably come in,' she said and opened the door wide.

Rosey sipped his tea and got Laura to tell him everything he needed to know by using one of the oldest and most effective techniques which his younger colleagues, with their modern methods of policing and counselling, seemed to have forgotten: that of keeping his mouth firmly shut.

He looked around the kitchen, impressed despite himself. The leafy upper-middle-class suburbs of Solihull were way beyond his normal stamping grounds; most of the ground floor of his own house would have fit in this room. It must have taken a lot of guts for Laura Bishop to move into a two-bedroom flat on the outskirts of Northfield with her drop-out boyfriend – or so her parents would have seen it. Father was most probably something in finance, and Mother was clearly a lady who lunched. The flat had been a young woman's fierce declaration of independence from her well-heeled family, and coming home had almost certainly been seen as a gesture of defeat, though never acknowledged as such.

He wondered how the engagement had been received in the first place, whether there had been earnest conversations about the young man's suitability, his prospects, and he wondered especially how Andy's disappearance was being taken. Not well, he suspected. She would be defending him to the hilt as part of herself and her own life. There would have been arguments before it happened; things that she was keeping from parents and the rest of the world, as a defence against the I-told-you-so's which would strip her right back down to being a little girl again.

'Sorry about earlier,' she said, picking up the thread of her thoughts. 'The last twenty-four hours have been ever so slightly stressful. Did you say you were retired?'

'Pensioned off. Bad back.' He smiled ruefully. 'Not very dramatic, I'm afraid.'

'It's just that, and I don't want to be impolite, but if you're not on active duty, or, you know, whatever the word is…'

'Why am I here?'

'Exactly.'

He hesitated, unsure of how much to tell her – or, more precisely, unsure of how much Andy had already told her. 'I can tell you why I'm *not* here,' he said. 'I'm not investigating a crime; I'm not interested in getting Andy in trouble.'

'Well that's something of a relief.'

'I suppose you could say I'm something like an old friend of the family.' Half-truths, the most credible kind of lie. 'I feel like I'm wasting your time, really. Typical of my bad timing to try and get back in touch the day after this happens to you. Stupid coincidence.'

'Andy had – *has* – this theory about coincidences. He says that events follow patterns like a grain in wood, and if you follow the coincidences – work with the grain rather than against it – life goes a lot more smoothly for you. I'm sorry, that probably sounds stupid to you.'

'When I was in uniform, I saw so much random stupidity and coincidence that I'd have agreed with his theory. But then I have a friend who's been a Detective Sergeant for a while now, and his whole ability to do his job relies on there being reasons for everything and connections between things, no matter how vague or deeply buried they are.' He shrugged. 'I don't know. Better minds than thee and me, eh?'

Very quietly he added: 'I think that it doesn't matter which way you look at it. I think the important thing is that a person takes responsibility for their own actions, don't you?'

She sipped her tea and regarded him for a long time, and Rosey was struck by the power of frank appraisal behind her eyes. It seemed to age her, and he felt a surge of sympathy for how the last few days must have affected her.

'If you're going to look for him,' she said finally, 'there are some things you need to know about.'

Mouth firmly, *very* firmly shut.

She glanced at the kitchen door, even though the house was empty but for them, and he knew that this was it – the thing she hadn't told Mummy and Daddy. Her defence against the I-told-you-so's. The thing about Andy which he needed to know if he were going to figure out why he hadn't come back.

'He's been acting strangely for the last couple of weeks.'

And he listened with perfect stillness as she explained to him what had been happening.

Afterwards, feeling that he owed her something more of an honest explanation of himself, he said: 'You should know, I suppose, that I was the one who found him. At the beginning.'

She stared at him in silence. He took the mug from her carefully before she could spill it.

'Sixteen years ago,' he continued. 'I was in uniform, very new to the job, and we got a tip-off that a child had been abandoned in a house, and we found him. Simple as that. He was a very lucky little boy.' It was only a small lie.

'My God,' she said in a very small voice. 'It was true.'

'You thought it wasn't true?'

'No! Not exactly. I mean, he wasn't lying to me. He believed it, anyway. It's just – it was so incredible, do you understand? Like something off the news. It's just you being here now – it makes it more real. Physically real. What happened?'

Rosey glossed over the details, as he always had done. It wasn't necessary for her to know everything, especially if Andy himself didn't. Not even Pete Sumner knew the full truth, just that there had been a criminal element involved.

'The thing is that most foundlings are babies, abandoned by young mothers who can't cope and don't know how to ask for help. It's very rare that a child is found as old as Andy. There was some idea that he was the kid of a junkie who got into trouble and disappeared, but I don't know. I only tell you this because I promised his father that if anything happened I'd look out for him. 'Course, at the time I thought I'd still be in the force instead of civvies, but there you go.'

'Do you think he's in some kind of trouble? Can you really find him?'

He shrugged. 'I still have a few mates who can help out with the odd favour or two. Just need somewhere to start.'

She took out her phone and paged through to the 'received calls' screen. 'Will this do?'

He smiled. 'I think it just might.'

5

DEVELOPMENT

Rosey told himself that he shouldn't be surprised to find that 144 Tyler Road had long since been torn down. He sat in his car and looked out at the demolition site where it used to be with the same kind of satisfaction that he might have felt had he been watching a rabid dog being put down – preferably by a bullet in the head.

'Sow the ground with salt too, while you're at it,' he muttered, unaware that he was talking to himself.

A lone yellow bulldozer was methodically chewing its way along the empty street; a row of dead houses lined up neatly ahead of it, a trail of pulverised brick and splintered wood behind. The bright December sun created a false mist out of the permanent haze of brick-dust which he could smell even with the windows rolled up and the heating cranked to full. All the same, a chill seeped outwards from his bones. Soon other trucks and diggers would come to clear away the rubble and start laying the groundwork for whatever new development was planned here. Business park, supermarket, Rosey didn't much care. Just as long as 144 was crushed into the dust.

He got out of the car and found a gap in the chain-link fence (a sign declared this as the property of a company he'd never heard of called *Jerusalem Construction*, that *Heavy Machinery was in Constant Use* and that trespassers could expect *Heavy Penalties*), approaching the rubble slowly.

He paced the perimeter of where the house had once stood, as if to assure himself of the actual physical limitations of the building which had once stood here: *this* wide and no more, *that* long and no more. His heart stopped when he saw something thin and metallic gleaming in the dust, but it turned out to be nothing more than an old nail. No magic. No terror. Just wreckage.

Two large men in hardhats stencilled with the words *Site Security* and carrying large walkie-talkies were approaching. They wore yellow hi-viz jackets and determined expressions. That was quick.

'Excuse me sir,' said the first. 'You are aware that this is private property?'

'Yes, I'm sorry. I'm just going.' That should have been the end of it. These guys weren't going to make a fuss – he clearly wasn't trying to nick anything, they could tell that. Depending on how bored they were, they'd send him on his way with a bit of face-saving macho bullshit and then go back to their tea and copies of the Daily Mirror.

'One moment please, sir.'

'No, really, I am just –'

But the second security guard produced his mobile phone, aimed its camera at him and took his picture.

'Hang on a second. What was that for?'

The first guard looked at him blankly while his companion, who had not yet said a word, tapped at the keypad of his phone. 'Security, sir.'

'What kind of security involves taking my photograph?'

'Most kinds, sir. Ever walked down a city street?' There was a sudden, casual contempt in the man's voice, and every policeman's instinct in Rosey's retired body began to scream at once. He turned to leave without another word, and found the first guard's hand clamped around his upper arm. 'As I said, sir: one moment, if you please.'

That was it. The man could be king of his own little rubble castle any way he liked – fair enough, as Rosey *had* broken through the fence, and he was content to play the alpha-dog game as a small price to pay for satisfying his curiosity about the house, but no hands were going to be laid on the man who had once swung Big Eddie. He turned, pivoted.

The kidney punch that the second guard delivered was precise and just strong enough to explode the crushed nerves near his fused vertebrae, and sudden volcanic pain erupted in his hips and down both legs. He screamed and collapsed to the ground.

The second guard's phone began to ring. He listened, hung up and nodded to his companion. 'It's not him, but Mr Barber said he's close enough. He'll be here in ten minutes. Said to make our guest comfortable.'

The first guard looked down at Rosey, who writhed, sickened at how old he felt.

'Oops,' he said, without any detectable sympathy.

'It's okay. I think he was being ironic.'

***

The guards' office was the standard template for site offices and used car yards – a squat, rectangular fibreglass and aluminium portacabin with a wonky desk and a paraffin heater which managed to warm the surrounding three feet to blast-furnace temperatures while leaving the rest of the interior feeling like a walk-in freezer.

Barber was a dapper, well-groomed man of indeterminate middle-age, wearing a long coat and the kind of pencil-thin moustache which Rosey had only ever seen in black and white films.

'So,' he said cheerily. 'The police constable. I was expecting you to have paid a visit years ago. I must admit, I was beginning to give up on you.'

Rosey said nothing. Barber smiled. 'Very good, Mr Penrose. You have decided that you don't care who I am or what I want; you refuse to say a single thing after having suffered such shabby treatment. I must say I don't blame you. Have these thugs even made you a cup of tea?' He glared at the two security guards, who glanced sheepishly at each other. 'Thought not.' Barber moved to fill a kettle.

'No thanks. I've just had one.'

'Hm. You're now thinking that this is all very predictable bad-cop, good-cop stuff and that you're still not going to say anything regardless of how many cups of tea you get. Not even –' he flourished a packet of biscuits theatrically '– for custard creams. You're a tough nut to crack, Mr Penrose, for sure.'

Barber busied himself with mugs, teabags, spoons. 'Frankly, I give up. You've beaten me. I'll tell you everything I know.' He made himself a drink and settled back opposite Rosey, on a plastic school chair.

'Actually, sorry, that was unfair of me. I'm sure that me being terribly clever and sarcastic is the last thing you need. I genuinely did want to simply have a chat. Sooty and Sweep here overreacted abominably and owe you an apology. Gentlemen?'

Mingled expressions of confusion, alarm, and embarrassment flushed their faces as they mumbled apologies like schoolboys and immediately found more important things to do. Rosey found himself having to contain a smile but remained stubbornly silent.

Barber sighed. 'I know everything about who, where, why, when and how you are, Mr Penrose; that's the long and the short of it. Nothing which isn't already in the public domain, don't worry about that; I haven't been snooping. Well, not much. It's alright if you don't want to talk. I wouldn't be able to trust anything you said anyway. All I really want to know is whether or not you've had any contact with young Andrew

Sumner in the last few days. He's popped up again, you might say. Sort of keeps popping up in a really rather irritating manner. Oh I know that you've had nothing to do with him since the day you brought him out of that house, but those sorts of connections between people have a way of shaping events much more strongly than you'd believe.'

Rosey concentrated on the glow of the paraffin heater.

'I could threaten you, of course – I know you have family – but you too have all sorts of connections, and that would only escalate matters and take a great deal of time and effort which I can ill afford at the moment, especially since you are what one would properly call a peripheral line of enquiry. Yes,' Barber chuckled. 'Quite peripheral.' He dunked a custard cream and nibbled at it. 'I am, however, extremely thorough, and I have more direct methods of making enquiries.'

'Sounds like a threat to me,' Rosey replied evenly. 'Mate, if you know so much about me, then you also know that messing around with someone whose friends are all cops is a very silly thing to do.'

Barber brushed the crumbs fastidiously from his coat and produced from one pocket a long, flat, metal stationery tin. 'It wasn't really a threat. I was going to do this anyway.'

From the tin, he started to unfold a long strip of linen. 'The wonderful thing about the human aura, Mr Penrose, is that it displays the soul directly, truthfully, without the murky lies and ambiguity of words – it is a language of the spirit for those who know how to read it. You're a policeman; you know about lie-detectors and galvanic skin response and such. That's just one surface manifestation of what I'm talking about. These, however, are capable of getting to the, ah, *deeper* truth of things.'

Rosey saw that the strip of linen was threaded along its length with serried ranks of gleaming acupuncture needles. He panicked then but, before he could leap from the chair, found that the guards were a lot closer than he'd thought, and they held him firmly.

Barber was humming happily to himself as he laid out his instruments. Rosey recognised the tune. It was, of all things, *Jerusalem*.

'England's other national anthem, they call it,' said Barber, as if reading his thoughts, and Rosey was starting to think that might be entirely possible. 'But I'll bet you already knew that. I bet you're a bit of an old rugger-bugger, Last-Night-of-the-Proms sort, aren't you?' He laughed softly. 'Still, you have to love the irony of it. Blake was a revolutionary and a heretic who was accused of treason, and it's his words we love as one of our most patriotic songs. It's so deliciously perverse.'

He stopped what he was doing and hunkered down close with a conspiratorial air. 'Here's something I bet you didn't know. You know that famous line, the one about those "dark Satanic mills"? Everybody assumes he was writing about the Industrial Revolution and what-not. However...' and he leaned in so close that Rosey could smell sweet, strangely old-fashioned cologne '...it's all part of a longer poem called 'Milton', and in his handwritten manuscript for that poem, the first time he mentions Satanic mills there's a little sketch, just a little doodle, not much more, sort of in the margins – and guess what it is. Go on, guess.'

Rosey didn't move. Didn't even blink.

Barber leaned in even closer, so that their noses were almost touching. 'It was a picture,' he whispered, 'of Stonehenge.'

The snort of laughter which escaped Rosey was completely beyond his control. In the frozen moment afterwards he was also convinced it would be the last sound he ever made, aside from screaming. But Barber was nodding and grinning.

'I know! I know! Mad, isn't it?' He moved away, back to his needles, selected one, and returned.

'I know why these terrify you, Mr Penrose, and you're right to be scared. But no, I'm not the man you put in jail, am I? You must be awfully confused.' He laughed, but there wasn't even the pretence of human bonhomie in the sound now – it was simple cold mockery.

'I've killed many people with these – youngsters, mostly, and in ways that would make you want to blind yourself for having seen them.' The cold in the room deepened, as if pouring off the man. 'As I said, you are entirely peripheral to the matter at hand, but he *might* come to you, and that is the only thing keeping you alive. I have no intention of killing you. However, I must be sure about what you know. I will be sure.'

'Who – what – *are* you?'

'I am a developer, Mr Penrose. I develop land. I also develop people. The two are often contiguous. Who knows? I might even be able to do something about that little back problem of yours. Call it an early Christmas present.'

Barber raised the first needle, and everything after that was bright and burning.

***

Rosey stood at the chainlink fence and watched as the bulldozers grumbled back and forward, pulverising the ground flat. The grim satisfaction he took in seeing this was undermined by what felt like the beginnings of a headache.

Driving home, he was nagged by the feeling that something important somewhere was out of place, until he suddenly realised how quickly it had grown dark. Either he had reckoned the time wrong, or he'd spent longer than he'd thought brooding over that house, because he was certain he'd gone there in the early afternoon, straight after seeing Ms Bishop, and now it appeared to be early evening.

By the time he got home, his head was throbbing fiercely. Definitely a touch of flu coming on. He had been planning to make a start on tracking down the phone number which Andy had called her from, but for some reason thinking about it only made his head hurt worse, so he took a couple of paracetomol and decided it could wait until the morning.

One thing though: his back didn't hurt nearly half so much as usual.

6

STAKED OUT

It was a routine matter for Rosey to trace the number of the phone box from which Andy had called Laura. He found it much as he expected: wrecked and filthy, although presumably somebody had been along since Andy had used it and finished the job, because the receiver was completely dead.

More plod-work with a photograph up and down the shops on either side of the street brought predictably disappointing results. Nobody had seen him, or if they had, couldn't recall having done so. Short of Andy having actually robbed anyone, he would have been totally inconspicuous.

Most places these days had CCTV for security (and why did he get a funny prickle of déjà vu when he thought that?), but he had neither the authority nor the time to bother.

It was while he was passing the entrance to a narrow side street between Ranjit the Wine Lord and the Ichbal & Paramanathon Cypriot Real Estate Agency that he saw the graffiti rainbow-scrawled on the brick walls either side, and his pulse quickened at the recognition: repeated everywhere, in a hundred different colours and sizes, was the motif of a spoked wheel.

The name of the street, almost illegible beneath layers of spraypaint, was *Moon Grove*.

As soon as Rosey set foot off the main pavement he became uncomfortably aware of how much darker and quieter it was. The scribbled walls of the shops on either side gave way to service alleyways rancid with overflowing wheely bins, and then – in a contrast so sudden it actually made him do a double-take – a short cul-de-sac of rambling, boarded-up houses. At the furthest and dimmest end, a vacant lot sat proud by virtue of its emptiness, like the stump of an amputated limb. It had a gravity and authority, as if it were the apotheosis of neglect to which the other mouldering buildings aspired.

It drew Rosey completely, like the dead zone on Wychbury hill.

He saw weed-choked piles of crumbling brick and, further back, the jungled shadows of a long-overgrown garden. He explored it as fully as he could, right the way back to a sagging wooden fence, and found nothing but more empty remains. There was no sign that anybody still lived here, just the broken mementoes of small, desperate acts of escape: alcopop bottles, solvent cans and used condoms.

This was a mistake. The graffiti had just been a blind coincidence. The boy clearly didn't want to be found, and he should just leave it at that.

Which was exactly what he did. There was a limit to how much he could be expected to do. Hundreds of people went missing every day across the country, and despite a few well-publicised cases of idiots getting caught after faking their deaths for the insurance, the truth was that if a person was serious about disappearing, it was all but impossible to find them.

All the same, the vacant lot on Moon Grove exercised an inexplicable fascination over him, and he managed to find an excuse to keep driving past it briefly over the next few days, sitting in his car with the engine idling, staring out at the weeds until he felt ridiculous again and left. And then came back the next day. He couldn't call it anything as melodramatic as a stakeout, because there was neither person nor place to stake out. It was like trying to do a jigsaw without the picture, not knowing if any of the pieces were missing or even whether they were all from the same puzzle.

And then on the eighteenth of December, a large piece of it literally fell into place when, just as he was about to give it up for good, he heard a scream of pain and saw a young woman with blood all over her face stumble out of the empty air and collapse to the rubble-strewn ground.

7

DOWSING FOR BEGINNERS

'So,' said Andy. 'Now what?'

'This what,' replied Bex, frowning at a sudoku puzzle.

'That's not very helpful.'

She sniffed and filled in a four.

They were lying each to a sofa before the fire in what Andy was now calling the Big Room, because everything in it was huge, overstuffed, and threadbare.

The whole of Moon Grove was much emptier and uncannily quiet after the upheaval of the last twenty-four hours. It seemed that only the hardcore Narrowfolk had chosen to stay – either that, or they were the only ones who had been able to scavenge enough provisions to earn their keep.

Andy wondered where the rest of the 'normal' just-passing-through squatters had found refuge. Shelters? Friends' floors? Doorways? He kept remembering the young man on the Pallasades ramp and wondering what had happened to him. So many people seemed to just appear and disappear at random, like dust motes drifting through a beam of sunlight in an empty room, drifting into the Narrows, invisible, unreal, falling out of the circles of the world.

He had, as a matter of pure pragmatism, quickly reconciled himself to Walter's talk of ley lines and energy streams and cosmic onions. Apart from anything else, it was the only plausible explanation so far for everything that had happened to him.

It didn't make it any easier for his eyes to accept what was outside, however.

The Narrowfolk called it the Fane, and at first glance it looked like a wall of white mist surrounding the house and its grounds. Closer, however, there was nothing cloudlike about it; nothing swirled or eddied; it was simply a point beyond which everything was completely blank, and to approach it too closely was to invite dizzying vertigo when it filled one's field of view completely.

When he tried to touch it, there was no fading or zone of transition; it appeared as if his hand had simply been cut off cleanly at the wrist. He'd felt neither temperature nor texture – no sensation whatsoever, including when he made a fist. In a panic he drew his hand out again and found it to be unharmed and working perfectly. He'd thought about sticking his head in to discover whether or not he could see his hand on the other side, but decided it probably wasn't a good idea. Apparently it was easy enough to leave Moon Grove – you just walked into the void and kept on walking. Once you were in, you couldn't turn around, and once you were through there was absolutely no coming back. He wasn't prepared to risk that.

Inside the Fane's protective circle there was no weather to speak of – no rain, bright sun or breath of wind. By Walter's decree the Grove had no television, radio, telephone or internet connection, and those few of the Narrowfolk who possessed such devices found that no signals from the outside world made it through either.

Instead, the evenings were times of feasting, warmth and firelight, but after two doldrum days of trying to find odd jobs to keep himself busy, Andy was surprised to find that he was bored stiff.

'I thought you were desperate to get out there and do something,' he said, as Bex continued to ignore him. 'You know, find the man with the staff and do a Buffy the Vampire Slayer job on him.'

'I am,' she said. 'And I will. Just not now. You saw what happened when we left your place. You and me are no good to anyone if we're stuck out in the middle of nowhere. And I don't mean nowhere as in Redditch, either. I mean really: No-Where.'

He couldn't argue with that, so he took himself off to stare at the void again.

**

With little else to occupy her time, Bex finally got around to the painful task of sorting out Dodd's things.

The clothes were the easiest – they were thrown into the common store of spare clothing in the cellar, which was probably where they'd come from in the first place. She found bundles of battered old Ordnance Survey maps so folded and refolded that they hung in tattered oblongs. There were dozens of books, mostly a lot of old science fiction and horror novels (including something called *The Borribles*, which she kept to one side; she wasn't much of a reader, but that one didn't look quite so sad and geeky), but the majority were about leys, standing stones, earth mysteries, geomancy, feng shui and even yoga.

She discovered, folded into the back of one, a page torn from a magazine; the "Missing: Can You Help?" page from an edition of the Big Issue several years old.

Rodney Stokes

Rodney, known to his friends as Dodd, will be 22 this year, and disappeared from his home in Nuneaton, Warwicks., on the 13th of November, aged 19. He was last seen at Coventry Station, and it is believed that he was going to spend the weekend with friends in Birmingham.

His parents, Bob and Irene, are desperately worried for his well-being and want only a phone call to know that he is well.

If anybody has seen Rodney or knows of his whereabouts...

But she couldn't read any more, because her tears were making everything blurry.

Then, at the very bottom of the box, she caught a gleam of metal. When she brought out what she found there and held them up to close inspection, suddenly everything made sense.

***

Andy was walking the perimeter of the Fane for the umpteenth time when Bex came running to find him.

He was at the back of the Grove, in the thin belt of uncultivated ground between rows of winter crops and the white wall. There was a crazy-paned greenhouse nearby, where Lark and her partner Cameron were doing whatever it was one did in a greenhouse, whilst cheerfully singing Christmas carols with a total lack of self-consciousness. He spotted Bex's small, coat-muffled figure tramping at speed straight through the parsnips, waving something thin and metallic over her head and grinning like a maniac.

'I've cracked it!' she yelled. 'I know what he was doing!'

'What? Who?'

She reached him and showed him what she'd found: a pair of long L-shaped pieces of wire, the shorter ends of which were sheathed in narrow copper tubes.

'What are these?'

She whacked him. 'God, you are so bloody slow sometimes! They're dowsing rods, of course! Dodd was dowsing the Narrows! All those funny little squiggles in his A-to-Z. He

169

wasn't just mapping the closures. I don't even think they are closures anyway, not really. You know what I think they are?'

'If I say I don't know, will you hit me again?'

'They're diversions. Those Narrows aren't being blocked – they're having their energy diverted somewhere else. Dodd was trying to work out where. It explains everything, don't you see? It's perfect!'

She bounced up and down in front of him in excitement while he took the rods and examined them sceptically. 'I don't know about this…' he said slowly.

'What?' She snatched them back. 'Everything you've learned so far, and you can't take this?'

'Just because one mad idea turns out to be true doesn't mean they all are.'

'But it's *all* true, Andy! Everything! Aliens built the pyramids! Narnia's inside a wardrobe! Fairies exist, and they hate holly! And a couple of bent coat-hangers can show you where the lifeblood of the earth runs. Watch!'

She took the rods, one shorter end in a closed fist so that each rotated freely in its copper sleeve with the long arms pointing straight ahead, weaving gently to and fro like a pair of antennae. With slow, careful steps she approached the Fane, and as she neared it the dowsing arms spread gradually apart so that when she was within a few feet of the white wall they pointed left and right, parallel with it.

'See?' she said. 'They point in the direction of the energy flow. It's dead easy.'

'It's dead bollocks,' he retorted. 'All it is, is the muscles in your hands and arms making tiny unconscious tweaks to move the rods in the direction you want. There's nothing mystical about it at all. It's just boring old physiology and a bit of wishful thinking. Give them here – I'll show you.' He took the rods, ignoring her poisonous glare, and moved back a couple of yards to come back at the Fane in the same way she had done – but this time he would make sure that they didn't move.

It was with considerable surprise that he found them starting to rotate.

They were turning very slowly in opposite directions. He shifted his hands to try and make them stand still, but without success – they rotated faster the closer he got to the barrier. Soon they were spinning like pinwheels.

'Yes, yes, very clever,' said Bex. 'You can stop taking the piss now.'

'I'm not!' he protested. 'I'm not doing anything at all!'

He stopped walking, but by now the rods seemed to have acquired a life of their own and were spinning freely, madly. Soon they were just blurred circles and he could hear the high-pitched whine of the wire whistling through the air like two miniature propellors. He appealed mutely to Bex, who simply shrugged, as dumbfounded as himself. The rods were shuddering now, rattling in his fists and growing uncomfortably hot.

He was just considering throwing them to the ground when, without warning, the copper sleeves split and the dowsing rods tore themselves from his hands, slicing thin gashes across his palms.

Bex screamed and flung herself to the ground as one arrowed over her head and disappeared into the Fane. The other shot like a slim, lethal dart across twenty yards of open space to the greenhouse and straight through both sides of it, shattering two large panes of glass which rained tumbling shards down onto the surprised, upturned faces of Lark and Cam.

They ran blindly from the greenhouse, Lark with both hands pressed to her forehead and blood streaming from between her fingers, neither of them taking much notice of where they were going.

Andy couldn't tell who yelled first, a chorus of panicky voices from all directions – 'Lark! No! Stop! Come back!' Confused, she turned, crying out 'I can't see! Why can't I s…?'

tripped over a furrow of earth, fell backwards into the Fane, and before anybody could get a hand to her she was gone. Her cry of alarm was sliced off as neatly as if it had never been uttered at all.

8
RE-ENTRY

'Lark, no!' Cameron lunged forward to follow her, but Bex was already there, blocking his way.

'Cam! Think! She's gone out – you can't do her any good going straight after her.'

'She's hurt! She's out there on her own. You know what it's like this time of year.'

'I know. But she's a clever girl, Cam. She'll realise what's happened, and she'll sit tight, and she'll…'

'The skavags will…'

'…*she'll wait for you to join her*. After you've got her stuff, and yours. You can't go out there with nothing. Starvation and hypothermia are not very romantic, you big idiot. *Think*. And you should get those looked at first, too.'

Cameron was covered in numerous small cuts which he appeared to notice for the first time. Gradually he calmed. Kerrie, who had come hurrying over from the house, appraised his wounds, pronounced him to be a big baby and led him back towards the kitchen. Bewildered Narrowfolk began to clear up the pieces of broken glass.

Andy said quietly to Bex: 'I think I'd better go get her.'

'That's not funny.'

'I mean it!'

'Really. Just like that.'

He shifted uncomfortably, as if embarrassed. 'The thing is, I've been watching this Fane thing for the last couple of days and I'm not sure that it's as one-way as everyone seems to think. I swear, every so often I can hear things through it.'

'Like what?'

'Nothing very exciting. Traffic. Music. Once, a siren. It just makes me think, maybe if sounds can get in – not to mention light and air and gravity and all those really basic fundamental things – maybe people can, too, and nobody's been looking hard enough.'

'Interesting theory. I'm sure that's never, ever occurred to Walter at all.'

'Well, since he hasn't bothered to show his face since we came back,' Andy retorted, stung, 'I might just not bother taking it up with him, if it's all the same to you.'

'Okay, alright, calm down.'

'Look, the upshot is this: if I'm right, Lark doesn't have to spend midwinter fighting off drunks and junkies in a shelter. If I mess up, you don't have to drag my sorry arse all over the city any more. I broke it; I pay for it.'

She regarded him speculatively for a long moment and then said, 'Think you can manage it?'

'I don't know. There's only one way to find out.' He knelt down and pulled up a parsnip, wincing at the sharp pain in his palm, and tossed it into the Fane.

'Well that was big and clever,' she observed drily.

Still kneeling, he reached in up to his armpit and felt around on the ground in the blank, white nothingness. When he drew his hand back, he was holding the parsnip again.

'And again with the impossible,' she breathed, eyes wide. 'My god, you might just be able to do it.'

'Maybe.' He pulled two more parsnips and threw all three into the void.

'What was that supposed to prove?'

'Nothing. I just don't like them very much.'

***

He held the iron stake and stood facing the Fane, a blank wall of apparently motionless mist so close that it filled the entirety of his vision, and for a moment it seemed that gravity had inverted itself by ninety degrees, and he was hanging miles above a featureless, arctic landscape. He wasn't sure whether he stepped deliberately or swayed forward, but there was a momentary sensation of being violently sideswept by a powerful tidal force, like surfing the outer edge of a whirlpool, and even as he formulated the panicked thought *Jesus Christ, it's going to tear me apart*, he was suddenly facing brick walls, tarmac, and the clouded sky of the real world again.

Here, Moon Grove was a vacant lot that gaped like a broken tooth where the house had once stood, even though he knew it was still there in some fashion, just behind him. He could feel it, or at least he could feel the forces which hid it, swirling behind his breastbone like heartburn.

It didn't take long to find Lark – and that she was not alone.

She was sitting on the pavement at the front of the lot, with her arms braced behind as if caught in the act of trying to crawl backward, and a strange man was doing something to her face.

Andy panicked, thinking that his delay had already been too long, and lurched awkwardly across the rough terrain, brandishing his stake. 'Hey!' he yelled. 'Hey, leave her alone! Get the hell away from her!'

Rosey looked up in surprise from where he'd been applying a bit of basic first aid, to see a young man in mismatched clothing running towards him waving what looked like a crowbar.

Lark stared around at Andy in surprise, and he realised his mistake when he saw the wound strips which dressed the cuts on her forehead. 'Andy?' She was quite gobsmacked. '*Bex's* Andy? What are you doing here? Where's Cam?' She jumped up and peered eagerly behind him.

'No, it's just me, I'm afraid. Sorry. Who's this?' He eyed the older man suspiciously.

'Andy *Sumner*?' Rosey's stunned expression mirrored Lark's.

'Yes? Hang on – what? Who are you?'

'Andrew Penrose.'

'*Who*?'

'Where's Cam?'

'He's back inside. Kerrie's trying to stop him doing anything silly.'

'Pete Sumner's boy?'

'*Right – stop!*' Andy yelled. This was starting to get out of hand. 'Lark. Calm down. We're going back inside soon and everything will be cool. Okay?'

'But that's…'

He held up a warning finger, and she subsided. 'I know. But we're going to do it anyway.' He turned to Rosey. 'You, whoever you are…' Then he stopped and thought for a second. 'Actually, it doesn't matter. Thanks for looking after my friend here. Have a merry Christmas. Bye.' He turned to go, wondering how on earth he was going to make good on his boast to re-enter a place that didn't exist any more.

Rosey had known that he was going to have to choose his words carefully if the boy wasn't going to take fright and simply run. 'Aren't you even curious about how I know your name?' he asked.

Andy turned back. 'Honestly? No. If you had any idea of the weird shit that's been happening to me so far this week, you wouldn't be surprised either. You're pretty low down the food chain – no offence.'

'I saw what happened to your flat,' Rosey replied conversationally, 'If you like, I think I can probably help you work out why it happened and what's going on.'

Andy simply laughed as he began to retreat across the rubble to where Lark was waiting for him.

'Please understand,' Rosey pressed, 'I haven't been sent by anyone. I'm not with the police or social services or anything like that. I don't want anything from you. I really just came to see...' he laughed. 'It's going to sound stupid.'

'What?'

'The plain truth of the matter, Andy, is that I've just been looking for you to make sure you're alright.'

Andy hesitated at that. 'But you don't know me from Adam.'

'That's true. Although we did meet once, a very long time ago.'

'When?'

Rosey glanced around, taking in the dereliction; the littered streets and lurking shadows. 'With all due respect,' he said, 'I don't really think this is the best time and place, do you?'

Andy conceded the point. 'I can't take you back in with me, though,' he added. 'The others would kill me.'

'Fair enough,' Rosey nodded, still careful not to push his luck. 'I can always come back. I can meet you here any time you like.'

Behind him in the empty street, he'd left his car with the engine running to keep the heater going, and its side-lights on so that he could better see to treat the girl's cuts. Now, suddenly, the engine coughed and died, while the lights faded to a sickly amber colour.

'Fuck me, but I love family reunions,' called Carling from the darkened mouth of the cul-de-sac. 'It almost makes me not want to kill every last one of you.'

At that, the shadows behind him surged into life.

Humped and glistening skavags boiled past him, filling the street from one side to the other just as their weird ululating cries looped upwards, echoing between the blank rooftops and boarded up windows.

'Fetch that one!' Carling's roar rose over the din, and his outflung arm pointed at Andy. 'Kill the others!' And he laughed with utter delight. This was what he was made for.

Rosey stayed only long enough to see a pack of creatures which defied reason tearing the doors and wheels off his Astra before turning to chase after Andy and Lark, who were both running for their lives back across the vacant lot. He caught up with them as they scrabbled through the overgrown bushes and hid against the sagging wooden fence at the very rear.

The skavags bounded across the pavement and up into the rubble. It did not matter to them that their prey had found cover; their sense of smell was acute. Carling, striding behind, shared snatch-glimpses of sensation with the more sentient of them, and felt an upwelling of pride as he watched his pack at work.

'Andy,' panted Rosey, 'those things…'

'I know. Shut up – I'm trying to think.'

'Whatever you're going to do, do it fast,' suggested Lark, her eyes wide in a pale, blood-streaked face.

'It's okay. I've done this before. Sort of.'

'*Sort of?*'

'Shut up!'

'Andy, what are those things?'

But he couldn't hear them any more. 'Big picture, got to see the big picture,' he murmured to himself. 'Straight across, cutting the lines, not such a good idea. Perpendicularity sucks, we know this. It's basically a big spirally, circley barrier thing, so let's go with that. Of course – *of course!*'

He grabbed Rosey and Lark, grinning like a madman. 'It's the Pattern – the grain of the universe. Cut *across* the grain and you get splinters, don't you? Go *with* it and you can carve any shape you want!'

The skavags, who had slowed as they sniffed out the cowering humans, were nevertheless halfway across the lot. Rosey decided to take matters into his own hands – or rather feet – and started to kick at the fence panels behind him. They were rotten and quickly began to collapse.

'What are you talking about?' Lark was close to becoming hysterical. 'We've got to get out of here!'

'Exactly! We've got to go around, not through! Around the edge! Follow the spiral! That's the way back in!'

'Go back *out* there? You're insane!'

The fence panel collapsed in splinters, and Rosey took each of them by an arm. 'Right, you two,' he ordered. 'Out. Now.'

'No!' Andy twisted free. 'We can't outrun them. We have to go out and around. I know it doesn't make sense but it's the only way. You have to trust me. And we have to go *now!*'

Rosey shook his head firmly. 'Not going to happen. You're crazy, lad. Let's go.' He started to push Lark through the hole in the fence.

'NO!' Sudden fire burst from Andy's fist where it still gripped the iron stake, and the other two flinched away. The same fury which had seized him first on Gramma's boat and then again when he'd killed the skavag in his kitchen was burning through him once more. Why did nobody ever listen to him? Why must he always be in the wrong? Traceries of blue fire crawled along the stake and crackled from each end with the smell of thunderstorms.

The skavags, only yards away, felt the power in his anger and paused, milling uncertainly. Carling sensed it through them and didn't like it. Something was amiss.

'I don't know who you are,' Andy growled, 'and I couldn't give a toss. Go wherever the hell you like; you're no concern of mine.' He turned to Lark. 'But you are. I'm taking you home.'

He grabbed her hand and they ran.

After a moment's agonised indecision, glancing through the hole in the fence to the escape offered there, Rosey followed.

The three of them burst from the bushes right into a knot of skavags, who scattered in alarm. Andy laid about wildly with the stake, lacking any kind of skill, hitting entirely through luck. Bright blue-white detonations flashed where he hit them. To their eyes, already half-blinded by the glare of watery midwinter daylight, he appeared unbearably incandescent, and for a brief second they fell back.

'No, you fuckers!' screamed Carling. 'Kill them! Tear them apart!'

Then the skavags' terror of their master caught hold once more and they swarmed forward across the open ground towards the running figures. His prey must have lost their senses, because they seemed to be trying to escape by the supremely stupid method of just doubling back around the outside. They were heading almost straight towards him. He changed direction to intercept them, his momentary worry eclipsed by the triumphant joy of imminent blood-letting.

That moment's hesitation had been enough for Andy to cover maybe a quarter of the lot's perimeter, and even though he could see that he was heading right for where the press of creatures was thickest, each step took him not just forward but fractionally *deeper*, following the curving track of ley energy which Walter had bent to hide Moon Grove.

He just had time for a sudden nauseating doubt to twist his guts (*I've killed us oh shit oh christ I've killed us*) and then he was surrounded by a nightmare of flailing claws and tooth-filled muzzles. But even as they tore at him they were little more than feeble, futile clutches at his clothes, and the howls were getting fainter as the air thickened and brightened. There was that sensation again of being buffeted by cyclonic winds – except this time they were coming from behind, because he was following their track instead of cutting across it – and then the three of them were stumbling into the bland sanctuary brightness of Moon Grove.

9

EROSION

The closest thing that the Grove had to an infirmary was the kitchen – not because it was any more hygienic, simply that, due to the Kitchen Tarts' methods of cookery, it was where most of the cuts, burns and minor injuries occurred.

Rosey sat on a stool before a huge Aga stove which seemed to be providing heat for the entire building, while Kerrie cleaned up his wounds with iodine and a complete lack of sympathy for his hisses of pain. His hesitation in following Andy and Lark had cost him a row of shallow but painful claw wounds down his left side.

'Sure, and you're just a big baby,' she tutted and launched into a lecture on the deficiencies of men in general – the idiocy of the young and the feeblemindedness of the older ones for letting them get away with it in the first place. It didn't seem to matter to her that Rosey was a complete stranger; she treated him with the same disdain as she did everybody else. But the look she gave Andy as she packed away was clear: *your guest, your mess.*

Mess. Pardon his French but what a fucking understatement *that* was turning out to be.

The house was buzzing as news of Andy's return evolved from rumour to gossip and then hotly contested debate all in a matter of minutes. Kerrie had shooed the crowds out of the kitchen in short order, and Lark was currently the centre of attention out in the dining room, but it was only a matter of time before Walter appeared, and then the really awkward questions would begin.

She stood looking at them both, arms folded over a disapproving bosom.

'You've got five minutes,' she said. 'And if my mince pies burn, you'll be in the next lot.'

She swept out, into the clamour of a dozen shouted conversations.

Andy sighed and fidgeted with the dressings on his hands. 'So. You came with something to tell me, but I'm sort of thinking you probably have more questions now, right?'

'Where do I start?' Rosey laughed and immediately regretted it. There was a slight edge of hysteria to the sound which he didn't like at all.

Andy shrugged it off. He didn't want this conversation, or this man's questions. He just wanted him gone. 'Sorry, but no. Any answers I could give you would just suck you in deeper, and you really don't want that. Believe it or not, I'm trying to do you a favour. I told you not to follow me.'

'Not that I had much choice,' Rosey pointed out, ticked off by the boy's attitude.

'A less sympathetic soul might suggest that it was your own bloody stupid fault for butting in where you weren't wanted, but who am I to judge? I think I know what you've come to tell me, and sorry, but I'm not interested.'

'Due respect son, but I don't think you have the first idea why I'm here.'

'Really? Try this, then. You're from NORCAP – the adoption people. Someone's come forward and said that she's my birth-mother and wants to get in touch, so you've come to make First Contact. Well you can forget it.

'I went through all of this when I was eighteen. Mum and Dad were always completely open with me about being adopted, so there was no big soap opera moment or, you know, 'I am your father, Luke' kind of thing. But still, it had to be done, so I phoned your people and they told me that there were no details of my birth parents. None at all. Hard enough being adopted normally, whatever that means, but a foundling? No chance. I hate that word, anyway. Makes me think I should be wearing a big floppy cap and dancing around singing 'Food, Glorious Food' or some such bollocks.

'So anyway, I did the very-angry-young-man thing for a year or two, helped along by a fair amount of recreational drugs and general silliness involving completely buggering up college, before I finally came to the realisation that it didn't matter. It just didn't matter. I am the person I am not because of whose DNA I carry but because of what I've done and how I've been raised – which, incidentally, was by two fantastic people who are just Mum and Dad. They're not 'foster' or 'adopted' or anything. They're just my folks. And I'm not in the market for any more.'

In the strained silence that followed it occurred to Rosey that Andy had a lot of steam to blow off about something which he claimed to be reconciled with, and almost felt apologetic about having to let him down. 'I don't know who NORCAP are,' he admitted, 'or what they do. I'm not from them. Sorry.'

'So…' Andy shoved his chair aside in angry confusion and stalked to the other side of the kitchen where he stood with his arms folded tightly. 'What, exactly? You said we'd met before, a long time ago. What's this all about?'

'I thought you didn't want me butting in.'

'I don't. But…' Andy floundered. '*You* followed *me.*'

'Yes, well. Obviously the situation is a lot more complicated than I thought,' Rosey replied, picking at his dressings thoughtfully. He was seized with a sudden and inexplicable conviction that there was something incredibly important that he'd forgotten. It felt like being watched, or followed, and it made him nervous. Made him want to keep his mouth shut until he could better measure the consequences of anything he said. 'I think I'm going to take your advice for now and keep my nose out of things. If you don't want to explain anything about where we are or what those things were, then that's fine by me. I'll pick it up as I go along.'

Rosey never knew what Andy's response to this might have been, because at that moment the kitchen door swung open, and Walter strode into the room like a branch of forked, grey lightning.

'Sumner,' he demanded, 'I need to know everything about what you did just now.'

Then he saw Rosey, and his face crumpled in a look of shocked horror so sudden it was like watching something age a thousand years in timelapse photography. His mouth worked soundlessly, like a toothless old man chewing something tough and bitter.

For some reason, Rosey wasn't surprised at all. Walter Lyttleton was older than the last time he'd seen him by the best part of two decades, and the trenchcoat was long gone, but he was undeniably the same lanky streak of child-molesting piss he'd choked half to death all those years ago.

'Well isn't this a nice coincidence,' Rosey observed.

***

Carling forced one foot in front of the other as he stumbled through the Fane, scoured blind and deaf by its relentless battering. It tore at his back and screamed through his head, eroding coherent thought and leaving nothing but the single-minded bedrock of his predatory rage. He would bring Sumner to ground or die in the hunt, and that was just fine.

It was preferable to whatever Barber would do to him for having lost the fucker a third time.

184

He had no idea how long he'd been walking or how long there might be to go, but if it didn't end soon, the Fane would kill him itself and solve everybody's problems. He'd watched the two skavags which had been close enough to attack Penrose lope in after him – close enough to be overcome by their hunting instincts but too far away to follow with any accuracy, and as they plunged deeper, he saw the Fane catch them and tear them apart in long, shrieking streamers of flesh.

But the blood-taste of Andy Sumner was strong; Carling was close enough to track him almost exactly, yet even so the unevenness of the ground and the squalling ley energy made him miss his step every now and then, and the Fane would snatch at the very substance of him.

It was not, strictly speaking, a physical force – it didn't scour the ground; it flung up neither dust nor debris, and the weeds which he moved past were completely unbent by it. However, he was at a level of the world where there was no clear distinction any more between the physical and the immaterial – and it felt pretty damned solid to him. It was quite literally eroding him.

Every time he stumbled it took a little bit more, like a desert statue suffering a thousand years of sandstorms in a few minutes. In a previous life, some teacher had tried to make him learn a poem about a statue in the desert that had been all worn and beaten to shit, and he could remember something about 'two vast and trunkless legs of stone' but that was about it. It was funny what came back to you when you were dying, he thought. It got mixed up in his head with snatches of a Nine Inch Nails song which looped *it won't give up it wants me dead god damn this noise inside my head* over and over. If this nightmare didn't end soon, it was likely that was all that would be left of him: blunt stumps and an endless, circling scream.

His hair had been the first to go, shredded like smoke. His exposed scalp – and in fact every inch of exposed skin – was now pitted and cratered as the windless hurricane scooped out chunks of his flesh. He had his fingers jammed protectively in his armpits, because the last time he'd looked several of them were quite a bit shorter. Christ alone knew what was happening to his face.

When he found Sumner, he'd tear the face from his living skull and wear it himself.

...god damn this noise...wants me dead...

Unable to see, hear, or sense anything properly beyond the blood of his prey which compelled him forward, Carling retreated into himself. His feet plodded forward on their own, and he entertained himself with fantasies of what he'd do to Sumner when he finally caught him. Then he reminisced over the glories of past violence; all the people he'd fucked up for acts of disrespect real or imagined. He revisited old arguments, thinking up better comebacks and more satisfying humiliations.

But eventually these too were scoured away by the Fane, until he was nothing more than a knuckled-down thing setting one foot in front of the other, two trunkless legs which had forgotten their destination, and continued to move only from a mute inability to imagine stopping.

...noise...

He disappeared into the Fane, erasing himself one step at a time.

***

'This is my house,' said Walter, 'and my children under threat, so you'll both sit tight there and listen. There are things you need to hear,' he directed at Andy, 'never mind what you do or don't want to know. If you abandon us, then so be it, but you've brought death to my door, and you'll not leave ignorant of it. As for you, policeman,' he turned to Penrose. 'You have no authority here, so please, spare me your self-righteous judgement.'

He'd recovered his composure quickly after the surprise of seeing Penrose in his kitchen, and he now regarded them both coldly over the paper-strewn expanse of his desk.

Walter's study on the topmost floor was book-lined and dark. In its arcane clutter it reminded Andy of Gramma's narrowboat, except that instead of bundles of drying herbs there tottered piles of atlases and ancient Ordnance Survey maps. What little wall-space remained was crammed with astrological charts, aerial photographs of the Nazca lines and Stonehenge, maps of the solar system, and even – Andy recognised with a jolt – a full-size diagram of the human body's acupuncture meridians. On the shelves behind him clustered dusty photographs which looked to be at least half a century old. Pride of place was given, not to an image, but a framed verse of handwritten text:

> *There all the barrel-hoops are knit*
> *There all the serpent-tails are bit*
> *There all the gyres converge in one*
> *There all the planets drop in the sun*

The last line in particular made his spine shiver. Somewhere a clock ticked away the dry silence like falling leaves.

'You'll recall that when you first arrived here I was concerned with your unskilled interference, that it would draw unwelcome attention.'

'Something about being an ignorant suburbanite, wasn't it?'

'Quite. Well, I did some asking around, and it turns out I was right.'

'Imagine your surprise,' Rosey muttered with heavy sarcasm.

Walter ignored him. 'The man who hunts you is called Simon Barber, though I use the term 'man' quite loosely. I doubt by now that there's much left of him which could be described as human. The tragedy of it is that he was originally a brilliant scientist – he even worked briefly for the Ministry of War – but he drifted into studies of occult interest which would never appear in any sane peer review journal.

Leys. Geomancy. The forbidden *dim mak* points of human acupuncture. Everything. And it has corrupted him utterly. He has walked alone through the deepest skins of the world, and whatever secrets he has found there have twisted his soul into a splinter of the black hole at its heart. He has long since been pursuing his own insane goals – I have no idea what these now are, but rest assured I equally have no intention of interfering with them.'

'Hang on,' Andy interrupted, 'You sound like you actually knew him.'

'Does that surprise you? Who do you think I learned from? Yes, I once knew him very well. We collaborated together on a great work, but…' a shadow of pain passed over Walter's face '… we had something of a falling out over its methodology.'

Andy was almost afraid to ask. 'What was this 'great work' of yours?'

In the silence which followed, he could feel the Pattern coalescing in the room, thicker than ever before. So thick, in fact, that he could now actually see it, linking the three of them in bright whorls of energy which hovered on the periphery of his vision.

'You,' Walter replied simply.

10

STEVEN

Rosey could barely contain his scorn. 'Andy,' he said, 'let me tell you about the 'great work' that this scumbag was doing to you when I found you,' and he went on to describe the horrors that he'd seen behind the door of 144 Tyler Road, almost two decades ago. What Andy heard was so outrageous that might have been tempted to disbelieve it, despite everything he'd seen and done so far, were it not for the whorls of energy surrounding Rosey which indicated that the old policeman believed it to be the truth. Both men, Andy saw, were linked with thick, dark ribbons of mutual enmity. 'Andy,' Penrose concluded, 'the things this man has done to you... you can't possibly believe anything he says.'

Walter seemed unmoved by the accusations, but Andy saw guilt circling with a deep and abiding shame in his aura. 'Do you recall any pain, Andrew?'

'Of course he doesn't, you bastard; he was *five*!'

'Are you physically scarred?' Walter turned to Penrose. 'Did the doctors who examined the boy find any sign of injury whatsoever?'

'You used needles, man! Red hot needles! I felt them myself! You were *burning* him!'

'Show Mr Penrose where you were burned. Show him the scars, Andrew.' Andy couldn't, because there were none. 'You had chickenpox where you were three, did you know that? I'm sure you have the marks from that somewhere.' Andy's hand went involuntarily to his neck, where a triangle of three white dimples nestled under his collar bone – they'd been there for as long as he could remember. 'Can either of you explain to me how I could have maimed a child so appallingly and yet have left no mark even so small as a chickenpox scar?

'They were acupuncture needles, and the heat you felt was coming *from* the boy, not *into* him. But of course a great clumping blue-uniformed oaf such as yourself would not have appreciated the distinction, much less stopped to consider the damage caused by just ripping them out thoughtlessly.

'When you barged in, I was in the middle of trying to reverse what Barber had already done. Do you have any conception of the complexity of the human bio-electric field or the system of chakras and meridians which regulates it? Of course you don't. Try to imagine a system so beautifully intricate and subtle that the art of its manipulation has taken three thousand years to evolve, as against the paltry two hundred or so of fumbling and butchery that in the West is called 'medicine'. Are you aware on any dim level of how much damage can be caused by simply tearing out great handfuls of needles which have taken hours or even days to place carefully so as not to injure the child? You might as well pull the plug on a nuclear reactor. Frankly, Andrew, I'm amazed that you didn't die right then and there. Even so, your *ch'i* had almost certainly been knocked so catastrophically out of alignment that you should have been rendered blind, or hopelessly autistic, or dead of cancer before puberty.

'The miracle is not that you were rescued, but that your brave rescuer here didn't kill you with his heavy-handedness. And yet here you are.'

'No thanks to you, apparently,' Andy retorted, but it lacked conviction.

'No? Who do you think called the police in the first place?' His question hung in the air like the aftermath of a lightning strike. 'My one mistake was in underestimating the speed of their response and not being able to bring you back down safely from your heightened energistic state before they kicked down the door.'

'This is a pack of lies,' spat Rosey. 'I was there in court; I read the witness statements. There was a call from a concerned neighbour who heard a child's cries. Andy, this is all bollocks. Don't listen to him.'

Walter's eyes never left Andy's. 'So much about that trial was completely different from what you or anybody else saw. There was no witness. There was no crying child. You trusted me – you'd known me all your short life. I helped *deliver* you, for goodness' sake. Those sharply-dressed young men of the prosecution were no more barristers than I am the Duke of Cornwall. Barber had been out of the game for years, but he still had enough friends in high places to make sure that I was put away for a very long time.'

'I'll tell you what you are,' Rosey snapped. 'You're an insane, paranoid-schizophrenic nut-job is what you are. Andy, this man has a documented history of drug abuse and mental illness…'

'Which no doctor was *ever* found to…'

'… a record as long as your arm…'

'…fabricated, all fabricated…'

'*Enough!*' Andy yelled, and watched in amazement as twin spikes of energy lanced out of him and into their auras, setting them to spin dizzily. Walter and Penrose rocked back as if slapped. Silence crept back into the room. He felt it filling the rest of the house, knew that the rest of the Narrowfolk were listening – not to every single word, just waiting to see if the thundercloud would blow past or open over their heads.

'I told you before that I don't care,' he said, 'and I meant it. Genuinely, I don't give a toss about what happened sixteen years ago. *You*,' he stabbed a finger at Walter, 'fucked with me, of that I have no doubt. Dress it up any way you like in truths and half-truths, but you dragged me into something unspeakable, and trying to ease your conscience about it now doesn't make any difference.

'*You…*' he turned on Rosey, 'just couldn't leave well enough alone. You had to drag all of this up again. It never occurs to people like you that some of us are truly happier not knowing all the crappy stuff that happened to us in the past. So now I know, and thanks, but at the same time, there goes my childhood, you know?

'Reasons, whys and wherefores, who's to blame and all of that –' he made a dismissive, cutting gesture '– not important. You can fight it out between yourselves when I'm gone. Whatever it is I can do, whatever I *am*, I'll figure that out on my own, thanks very much. All I want to know right now is where am I from? *Who* am I from?'

Walter heaved a great sigh, as if a burden had just been lifted from his shoulders, and began rummaging through the crammed shelves of old maps. 'You were born in a small village called Holly End, a few miles south of Birmingham, on the edge of the Cotswolds. It used to be very pretty, once upon a time. It had a church and post-office, and a little cottage hospital where you were born. Your mother was a local girl called Anna Pickett. You are her only child. The name she gave you was Steven. Ah, here we are.'

While Walter carefully unfolded an ancient and yellowing map across his desk, Rosey turned to Andy, his aura swirling and agitated. 'Andy,' he pleaded 'you have got to understand that this is all lies. Listen to what he's saying. Babies aren't born in cottage hospitals in this day and age; he's living in a dream world. When he told all of this to the arresting officers, don't you think that was the first place they went to? They tried, at least, but they couldn't find it. Andy, *there is no such place.*'

But all he could think was *Steven. My name was Steven.*

'You'd be amazed how many places there are dotted around the country which don't exist, Mr Penrose,' replied Walter. 'I think you'll find that you're in one of them right now.'

To that, Rosey had no reply.

'All the same,' the older man continued, 'best if you believe him. I know what you're thinking, but you can never return to Holly End, Andrew. If it were possible, I would have done so many years ago.'

Andy roused himself. 'What? Why not?'

'For one thing, it has been taken out of existence, just like Moon Grove.'

'I found my way back in here, didn't I? I can find that place, too.'

'I don't doubt it. But even if you could, it would be the single most dangerous place in the entire world you could go. It is the place where Barber and I began our work, the place from which I fled with you when I learned the monstrous truth of his ambitions. He removed it from the skin of the world himself, and it is still the centre of his power. Make no mistake: he knows who you are by now, and he is not hunting you out of some silly old man's nostalgia, like the two of us. He will take you apart screaming and dissect your living soul out of nothing but simple curiosity, just to see what makes you tick.'

Andy sat back and sighed darkly. 'Yeah, well,' he said with bitter irony. 'It wouldn't be Christmas without a few dodgy relatives, would it?'

***

Bex found Andy in the kit room, stuffing a rucksack with clothes and other items from the storage bins of leftover supplies. She hefted her own bag higher on one shoulder and said brightly 'So! Where are we going?'

Andy kept cramming. '*We* are going nowhere,' he replied bluntly, without looking around. '*I* am making like a bread van and getting out of this place before I get somebody killed.'

'You mean "hauling buns".'

'Whatever.'

She watched him silently for a moment while he packed. He could feel her behind him in much the same way as a blind man can feel the sun on his back.

'I would just like, for once,' he said suddenly, spinning around to glare at her, 'for there to be somebody in this world who I don't have to argue with, or have to justify myself to, or fight to get anything from, you know?'

'Oh, I know,' she replied. 'I know that one alright.'

'You can't come with me,' he insisted.

'You'll note that I'm not arguing about it.' She looked at what he had unthinkingly stuffed in his bag. 'You've just packed a pair of board shorts,' she observed. 'Long trip, is it? Just as long as you understand that you're not going anywhere stupidly dangerous, like this Holly End place.'

He stared at her in surprise. 'Were you eavesdropping?'

'It's sweet how you think anybody has any secrets here,' she answered innocently. 'But you've got it arse-backwards, as usual. You're the one who's coming with me. Lead skavags to my front door, will you? Not if I can bloody help it. I'm making sure we're well shot of you.'

'Neither of you is going anywhere.'

Walter stood behind them, wearing his walking boots.

'Andy,' he continued, 'it wouldn't make any difference – he'll come here looking for you regardless. In any case you're not responsible for these people or what happens to them. That's my call. Barber and I were close once; I'm going to find him and try to put a stop to this madness.'

'But he'll kill you!' protested Bex.

'With any luck, they'll kill each other,' Andy replied bitterly.

Walter grunted. 'It's been a long time coming, if so.' He reached into his shirt and drew out a fine chain, from which a spoked-wheel medallion spun in eye-watering concentric orbits. He unclasped and offered it to Andy, who recognised it vaguely from somewhere. 'Take it,' said Walter. 'You liked it once upon a time.'

Andy shook his head tightly. 'That wasn't me. I want nothing from you. Do you understand? *Nothing*. Haven't you done enough already?'

Bex fetched him a slap behind the ear. 'Don't be such a child,' she scolded. 'Can't you recognise when a man is trying to make amends? Here,' she took the medallion, 'I'll look after it.'

'Stay here,' ordered the older man as he headed for the front door. 'If I'm not back by morning, get everybody out of here. Get them anywhere else you can. Don't wait for the Fane to stop on its own. And for God's sake, try not to do anything else stupid.'

***

The Carling that collapsed over the threshold into the sanctuary of Moon Grove was a stripped, skeletal thing dressed in rags and clutching in its mind just a few glittering shards of murderous intent.

It was night. He lay on his back in the thin margin of long grass at the very edge of the Fane and stared up at the sky with his eroded face. He could see neither moon nor stars. For some reason this struck him as immensely funny, and he began to laugh, but it soon degenerated into weak spasms of coughing, so he stopped.

'Made it in, boss,' he croaked, and was shocked at the sound of his own ruined voice. Not doing that again in a hurry, either.

While he was resting, he watched a bright doorway open briefly and a lone figure stride across the empty ground to disappear into the barrier. Rats leaving the sinking ship already, he thought. No matter. There would still be plenty of them left when his master arrived.

Carling began to crawl with agonising slowness around the perimeter of Moon Grove, searching for a way to let himself in.

11

COLLAPSE

Barber wasn't particularly surprised to find Walter at the door to his office; with events surrounding the Sumner boy converging at an ever-increasing rate, it was almost inevitable. Nevertheless, there was something about the way the man had made it up six floors past all manner of security that irked him. He was going to have to have words with the concierge.

'Well now. Father Walter Lyttleton.' He rose from his desk and moved around to greet him, hand outstretched for shaking as if they were nothing more than old business partners. Walter looked like he hadn't eaten or shaved in days. He refused the hand, and Barber put it away with a shrug as if to say *Oh well, you can't say I didn't try.* 'You look old, dear boy. Older than you should. Old and weak. How long has it been for you?'

For Walter, words wouldn't come at first. There was so much to be said and no possible way to say it all, his throat was choked. 'Almost sixteen years,' he managed thickly.

'*Sixteen?* Good grief, man. If you'll forgive me for saying so, they haven't been kind to you. And you living here all this time, right under my nose like a cockroach. That's quite some achievement; well done.' Barber resumed his seat. In the darkness of his office, the only illumination came from the Christmas lights strung across New Street outside. They bathed his face in shifting tones of glacial blue and white.

Walter could only plough on, and say what he had come here to say. 'You are aware that Steven is with us too, I take it.'

'"Here all the barrel-hoops are knit." Isn't that right? Yes, I am aware. All the gyres are converging in one, Walter. Everything is converging. Something has woken up in the boy, despite your sabotage. He is growing in power; I can feel it. It was always going to happen, but now there's nothing either of us can do to control him, is there?'

'I'm not here for old arguments, Simon.'

'Well your tone has certainly mellowed with the years. No self-righteous holier-than-thou lectures about the sanctity of this that and the other. What are you here for, then? Could it be that you have come to ask me for something? Please don't say that it's forgiveness.'

'I have him. Call off your dogs, Simon, leave my people alone, and I'll give you back the boy.'

Barber shook his head slowly in wonderment. 'It's incredible. You really have no sense of loyalty, do you? Personally, I think treachery is programmed into your genes. But my dear Walter,' he laughed, 'what makes you think I even want him? He is absolutely no use to me whatsoever now. Your betrayal set me back years. Decades. Did you think I wouldn't have moved on since then?'

Walter hesitated.

'I'll tell you what, though, I've just had an even better idea. How would you like to come back to Holly End instead?'

Barber left the question hanging in the air between them for a moment, enjoying how its sudden allure made Walter's eyes glisten. 'It's still there, you know,' he continued quietly. 'All just as you left it. The green is still there, the Clee boys are all grown up and terrorising the village; there's a holly wreath on every door and a Christmas tree at every hearth, and even some drinkable homebrew at the Black Horse at last.'

Walter responded as if the words were being forced out of him by torture: 'There's nothing I'd like more, you bastard, and you know it. This isn't about me for once.'

'St Kenelm's needs its vicar, Walter. The villagers have been cut off for so very long and they need guidance more and more each day. Will you not come back to us?'

'My god, if you knew how much I've dreamt of it...'

'Then don't bother with the boy, old friend.'

'What do you mean?' Walter edged away in suspicion.

'I don't need him, so you don't have to betray him. Well, not him alone, anyway. Give me all of them.'

'*What?*' It came out as nothing more than a gasp. He felt like he'd been punched in the stomach.

'Yes, Walter.' Barber's smile was cold and feral. In the shifting blue light, the black pits of his eyes and white gleam of his teeth made him look like a shark. 'The Narrowfolk. Give them to me, and you can come home.'

'Never. You're insane, Barber. You always were.'

'After sixteen years, haven't you grown tired of the filth and vulgarity out here? Living like a beggar, scrounging an existence out of other people's bins. And what thanks do you get from those whores and addicts? You say that they are 'your' people, but what do they ever do except leave when they have taken what they can from you?'

'Please...'

'Your people, Walter, your *real* people are baking mince pies and waiting for someone to lead them in a proper carol service. Steven can come back with us. We can reunite him with his family, and all of this will have been nothing but a bad dream. A genuinely fresh start, Walter – how many people ever get that chance? We can be there in two hours. What do you say?'

'You're lying.'

'Then say no. It's that simple. Say no.'

He couldn't. He thought of Dodd, Bex, Lark, and all the others exactly like them who had come and gone over the years, and yet he could not refuse this man. Had he ever made the slightest bit of difference in their lives? What right had he ever had to draw them away from normal society and into the insanity of the Narrows? Ashen-faced with shame, self-loathing and world-weary desperation, Walter whispered:

'*Yes.*'

Barber's mocking laughter filled the room. 'Oh Walter, it's so nice to know that in this world of flux and mutability some things can always be relied upon. You know as well as I do that there can be no going back, but you just can't help yourself, can you? Nobody needs you. I don't even need your betrayal – my man Carling telephoned hours ago to say that he's followed Penrose right to your door. Your Narrowfolk are already mine. You've simply demonstrated that you have no right to beg anything on their behalf, that's all.'

From the inside pocket of his jacket he removed the flat stationery tin of needles, and began to unfold the linen strip along which they were ranked.

'However,' he continued, 'you also know that I cannot possibly trust you. You're going to tell me everything about what the boy is and what he can do. Then maybe I'll give you the death which is all you deserve, and what you really came here for after all.'

At his signal, the door opened and two security guards entered.

Walter, trapped against the window facing the street, threw himself at it as hard as he could. If Barber had allowed any modernisation of his inner sanctum the window would have been suicide-proof safety glass too tough to break, but instead the brittle old single-glazed pane exploded into jagged shards, lacerating him in a dozen places as he plunged into the night.

He fell into a row of glowing, six-foot high blue and white snowflakes stretched high across the street and his limbs tangled in the construction wires as bulbs shorted out and exploded around him in showers of sparks. Even though the high-voltage electrocution killed him instantly, the high-tension cables – strong enough to withstand heavy winds and rain – held aloft his burned and bleeding corpse to the horrified gaze of upturned faces for hours before it could be cut down.

**

The stake was easy enough for Carling to find: a foot of oak protruding from an elaborate piece of graffiti painted on the ground, wrapped in copper wire that gleamed faintly in the dark. He grasped it with both hands and pulled, exerting the last gasps of the stolen strength which had allowed him to survive the Fane in the first place. There was no point in pretending any more that he was ever going to get his hands on Sumner, but this would have to do. Bring down the walls of his castle and if he was lucky, live just long enough to see the fucker eaten alive.

'I'll huff…' he grunted as he hauled upwards, 'and I'll puff and I'll…'

With an almighty wrench which tore something deep, deep inside, he pulled the stake free in an explosion of frozen soil and collapsed backwards, gasping for breath and staring up at the sky.

This time he could see the stars.

**

'All I'm saying,' Andy insisted, 'is that we should have some kind of fall-back just in case he doesn't come back.'

'Like what?' demanded Cam. He had his arms wrapped protectively around Lark and glared as if Andy were the one threatening her.

Andy was very nearly at his wits end. The Narrowfolk had mobbed him in Butlins, alternately demanding to know how he had got back in and where Walter had gone. Half of them refused to believe that they were in any sort of danger while the other half were waiting for him to tell them what to do, which was even more frightening.

'I don't know, do I? You're the ones who live here! What do you normally do when someone tries to attack you?'

'People *don't* normally try to attack us – that's the point.'

'It's not exactly people you need to be worrying about.'

'And you led them to us! So what are you going to do about it?'

Moon Grove suddenly shrugged around them in a jolt which felt sickeningly familiar, and he stumbled into Bex. Crashes and screams sounded in distant rooms.

'Jesus, no!' he moaned. 'Not here too. Not *here*!'

Seconds later Stirchley appeared in the opening, his eyes wide with shock. 'The Fane!' he gasped. 'It's fallen! They're coming!'

Cursing, Andy threw himself towards the stairs.

***

An army of skavags poured past Carling and across a broken landscape of concrete and churned mud towards Moon Grove, which stood high and vulnerable against the orange sky. One or two stopped to sniff at him, but now there was nothing left to inspire even an animal's curiosity, much less fear.

The baying, yammering horde quickly surrounded the house, tearing apart the outbuildings and fighting to find a way in, and after them strode Barber's tall figure. His greatcoat swept about his ankles, and serried ranks of needles gleamed down its wide lapels. He stopped for a moment by Carling's inert form and knelt. Very gently, he brushed a crumb of dirt from the ravaged face.

'That's two you've cost me now, Lyttleton, you faithless swine,' he growled. At his touch Carling's eyes flickered open and his lips moved feebly.

'Got you in, didn't I?' His voice was the whisper of winter in dry grass.

'You did at that,' Barber replied. 'Bless you my boy, but you actually did it. So strong. So very, very strong. Rest now, boy. You've earned it.' He watched as the last shreds of Fane-cloud dissipated from around the house, listening with satisfaction to the screams of women and children. The skavags paused in their frenzy, awaiting his orders.

Sieges had always bored him to tears.

'Kill them all.'

***

The house was chaotic with panicking Narrowfolk. Children howled, adults grabbed their belongings together and shouted desperate warnings to each other as they ran from room to room, finding no escape through any door, any window.

'Get everybody upstairs!' Andy yelled, but he was completely ignored in the panic. In the hall he collared Stirchley, who was trying to run and stuff a carrier bag of Rizzlas into his rucksack at the same time. 'Get these people upstairs!' he demanded, 'and switch on every light you can find!'

'Lights?' Stirchley's eyes were wide and darting.

'They're nocturnal aren't they, those things?'

'Yeah... but...'

'Well then!'

The two of them ran down into the chaos, grabbing people by the arms, the heads, whatever, and yelling at them to get upstairs, get up there *now*, as far as they could go, and flicking on every light switch within reach as they went. Stirchley stripped the Christmas tree of its fairy lights and wound them around his head.

'Stirch?' Andy looked on incredulously. '*What?*'

'It's okay!' he grinned. 'They're battery powered!' And he waved the battery pack at him. Andy had just enough time to think that he looked like some kind of mad-eyed disco Messiah before the first of the skavags crashed through the front porch. Somebody screamed 'They're in! They're inside the building…!' and tailed off into a gurgling shriek which was drowned in high looping cries; the creatures were smashing their way in through every ground-floor window. They clambered through broken glass, pale-eyed and blinking, cutting themselves but not apparently feeling it, or else their hunger was overriding the pain. The black-red of their blood smeared over each other and the floor like oil.

Andy was in the Big Room when they tore through the window, where it seemed that a hundred years ago he'd pinned up a holly sprig and listened to the winter wind, dreaming fairy tales of Holly Kings and Oak Kings. A skavag leapt up and half-sat on the window ledge, its head moving in quick darts as it scanned the room. It saw him and keened.

It was answered a thousandfold, from every direction.

He scrambled backwards, dragging the door shut as bodies slammed heavily against it on the other side, claws tearing at the wood, scrabbling at the doorknob.

Back in the hallway, towards the front of the house, skavags were in the graffitied porch, tearing furiously at the walls as if bent on shredding every sign of the Narrowfolk. From the other direction, the kitchen, he heard loud shrieks and heavy metallic clanging sounds accompanied by a frenzied female Irish war cry of 'Get out of me fecking kitchen, ye little feckers!' Ceridwen was defending her realm, for the moment.

People were fleeing to the upper floors, and he could hear Bex shouting orders shrilly over the din; he prayed that she was organising some kind of defence up there. Then clawed arms burst through the panel of the door at the same time as the porch door shattered, and the hall was filled with leaping monstrosities. He ran for the stairs.

On the first-floor landing, he met a line of Narrowfolk ranged across it – Bex, Stirchley, Cameron, Lark, and half a dozen others he didn't know – pale with fear but armed with whatever makeshift weapons had come to hand. Several had torches. Bex handed him his iron stake. 'Thought you might need this,' she said.

'So what's the plan?'

'Plan? You think there's a plan?'

Any reply he might have made died in his suddenly dry throat as skavags boiled up the staircase. Everything after that was a jumbled nightmare of screams, thuds, flailing limbs, claws, and teeth. Those defenders with torches flashed them directly into the skavags' light-sensitive eyes while the others bludgeoned them with golf clubs and cricket bats, but there were simply too many.

Stirchley's torch began to dim almost immediately; he shook it and peered at its dying bulb. 'Solar-powered piece of crap!' he complained and threw it at the head of the nearest creature. Then a sudden savage tug on his right ankle brought him to his knees. In the melee he'd found himself at the very edge of the landing, hard up against the balustrade, and as he looked down over it he saw that a skavag had clawed its way up the side of the stairwell and reached through to grab at him. It was funny; his foot looked oddly short. Then he saw his own toes, still wrapped in half an army surplus boot and a shred of sock, being chewed in the creature's wide muzzle. His blood was squirting down its face – he heard it *gargling* on his blood – and his shriek cut wide through the sounds of fighting.

Heads turned. Guards dropped. Weapons wavered. Cameron was seized by a dozen clawed arms and dragged into the seething pack. Lark shrieked with fury and tried to go after him, but Andy and Bex dragged her back.

'This is fucked!' Bex spat. 'We can't do this!'

There was a sudden resounding crash from somewhere up on the next landing, as if a large piece of furniture had fallen over, and Penrose shouted down 'You lot! Get back up here! Right now!'

They fled backwards up the next flight, flailing wildly at anything within reach, helped only by the narrowness of the staircase which forced the creatures to climb over each other, choked by their own numbers.

At the top the defenders found that Penrose and several others had indeed dragged a wardrobe from the nearest bedroom and flung it on its side as a makeshift barricade at the edge of the second floor landing. Stirchley was unceremoniously posted over and dumped in a moaning heap on the other side.

As they squeezed past, Rosey upended a bottle of home-brewed sloe gin over the wardrobe's length and struck a match. It ignited with a dull *fump!* and the smell of burning sugar, eliciting yells of alarm.

'How the fuck are we supposed to escape now?' Bex shouted at him.

'Escape?' Rosey laughed shortly. 'I'll settle for not getting eaten, thanks.'

As far as fires went, it was dismally weak and short-lived, barely hot enough to blister the varnish – but for a moment it kept the skavags at bay, and they milled on the stairs, mewling uncertainly in their near-human voices. Elsewhere in the house, they could be heard running amok; Andy wondered if Kerrie and any of her Kitchen Tarts had survived. It was possible. They had a big lockable larder and a walk-in fridge. Then a thought struck him.

'Why have we still got electricity?'

Bex blinked at him. 'Relevance?'

'This happened before at my flat, didn't it? Somehow he dropped the whole building into a Narrow, and the first thing that happened was the power got cut. So why not now?'

'Easy,' she replied. 'Power's running off the gennie in the cellar. There's nothing to cut off. What *are* you on about?'

'I mean the light's the only thing slowing them down at the moment…'

'That was *slow*?' Stirchley's voice was raw with hysteria. Rosey was trying to wad the stump of his foot with a bath towel; there was blood everywhere. 'Calm down,' he growled.

'… but what happens when they find the generator and cut the power?'

Stirchley laughed a high bubbling laugh. 'How can they cut the power, man? They're animals!'

'No, they're not animals. At least, they are normally, but they're being controlled aren't they? So all bets are off as to what they can and can't do.'

'And this is getting us where, exactly?' protested Bex.

He wasn't sure. But he'd seen something, both outside the Fane earlier that day and just now as the skavags had come swarming up the stairs. Their auras were simpler than those of human beings: cruder, the connections between them coloured in muddied shades of fear and dominance. The rank and file were held in thrall to their pack alphas who were in turn driven by a terror of something outside which walked in the shape of a man but was more monstrous than any of them. It compelled them to attack a brightly lit house full of people when every instinct said to run, hide, seek the shadows and narrow places. *What are you?* he wondered. *Anything more than just attack dogs?* He remembered Gramma's dog, Spike, and the skavag in his kitchen – the way its skull had shifted and imploded under his fingers. In that flash of connection knew how he could fight them, even though his heart shrank at the thought of what it might cost him.

The flames were dying, and the skavags milled more bravely in response.

Looking at the faces of his friends Andy realised that the cost of inaction would be immeasurably dearer.

'Hold this,' he said to Bex and passed her the iron stake.

'What? What are you…?'

He climbed up onto the side of the wardrobe and stood looking down. Below him, gangrel monstrosities filled the staircase from wall to banister. The dying flames threw distorted shadows of their already grotesque shapes up the walls, shining redly on claws, teeth, and eyes, and they set up a ululating chorus as they saw him: their hunting call. If this was not a vision of hell, thought Andy, then death would be fine, because no afterlife could boast anything worse.

'*Andy, NO!*' Bex shrieked.

He jumped.

***

There was no hope of defending himself; Andy was driven to the floor instantaneously. He simply curled himself into the tightest of foetal balls and waited for the biting to begin.

He didn't have to wait long.

He'd once seen a documentary about shark attacks in which the victims had described feeling no pain but a violent tugging sensation, and that this had been put down to a combination of shock and the incredible sharpness of the sharks' teeth. The skavag attack felt nothing like that. It was the worst pain he had ever experienced in his entire life. They worried at him like a toy from all directions.

He'd been afraid that he wouldn't be able to call up the same responses which had saved him first on Gramma's boat and then again at the flat, but in the end he didn't have to think about it at all. His flesh responded instinctively – the same instinct which crushes the wasp as it stings, or keeps a cornered animal fighting even as it is ripped apart.

Wherever teeth or claws pierced his flesh, his *ch'i* surged in gouts of ravening blue flame. It burned into the heads and limbs of his enemies, warping their own energy meridians and the flesh within which these were anchored, causing sudden catastrophic malformations of muscle and bone which were at best crippling, and in most cases instantly fatal. Limbs twisted and snapped. Internal organs burst. Skulls imploded. Within a few moments he found himself bleeding from innumerable wounds but surrounded by a ring of twitching, dying creatures.

'*Andy!*' Bex screamed. 'Andy, speak to me, *please!*' Tears were streaming down her face as she tried to climb over the barricade, and it was only with great difficulty that Rosey and Lark were able to hold her back.

Andy tried to struggle into a sitting position, and the skavags came for him again. Clenched into a screaming ball, his *ch'i* raged out of the holes they made in him and burned them back once more.

They came for him three more times before they learned that attacking him simply meant their own deaths, and retreated to a respectful distance, snapping at each other in baffled frustration. By that time Andy was completely motionless, buried beneath a pile of contorted bodies.

The only other sound was Bex's hysterical sobbing.

Slowly it seemed to occur to the skavags that there was still prey hiding up there that didn't burn them when they bit it, and they began to edge up the stairs again.

'Let's get this thing reinforced,' ordered Rosey, and the Narrowfolk set to work.

12
OLD BONDS

Andy was standing in a child's bedroom. It looked like it had been decorated following the instructions of a prison inmate who had lived in solitary confinement for most of his life and had only the haziest notion of bedrooms, let alone those belonging to children. Everything was slightly too bright, and none of the walls seemed to meet each other at the right angles. There was a Transformers lightshade hanging from the ceiling, and from underneath it spun a small brass medallion which he seemed to recognise from somewhere. Beneath that, on the bed, lay a boy – not much more than a toddler – apparently asleep.

He walked towards the boy across rough, unsanded floorboards vicious with splinters, and then a rug on which plastic cowboys and Indians were fighting. They were the kind which could be pulled apart and swapped around, and whoever had set them up had mixed them together so that Indian braves had cowboy heads, and cowboy bodies walked in buckskin and moccasins.

The boy woke up as he approached and sat up, regarding him calmly. 'Who are you?' he asked.

'I'm Andy,' he replied. 'What's your name?'

The boy's face crumpled into misery. 'I don't know,' he answered and began to cry. 'I can't remember.'

'Well,' he said, 'you could always borrow mine, I suppose.'

'Really?' the boy brightened momentarily, then looked doubtful. 'Is that allowed?'

Andy shrugged. 'It's my name. I can lend it to anybody I like.'

The boy's grin was like the sun chasing away clouds on a wind-driven day. 'Then I'll be Andy too.'

'Okay. But see, names are a serious business. We'd have to shake on it.'

'Shake?' Boy-Andy tried an experimental shimmy and looked confused.

Grown-Andy laughed. 'No, you big pudding. Shake. *Hands*.'

'Oh!'

Solemnly they shook on the deal. As they did so, Boy-Andy inspected the bites and cuts all over Grown-Andy's forearm. They were no longer bleeding, but still fresh and raw.

'Does it hurt?'

Grown-Andy examined himself gingerly. 'Not at the moment. I expect it will do, though, soon enough.'

They traded anxious glances, the reflections from the slow-turning brass mobile drifting in curled shavings of golden light between them.

Boy-Andy said: 'The man with the needles will be coming back soon.'

Grown-Andy replied: 'I know.'

'He scares me.'

'He bloody *terrifies* me!'

Boy-Andy giggled and clapped a hand to his mouth. 'You said a swear word!'

'Too bloody right I did.' Grown-Andy wasn't joking.

Golden shavings of light. Drifting, drifting.

Boy-Andy said: 'You can't stay here, you know.'

Grown-Andy's reply was a reluctant whisper. 'I know.'

'You have to go and meet him, or your friends will die.'

'I don't know what to do, though. I don't know how any of this works.'

'Here.' Boy-Andy reached up, and even though he was far too short to reach the Transformers light-shade, he managed to take down the brass medallion. 'You gave me something, so you should get something too.'

Now that he was able to examine it closely, Grown-Andy saw that it was a series of concentric rings with delicate spokes – it looked like a sun, or a burning wheel.

'What is it?' he asked.

'It's you,' came the reply.

***

When Andy regained consciousness, he was lying brokenly on the stairs as creatures climbed around him, carefully avoiding any contact. Their smell was overpowering, like the ripeness of burst bin-bags.

Everything hurt. Even the darkness behind his eyelids seemed to be nailed to the back of his skull. Up behind him, as if from a great distance, he heard the commotion as the skavags renewed their attack on the barricade, and then full awareness uncorked his ears and it all came rushing in, a tumult of noise: yells, screams, and hoot-howls.

He levered himself painfully up the wall at his back. The skavags nearest to him recoiled, yowling, made as if to attack him, and then recoiled again as instinct warred with the hard-won lesson of their dead packmates.

'What are you going to do about it?' he snarled at them and lunged. They fell back over each other, snapping at themselves in confusion, and he laughed weakly; it was nice to see something else cower for a change. He was able to ease his way past them and down along the wall.

A sudden cheer from upstairs made him pause and look back.

'Oi! Sumner!' Bex was grinning like a maniac. 'If you're going out, get us twenty Marlborough Light, yeah?'

'And a curry!' shouted Stirchley raggedly.

Reluctant to provoke the skavags any further by replying, Andy settled for simply grinning in return and giving them the finger before continuing downstairs. It was time to a put a stop to this.

The creatures parted ahead of him and closed in behind as he reached the ground floor. He was bracing himself for the inevitable moment when one of them got up enough nerve to come for him, because he didn't think he had enough left in him to survive another onslaught, but it seemed that whatever pack mentality ruled their aggression also controlled their fear. He saw it webbing them together like a low-grade telepathy. Too many were afraid of him for any single one of them to attack alone, and so he reached the shattered remains of the front door unmolested.

He made his way across the churned up chaos of Moon Grove's once-proud allotments and the splintered wreckage of sheds and greenhouses, to where Barber stood. At his feet, an emaciated figure lay clad in rags.

'You've made them fear you,' Barber remarked. 'It feels good, doesn't it?'

If he was at all surprised to see Andy simply walk out of their midst, he didn't show it. For his part, Andy could barely stand, let alone engage with this. He brushed Barber's words away.

'Enough. Call them off. You've got what you want. I'm here. The rest are no threat to you.'

'Dear boy,' laughed Barber. 'What on earth makes you think that I want you for anything?'

Andy swayed, confused. 'Then why… why all…?'

'Dear lord listen to you, trying to find reasons for everything, as if that would make a difference. Because, you meddlesome little by-blow – and please stop me if this gets too technical – quite simply you are fucking up the programme. Every time you set foot in the Narrows, you end up disturbing the delicate system which has taken me decades – and I cannot emphasise that enough: *decades* – to develop. I desire nothing from you at all except your immediate and permanent *absence*.'

His coat began to billow and unfurl, the glittering rows of needles in its lapels flashing as they began to squirm free. Distantly he could hear the sounds of renewed fighting in the house: smashes and screams as his friends died. Barber's grin was as wide as a lake of broken ice. Andy seized on the only thing which seemed to offer even a whisper of hope: the image of a brass sun ornament spinning in impossible geometries. He still had no idea what it meant but it did at least remind him of something.

'Do this, and you'll never find out where I planted that stake I took,' he warned, sounding far more confident than he felt.

Barber's eyes narrowed.

'You see I do know a little bit about this fabulously delicate system you've got set up here. I know that you tried to do something to me with those needles when I was a kid, except that Walter stole me away, and so it didn't take. I know that now you're trying something similar, just on a bigger scale.' Even as he was improvising wildly he felt the rightness of it, and the words tumbled out of him as if trying to catch up with his racing mind. 'I don't know what it is exactly, but I know you've got these stakes planted all over the city doing something to the energy patterns. You know I took one – because I'm so *meddlesome*, aren't I – but you don't know where I put it back in, do you? You'll never find it, trust me. Needle in a haystack. You'd better hope that whenever you switch this thing on, or fire it up or whatever, something doesn't go pop. Because it'll probably be quite a big pop, don't you think? Sorry if that's not technical enough for you.'

'You lack either the wit or the forethought for that, shop boy.'

'And don't you just wish you could take that chance,' he shot back. 'But you don't do chance, do you? As for these sorry things,' he indicated the skavags who were lurking nearby, 'breaking them is nowhere near as satisfying as the look on your face right this minute. Call them off. Now.'

'You're lying. You're lying to me, and I'm going to tear the truth of it from your living soul, you arrogant pup…'

'You might find that harder than you think,' Andy warned in a low voice. Motes of energy crawled down the meridians of his arms and burned from his fingertips like brief-lived fireflies. 'I'm sure you could, but then, I've just walked right through everything you could throw at me, so you work it out. You have no idea what I'm capable of. Why make things harder than they have to be? I'll give it up to you willingly – you can tear me apart, find out what makes me tick, fine. Just call them off and let my friends go. Third and last time, or things between you and me start to get awkward.'

'You *lie.*'

But the momentary cloud of uncertainty which crossed Barber's face was enough to tell Andy that he'd won. He just prayed to whatever force was keeping him on his feet that Bex didn't take it into her head to come running out at that moment waving the stake over her head.

'Very well. Your friends will live to squat another day. What few there are left of them.' The sounds of fighting in the house ceased abruptly, and a swarm of dark, hunched shapes poured out of windows and doorways as quickly as they'd come, disappearing into the gloom. Andy heard a distant, ragged cheer rise from inside. Too few voices, though – far too few.

Barber's ambush happened so quickly that he barely had time to register the flash of movement before the needles struck him.

At nine points from just below his hairline, down the length of his body to the back of his left knee, they were driven with such force that in most cases they pierced through several layers of clothing and into the meridian points of the flesh beneath. When he tried to run, or indeed react in any way, he found that he was completely paralysed.

He hadn't been deprived of his sight, however. He saw the lines of his own aura stretched tight through the needles and into Barber's own, wrapped and knotted, held fast, flickering wildly in ribbons of dying neon. It made him sick, like watching himself being operated upon. Barber examined them briefly, made a satisfied-sounding grunt and stepped back to regard Andy contemptuously.

'Walked through everything I could throw at you, did you? I think not. I *am* going to burn the truth out of you, make no mistake about that, but don't worry – I'm not going to kill you. Not as such.

'Well!' he said brightly, clapping his hands and looking around at the devastation. 'This has been a lot of fun, but I mustn't overstay my welcome. You know what they say: no rest for the wicked. Thank you all so much for entertaining me. You really must come to my place some time. Why not right now? What a cracking idea! Come, boy. Heel.'

A marionette, Andy had no choice but to follow. As they passed the corpse on the ground, he was horrified to see it struggling to prop itself up on one elbow; he hadn't thought anything so damaged could possibly live.

'Wait…' Carling gasped. 'Boss, where're you… wait for…'

Barber stopped and looked down at the crippled thing. 'My boy,' he murmured, almost regretfully. 'My poor, faithful boy.'

'…got you *in*…' Carling insisted, though the effort was almost too much for him.

'Yes you did. Nobody else could have. You have been given such strength, and you have used it so well.'

'…then… help…'

Barber shook his head sadly. 'No, Carling. I'm not going to help you. I'll be honest with you there. You deserve that, at least.'

'…promised…'

216

'Yes, I know I did, but the circumstances have changed.' He indicated Andy, an impotent witness to this latest betrayal. 'He has proven to be considerably more difficult to subdue than we anticipated, and I'm going to be forced to make use of some additional resources. I fear that the system will not cope with both breaking him and healing you. I am truly, truly sorry.'

'...fuck your sorrys...'

'Goodbye Carling.' Barber turned back to Andy, his eyes dark with accusation. 'You should take a lesson from this. Everything he has done has been in complete accordance with his nature, even at the cost of his own life. That's your place he's lying in, Sumner. Remember that.'

And he led Andy away into the narrow places of the world.

***

The skavags drifted away into the shadows, along with the last shreds of Fane-cloud, and reality settled itself back around the devastation of Moon Grove in stunned silence.

***

When the survivors emerged, they found Carling crawling with agonising slowness across the scarred ground towards the undergrowth. He was covered in freezing mud and shivering uncontrollably.

'What do we do with this?' asked Rosey, staring down at the struggling figure with wary disgust.

'Stupid question,' replied Bex, and hefted the iron bar over her head. But she hesitated as Carling rolled over onto his back and started to make a thin, hitching, tearing sound that took her a while to identify as laughter. 'What are you laughing at?' she demanded. 'You don't get to laugh, you piece of shit, not after what you've done! *Not after what you've done!*' She raised the point of the stake to bring it down – and found that Rosey was in the way.

'You don't want to do that,' he said.

'What do you know about it?' she yelled in his face. 'Just who the hell are you to tell me anything, anyway? You're not one of us, *policeman*. He did this! And everything else! He killed Dodd, I know he did!' she shoved Rosey aside roughly – no mean feat given how much bigger he was – and raised the point of the stake again. 'I'll do it, by Christ, I will.'

Carling wheezed with mocking laughter. "f you was going to... you'd've already done it... weak bitch... besides, they won't let you.'

'They?'

'...them..' he pointed a frail finger ahead at the bushes towards which he'd been crawling. There, half-hidden in the dripping gloom, crouched three skavags.

They made no move to attack. Instead they sidled warily out of the shadows towards Carling, flinching and snarling in fear at the small group of Narrowfolk. They were clearly female and apparently quite old, judging by their flat, wrinkled dugs. It was the first time Bex had even considered the possibility of skavag sexes. Up until now she'd seen them as neutered and anonymous threats with nothing to differentiate them, but to think now that there were skavag females and therefore skavag males, and presumably by extension skavag *babies*...

Right at this precise moment in time she couldn't allow herself to care about anything more than that they looked old and frail and very possibly hittable.

'I don't think they're in much of a state to stop me,' she suggested and stepped over him again. 'You want to see what "weak" is?' She held the rusted point over his chest, like a tiny soot-and-tear-streaked vampire hunter. The skavag-crones became agitated, mewling piteously.

'Not them,' he croaked. 'The ones you can't see.'

The shadows around them suddenly seemed to be very busy.

'They've come for me,' he continued. 'They are scared of you, yes. Barber's cut them loose. Cut us all loose because of what your boy did. Only got their own strength now, don't want to hurt you, but they will if you don't let me go with them.'

Bex was trying to look in every direction simultaneously. 'That's not going to happen. You don't get to walk away from this.'

Carling made that awful tearing noise which was as close as he could get to laughing. 'Stupid. Look at me. Walk away?' He spat. 'Okay. Make it easy for you: tell you where he's taken your boy.'

'Why would you do that?'

'Mended my ways, haven't I? Sorry for all the bad shit I've done.' He laughed again, mockingly. 'Why do you think? So that you can go and take him down, that's why.'

'And if I can't?'

He shrugged. 'No skin off my banana, is it? I'm still fucked.'

She shook her head in disgust and disbelief, but dropped the point of her stake all the same. 'Fine. I hope you're happy. You deserve each other.'

The three skavag crones shuffled forward and gathered him up in their gnarled arms like a pile of loosely-jointed driftwood. Rosey started to slip away in the opposite direction, drawing her gently with him. 'Why are they doing this?' he whispered.

'I don't know,' she replied. 'Maybe they recognise one of their own.' She called out after Carling: 'So what about it, then? Where's he gone?'

Carling seemed to have regained some of his strength already, because his answer returned clearly. 'Barber's taken your boy back to where this mess all started. He's going to finish it once and for good. It's a place called...'

'Holly End. I know.' She could have kicked herself; it was so obvious.

'Yeah, well here's two things you didn't. First, it's also the place where he's strongest.'

'Fabulous.'

'Plus it's hidden, like your place here used to be,' he chuckled. He had nearly disappeared, borne into the night, and all she could see of him was a pale gleam, like old bones at the bottom of a well. 'But if you can find the stone that anchors his power, it would seriously fuck him up. You might even get out alive again.'

'What stone?' she called desperately. What do you mean it 'anchors his power'?'

'Big brave clever girly like you should be able to work it out.'

'You son of a bitch!' she yelled after him. 'Tell me!'

But all that came back to her was the echo of his mocking laughter.

PART 3: VILLAGE

1
TED

HOLLY END, THURSDAY DECEMBER 19ᵀᴴ, 1957

'Ted!' called his mother from the kitchen. 'Make sure you take Sam with you!'

Twelve-year old Ted slumped in the act of putting his duffel-coat on and groaned. 'Oh mother, must I?' he complained. Another ten seconds and he would have been safely out of the front door and on his way to an adventure in the Rimwoods, but now...

'Edward Clee!' she replied in the sharp, no-nonsense tone which every hand on the farm feared, even his father. 'It won't kill you to look after your little brother for a few hours, and it might make you think twice about going anywhere silly!'

How did she know? How did she always seem to know?

'And make sure that you get branches with plenty of berries. We need all the good luck we can get this year.'

'Yes mother,' he intoned.

He dutifully checked that in the old burlap sack there were some secateurs and a pair of workman's gloves (not her good gardening ones, not on his life), by which time Sam was standing by the back door, his wellies shining almost as brightly as his eyes.

'So are we going somewhere silly, then?' his eight-year old brother asked.

'Not now,' Ted grumped.

But a hundred yards down the road, he'd already changed his mind.

***

Collecting holly branches so that his mother could make wreaths for everybody in the village was the last thing Ted wanted to do, but volunteering for the job was the best way of getting out of the house without having to either run errands or chop wood. It gave him licence to roam far and wide – at least, as far and wide as it was possible to go in the valley without running afoul of the Spinny – to delve into gullies and forge his way through thickets as if he were exploring a tropical jungle. Though if the truth be told, there weren't many gullies and thickets left whose secrets he hadn't already plundered, and his recent forays had taken on a bit of an air of desperation. More and more he found himself edging up into the forbidden Rimwoods, and the Spinny which lurked there ready to turn you about and plop you back in the valley when your eyes and feet told you different. The Professor told them that the Spinny was protecting them from what was left of the world outside, but it didn't feel like that to Ted. In Ted's one and only experience of the Spinny – having run away from home when he was younger than Sam, due to a dispute over bedtimes – it didn't feel like he was being protected at all.

It had felt like he was being laughed at.

'What's the plan, Desperate Dan?' Sam chanted as he bounced alongside, stomping puddle-ice with his wellies. They were on the main road through the village, though 'road' was a bit grandiose for it. After five years with no traffic but horse-carts, it was rutted and overgrown.

'Well,' replied Ted archly, and performed an elaborate pantomime of looking to make sure they weren't being spied upon, 'I thought we might go for a spot of target practice. What do you say?' From the deep pocket of his duffel-coat he produced a sturdy-looking slingshot. He'd made it himself from a fork of yew, with a cord-whipped handle and a band of thick inner-tube rubber. At full stretch he'd measured its range at over a hundred yards, and close-to he'd once put a stone through a baked bean tin. It was, as far as he was concerned, quite the most lethal weapon known to man or rabbit.

Sam's eyes widened. 'Can I have a go?' he begged.

'As long as you don't take any of your own fingers off, of course, but only on one condition.'

'What? Yes! Whatever it is!'

'That you don't tell anybody where we're going. Mother will have absolute kittens if she finds out.'

'Where *are* we going?'

'Can't have target practice without any targets, can you? We're going to see Rabbit John.'

They passed a few more cottages, then the Black Horse, and St Kenelm's church with its square, ivy-covered bell tower. One of the many secrets which none of the adults suspected he knew was that the crypts of the church were still nearly half-full of the supplies which the Professor and Reverend Lyttleton had put aside before they'd raised the Spinny. Life in Holly End was hard enough these days; he imagined that without those stockpiles, his father and mother and all of their friends would be dead of starvation or disease, or else forced to find some way out through the Spinny and into the radioactive wastelands beyond, to be preyed upon by the bands of marauding Rouslers who lived out there. Ted also knew that of all the bogeyman stories which grown-ups told children to make them behave, the Rouslers were actually real. He'd seen them himself.

Now they were passing the Burnouts – the blackened ruins of cottages at the village's edge which had been destroyed in the one and so far only Rousler attack. There had been mercifully few deaths; most of the village families had, as usual, been gathered for the evening in the Black Horse. Rabbit John had come tearing down from his poacher's hut in the Rimwoods, shouting the alarm, and prompting a very calm sort of panic such as only people who had survived the Birmingham Blitz could manage. In the brief chaos while the women herded the children down into the shelter of the pub's cellar and the men dashed off to find weapons, Ted had caught sight of a screaming band of wildly-dressed figures throwing flaming torches into the thatched roofs of the outlying cottages. It was all he saw before being dragged to safety, but he still heard the sounds of fighting clearly enough – the gunshots and screams. He had made his slingshot the very next day.

Strangely – at least to Ted – the attack seemed to make people think that Rabbit John was even more of an Odd Sort than before. As if he'd somehow brought it down by living apart from them, and so close to the Spinny. Spending any time with him beyond bartering for rabbit meat or fur was heavily frowned upon.

This, of course, was why Ted did it. Plus the fact that Rabbit John was teaching him all kinds of super things, like tracking and trapping.

Uphill into the thin outliers of the Rimwoods, and Sam was chattering away brightly about what he thought he might get for Christmas, when the world unexpectedly *shifted*.

For a moment – no more than the space of a few footsteps – it seemed that the path was lengthening away beneath his feet, and that despite his legs telling him that he was still moving forwards his eyes insisted the opposite. Disorientated, he stumbled.

'Did you feel that?' he asked Sam shakily, but his little brother was oblivious. 'Sam, I said did you…'

Sam shushed him violently. He was staring ahead, pale and trembling.

There was someone on the path ahead of them.

They couldn't see the figure clearly – just hear its clumping footfalls on the hard earth and its ragged breathing – but soon there was a glimpse of tattered clothing and wild eyes staring out of a grime-streaked face.

Rousler.

Sam whimpered, a small animal noise of terror.

With shaking fingers Ted slipped a stone into the cup of his slingshot. He aimed and, convinced that he was going to miss, let fly.

His stone struck the Rousler square in the centre of its forehead, and before it could react Ted fired again, pulling the band right back to his ear. *Baked beans!* he thought and laughed a little hysterically. His second shot was as true as his first; the Rousler grunted and collapsed backwards into the bushes.

'Oh cracking shot, Ted!' Sam yelled, and together they approached cautiously to inspect their prize.

2

WRECKAGE

Bex wandered the ruins of Moon Grove long after everybody else had abandoned it. The building was beyond repair, uninhabitable. Even if the skavags hadn't inflicted so much damage, their invasion of what should have been the safest of refuges would have made the Narrowfolk leave. Nobody could feel safe here again.

Nevertheless, she found it surprisingly difficult to tear herself away. Running away from Mum and Shithead Dave had been a doddle in comparison: empty her purse, pour a pint of milk into the engine vents of his Beemer and disappear into the night.

Here, though.

She trailed in and out of rooms, picking her way over smashed furniture, gouged floorboards, and – in too many cases – large, dark bloodstains.

She salvaged what she could from the kitchen. Kerrie the Kook's cauldron lay overturned, cold and empty, next to the corpse of a skavag with a crushed skull. Of Kerrie herself or her Kitchen Tarts, there was no sign. The great blackboard in the dining room had been torn down and broken in half across the refectory table. Everywhere, rain blew in through broken windows and through cracks in the ceilings, in steady pattering streams down the wide, gutted stairwell, pooling on the floors and bloating the carpets. The whole building wept.

When Rosey came back, he found her in Walter's study, surrounded by a strewn mess of maps and books. She'd heard him clumping up the stairs and had stuffed several maps into her rucksack along with her few other treasures: Dodd's A-to-Z, his dowsing rods, Andy's stake with the weird cross-quartered circle stamped into its head, several ounces of rolling tobacco and an eighth of hash traded off Stirchley for some spare Christmas light bulbs which she'd nicked from Andy's flat. Remembering the look of hopelessness on Stirchley's face as the ambulance doors closed on him, she came close to tears again.

'I'm glad to find you still here,' he said.

She sniffed hard. 'Elementary, my dear flatfoot,' she replied. 'The others okay?'

He so-so-ed. 'The ones that would come with me, yes, mostly. You are very stubborn people.'

'We're not charity cases, or scroungers. We keep out of everybody's way and help each other because we've learned that no other bugger will. Used to, anyway.'

'The ones that got hurt are at casualty in Selly Oak. The mothers with kids have gone straight into B&Bs. That was easy enough. Some of the men – I pulled some strings and got a few into Snow Hill and Firside. That was out of the few that would even agree to let me try. The rest have disappeared off somewhere to another squat. As I say, stubborn.'

She squinted at him, calculating. 'You'd do the same to me if you could, wouldn't you? Get me in a hostel, call the social workers.'

'In a heartbeat. Look at what happened here.' He gestured around at the wreckage. 'How can you prefer this? How could you, even before?'

'Put it this way: do you know how many social workers saw that little girl Victoria Climbie while her religious nut-job of a mother and her sicko boyfriend kept her tied up in a bin bag in the bath and stubbed cigarettes out on her thighs?'

'That's hardly the…'

'*Five*. Guess how many times your precious social workers and doctors and police saw Baby P while his mum and boyfriend broke his spine and eight of his ribs. Go on, guess.'

'It…'

'Over *sixty*.' She was coldly furious, advancing on him, knowing that none of this was his fault but helpless to stop. 'Don't tell me the system works or that it's imperfect but the best we've got, because it fucking *doesn't* and it fucking well *isn't*. I'll take my chances with the monsters I can see rather than the ones pretending to care for me.' She pulled up her left sleeve and showed him the cuts running along the underside of her forearm. 'The only one cutting me is me, and we're both fine with that, okay?'

If she'd been hoping to provoke him, it failed. 'Okay,' he answered. Some of the cuts were very fresh, inflicted in the last few hours, while he'd been away. 'It's not your fault, you know,' he added. 'What happened here.'

There was no point trying to respond to such hollow platitudes, no matter how well-intentioned they were. Of course it was her fault. She'd brought Andy here and everything that had followed him. She'd insisted that he stay and try to help them, not because he had anything to offer the Narrowfolk but because she'd wanted payback for Dodd's murder.

'I need answers, Mr Penrose,' she said, shoving her sleeve back down and stooping to strap up her rucksack. 'If all of this is dead and finished, I have to know why before I let the nice men in white coats take me away, do you understand that?'

'I understand that you're going to follow me to Holly End whether I take you with me or not, so I might as well keep you where I can see you. Did you find the map?'

'Right here.' She patted a pocket, and straightened up. 'No, scratch what I just said. I'm only a scavenger, Mr Penrose; I trade fags and food for a roof over my head, and that's pretty much it. I'm not in this to solve the mystery of whatever mad scheme Barber's got planned. All I know is a friend of mine has got himself into trouble on my account, and I'm not going to let that happen a second time.'

'That's the most sense I've heard from any of you lot since I got here,' he replied.

'It's just that...' she stomped out onto the landing, waving around at the empty shell which the house had become. 'This, you know? What happens if I come back and this is all...' she couldn't finish and stood gazing around helplessly.

'If it's all gone?' he finished gently. 'Look around, Bex. It already is. There's no coming back here, whatever happens.'

It was easy to leave after that, as if hearing it from somebody else made it alright, made it less like she was abandoning something that still needed her. She found that for all that he was a similar age to Walter, Penrose had none of the secret smugness which had prevented her from ever truly trusting him. She suspected that he was simply being kind. Her stubborn, self-destructive streak rose up against the idea like bile – wanting to tell him to piss off, that she didn't need his pity or his help – but for the first time in her life she swallowed it back down again and followed him out of the house.

***

Walter's map located Holly End in the Warwickshire countryside south of Stratford-Upon-Avon, but that was where its usefulness ended. It was ancient, made from some kind of heavy cloth-card, and had seen so much use that the folds between its panels had disintegrated until they were held together by nothing more than the underlying fibres. The place-names were miniscule, written in a font which seemed to be all verticals, and there was no distinction between A and B roads – all of which were helpfully marked in red ink that turned almost invisible in the sodium streetlight as Rosey drove them down the M42. Not that it indicated any motorways, either, of course.

Bex suggested that the bloody thing must be pre-war – pre *Trojan* War, possibly – and after wrestling with both it and a huge modern road atlas for half an hour in the passenger seat, eventually gave up and demanded that they stop at the next services before she threw the lot out of the window.

She climbed back into the van's interior and began rummaging through its tiny cupboards. 'Where do you keep the kettle in this thing?' she asked.

'I told you,' he called back over his shoulder, 'not while we're moving!'

With his Astra wrecked by the skavags, Rosey had been left with no choice but to pull the winter covers off what he called his 'shed on wheels': a 1972 Volkswagen campervan with bay windscreen, pop-top, and a marmalade-orange paintjob which made Bex think of old penguin paperbacks. She understood that he called it a shed in the sense that it was his manly refuge from the world, but it was also a fair description of its shape; it had all the aerodynamics and maneuverability of a loaf of bread. She'd fallen in love with it instantly. Secreted ingeniously away in little cupboards were a fridge, stove, sink, and all manner of space-saving gadgetry, but he'd expressly forbidden her to explore or tamper with anything while he was driving. Needless to say, she paid absolutely no attention.

At Warwick services, they found that the commuter frenzy had trickled away, and they were able to spread their maps over two tables as they ate. Bex discovered that she was ravenously hungry, and Rosey watched with a bemusement bordering on alarm as she demolished first a huge Cumberland sausage, coiled python-like in a lagoon of red-onion gravy, and then most of his scampi. And then a sticky toffee pudding.

He found himself wondering where she stored it all,

especially someone so small that she looked like if you kept peeling back the multiple layers of clothing she'd disappear completely. Then he found that thinking of peeling off her clothes made him feel very awkward indeed, and he went to get a coffee. As he stood at the counter being served by a bored-looking young woman who couldn't have been much older, he realised that never mind monsters, murderers, and geomantic sorcery – at some point he was going to have to explain to a mother or father why he'd gone off gallivanting around the countryside with their teenaged daughter.

And that *really* scared the shit out of him.

He headed back to their table, seriously considering calling the whole thing off and hauling her back to Birmingham, but as he did so he saw that her sleeves had ridden up as she'd leaned over the map, exposing an inch of the clean bandage which he'd insisted on applying before they left. Maybe she was better off with him. He knew that he was no cradle-snatching perv, and that should be enough.

It didn't make a blind bit of difference to the smirking check-in clerk at the Ramada Holiday Inn next door. As Rosey paid for two single rooms he got a look which as clear as day said *You aren't fooling anybody, old man.* Paying cash was probably what did it, but it was the lesser of two evils; he didn't *think* Barber had the connections to trace his credit card, or would even bother, but he was taking no chances. He'd withdrawn as much as the ATM would allow and had been paying cash for everything since Moon Grove. Let the spotty-faced little twerp of a desk-monkey smirk all he liked.

Bex had made a token protest of wanting to carry on as far as possible that evening, but had given in gladly enough when he asked her if she really wanted to spend the night stumbling around the pitch-black countryside in the rain, looking for a non-existent village.

She was even able to ignore the room's corporate sterility and indulged in the guilty pleasure of a full, steaming hot bath without having to worry for once about how much hot water she was using. She slid gratefully between impossibly clean sheets and collapsed into a sleep so profound that it formed Narrows in her own mind, down which she could flee the nightmares which threatened as soon as she closed her eyes.

Running. Always running.

***

It really didn't matter whether or not the reception clerk believed that he was Bex's father, Penrose thought as he let himself into her room. The important thing was that he'd been given a duplicate key-card.

She was sound asleep and snoring amidst a drift of clothes and belongings from her rucksack. A can of Special Brew stood on the bedside table. It was a good job they'd only taken cheap rooms; Lord only knew what damage she could have inflicted on an actual mini-bar.

He watched her for a while, wondering at how long it had been since he'd watched his own boys sleep like this and what had happened to all the time in between. Why it wasn't her *own* Mum and Dad who were watching her like this – what had gone so catastrophically wrong that their daughter had ended up in a poxy motorway motel like this with a strange man? Jesus, she couldn't have been much more than sixteen. The world was getting sicker by the day. Who could blame her for wanting to run away and find a better one?

Taking care not to disturb her, he rummaged in her bag until he found the A-to-Z, and left the room as quietly as he'd entered.

Back at reception, he did at least have the pleasure of seeing the clerk's smirk replaced by dim confusion when he asked 'Excuse me son, you don't have a photocopier I can use, do you?'

Penrose let her sleep long the following morning and insisted that they have a decent breakfast while they worked out exactly which way to go next.

'What's this really long straight road?' she asked, pointing at the road atlas.

Rosey glanced at it. 'That's the Fosse Way. It follows the line of a Roman road all the way from Leicester down to Bath, I think. Dead straight for hundreds of miles.'

'Where's Bath?'

'There.' He made a pained noise. 'Do they teach nothing in schools these days?'

'And where's England again?'

'Shut up.'

She grinned. 'Okay, but seriously. I'm trying to work out why Walter ended up in Birmingham. Holly End's here, right?' She indicated a point at the northern edge of the Cotswolds. 'So?'

'So he grabs baby Andy because he wants to put an end to whatever Barber's been doing, and he goes looking for a safe place to hide. But there are loads of places closer than Brum, look: Cheltenham, Stratford, Banbury. Why not them?'

'Maybe he thought he could hide better in a big city rather than a medium-sized town.'

'Maybe. Or maybe it's not about where you go so much as how you get there.'

He sighed. 'Ley lines again, right?'

'Yes,' she said defiantly. 'Tell me, Mr Penrose, exactly how *do* you explain what you've seen and everything that's happened to you?'

'Just because I can't explain it doesn't mean I have to swallow every crackpot piece of New Age crystal-clutching rubbish that claims to.'

'None taken,' she replied acidly.

'Roman roads aren't ley-lines though, are they?' he pointed out. 'Even I know that.'

'Not necessarily, no. But leys are just channels for the earth's *ch'i* energy – either they occur naturally or they can be created by people travelling the same route for hundreds or thousands of years. Like the difference between streams and canals. Anyway, Fosse Way's no good. Look, it goes off on the other side of Coventry, nowhere near Birmingham.'

'Well the only other Roman road I know anything about is Icknield Street,' he said, flipping through her battered A-to-Z. 'There are parts of it still visible in Sutton Park, and…'

But whatever he was about to say was drowned out by her cry of 'OhmigodYES!' as she slapped the table in excitement. Bacon and hash-browns bounced. Heads turned. 'That's it! That makes so much sense!' Her eyes were shining and she was grinning widely, and Penrose couldn't help noticing how badly she needed a dentist. I *am* getting old, he thought. 'All the Narrowfolk know Icknield Street – it's one of the oldest, quickest narrows – or it was until it closed. It was the first to close, now that I think about it. But of course, it would be the first one that Barber targeted, wouldn't it? We all used to travel it. It's where Andy's flat was – he practically lived on it.'

'I know. I saw what was left.'

'Yes, but look where it ends!' She swept the map around and shoved it at him across the table. 'Follow the line!'

He did so, tracing the line of Icknield Street nearly due south through the city and out into the countryside, where it was renamed Ryknild Street in quaint olde worlde lettering, becoming A-roads, then B-roads, and finally dwindling into farm tracks as it was lost in the rising slopes of the Cotswolds, barely a mile away from where Walter's map indicated that Holly End should be. He felt a strange plummeting sensation in his stomach, as if he was in a lift that had suddenly dropped one floor too many.

'I don't care what you say,' Bex insisted. 'There is no way that could be a coincidence. Andy must have felt it way before any of this kicked off. That's the way Walter got out, and it's the way we're going to get in.'

3

RYKNILD STREET

A few miles west of Stratford's carefully manicured tourist traps, they caught Ryknild Street as it crossed the river by an ancient, single-lane stone bridge at Bidford-on-Avon, and entered the Vale of Evesham. Shortly after they'd crossed, Bex asked Rosey to park the Shed and got out with Dodd's dowsing rods.

'Look,' she said, seeing the expression on his face, 'there's no New Age crystal clutchery involved here. All these do is amplify the effect of the interaction between the human central nervous system and the Earth's ley matrix.'

'Of course. Silly me.'

'Involuntary tics and twitches in the arm muscles, right? They get translated into a swingy-pointy movement of the rods.'

'Swingy-pointy movement.'

'Shut up, it's perfectly rational!'

She stood in the middle of the road with the dowsing rods outstretched (she'd replaced the split copper sleeves with bright pink drinking straws from the service station), and before she'd had a chance to try and relax or concentrate, they immediately flew to cross themselves. Simultaneously she felt a tremendous jolt of energy spiral upwards through her body: in from the ground through the soles of her feet, setting off explosions between her legs, behind her navel, at the tip of each breast and at the base of her throat, before shooting out through the top of her head. She yelped, dropped the rods and staggered back against the campervan.

Rosey was out and at her side in a second. 'Are you alright?'

'Well I think we can definitely confirm there is a ley running along here,' she replied, dazed and flushed. 'Bit of a kick to it, actually.'

'What happened?'

'It was like – no, I don't think I should really say.'

'Why not?'

'You'd probably say it wasn't very ladylike.' She giggled, blushed to the roots of her hair and got back into the van.

The Roman road arrowed straight towards the grey shadow of the Cotswolds' most northern edge. It was built up slightly higher than the surrounding fields, which were flat and shining with floodwater mirroring the grey sky, and cross-hatched with winter-bristling hedgerows. By the roadside these were overgrown – long-fingered ash, scribbly beech, and hawthorn stripped bare to the thorns – punctuated occasionally by gaunt, black-limbed oaks. The only sign of green came from stands of holly which seemed gleefully oblivious to the emptiness of the season.

Bex grew ever more uncomfortable, all too aware that this was the very worst time of the year to go exploring ley paths or hunting for lost villages – especially those named for trees which were at the height of their power. She remembered what Carling had looked like for having run afoul of it, and she shivered. The sheer, flat openness of the landscape was making her twitchy too – there were no roofs to shelter under or alleyways to hide in. She felt exposed and defenceless.

Rosey too found it disconcerting, being used to the stop-start labyrinth of city driving or else just tooling around tame country lanes in the Shed on a weekend. This wasn't the chocolate-box England of bank holidays, however. Driving for so long in one direction was something you did in America or Australia.

The hills grew nearer, becoming low, wooded ridges, and they passed through a few villages with names which made them sound like they should have been inhabited by hobbits: Bickmarsh, Bucklestreet, Honeybourne. At last the land started to rise, and they stopped at a village called Weston-sub-Edge which was the first they'd seen built in the characteristic toffee-coloured Cotswold stone and, true to its name, nestled at the very feet of the hills. Up close, they undulated in wooded waves east and west, folding around themselves in deeply shadowed coombs and vales.

Weston was also the point where the road turned away from Ryknild Street, which continued its southerly course as a walking track up into the hills. Rosey suggested they stop and gather their bearings, though he wasn't optimistic about the chances of the locals being either able or willing to tell them anything. Bex was more philosophical, figuring that they should at least be able to get a decent lunch.

'How can you possibly be hungry again?' he asked, aghast. 'You've done nothing but sit in the van for two hours.'

'Come on, old man,' she laughed. 'Let's get you a nice ploughman's, shall we?'

They had parked outside a plain, square-fronted pub called the Seagrave Arms. She'd been expecting it to be hideously touristy, full of yompers and chompers, but was pleasantly surprised to find the opposite. Instead of pool tables, one-armed bandits and televisions ramming Sky-bloody-Sports down your eyeballs, there was a fireplace, brass-handled beer-pulls, and the dark-warm smell of beer and oak. It reminded her of Moon Grove a little bit. There was even a community noticeboard next to the bar, which she checked out of habit while Penrose ordered drinks.

She skimmed over cards advertising Christmas cakes, home accountancy, central heating repairs – village life in minutiae – and wanted to point it out to Penrose.

See? she wanted to say. *It's not us who are odd, swapping this for that and trading favours, it's you lot. You people, who have your finances looked after by Bangladeshi call centres, who pay the supermarkets to fill your homes with rubbish which you then have to pay the Council to take away again, who can't touch the soil that your food grows in. Us Narrowfolk, we're not living some kind of New Age alternative lifestyle – this is the oldest lifestyle there is.*

But he'd just bought her an orange and lemonade – bless, as if she couldn't drink him under the table – and she thought it might have come across as a bit churlish.

Then her eyes lit on a flyer for the Ryknild Ramblers' forthcoming Boxing Day expedition, which sucked the air out of her lungs and set her heart hammering in its cage.

Ryknild Ramblers Boxing Day Woodwalk

Come and burn off some of that Christmas pudding with a traditional Boxing Day ramble through the beauty of our local woodland! Starting from the Seagrave Arms, we'll follow Ryknild Street up into Weston Woods, along the Narrows to the Kiftsgate Stone and back down in time for a lunchtime pint.

Contact details followed, but by that time she was grabbing for Penrose. 'Look!' When he'd read it she snatched the flyer from the noticeboard and went over to the landlord, who was chalking the day's lunch menu on a small blackboard.

'Excuse me,' she said, showing him the flyer, 'but where is this?'

He glanced at it and then her. 'Which part, m'dear?' he asked genially.

'The Narrows! Are there some nearby?'

'Wouldn't know about "some" there. There's just one – road at the top of the hill. That's what it's called; don't ask me why though. Goes to Chipping Camden, it does. That the way you're heading then, is it m'dear?'

'What about this Kiftsgate Stone thing?'

'Ah,' he said sadly, 'I think that might be what you'd call a bit of poetic licence, seeing as how there isn't one. Not now, leastways. Got stolen, it did, maybe sixty years ago now. But people's memories are long, especially for something that's been here longer than most of the villages around abouts.'

'What kind of stone was it?'

He paused, laid down his chalk and leaned on the bar, looking at her properly for the first time. His hair was a shock-white thatch, and he had the bushiest eyebrows she'd ever seen. 'Well now, if you'll forgive me for saying so, but we don't often get young people like yourself interested in the old paths and stones. Getting dragged around the countryside by your dad, then, is it?' he nodded at Rosey.

'Yeah,' she drawled. 'I have a passion for old things.' Out of the landlord's eyeshot she tipped Rosey a saucy wink. He nearly choked on his pint of the house ale.

'She really loves Time Team,' he coughed.

'Well then m'dear,' said the landlord, warming to an unexpected audience, 'the Kiftsgate stone was, *is*, a big standing piece of limestone, like them chappies up at the Rollright Circle, if you've been there. These hills are covered in 'em. People have been burying their dead up here since the Stone Age. But the Kiftsgate Stone now, that was what you'd call a *moot stone*. Anglo-Saxon, that is: a meeting place for all the villagers hereabouts to settle their business with each other in the old times. They say that George the Third was proclaimed king by it.'

'What we're actually looking for is a village called Holly End,' said Rosey, anxious not to get sidetracked. 'Is that somewhere nearby?'

The landlord's brow furrowed in thought, causing his eyebrows to collide alarmingly like two wrestling caterpillars. 'No, I think you're wrong there,' he replied after some thought. 'There's nowhere hereabouts by that name. There's a Hill End,' he added hopefully, 'about six or seven miles east of here, out by Ilmington – maybe that's what you're looking for.'

'Cheers – we might give that a try.' But it was as they'd suspected. He took a long swallow of his pint and turned back to Bex. 'People's memories may be long,' he said out of the landlord's hearing, 'but it seems they're also selective. I suppose we're walking from this point on.'

'Skates on, *Dad*.' She headed out to the carpark.

'All in good time,' he said to himself. This bitter was very good indeed. 'All in good time.'

***

The left the Shed at the Seagrave Arms and continued on foot.

The line of Ryknild Street began as a farm road, which was easy enough to follow, but as it climbed higher it degenerated into a track of thick grey-yellow mud which clagged and clung to their boots. They were soon amongst the winter-dripping ash and birch trees above the village, and the difference in their ages quickly became apparent: Rosey, whose own slow ramblings in the fields outside Halesowen had been mostly in stubborn defiance of his bad back, found himself stumbling breathlessly, while Bex, who literally walked for a living, powered upwards in great yard-eating strides that he wouldn't have though possible for one so small.

She stopped, waiting for him to catch up, and used the time to conduct another dowse. She braced herself for the jolt, but nothing happened. The rods swung randomly, listlessly. Something was wrong. 'That can't be right,' she murmured, puzzled.

'Don't worry about it,' panted Rosey, resting against a tree. 'It happens to us all at one time or another.'

'No, this is serious. I'm not getting anything. It's like the ley isn't there anymore. Maybe we've strayed off it somehow.'

'Maybe it was never there in the first place.'

'Not helping!' she rebuked him. 'No, we're on the line, I'm positive of that. There's something weird going on here.'

Ironically enough, he thought, but he didn't say it. This was her territory.

They eventually emerged onto a narrow lane that bordered the far edge of this small wood. On their side, trees clustered thickly right up to the road's verge, overhanging a mossy stone wall. On the other, the path continued over a stile into rolling fields and bare hedgerows. A little way off to their right the road forked, marked by a leaning cast-iron signpost which Bex approached with the air of someone completing a pilgrimage. The roadsign said simply: *The Narrows.*

The world was silent, the sky a hard white, and the temperature had dropped considerably. Their breath plumed.

'Feels like it's going to snow,' gasped Rosey and then concentrated on regaining the ability to breathe.

'It's here,' she whispered. 'It's very close. I can feel it. Can't you feel it?'

He could certainly feel something – beyond the burning in his lungs and the chill in the air there was a sense of hushed expectation, a preternatural stillness, as of the pause between inhalation and exhalation, when life hangs in the balance and whole worlds can be spun into being or lost forever.

She shook herself. 'I have to see this Kiftsgate Stone,' she announced and set off down the lane in the opposite direction.

'What?' he called. 'The one that was stolen sixty years ago?'

'Cynic!' she yelled back.

A few hundred yards further on, in the woods to their left, they found a small clearing just on the other side of the stone wall. Had it been summer and the trees full of green growth, they might not have spotted it, but in the dead of winter there was nothing to obscure the three-foot wide pit which showed where something large and heavy had been dug out of the earth a long time ago. It looked like the puckered scar of a traumatic wound. Bex's hands were shaking as she took out the dowsing rods again and tried to get some kind of reading from the site, but once again they remained stubbornly apart.

'Still nothing?' he asked.

She shook her head, confused and irritated – and most of all, scared. 'This isn't right. This *can't* be right. It was there, back at the crossroads, definitely there. But now…' She climbed over the wall and into the clearing, walking to and fro around the hole in the sodden leaf-mulch, trying the rods at all angles, still without success. 'Now it's like it's disappeared completely. This is just wrong. Something should be *there*.'

Rosey climbed over to join her. 'Whatever used to be here was stolen a long time ago,' he reminded her, 'before you or I or anybody involved in this was born, so I'm not sure how this helps us.'

'Because it's all connected, don't you get that yet? There are no coincidences! Everything's connected. You, me, the earth, the stone, Dodd, Andy, that bloody sign back there – all of it. Not because it just is, but because we *make* it like that. We make the connections, the human link, human souls and thoughts and actions. Can't you see that?'

'I can see that we're stuck, and that you obviously feel very strongly about this, but it seems to me that shouting at a hole in the ground isn't going to do us much good. We need to stop charging around on a wild mystical goose chase and do this properly. If the village existed there will be records, relatives of people who lived there…'

But she wasn't listening. 'You're right,' she said, half to herself. 'Shouting at it's no good at all.' The answer had come to her so neatly and obviously that she couldn't believe it was a coincidence. It simply couldn't be that easy, could it? 'We have to heal it; that's what we have to do.'

She pulled from her rucksack the three-foot long iron stake. She'd brought it along in the hope of somehow returning it to Andy, as a symbol perhaps of whatever strange control he had over the narrows – a control which she now knew was simply an accident of circumstances rather than something innate and unreachable by her. And why *not* her? He'd done nothing more to earn it than be in the wrong place at the wrong time as a child, whereas she had made this world of shadows and shortcuts her life. He could be dead, for all she knew. In which case the responsibility fell to her anyway, but only because she chose it. Even if there were no more Narrowfolk left to defend, then so be it: she'd fight for herself, which was all she'd ever done in the first place.

She took the stake, and with as much strength as she could muster drove it deeply into the damp earth at the centre of the pit.

And the world around them changed.

4

THE RIMWOODS

The first thing that happened was that it began to snow.

There were no warning flurries of sleet; it was immediate – the temperature plummeted, and large drifting flakes started spiralling out of a windless, white void all at once. It grew darker as the clouds started to shed their weight, or else it was because the lane was suddenly narrower, and no longer asphalt but hard-packed earth, rutted and crusted with frozen puddles. The wood was thicker and more wildly overgrown than ever, completely burying the stone wall and thrusting right up against the lane's edge.

A hundred yards further along, where before there had been only unbroken trees, there was now a small gap and a trail leading down into the dripping gloom.

Bex caught Rosey's look. His eyes were shining as excitedly as hers.

Then it all began to fade again.

'Quick!' she yelled, and they ran for the gap.

The zone of briefly-awoken earthpower which had sprung out of the pit was contracting back towards the stake at its centre. She could see the edge of it rippling towards her, asphalt erasing the hardpacked lane and the wildwood subsiding as the bubble shrank and reality flooded back to reclaim its rightful territory. Within moments, it would reach the gap and the trail which she was certain led to Holly End.

She ran harder, gasping for breath, and not for the first time wished that she didn't smoke so much. Fifty yards, a dozen paces. Behind her, Rosey shouted for her to wait, wait for him, but there was no way she was going to do that. She couldn't even afford to sacrifice what little speed it would cost to look back and see how far behind he was.

On the other side of the trail's entrance were two big scraggly birches; she watched as the furthest was wiped out and replaced by a fencepost and another yard of tame stone wall.

Twenty yards.

Ten.

She threw herself forward, falling, feeling gravel bite into the side of her face and something like a warm wave of pins and needles slide through her. Rosey's despairing cry was suddenly cut off by silence.

The almost-silent hiss of snow sifting through bare branches.

**

Bex sat up. She was at the very threshold of a narrow dirt road which wound away through tangled woods, and there was no sign of Andrew 'Rosey' Penrose anywhere.

She pulled her woolly hat down low to the line of her eyebrows and gathered up her rucksack. Of the stake, there was no sign. She wondered if Rosey had found it, trying to imagine the gulf that lay between the world she'd left and… well, whatever this was. She'd walked some deep narrows in her time, but this was something else altogether. What would he do? Hang around and try to find another way in (through? across? between?) How long before he gave up and went back to the van? For another thing, it was getting colder by the minute. Even under the shelter of the trees, the snow was beginning to stick. She was going to have to find Holly End quickly, whatever it was like or whatever might be there, if only to simply find shelter.

She set off along the woodland track.

At first she made reasonably good progress – the track was level and hardpacked, having obviously seen regular use, and she soon saw the reason: several hundred yards further there was a gleam of metal amongst the trees. Approaching cautiously, she discovered that the track widened into a small clearing, where an expensive-looking car sat partially covered with a heavy tarpaulin. Bex knew nothing about cars, but its wheel arches were mud-spattered, and the exhaust still felt warm to the touch, so she thought it couldn't have been there much longer than a couple of hours. This must be Barber's car. It briefly crossed her mind to try breaking in, but she didn't want to risk setting the alarm off.

It also looked like something bigger had been parked next to it, because the ground was churned by deep tyre tracks which were now filling with snow. Why stop here and swap vehicles, though?

The reason soon became clear as she pressed on – beyond this clearing the track angled downhill and narrowed into little more than a rutted trail, treacherous with potholes. Her snowy woodland stroll turned into an uncomfortable frozen stagger as, no matter how careful she was, her feet strayed into ankle-deep puddles and her hands were numbed and scratched raw from clutching for support at sodden branches.

She guessed that she was descending the same hill that she had climbed earlier with Rosey, or whatever was analogous to it here, but she couldn't recall it being this high. Even allowing for the fact that the Narrows were always wilder, it was still taking an awfully long time to get anywhere. The Narrows were supposed to shorten distances, not lengthen them, and despite her eyes' evidence that the track ran straight both behind and ahead of her, she couldn't shake the impression that she'd actually been twisting and turning a serpentine route downhill without realising.

The effect of all this was so disorientating that when she finally came out of the trees and saw Holly End spread out before her, she didn't immediately take in what she was seeing. When she did, all the breath left her body in one awestruck 'Oh, *wow*!'

Holly End lay several miles distant and still further down: a picture-postcard English village of snow-covered roofs and lazily-smoking chimneys, complete with church steeple. It nestled in a landscape of white, glittering fields and a handful of farmhouses, neatly patchworked by hedgerows, with the whole valley occupying a shallow bowl surrounded by low wooded ridges. Above the protective hills was a completely circular band of thick snow-cloud, but over the valley the sky was the transparent blue of morning. Despite what her watch said, it was incontestibly morning: a pale midwinter sun had just risen above the girdle of cloud, and a light mist clung to the dips and hollows. It was quite simply one of the most beautiful sights she had ever seen in her life.

It was also terribly, terribly wrong. She couldn't pin down exactly what it was which made her feel that – just that something about the village set her Narrowfolk senses squirming.

By rights, from this vantage point she should have been looking north over the Vale of Evesham towards Stratford-upon-Avon, but that looked to be still well over the horizon. The Narrows, as she understood them, were called that because that was exactly what they did – they narrowed the distance between points in the real world by diving down under them. What she saw now was the exact opposite of that: a landscape folding out beyond the confines of its physical geography and occupying more space than existed for it in reality. The girdle of cloud around it was exactly like Walter's Fane. A building was one thing. This, on the other hand... she couldn't begin to comprehend the scope of power or ambition necessary to pluck an entire valley out of the world. She felt like a stone-age girl who had just been shown the pyramids.

Nor could she square the beauty of this place with what she knew of its master. How could this be the stronghold of a person like Barber? Carling had obviously been…

Something struck her hard in the middle of the forehead.

It hit with a sudden, stunning force that slammed her into the back of her own head, spreadeagled and paralysed against the inside of her skull, hearing only a dull ringing noise. The world had stopped.

She had just enough time to think 'Shit, that felt like…' before it happened again.

This time the world went away completely.

***

'Oh, cracking shot, Ted!' yelled Sam, and he ran forwards, whooping like a red Indian.

'Sam!' Ted called sharply, and the younger boy pulled up short. 'Be careful. He could be shamming.' Sam grinned back and carried on at only a slightly more restrained pace.

Together, the stood and looked down at Bex's inert form.

'Is he dead?' Sam asked breathlessly, excited and a little awed at being this close to an actual Rousler.

'I don't think so.' Ted knelt and peeled back the woollen hat which had cushioned Bex's forehead from the full force of his slingshot. A large bruised lump was already starting to appear. As they examined their captive, a horrible suspicion began to grow.

'Te-e-e-ed,' said Sam carefully, 'are you *sure* this is a Rousler?'

'What else could it be?' he snapped irritably. Sam knew that this meant he was scared too.

The face below the hat was that of a young boy – probably little more than Ted's own age, but pierced in a barbaric fashion with metal studs through the eyebrows and nose. His clothes were similarly outlandish: a thick army coat with dozens of pockets, even down the sleeves, at least three scarves, rainbow-striped fingerless gloves, a pair of badly abused jeans patched with a hundred different types of curtain fabric, and heavy army boots which, despite being covered in mud, could clearly be seen to have big yellow daisies painted on them. This was not the feral, ravening figure which the stories had lead them to expect from a Rousler. This looked more like Andy Pandy after too much cider.

'I think it's a girl,' Sam continued, and with rising horror: 'Ted, you just hit a *girl*!'

'Well how was I to know?'

Sam gave a low whistle. 'Cripes.'

'But who is she and how did she get in?'

'We have to tell Professor Barber. He'll know what to do.'

'Hmm.' Ted checked her pulse and her breathing again, like he'd been taught to do. She was getting cold. 'We'd better get her to Rabbit John first before she catches her death. Come on.'

They hoisted her up with an arm slung around each of their shoulders and her head lolling between them, and slight though she was, it still proved awkward since the trail was narrow for three abreast.

'You hit her twice, you know,' Sam reminded him.

'Yes, thank you, I had noticed. I think we can spare Rabbit John the details, don't you?'

'You are in *so* much trouble.'

'Oh, shut up.'

5

HOLLY END

Andy lay bound and gagged on a pile of army surplus blankets in the crypt of St Kenelm's church. It wasn't just blankets though; piled on every side were crates, cartons, and boxes of ex-military supplies: tools, medicines, freeze-dried food and gallons of diesel in huge metal drums. There was enough to keep a small community going for years. Evidently that had been the point.

He couldn't remember how long it had been since Barber had dumped him here. Couldn't think very clearly at all, as a matter of fact. There was something very close by – possibly in the church grounds – which was singing with ley energy of such intensity as to be physically painful. It was pitched beyond his range of hearing but at the frequency of his very bones, turning them into buzzing tuning forks; he ached all over as if with 'flu.

He'd felt it the moment he and Barber had entered the valley.

In the outlying woods, Barber had swapped his car for a battered jeep, but just before tying him up and throwing him in the back, he had abruptly changed his mind and turned to look at Andy as if a new idea had suddenly struck him.

'Come,' he said. 'There's something you should see.'

As he led Andy to the brink of the valley, he withdrew the tightest reins of his power, allowing a measure of freedom to return.

Andy stared around in amazement at the encompassing hills and the village below, where something far-off sang a discordant anthem of earthpower. The same thing that Bex had felt as an indefinable wrongness nagged at him like the sound of distant screaming, yet despite the feeling of revulsion, he found himself responding to its call – all other things aside, he wanted to see its source.

'It's a Fane,' he breathed. 'My god, it's a huge Fane.' He turned back to Barber. 'What have you done to this place?'

Barber shrugged. 'If you want to call it that, though it seems unnecessarily poetic. Technically, it's a Schumann-Watkins Displacement Field. The villagers simply call it the Spinny.'

'Walter copied it. Moon Grove – he was trying to recreate *this*.'

'A slave building sandcastles in flattery of his master's palace.' Barber regarded the frozen fields and said, half to himself, 'But I won't allow them to go the same way. When the end comes for them, it should be swift, painless and without fear. They deserve at least that.' He switched his attention to Andy. 'I'm afraid I can't offer you the same.'

Then he shook himself, clapped his hands together and said, 'Now then. A spot of history, I think. But before I begin, understand something. I tell you this not to gloat or revel in my own accomplishments. Nor to taunt you. I simply believe that a soul should not die in ignorance of its own nature. When death comes for you, you will understand its purpose and its rightness. That is what I *can* offer you.'

'Great. Allow me to weep with gratitude.'

'Hiroshima and Nagasaki gave us something new to fear – atomic annihilation – and so when the war turned Cold, it was necessary to manufacture a new global monster. Everybody naturally looked to the Soviets. Throughout the war there had been boffins squirrelled away around the country, coming up with all sorts of top-secret wizardry, some of which involved tinkering with electromagnetic fields to hide our planes from enemy radar. Stealth, they call it now. Then some bright spark came up with the idea of, well, why can't we hide ourselves from the enemy's planes too? There's only so much you can bury in a bunker, but what if we could find a way to protect entire towns and cities by manipulating the subtle energies of the very landscape itself?

'Did you know that during the First World War "earth-current signalling" devices used the ground's own electrical conductivity to transmit messages between trenches where enemy shells had destroyed the telegraph wires? Oscar Schumann's early work on the resonant frequencies of the earth-ionosphere cavity provided a conceptual framework, after which it was only a question of developing an appropriate mechanism for manipulating the field – and that we took from the practice of acupuncture.'

'Stakes in the ground.'

'Exactly. When the Jerusalem Project was set up, the War Office had already commandeered hundreds of villages for its own purposes, usually as gunnery ranges. In most cases, the inhabitants were simply turfed out and there are still ghost villages like Tyneham and Imber, where they've never been allowed back since. The original project's location was one such. But despite all our efforts we were unable to establish a stable Schumann field until we realised that what was missing was the presence of people. The human bioelectric field and the earth's own iso-electric field interact in subtle, symbiotic ways which we don't yet fully understand. For example, the original neolithic 'old straight tracks' didn't just follow pre-existing energy channels; somehow they came into being simultaneously.'

'Walter said that we walked them into existence, like aboriginal songlines.'

Barber glared. 'Walter had the soul of a poet, and that made him fundamentally unsuited for Jerusalem. If I'd seen that earlier I might have been able to spare him.'

'But not me.'

Barber regarded him for a long, silent moment. 'No,' he said. 'Not you. But then your fate was never part of the plan to begin with.

'The original residents of Holly End were, of course, delighted to be allowed home so soon after the war. The prospect of having a few soldiers billeted on the outskirts and a pair of mad scientists conducting their odd experiments in the woods must have seemed a small price to pay. It wasn't until we actually succeeded that any of us realised how dear that price truly was.

'The Schumann field was an unqualified success: we were immediately and totally cut off from the outside world. Which, as you can imagine, posed some tricky logistical problems.'

'You mean like how to stop all the villagers from starving to death? That sort of thing?'

Barber flapped a dismissive hand. 'That was never an issue. We'd stockpiled plenty of supplies and worked out a sustainability programme based on old-fashioned crop-rotation techniques long before they ran out. But it took nearly a year to re-establish communication with the outside world. This was in 1954. A year later, when I finally stumbled out on the road to Chipping Camden, it was 1963.'

'Bullshit.'

'A week after the assassination of President Kennedy, and a year after the world had nearly blown itself to smithereens over Cuba.'

'Bull*shit*!'

'If I remember rightly, Doctor Who had just started on the telly.'

'*Nine years?*'

'It's not so surprising if you think about it. You and your Narrowfolk utilise a much weaker version of the same displacement effect to sneak around parts of the city where you don't belong.'

'But of course,' Andy replied, 'you never told the villagers what you found, did you?'

'A lot can happen in one year, never mind nine. The Jerusalem Project was officially dead. We'd been forgotten about by the War Office, by friends and relatives, and even disappeared from the maps as if we'd never existed in the first place. And yet, it was the best thing that could have happened. At a stroke we were liberated from the petty demands of our war-mongering paymasters and free to set our own agenda – to use Holly End for an altogether more profound and lofty purpose: the secrets of the human soul and reality itself.'

'Here we go.'

Barber pointed at the village below. 'Down there, oh righteous one,' he said with heavy scorn, 'there is no crime, no addiction, and no deviance; no suicide bombers, no genetically modified food, no oestrogens in the water supply; no ASBOs, spam email, reality television, 20-20 cricket, or GPS navigation systems. Do you understand yet? The people who live down there brew their own beer and eat food that they've grown themselves. They have a bit of a sing-song and dance in the pub on a Friday night, and they say their prayers for Queen and Country in church on a Sunday. The girls make cakes, and the boys catch newts, and at school they all read Kipling and Shakespeare. This place is as close to being perfect as anywhere you are likely to see.'

'Funny. I keep hearing that. It's all still a lie, though. They deserve to know the truth. They should be able to choose for themselves.'

'Deserve? Should? Don't bandy moral absolutes with me, boy; don't you think I heard this bleating a thousand times from Lyttleton? What would you do? Give them to the care of the so-called Welfare State so that they can be housed in high-rise slums, with access to all the best crack and pornography that money can buy?'

'Don't pretend that you care. Not after what I've seen you do.'

'The fact that I have a sense of loyalty and responsibility to them does not stop me from doing what must be done, however unpleasant it might be.'

'That's just self-justifying crap, and you know it.'

'I imagine you told yourself much the same when you left your fiancée,' Barber shot back. 'Or am I wrong?'

Andy found he couldn't answer that.

'In any event, the adults are altogether useless as test subjects. Their meridians are already set and fixed, and they're not susceptible to the kinds of manipulation which are necessary. They were all born Outside; they're like colonists on a new planet with different gravity – any scientist trying to research human development in such circumstances would have to wait for the first native generation to be born.'

'The children.' Andy felt sick.

'Yes. But you see, the children of Holly End had all come in from the Outside too. What we really needed, Walter and I…'

'…were the ones born Inside.' The implication of what he was hearing struck him suddenly. 'Dear God – how old am I?'

'You were born in nineteen fifty five, the firstborn son of Holly End. You were three when the good doctor spirited you away. That was two years ago – nearly eighteen Outside. In one sense, you're over fifty years old. That's older than I am.'

Barber then told him the story of a young woman who had found herself pregnant by a soldier stationed at one of the nearby army camps; of how, despite pressure to have the child adopted, she'd borne both the shame and the boy and moved to Holly End to make a fresh start. Of how after the Spinny had cut them off, she had fallen in love with a farmer who'd wedded her without a second thought for curtain twitchers or post-office gossip. Of devoted step-fathers and new half-brothers. Of the first devastating Rousler attack which destroyed crops, houses, and families, and a community too shocked to properly realise that not all of the bodies were accounted for.

'What family you might have had here are long gone. The gates of the garden are shut, son of man, and there is nothing for you here except death.'

But it was just another story. It connected with nothing in him which could envisage having ever lived here, because the buzzing in his head was getting stronger, and he felt himself becoming dislocated just like when he'd been on the payphone to Laura. If only he could think it through, if only it would let up for a second, he might be able to get his head around all this.

That was when Barber threw him in the back of the jeep, under a pile of tarpaulins and spades and drove him down into the village to be locked in this crypt.

***

He must have fallen asleep at some point, because the sound of the crypt's heavy door crashing open startled him awake. He'd lost all sense of time.

'Get up.' Barber stood at the top of the crypt steps, looking dishevelled; he was covered in mud and leaf-mould. His needles, and thus the power which controlled Andy through them, had been withdrawn when he'd been dumped down here while Barber had been off doing whatever had made such a mess of his nice long coat. It gave Andy the freedom to at least lie there and squint up at him.

'Spot of gardening, is it?' he mocked in weak defiance.

Barber smiled mirthlessly. 'Something like.'

Unfortunately, freedom wasn't the same as strength. Despite the fact that his wounds were almost healed, he could do nothing to stop Barber dragging him up the steps, through the church, and out into the snow-blanketed graveyard, where he finally saw the source of the tortured earthpower by which Barber meant to end his life.

6

RABBIT JOHN

Bex became aware of the dry-sweet smell of herbs and woodsmoke, the sound of cheerful whistling, and a monstrous pain as if a railroad spike had been driven straight into the middle of her forehead.

She found herself lying on a narrow cot in a small, dimly-lit shack. The ceiling was raftered with rough-hewn timbers from which hung all manner of tools, traps, and animal skins in various stages of preservation. She tried to sit up, winced at the pain in her head, and discovered that someone had bandaged it. A thick poultice was wadded between her eyebrows; her fingers came away covered in green guck. She tore it off in disgust.

A second stab at the whole sitting up business was slightly more successful, but a sudden wave of dizziness turned the world inside out and upside down, and she fell back, knocking over a small bedside table that had been set with a tin mug and a jug of water.

At the noise, a man appeared in the low doorway. He was dressed in army fatigues which had been heavily customised with animal furs, but despite this, and the generally unkempt state of the shack, he was clean-shaven. She found this oddly reassuring, although it made telling his age impossible. He had the look of a young man ridden hard by life.

Rabbit John regarded her with concern. 'You've woken up, I see.'

Bex lurched to her feet. 'Where am I?' she demanded.

'Come outside when you're feeling up to it,' he replied by way of an answer. 'There's a brew on.'

It took a while to gather her marbles together. Outside, she found that the shack occupied a small clearing in the snow-cloaked woods; a wide lean-to porch ran the length of it, under the shelter of which the man was boiling a kettle over an open fire. Two boys were hovering nearby, and when she appeared, they drew back fearfully, whispering. Wordlessly, Rabbit John handed her a chipped mug of tea. It was black, unsweetened, and cut clean through her mental fog. She sipped carefully as he left the fire and approached to inspect her forehead.

'You took the dressing off,' he observed.

'It smelled of tree.' This close, she noticed that his eyes were exactly the same colour as Maltesers and found herself blushing inexplicably.

'It took half an hour to make,' he chided.

'Sorry, but… You haven't got any paracetomol, have you?'

'I'm afraid I don't know what that is. How many fingers am I holding up?' He showed her three.

'Three. Is this some kind of concussion thing?'

'Yes. Can you count backwards from ten?'

'Certainly can,' she replied and simply returned his gaze. It wasn't easy – he was nearly a foot taller.

'Humour me.'

She sighed and counted backwards from ten.

'What's your name?' he continued. 'This isn't a "concussion thing," I should add.' There was a hint of warning in his voice.

'What's yours?' It came out more aggressive than she'd intended, but she let it stand.

'John,' he answered amiably. 'Most people add a Rabbit to it, but you can't blame them for that.' He gestured self-deprecatingly at his coat. 'It's not like I don't invite it. There,

I've told you mine. Rousler or not, you can't really be so ungrateful as to not return the favour, can you?'

'Actually, yes I can. Nothing personal, you seem like nice boys, but I don't want to get you mixed up in all of this. I'm just looking for a friend of mine. If you'll let me have my stuff, I'll be on my way and out of your hair.' She didn't sense any harm in these three, for all that they looked like rejects from a bad costume drama, but Carling had said that Holly End was the centre of Barber's power, and she wasn't taking any chances.

Rabbit John merely settled back onto his tree-stump chair with an amiable smile, as if to suggest that it was all the same to him whether she talked or walked – then she saw that his foot was resting on her backpack like a footstool and swore aloud. There were shocked gasps from the two boys.

She turned on her brightest, sunniest fuck-you smile. 'Angela,' she said, 'Angela Parkhurst,' and held out a hand, which Rabbit John shook with dry amusement. It was the name she habitually gave in doubtful company; 'Nosey' Parkhurst had been the biggest bitch and gossip in Year Nine, and Bex had no qualms about dropping her in anything nasty. 'I'll play, but I'm not sure how much of this you're going to believe.' She launched into a heavily truncated version of the events that had unfolded since Five Ways tunnel, leaving out as much as she could about Barber until she knew where this strange woodcutter's loyalties lay.

As she spoke, his face grew pale, and his mouth set in a thin, hard line; clearly he was trying to contain a turmoil of emotions – but whether they were anger, fear or excitement, she couldn't tell. Ted and Sam were exchanging increasingly bewildered looks and whispering together urgently. It wasn't at all the reaction she'd expected.

'I think,' he replied slowly, piecing together his thoughts, 'that you've probably told us less than half of what you really know. I'd have done the same in your position. But I don't think you realise how much more you've told without meaning to.'

He reached into her backpack and brought out Dodd's A-to-Z. 'I was having a look through this, back when I thought you were a Rousler. I know better now.'

'That's the second time you've called me that. What is it?'

'It doesn't matter now.' He looked like he was about to be sick. She couldn't work out what the problem was. 'In the front here, it says this was printed in the year two-thousand and four.' He laughed shortly. 'Birmingham's a bit bigger than I remember.'

'So?'

'So this is quite battered by the look of it. What year is it now?'

'You're kidding, right?'

'Sam,' said Rabbit John, his liquid chocolate eyes never leaving hers, 'how old are you, son?'

'I'm nearly nine,' he answered proudly.

'And when were you born?'

'On the twenty-second of April. There was a 'lectricity cut. The doctor thought I was a *girl*,' he added in disgust.

'What year, Sam?'

'Nineteen fifty. I *can* remember, Rabbit John.'

Bex's hands went to her mouth. 'Oh my god.' *Nineteen fifty?* It wasn't possible. 'What's he done here? What's he done to you people?'

Rabbit John tossed Bex her belongings. 'I think I'm going to help you find your friend,' he said. 'Then I think I'm going to find our esteemed Professor Barber and ask him a few blunt questions.' He went back into the shack and came out again a few minutes later with an old army rifle slung over his back. 'On the way, you can fill me in on the rest of it.'

The first thing she filled him in on was her real name. Screw Angela 'Nosey' Parkhurst; this brooding dark young man with the gorgeous eyes was all hers.

'So tell me about these Rouslers,' she said to Ted, as they threaded a careful single-file down the trail out of the Rimwoods.

'I don't understand it,' he answered. 'We saw them. We all *saw* them. They attacked us – burned down some houses. People died! And you say that there just aren't any Outside. It doesn't make sense.'

'Maybe if you tell me a bit more about them we can figure it out.' She felt an unexpectedly deep sympathy for the lad. He wasn't that much younger than herself and having to come to terms with a lot of painful truths about his world very quickly. She knew how that felt. 'He probably paid a bunch of skinheads to do the job.'

'Skin-what? What are… why would anybody *do* that?'

'Fear,' she said simply. 'To keep you afraid. To control you. Which means he needs you for something. I'm betting it's not anything fun.'

'The Professor showed us a cine-film he took of them when he went exploring in the wastelands,' said Sam, trotting behind. 'I drew some pictures. I can show you them if you want.'

She grinned. 'That'd be awesome.'

'Awesome,' Ted tried the unfamiliar slang, liking the sound of it.

Sam was happily reeling off everything he'd learned about Rouslers from the cine-film, which had been meant just for the grown-ups because it was so disturbing, but that naturally he and Ted had sneaked in to watch. 'The fields are all desert because of fallout from the Ruskie bombs, and the Rouslers drive around in big fast scary cars made out of all bits and pieces, and their chief is a big bald muscley man called the Lord Humungous, except he wears a mask so nobody can see how badly scarred his face is, and there's only one small town

264

and it's pumping petrol...' He stopped, thinking he must have said something wrong, because Bex was laughing so hard that tears were running down her cheeks.

'I'm sorry...' she gasped, 'I'm so sorry... it's not funny...' Slowly she caught her breath and wiped her eyes. 'It's awful and tragic I know, but still...' and she was off again.

When she had calmed down enough to be capable of coherent speech, she did her best to describe the plot of the Mad Max movies, but it was hard to explain the Ayatollah of Rock And Rollah to people who had probably never even heard of Elvis. Underneath the surreal absurdity of it all, she felt her loathing of Barber deepen even further. How much he must have loved his little joke, fooling and terrorising these villagers into thinking that they were surrounded by a nightmare world full of psychotic monsters. How he must have laughed as their cottages burned. *I'll see you burn,* she thought. *Burn you down to the ground.*

But thoughts of revenge were driven from her mind when they all heard the church bell down in the village begin to clamour: a wild, arrhythmic alarm routing echoes around the valley.

They looked at each other questioningly. Then they began to run.

265

7

THE KIFTSGATE STONE

It had been placed in the small graveyard of St Kenelm's church, and indeed it was the same general size and shape as a headstone, but it was furred with moss and so weathered by long centuries that it looked like a giant tooth pitted with decay. One corner had been broken off in ages past, and at some point somebody had bored a hole right through the soft limestone. It was through this hole that Barber threaded the chain with which he manacled Andy.

It was also deeply, fundamentally *wrong*.

Wrong in the sense of a dislocated finger. Of nails scraped down blackboards. Of two-headed calves and beached whales and small sea-creatures flopping helplessly on the exposed seabed just before a tsunami. It shrieked its wrongness through his nerve endings and made his flesh crawl where he came into contact with it. It was so aberrant that he could barely see it properly, as if his brain refused to let his eyes acknowledge its existence.

Barber returned carrying a slim briefcase, which he opened in the snow. Seven neatly ranked daggers with ornate handles gleamed.

'I'm not going to pretend that this isn't going to hurt.' He used one of the knives to slice through the front of Andy's layered clothing, baring his pale chest to the chill. 'It's the worst kind of pain you can imagine, or so I'm reliably informed. These,' he gestured to the knives, 'are the least of it. Besides,' and he waggled the knife he was holding admonishingly, 'this was all your idea, remember.'

Andy's smile was ghastly. 'That's right. My idea. And guess what. I'm going to do to you what I did to those skavags, Barber. I'm going to turn you inside out.'

'Very brave. Very hollow. Now then boy, let's see what makes you tick.'

Moving with deft precision, he began to array his needles in Andy's *ch'i* meridians, forming the complex and forbidden *dim mak* configurations which would hyperenergise his system and siphon it out through the gateway chakras which swirled in lazy galaxies at seven points down the centre of his torso. The others that had been sacrificed in the city had taken a lot longer; an infinitely more complex procedure of self-incineration by which the entirety of each victim's soul had been liberated to help restructure the city's own energy pathways. Nothing so ambitious was required here. This was fast and brutal: all he needed was the boy's *vishuddi chakra*, the throat gateway through which he could interrogate his soul directly. Find out whether or not he was bluffing about the stake, and maybe, if there were time before he died, what changes had been wrought in him in the years since he had been stolen away.

He was hunched over Andy avidly, like a vampire, and Andy could see gossamer streamers of his own aura beginning to drift upward, drawn into the black thundercloud of Barber's own. Small points of heat, like cigarette burns, began to blister his skin under the needles. He could smell his own flesh burning. Instinctively he shrank from this, pressing back against the stone, revolted by it, wanting to bury himself in it, to crawl into the earth and hide forever, remembering as he did so a dream of stones socketed in human flesh.

And as if it had been merely waiting for an invitation, the stone sang itself into him.

In a flash, his perception spiralled out into the Rimwoods, past fields and houses, taking in as it did so every leaf, stone, and living creature on the way – passing Bex in surprised delight as she walked down into the valley with three strangers, and then gone before he could try to make contact. He was dimly aware of his own body as a sensation of burning and choking. Then he was arrowing out along the ley to its anchoring point eight miles away at the Bidford-on-Avon bridge where she had experienced her orgasmic dowsing, and he knew instantly what was so very wrong. The stone had been moved from its proper position, and the ley had moved with it, to be wrapped around this valley. Its discordant singing was the thrumming of an over-stretched guitar string, tightened too far and ready to snap.

This flight lasted barely a second before it recoiled back into the stone, and then catapulted him in the opposite direction – into Barber. Just like with Spike, just like with the skavags, for a fleeting moment he *was* Barber. He felt the towering arrogance of the man, the monomaniacal certainty of his own rightness, and much more besides. It passed, and he found himself looking into his enemy's awestruck and enraged eyes.

The burning had stopped.

'Impossible!' the dark man snarled. He'd been so close to forcing the boy's secrets from his flesh, when his meridians had inexplicably *moved*. This was impossible. They should have been as fixed and immutable as the network of his arteries or the swirls of his fingerprints, and yet they had slithered out from under his needles and twisted like serpents throughout Andy's body, escaping Barber's reach. It was simply, physically impossible. When you dammed a river, the river changed, yes, but it didn't get up and go flowing somewhere else.

'You're...' Barber struggled for speech. 'Unfixed! How can you be unfixed and yet live?' He didn't seem to have noticed Andy's brief intrusion into his soul.

'You tell me,' Andy grunted, struggling to his feet. The needles fell from his flesh, twisted and smoking. 'You're the *scientist*.'

'Professor?' a timid voice queried from behind them. 'Is everything all right?'

An old man dressed in a flat cap and waistcoat hovered at the edge of the graveyard, a bicycle clutched defensively in front of him. Quite how he thought the sight of the trustworthy Professor brandishing a knife at a half-naked young stranger could be anything other than *not* all right was a question Andy never got to ask.

'Sandy, old chap,' Barber said without looking around, the effort of maintaining civility straining his voice. 'You know I have nothing but the deepest affection for you, but now is really not a very convenient time.'

'But he's… is that a…'

This time he looked at the old man. 'Yes. He is. The Rouslers are here again, and in greater numbers than ever before. Best you go sound the alarm, dear chap.'

The bicycle clattered to the pavement as Sandy took to his heels and ran for the church. Moments later, its bell began to ring out a ragged alarm, and rooks fled like a cloud of complaining shadows from the tower.

'You could never have hoped to keep me a secret,' said Andy. 'You knew someone was bound to see this. That's why you went up into the woods just now. You've untethered the Fane around this village. You're bringing it all to an end – this place, all of these people. What's the matter, finally tired of playing god?'

'It was going to end soon anyway. You were just a bonus. As for playing god…' he shook his head and chuckled '…boy, you have no idea.'

'Oh, I have a very clear idea. I've seen inside you, and I know *everything* now. I know you killed Walter. I know what the Closures are for. I know about the Gates, and the Rotunda, and the *urdrog*. Why do you think I let you bring me back here in the first place? Did you think I actually came here to let you kill me? I know all of it, and now I'm going to stop you.' Uncertainty played across Barber's face, and Andy could imagine how uncomfortable that unfamiliar emotion must be to him.

But the dark man rallied quickly. 'Very well then, if you know so much, you also I know that *I do not play!*'

Darting forward, he clamped one hand over the crown of Andy's head, digging his fingers hard into his scalp, and the other hand just as hard onto the Kiftsgate Stone. Both Andy and the stone screamed with the same voice as he brutally hauled raw power from one and poured it into the other.

'This is it, boy!' he raged, now completely beyond the pretence of humanity. 'Invade my mind, would you? This is what you get for fucking with me!' His fingers began to curve inwards, pressing through flesh and bone and stone, tearing energy out of the Schumann-Watkins field and ramming it down into Andy's spasming body. 'Is this what you wanted? Do you understand? All your pissing around in the Narrows is *nothing. This* is what the world feels like!'

The field began to collapse inwards under Barber's relentless pressure, squeezing down from the encircling hills in a rapidly tightening noose which drained the living vitality out of every molecule as it fought to meet the demands of its creator. Trees collapsed in columns of dust, wildlife fled its approach and died as desiccated skeletons – snow exploded into vapour, and the very soil beneath was sterilised of bacteria. The villagers, who had already been roused by Sandy's alarm, peered fearfully from doors and windows.

'It's myself I blame,' Barber continued through gritted teeth, as earthpower howled around and through him. 'I should have chased you down as soon as Walter stole you. I should have killed you when I could. Now, you see what you drive me to? You *see?*' He pressed harder, viciously, and the earth began to heave in convulsions which spread outwards from the stone like ripples on water. 'I have given *decades* to protect this place and further this work. I have taken *lives*. I have made myself a *monster* for it.' With each phrase, he rammed power harder and harder into the screaming figure before him, and he leaned in close, speaking against the burning skin of Andy's forehead. 'But I will destroy it all – *all life, in all worlds* – before I will suffer a rival.'

The surface of Andy's body exploded into a thousand miniature suns as his meridians attempted to dump the appalling energy overload. His nostrils were filled with the stink of his own skin and hair burning. He couldn't do this. He'd underestimated; this wasn't a dog or a scavenger beast. This was a man with the secrets of the universe at his command. Andy was going to die.

8
LEY OF THE LAND

Bex, Rabbit John, Ted and Sam were on the outskirts of the village when the first earth convulsion swept past, knocking them flat.

'What the bloody hell was that?' she yelped, picking herself up again.

'*Another* one?' Ted's eyes were wide with incredulity.

'It was stronger that time!' said Sam, bouncing up. There were leaves in his ears.

'But what *was* it?'

'Nothing good,' suggested Rabbit John. 'I think we'd better hurry up.'

***

Alice Clee left her baking and hurried to the front door. The sound of the church bell hadn't really impinged on her awareness; if she'd heard it at all she'd thought it was only old Sandy Wilkins getting in a spot of campanology practice for Sunday. But then the whole cottage had lurched and sent her best Mason Cash mixing bowl crashing into shards, which was a real tragedy, because there were no more of those to be had in this world, and she ran outside to see what was going on.

A pale haze was sweeping down out of where the Rimwoods used to be, flowing over the fields like the photographic negative of a cloud-shadow, and in its wake she could see – well, couldn't understand what she was seeing but saw it nevertheless – things crumbling. A small flock of their precious black-faced Cotswold sheep were caught up and, bleating their terror, reduced to bundles of woollen rags and stick-like bones.

Her first thought was *This is it. They've dropped the Bomb. They've finally found us, and they've dropped the Bomb. It was never safe at all.*

Then: Tony was somewhere out there with the men, working on some wall repairs. She had no idea at all where Ted and Sam were. Her husband and her boys.

Alice dropped everything and ran towards the haze, crying their names.

***

The stone began to fracture under the intolerable strain. Chunks of limestone crumbled away as hairline cracks spread upwards from the ground, but Barber dug his fingers in deeper, commanding it to hold together and obey his will. His other hand pressed deeper into the boy's skull, his fingers like stakes searching out the landscape of his mind, not to reorder or control but to burn utterly.

Yet, incredibly, Andy continued to resist. He was drawing power of his own from somewhere – out of the air, out of the ground, Barber couldn't tell. Frustrated and enraged, he hauled harder at the earthpower. The stone screamed louder, and the fractures grew.

***

The street was rapidly filling with her friends and neighbours – shouting, calling, crying. Alice thought that if she looked anything like as wild-eyed and frightened, then she must be in a real state. Then four mud-spattered figures appeared at the end of the street, outracing the death zone, but she had eyes for only two of them. Sam was riding piggyback on Rabbit John. Weeping with relief, she gathered her boys into a fiercely protective hug.

'Thank you, John,' she sobbed. 'Thank you so much.' Her eyes searched Ted's face intently. 'Have you seen your father?'

He shook his head mutely, and she moaned, turning to appeal to Rabbit John once more. 'What's going on? What's happening? I don't under… *who is this?*' Her voice broke on a high note of near-hysteria. She'd noticed Bex for the first time, and somehow this seemed to be the worst thing so far: the first completely strange face she'd seen in five years. *Who is she, John?*'

Bex had no time for this. 'You've got to get them somewhere safe,' she told him urgently. 'Everybody you can find. Get them somewhere *deep*. This place is toast.' *Not again*, she told herself. *I will not let this happen again.*

'What are you going to do?'

She grinned at him. 'What I do best: stick my nose in where it isn't wanted.' She sped away towards the centre of the village. Just before she passed out of earshot she thought she heard Sam's excited voice shrilling 'Mummy, she's a girl! And Ted hit her! Twice!'

***

Bex skidded around the village green to the far corner of the churchyard and pulled up short, gaping. Even though she was an avowed atheist, had never been to church in her life and actively despised the stupid credulity of pretty much everybody who did, the only way she could describe the confrontation before her was 'biblical'.

Andy was alight. Constellations burned within his flesh, shifting, racing and reordering themselves in frantic geometries as they tried to cope with the torrent of power being directed through him. He knelt as if receiving benediction from a tall, stooped figure of impenetrable darkness which had one hand clamped to his head as if trying to drive him into the ground, whilst drawing power from a large standing stone with the other.

The stone that anchors his power, Carling had called it.

The impasse between the two men was throwing the earth into further turmoil; concentric ripples were pulsing outward, tearing fissures in the ground and tumbling buildings.

With sudden dismay, she realised that the closest thing she had to a weapon or even a tool was the iron stake – and that was stuck in the ground several miles and an entire world away. She looked around desperately and seized the nearest thing to hand: a pair of cobblestones from the ruined road. Running forward with a yell, she flung one at the Kiftsgate Stone with all her strength.

And missed.

Closer, still running, but with her offhand she hurled the second. Amazingly, her aim was better. Slightly. It hit Barber square on the shoulder and bounced away.

He turned and looked at her. There was nothing remotely human in that gaze. With a dismissive flick of power he swatted her away.

She landed in a tangled heap by the church lychgate but barely felt the impact; her nerves were crawling with black fire from his touch. She had just enough coherence of thought to wonder how Andy could still be alive if that was what Barber's merest glancing blow felt like. The simple answer was that he couldn't. He was going to die, and there was nothing she could do about it. She shut her eyes and waited for the end.

***

All life. Barber's words burned in his brain. *In all worlds.*

***

'Are you all right?' said a trembling voice behind Bex, and a child's hand appeared on her shoulder. 'Can I help?'

She looked up. Ted's face was pale, and his eyes were slightly glazed with shock, but he was there. She nearly yelled at him to get out, to get back to his family and as far from here as he could, but then she caught sight of the catapult sticking out of his back pocket and remembered the bruise still smarting in the middle of her forehead.

'Depends,' she answered. 'Exactly how good a shot are you with that thing? Think you can hit that stone?'

'Watch me.'

He stood up, loaded a ball bearing into the rubber band and pulled it right back to his cheek, sighting carefully. The tendons in his neck stood out as taut as the rubber itself. Seeing the movement, Barber turned, and Ted nearly quailed under the naked animosity in his expression.

'Dear me now, Edward, what do you think you're doing?' he asked in tones of perfect reasonableness, as if he didn't at that moment have his fingers hooked into another man's skull. Andy sagged in the momentary respite. 'He's a Rousler, Ted. I'm saving everybody's lives. Don't be foolish now.'

'I'm not foolish,' Ted replied and shifted his aim fractionally.

Too late, Barber realised that the weapon was not intended for him, and his face dropped in alarm. 'Don't you dare!' he screamed. 'Oh don't you *dare*, you bad, bad boy!'

'I'm not bad, either,' Ted corrected him. 'I am *awesome*.'

His aim was true.

Subjected to stresses beyond endurance and held together only by the will of its master, the Stone exploded.

The one and only time Bex had been to the seaside, her big brother Nick had taken her beachcombing, and during their explorations they'd found a length of rope sticking out of the damp sand. They came to the only sensible conclusion that the other end was tied around either a treasure chest or the corpse of a pirate, or, ideally, both. Grasping the end – and on Nick's 'One… two… *three*!' – they'd hauled as hard as they could, but rather than being showered with gold dubloons (or bits of pirate skeleton, which would have been even cooler), the rope had simply *thrupped* out in a long straight line, flinging seaweed and sand in their faces. Six-year-old Rebecca had declared the enterprise to be stupid and gone off to torment some crabs, but that memory was the closest she could get now to an analogy for what happened when Ted's shot destroyed the Stone.

The life-devouring noose tightening around the village winked out existence instantaneously as the suddenly-released Ryknild ley tore itself out of the ground like a length of rope yanked out of wet sand.

It resembled something serpentine, a dragon-wall of blue fire, and she could see through it as if through a severe heat haze. Andy and Barber had been flung apart by the explosion; Andy was on the same side as herself, lying naked and as if dead, but Barber was a dimly blurred and wavering shadow limping away through the graveyard.

'Help me!' she shouted to Ted. 'We've got to get him out of here!' They each grabbed one of his arms and began to drag him away.

Then the dragon-ribbon began to move as it tried to earth itself along its original course. Eight miles in length, anchored at the Bidford-on-Avon bridge, but only one mile sundered from its true path, it began to describe a long and shallow arc across the Vale of Evesham. Close up, it looked like a slow-moving wall of blue fire stretching from one horizon to another, moving inexorably towards her. It was shot through with venomous black veins which resembled the symptoms of blood poisoning, as if the very life-energy of the earth were diseased. Now that it was free of Barber's rapacious demands, it was no longer destroying everything in its path, but it was still violent, stirring trees and plant life with hurricane-like force, and Bex didn't much feel like waiting for it to hit her.

For another thing, the landscape on the other side of it seemed to be changing. One moment it was fields; the next, marshland; then jungle, desert, primeval forest, and a hundred permutations in between, all layered over one another and shifting in and out of focus. It was like what happened when she'd opened the way to Holly End just a few hours ago – but infinitely more complex. An infinity of worlds nestled like the layers of an onion, and breaking towards her in a standing wave. If that thing hit them, Christ alone knew where they'd end up.

They hoisted Andy's dead weight between them and shambled away through the wreckage of the village, but Ted was only a kid, and she was barely a few years older. Out into the fields, the ground became steeper, and as the ley neared its true course, it picked up speed until they could feel it roaring silently at their backs. There was really only one thing she could think to do.

She dropped Andy and flung herself on him, hugging with one arm and drawing Ted down to clasp him with the other.

'Whatever you do!' she shouted as they were overborne, *'Whatever happens, don't let go! Do you hear me? DON'T LET…'*

And they were swept away.

The ley continued on its way for another half-mile before regaining its ancient course and quite literally earthing itself. The blue fire slowly dissipated amongst the trees and meadows and was gone as if nothing had ever happened.

***

The following day, quite a few locals who were driving through the area about their everyday business remarked to their loved ones or their mates down the pub that night as to how the roads all suddenly seemed slower than usual, as if they were longer, or there were more of them – except that was, of course, nonsense. And by the way, didn't you see a lot of strange vagrants about, these days?

9
THE DOBUNNI

Bruna was enjoying the view from the caral's roof deck when it threw a wheel, two days out from Caer Trefni. How it had happened, none could say. Being of a respectable middle-caste clan, they had been just forward of the Dobunni nation's centre, and dozens of carals of all shapes and sizes had passed over the same ground before them. The leather-smocked wheelwrights who clustered around the front of the great vehicle, pointing out bits of damage to each other and stroking their long moustaches sagely, came to the conclusion that the stone which did it had been gradually worked loose by the passage of many wheels before finally ricocheting up into the gearing.

One or two of the older and more superstitious engineers wondered whether it might have had anything to do with the violent display of blue wyrdfire which had lashed the eastern plains the day before, but the consensus argued against them – though with due deference to their seniority. The last thing anybody wanted was a coven of Seers poking around under there.

Certainly nobody suggested that the driver might have erred or that the family's maintenance of their caral was lacking – to have done so would have been the gravest of insults. Nevertheless, the fact remained that repairs had to be made, and the delay would be costly. Lady Holda herself laid no blame, but gave orders in her customarily terse, unarguable manner: the family's animals were to be cut out of the Dobunni's great communal herds which grazed like clouds in the grassland on either side, and the services of a wheelwright would have to be bartered for quickly.

The nation would not stop for them. It could not. Not even in the ordinary course of events – some of the high-caste carals were so large that they required half a mile to stop – and especially this close to Caer Trefni's great Overwinter Market, where a day's delay would mean the difference between the coming year being one of richness or simply bare subsistence. The unwed men would drift away to find more prosperous homes, and the nation would degenerate into a ragged caravan of vagabonds and rustlers. The central plains were littered with them. Lady Holda was fiercely adamant that she would not be the cause of such shame, and the nation's Council honoured her sacrifice by stationing a warband for her clan's protection.

Bruna stood on the caral's forward parapet with the other wieve-maidens and watched as the tall, clean-limbed young men rode back towards them. Their hair was chalked back into sweeping spikes, they wore checked warriors' britches, and their gleaming javelins were held aloft by well-muscled arms banded in gold. They laughed and sang as they rode.

But long after the other girls had gone back down to flirt, she stayed to watch the nation pass by. First the big carals like her own – each of which was home, nursery, school, and workplace for a clan – then the smaller four-wheeled wains of the lower-caste families, and finally the straggling collection of carts, ponyteams, and disreputable single riders. It was strange to see them go by. For as long as she could remember, they had always been behind her, just as those ahead of her might have moved up or back slightly according to the shifting fortunes of their clan but never really *moved*. She stood on that high place, below the bright midwinter sky, and watched her place in the hierarchy of her people slip away into the dustcloud of ten-thousand wheels.

It would have been unfair to say that they were left entirely alone. True, the caral was the clan's heart; more than just Lady Holda's residence, it was moothall and temple, workshop and goods store. But the extended families of the weavers, drovers, herdsmen, warriors and artisans who comprised the clan rode satellite in numerous smaller wains, and these pitched up in a loose circle around the caral, forming an instant village. In moments, awnings were guyed out, cookfires lit, and children took advantage of the unprecedented halt to go tearing around like small, dusty comets.

When the cloud of the nation's passage was nothing more than a lingering smudge on the wide, northern horizon, she looked around at the vast plains which stretched in a rolling sea of grass and the tumbled wolds behind, through which they'd passed yesterday – and despite the cheery chatter and bustle which surrounded her, was suddenly struck by the immensity of it all. The emptiness.

The wide world was no place to find yourself unguarded and alone.

***

Iaran and Edris of the warband let their mounts graze on a small rise of land overlooking the solitary caral and its village of satellite wagons. Despite the earlier excitement, there had never been any real prospect of fighting; the broad vale through which they were journeying was too open to provide much refuge for bandits.

'There's talk of sorcery at work, I hear,' remarked Edris casually.

Iaran smiled thinly. 'The only spirits at work here are likely to have come out of a bottle. He wouldn't be the first driver to blame a mishap on the Bright Folk.' He was a veteran of thirty-nine summers, an achievement which he attributed very firmly to steel rather than superstition.

'Ay, and not the only time today.' Iaran did not reply, plainly having said all that was necessary on the matter. Taking the older man's silence for indulgence, Edris warmed to his subject. 'Strange events have happened all along the line since that wyrdfire storm yesterday. Ox-teams running wild. Lights in the sky. A bag of flour in the mielcaral is said to have turned into sand even as it was being milled. One of the men in Cordmaster Gaeled's warband was bitten on the hand by a blue serpent which fell from the sky and crawled down his lance.'

'Hmph.'

'The whole warband witnessed it!'

'Ridiculous. Men of honour would not give credence to such prattling.'

'Then it must be true, must it not?'

Iaran flicked his horse's reins and moved it to graze a few yards further away. Edris knew he had pressed his patience far enough and let the matter drop. He remained where he was, watching the herdsfolk go about their business in the makeshift camp, listening to the murmurous ruminations of cattle and the high, ringing hammer blows of a forge flying out into the still, empty sky. A waiting sky.

'Mark me,' he murmured to Compa, patting his neck gently, 'the land is troubled. We've not seen the end of it yet.'

Compa munched grass and kept his own counsel.

***

Ten-year old Hael was getting very, very cross. The calf blundered away from him along a narrow stream, crashing through bushes in panic and blarting for its mama as if he were a wolf or something. If anyone had a right to be afraid, it was he, not this big, stupid baby. Night was coming on. Da was going to beat him for this. But then, Da was most likely going to beat him for something or other anyway; it was the men and women of the warband that Hael was most afraid of. He was terrified that they might go to his Da and say that they couldn't possibly allow the caral to be slowed down by a boy who couldn't even look after a single stupid calf and needed to be searched for after dark, and that it would be better for all if he were left behind. His Da might agree. Two thoughts made his blood run cold with terror: what if there really were wolves out here, and, worse, what if nobody came looking for him at all in the first place?

He put on a renewed burst of speed, but the big, stupid baby just rolled its eyes at him in fear again, charged away along the stream and disappeared. When Hael fought his way through the thicket and saw what was on the other side he stopped cold. Fear of losing the calf, fear of his Da's belt and the warriors' scorn, fear even of being eaten by wolves – all were eclipsed by the bowel-watering terror of what he found in the small clearing beyond.

It was a boy.

Much the same age as Hael himself, he wore an outlandish tunic which flapped open up the front like something disemboweled, and the sort of short hair that he had only ever seen on slaves or criminals. The calf had just galloped through his campfire, and he was half-rising with an O of surprise in the middle of his pale face. He hadn't seen Hael yet, and for a moment the herdsboy thought he might just escape, until a *second* figure came striding up. This one was even stranger: its hair stood up in ragged tufts, and it appeared to be dressed in multicoloured rags. It was pointing at him and yelling in an alien language.

Hael knew without a shadow of a doubt that these were two of the Bright Folk, and that the shouting one was casting a spell on him; soon he would be spirited away to be lost forever in their kingdom under the hills, never to see his Da or his clan or stupid calves ever again. Then the animal blundered back across the clearing, throwing everything into even greater confusion. Hael spared a second to thank the noble beast for this distraction and took to his heels.

**

'Stay here!' commanded Bex. 'Pack our things!'

'Why?' asked Ted. 'What are you going to do?'

'I'm going to stop that kid from letting everybody know where we are, what do you think? You're going to get us ready to move.'

'What kid?'

She snorted in disgust, muttered 'Some watch-guard you turned out to be,' and disappeared in pursuit.

'Sorry!' he called after her, but she was gone.

Ted went back to the crude lean-to which they'd built against the coming night. Andy lay beneath it, staring sightlessly up at its branches. He didn't respond to Ted's approach, just as he hadn't responded to anything either Ted or Bex had said or done since the wave of blue fire had stranded them here. He would move where he was put and obey the simplest of commands, but beyond that he was unreachable and insensate. Ted found his glassy stare deeply unsettling and kept away from it as much as he could. They had dressed him in what they could spare from their own winter layers, but with the onset of night, the temperature had started to drop rapidly, and Ted wasn't at all sure that he would survive the night. And now, to top it off, Bex had said to pack everything and move just when they'd got settled. It had taken him *ages* to get that fire going.

'Besides,' he said to Andy's blank expression, 'why shouldn't we let ourselves be found? We're doing you no good like this. The trouble with your friend is that she thinks everyone's out to get her, that's what. We need *help*.'

Abruptly, his stomach rumbled. He hadn't eaten anything since breakfast: toast and bramble jam. He'd picked the fruit himself in the Rimwoods, and his mother had baked the bread. Ted was suddenly, gut-wrenchingly homesick. He threw everything down and sat with his arms wrapped around his knees and his head buried against his forearms, and did what nobody could have blamed a twelve-year old boy in his position for doing: he began to cry.

***

Iaran and Edris were overseeing the ingathering of the clan's numerous small family herds when they were approached by an angular, sour-faced father and his cowering son.

'Tell them!' the man barked, propelling the boy forward. 'Go on, now we're here. You're keen enough to take a whipping from me – let's see what your nonsense earns you from these men. I hope you think it's worth it.' Turning to the two warriors, he was immediately fawning. 'My apologies, noble sirs. I did try to thrash the impudence out of him, but he insisted on seeing you.'

Iaran, who had taken an instant dislike to the man, addressed the son directly. 'What is so important that you would brave the anger of your father?' He saw the boy's head lift a little at the word 'brave'. Not a dullard, then. But the father weighed in again before his son could open his mouth to reply.

'Nothing but a lot of nonsense about the Bright Folk stealing a calf that he was supposed to be looking after...'

Edris turned with shining eyes to Iaran, who uttered a long-suffering sigh. 'I suppose I'll not hear the end of this until I say yes, will I?'

Edris grinned.

'But alone, mind! I'll not risk more than one good horse in the dark. If you lame your mount, you walk back yourself.'

Edris turned to the boy, who was cringing under a renewed cuffing from his father. 'Good drover,' he said, trying not to sound too sarcastic, 'I beg leave to borrow your son awhile.' The man did a plausible imitation of a gaping fish before managing to stammer out his permission amidst many a 'my lord' and 'honoured sir'.

Edris plucked the boy from the ground with a single deft sweep and set him in front of his saddle. Hael clung tightly to the twin saddle-horns, speechless with delight, smelling leather and steel and warrior's sweat. Edris thought it likely as not they'd find nothing but shadows and a boy's overactive imagination, but if he had to spend the rest of his life under the hands of such a father, then at least he'd have the consolation of knowing that the man had seen his boy riding with one of the warband – and if that stayed his hand by the measure of only one bruise, well then maybe that was noble enough work for a warrior instead.

10
HOLDA'S SONG

The caral set off again shortly after dawn, bearing three extra – and very unexpected – passengers. Drovers yoked up a half-strength team of their prized red oxen and the clan held its collective breath as the mighty-shouldered beasts stamped and strained, their breath steaming like pistons. The mud of the road was churned up in great gouts as their hooves fought for traction, and, inch by agonising inch, the massive many-tiered structure began to roll forward.

Amongst the wrights there was much anxious muttering and peering at axles, shafts and bearings, but as the caral picked up a ponderous speed, the new wheel turned smoothly, and the looms in the Lower Gallery awoke to life once more.

Satisfied with the repairs, Lady Holda ordered the remaining oxen to be yoked, the sails unfurled, and the caral resumed its rumbling northward course along the wide-rutted wake left by the rest of the nation. They had lost a day, but that could not be helped. They would not get the most favoured trades this year at the Overwinter Market, but the quality of their clothwork would remain unstintingly high as a matter of pride, and the careful thrift of previous years would hopefully mean little more than a few tightened belts.

To say that the Dobunni would find any excuse for revelry was an exaggeration, but not by much. Celebrations were brief, though full-throated. Lady Holda presented the wheelwright with a surcoat of the finest wool worked in intricate detail by her own hands, and a keg of dark valley ale to his prentices, who lingered no longer than propriety required before disappearing with it and a crowd of giggling wiever-girls down into the axle-hold, from which there issued such a din of carousal that some wondered if another wheel hadn't fallen off.

For the moment, the three otherworldly strangers in their midst were almost completely forgotten about. This was not surprising; they were unimpressive invaders.

The wild rumours which had spread like waves in plainsgrass from the drover boy's excitable babbling – everything from an attack by cattle-raiders to the very opening of the demon-infested pits of Annwn itself – were dispelled the moment that the strangers were brought in by Edris. Far from being threatening, and possibly even infernal beings, they looked pale and undernourished; one was plainly witless and had to be led everywhere by the other two. They were shorter than the smallest Dobunni by at least a head, upon which their hair was cropped like criminals. Most shocking to a wiever clan – for whom the quality of their garments was not just livelihood but art, identity and pride – was the filthy and ragged state of their clothing. Plainly, these were diminished creatures more deserving of pity than fear, notwithstanding the impossibility of their appearance in this wide expanse of uninhabited country.

Impossible or not, decreed Lady Holda, they were here and must be dealt with according to the traditions of hospitality observed by all the caral nations. For what use was tradition if not as a guide in extraordinary circumstances such as this? It was said that the measure of a clan-mother's generosity lay in how she treated not the richest and most powerful nobleman, but the meanest beggar – from whom there was nothing to gain but the honour of demonstrating her largesse.

Bex and Ted were therefore surprised, after being kept at swordpoint for an hour while their fate was debated in a language they couldn't understand, to find themselves ushered into a large, bright ambassadorial cabin on the caral's topmost tier.

***

To Ted's schoolboy imagination, fed only by dusty pre-war copies of Mallory and T.H.White in Holly End's tiny parish schoolhouse, it looked like the inside of a medieval pavilion. It reminded Bex of a yurt where she'd crashed for a night at her first Reading Festival; it had the same TARDIS-like sense of light and room in a confined space – but thankfully without the vomiting hippies.

The guest chamber was kept for the enjoyment of trading representatives from other clans and the occasional Settled merchant, and so was a showpiece of the clan's craft. Rugs of every shape and texture patchworked the floor around furniture that was just as lavishly carved and upholstered. The walls and ceiling were canopied in tapestries and long yards of richly embroidered cloth, except where windows looked forward over the rolling landscape and were screened with the thinnest gauze, which admitted the view but neither insects nor road-dust. Despite this, it wasn't cold; light and warmth came from many brass lamps, in the light of which the hangings scintillated with gold thread and semi-precious stones.

'Jeez,' murmured Bex to Ted, gazing around at the ostentation. 'Enemy *camp* or what.'

Ted had already found the food.

There were few vegetables and only dried fruit this close to the end of the road, but he found broad slices of unleavened bread, small triangular pastries and a stew thick with gravy, sweetly spiced.

'I wouldn't touch that,' she warned.

Ted chewed defiantly without replying. Now she was just being ridiculous.

'Seriously. You don't know; it could be poisonous. We don't know anything about this place. They could be about to...'

But Ted's eyes were suddenly bulging. He dropped the bread and fell to his knees, clawing at his throat and making hideous dry choking noises. She leapt forward with a cry of alarm, but his choking turned into giggles of laughter as he rocked onto his backside, grinning at her. 'It's fine,' he said around his mouthful. 'You should try some.'

'You little *shit*! That wasn't funny!'

'Yes it was. *You* should stop being so suspicious. Not everybody's out to get you, you know.'

'Yeah, well, when I've *met* everybody I'll...' She stopped. Sniffed. 'Wait a minute. What's that?' She picked at the food dubiously, then with rising astonishment and delight. 'That's not possible.' She tore off a hunk of bread and scooped a mouthful of the stew, suddenly laughing around it. 'No way!'

'Told you it wasn't that bad.'

'Not that bad?!' And then she did something which surprised him more than anything else she'd done in the brief time he'd known her: she flung her arms around his neck and hugged him like a python. He blushed furiously. 'Ted, this is more than 'not bad'. It's only a bloody korma!'

'...?...'

'It's a lamb korma, I swear!' She made a rapid, disbelieving inventory of the dishes. 'We've got naan bread, some kind of samosa there; that's – yum – yep, that's mango chutney or as near as. All we need are the poppadoms and lager and a bunch of drunk rugby players. Who *are* these people? Oh my god.' She suddenly remembered the last moments on the stairs of Moon Grove. 'It was the last thing before he left; Stirch asked him to bring back a...' but she couldn't finish, because she was choked up by something very different from naan bread.

She went to the curtained alcove where Andy had been laid upon a wide, low bed, surrounded by pillows and bolsters to prevent him from falling off with the caral's movement. She brushed some stray hair away from his eyes. 'Thank you,' she whispered. 'I don't know how you did this or where you are, but thank you.' She planted a kiss on his lips, which Ted thought lingered a little too long for simple gratitude.

They slept well into the next day and so missed the celebrations as the caral resumed its slow journey north across the plains.

***

Despite the small size of the community following the caral, it took Ted a surprisingly long time to find the drover boy. He discovered that the herds-families drove their cattle and sheep far from the broad swath of the heavily-trampled road, in the long plainsgrass sometimes over a mile distant – and in the winter, even further than that.

It was a relief to get out and stretch his legs. More than a relief; it was a revelation, because this land was unimaginably vast, far beyond his experience. Ted's earliest – and in fact *only* – memories were of Holly End. Of restrictions, and encirclement, the limits of his horizon bounded quite literally by the Rimwoods and the Spinny at their heart. He could walk the limits of his world in under a day. Every square yard was known: every tree, building, hedgerow and stone. There were no surprises, and the fun of exploration was quickly exhausted.

But *here*.

It just seemed to stretch on forever. They were travelling across a wide, shallow vale of grass and scattered woodland towards a range of low hills far to the north, under an azure sky so massive that when he looked straight up, it filled his entire field of vision and made him feel like he was flying.

There was no evidence of human habitation anywhere, except for the road and the large smudge on it a day distant, where the rest of their people had gone on ahead. The idea that you could travel, and travel, and keep on travelling for days on end without having to turn aside or turn back was both thrilling and terrifying. It was too much for him to fit in his head for very long at a time, so he reined his attention in and focussed on finding the drover boy.

Another odd thing was that wherever he went amongst the trailing carts and wagons, the people saluted him with a closed fist to the forehead, as if doffing invisible caps. As if he were somebody important. At a loss to explain otherwise, he simply smiled, nodded politely, and moved on.

He found the drover boy in charge of a small group of cows and their calves – shaggy, dark-haired beasts of some Highland breed, with blunt noses and straggling brows which gave them permanently bad-tempered expressions. The boy was wearing a scowl fit to match as he stomped along behind them, whacking at the grass with a stick. When he saw Ted, his eyes widened with alarm, and he made the same salute.

'No, please don't. It's fine, honestly,' he said, eager to reassure. 'I'm Ted.' He pointed to himself. '*Ted.*'

The boy imitated him. 'Hael.'

'Hael. That's a funny name. Pleased to meet you.' Ted stuck out his hand.

Hael was filled with dismay. There was only one possible reason why the stranger could be holding his hand out, and he only had one thing worth giving. From within his jerkin he drew out the leather pouch and, with deep resignation, handed it over. Ted peered inside. It was full of marbles. Crude ones, to be sure, nowhere near spherical, but obviously smoothed and polished with loving care – the sort of treasure only another boy could truly understand the worth of.

'No,' he said firmly, pressing them back. 'That's not what I meant.' He grasped Hael's right hand, placed it in his own, and shook vigorously. 'See? Pleased to meet you.'

Hael looked surprised, confused, and then grinned widely, pumping Ted's arm until he thought it might fall off.

'I'm the one who should be giving you something,' he continued. 'I'm sorry if we scared you last night. I think we made you lose a calf. My father's a farmer too, so I know how bad that sort of thing is. Once I left a gate open, and all the sheep got out, and he made me bring them all back in one by one, on my own. I was only eight. It took me the whole night, and I had to use my torch. Mother wanted to come out and help me, but he said, "No! The boy must learn!" And he still made me go to school the next day.'

Hael understood not a single word of this, but nevertheless recognised the sound of a Da being impersonated, and laughed.

'I thought you might be hungry,' Ted went on, 'so I brought this.' From his satchel he produced some of the spicy pasties and a big piece of the sweet flatbread which Bex had called 'Narnia' bread, which obviously must have been her idea of a joke. 'Call it a peace offering. No hard feelings?'

From the way Hael tore into the food, it appeared there weren't.

They ate as they walked together in companionable silence. Hael shared a skin of what Ted assumed was water, but which turned out to be slightly fizzy and tasted of sloe berries. At one point something small and furry darted away from them into the undergrowth, and, wondering whether this world had rabbits, Ted began to collect small stones for ammunition. When Hael asked him what he was doing, Ted showed him the slingshot with an evil grin and fired at the rump of a dopey old cow which had been slowing them down by stopping to graze every dozen yards. She gave an indignant bellow like an elderly matriarch and trotted ahead, scowling back at him through her shaggy brows as if to say 'Young *man*!' Hael hooted with laughter.

'Here. Have a go.'

As he passed the weapon over, Ted began to get an inkling of how much human experience is universal, and of the things that transcend barriers of language or even the walls of reality itself: hunger, friendship, and the gleam in the eye of a small boy armed with a slingshot.

***

To Bruna fell the honour of attending the strangers' needs. The fact that she even considered it an honour where most other wieve-maidens of her rank would have seen it as an insult was the very reason for her appointment in the first place.

Unsure of what was customary for people of their kind to wear, she brought a little of everything and did a creditable job of suppressing her mirth when Bex chose an outlandish combination of drover's boots, wiever's waistcoat and warrior's tartan britches. She brought soap that smelled of fresh grass and copper basins of hot water – the best she could do short of a proper bath, what with the drofcaral being a day distant – along with towels, brushes and combs.

She also brought the chirurgeon, accompanied by his wide-eyed prentice lugging a large apothecary's chest, and one of the tallest women Bex had ever seen in her life. Bruna was able to explain very basically that this was Holda – queen or matriarch or ring-master of this travelling circus. She carried the figure and grace of a much younger woman, even though the hair which hung far down her back in a long braid clasped with gold barettes was iron-silver in colour. She wore a dress of plain, snow-white linen over which was a long sleeveless mantle embroidered in gold with flowers and curvilinear knotwork. Only her hands, when she reached out to lay one affectionately on Bruna's head, really showed her age; they were deeply lined and calloused, the hands of a woman who has worked long at many hard and thankless tasks. Her eyes glittered with a wry intelligence, and when she turned their regard towards Bex, she felt that for the first time in her life someone was really *looking* at her.

Through a combination of simple sign language and educated guesswork Holda was able to introduce herself and find out the name of the chirurgeon's new patient. Beyond that, all she could do was hope that the girl who called herself 'Bex' was as intelligent as she looked and didn't misinterpret what was about to happen.

There was much excited discussion between the chirurgeon and his prentice when they bared Andy and saw that his numerous burns and bites were already beginning to heal cleanly. It seemed to confirm something that they had already suspected, and Bex wondered how advanced their medical knowledge was, for all that they looked like a pair of rejects from Hogwarts.

From the heavy wooden chest, they produced a carefully-wrapped collection of what seemed to be gold and copper jewellery: armbands, rings, torcs and brooches, each of which was an ornate latticework of curvilinear filigree set with pieces of highly-polished yellow quartz. If the ancient Celts or Mayans had ever invented electronic circuitry, she thought, this was what it would look like. They proceeded to fasten them all over Andy's body, but she became alarmed when some were pinned to his skin.

'What are those things?' she demanded. 'What are you going to do to him?'

Lady Holda spoke sharply to the chirurgeon, who managed to draw Bex away to the other side of the room. As *dama* of her caral, she was more than just a political leader or skilled artisan. There were powers over the wyrd which were hers to exercise by both right and responsibility. The next part of the sounding ritual was her prerogative, and it demanded her full attention.

Taking a moment or two to compose herself, she began to sing – though it was not singing as Bex understood it.

There was no melody, rhythm, or even discernible words (not that she would have understood them anyway); it was a long exploratory meandering up and down the scale, varying in tempo and volume apparently at random. In response to the song, the pieces of quartz began to glow – very faintly, with irregular, flickering colours. She changed the song in dozens of permutations, and it seemed to Bex that Holda was trying to chase those glowing motes, to pin them down and strengthen them, but for every one that brightened and stabilised, half a dozen others flickered at the edge of extinction. She persevered, though it was clear that the effort was taking its toll; sweat beaded her brow above clenched eyes, and several times Bruna had to step in to physically support her as she swayed. When she finally abandoned the song, she was near collapse, and the room was as hot as a sauna.

Bruna eased her into a chair as the chirurgeon and his prentice carefully removed the devices from Andy's body.

'Well?' she said impatiently. 'What? Did it work? Did you find him?'

Wearily, Lady Holda mimed two fingers walking away from her head and out into an open-palmed shrug. She wore an expression of helpless sympathy, which Bex thought must be universal amongst healers of every time and world.

The Lady's meaning was clear: Andy was lost, and he was never coming back. And without him, she was never going home.

***

The others had cleared away their things and disappeared – even Ted had gone exploring – but Bex lingered by Andy's bedside.

'You know,' she said, smoothing his bedclothes, 'this would be a lot easier if you were on a machine. Oh don't look so shocked,' she chided his completely blank expression. 'Like you weren't thinking it too.' She mimicked a flatline tone, and then sighed heavily. 'Humourless sod.' The shallow rise and fall of his chest was lost in the caral's gentle sway, and outside she heard distant calls and laughter. She hoped Ted wasn't getting into trouble.

'The thing is,' she continued, 'I think I did the right thing. I came after you. Was that right? He was killing you – it had to be the right thing to do. It's just that…' she swallowed hard. 'It's just that we're stuck here now, and I think Barber's dead, but what if he isn't? What if he's just going to carry on doing whatever it was he had planned, only now there's nobody who knows or can stop him?

'Plus, I've got one of the bloody Famous Five running around after me now too. How can I be responsible for looking after a twelve-year old kid? I didn't bring him here; it was all an accident! It's not fair!' Her flare of indignation subsided as quickly as it came. They were fewer these days and harder to sustain.

'The honest to god truth is that I'm afraid I've really fucked things up badly this time, and for once I can't run away.'

She unhooked the brass pendant from around her neck – the one which Walter had tried to give Andy – and tied it from the lamp which hung over his bed, so that it flashed and spun above his face. 'I don't think I'm the best person to look after this anymore,' she said. 'You were wrong.'

She left quietly and without looking back, and in so doing failed to see his eyes as they moved to follow the pendant's swaying motion.

11
PROOF

For Andy, the return to consciousness was like the re-forming of scattered droplets of mercury. Quicksilver flecks of awareness splashed across a hundred worlds ran together in fragmentary snatches of sound, taste and smell. They fought for coherence and lost it, spraying apart and back again – each time slightly more vivid than the last – eventually forming thread-thin trickles of thought which jumbled together in a blur, like the white noise of a city at night or the whine of blood in the ears.

Just above that, the rumbling creak of wooden movement. Voices, distant: calls and laughter. Closer: someone bustling nearby. A woman singing softly to herself.

Sight returned to his already-open eyes. A small brass wheel glittered and twisted above him, which he seemed to recognise from somewhere. Was it this that had called him back? Had he called *himself* back? Back to where? Where was he?

Who was he?

There was a dream of himself as a boy, lying much the same as he was now, looking up at the same bright talisman, and a nightmare vision of grey stones socketed in flesh. He knew now that this was not entirely a dream but was in part memory, but this brought its own uncertainty: because what if he were still that boy, dreaming himself forward into the fantasy of being a man? Two points at each end of a line that was his life from earliest memory to latest; or maybe the same point overlapping – a circle, not a line. A big, gaudy carousel with painted faces rising and falling. Except that he didn't have to ride it anymore because he was... because he was...

'Unfixed.'

The dark-haired girl who was rearranging things at the foot of the bed looked up in surprise at the sound of his voice.

'Hello,' he croaked, and tried to smile.

She gave a small shriek and fled.

Still got the old magic, he thought, but fell asleep again before he could appreciate the irony of it.

***

Bex's head felt like it was churning with bilge-water, the sloshing filth of a deep-keeled ship rolling in storm-wracked seas. It was an entirely familiar sensation, and one for which she had a tried and tested remedy.

There was no door as such to lock, but she knotted the bottom corners of her berth's curtain to the legs of a low table so that no-one could lift it aside and barge in. Not that anybody would, but the privacy was for herself, not from other people, and that was an important distinction to make. She especially didn't want Ted to see this.

She was relieved to find that her hobby knife with its red plastic handle was still in the rucksack and hadn't been lost in all the mad dashing about of the last few days. She could have used anything – a knife from one of the platters outside, or a bit of broken crockery – but the knife was an old friend and a small piece of home. She remembered using it for the first time up in her bedroom while Mum and Shithead Dave went for each other like hacksaws downstairs because Mum thought he'd been up in little Becky's room again, but of course he hadn't, he couldn't have been, could he, good old Dave, everybody's mate?

300

The bandages that Rosey had put on were a bit grubby by now, but he'd done a good job, and the flesh underneath was clean. The newest cuts looked a bit red, but there wasn't any sign of infection. All that remained of the others was a row of thin white scars, like tally marks on a prison wall, counting off the days of a life sentence with no hope of time off for good behaviour. *Bad girl,* he'd said, good old Dave, when he'd finished. *You know what happens to bad girls, don't you?* Whatever he thought it was, she bet it didn't include getting slashed by a red plastic craft knife. The look on his face.

It didn't stop him from being right, though. She *was* bad. Somewhere deep down, something essential inside her was broken, and it made everything she did broken too. She could fix it with her little knife – it was only a temporary fix, but it was all she had.

She found a clear space in the corrugation of white scar tissue, but as she put the tip of the blade to it, a small drop of oily black fluid oozed out of one pore.

She stared at it.

It was joined by another, and yet another, and still more, seeping out of her skin like beads of condensation forming on a mirror – and they stung. They stung like an absolute bitch, almost as bad as the cut would have done. They grew until they ran into each other and became thin trickles down her left forearm – and then she felt her right arm growing wet in its sleeve, which she rolled up and saw that the same thing was happening there too.

Where it dripped, it left smoking scorch-marks on the bedspread. That was what galvanised her into action. Not wanting to avoid the damage, but the explanation for it. Her first instinct as a self-harmer – to hide the act itself – shook her out of dumbfounded surprise. She cupped her hands together and tilted her arms forward so that it, whatever it was, ran into the bowl of her palms instead of the floor. It burned like acid but without leaving a mark, and it was only as it began to collect into a viscous black puddle that she realised that it stank too.

'Oh this is just charming, isn't it?'

Walter would have called it *sha*, life energy poisoned from being twisted out of its true course for too long. She remembered seeing it in the ley just before it hit them: twisting black streamers fouling the blue, like blood in water, the accumulated poison of Barber's corruption. *I healed it, though,* she thought with savage pride. Whatever the result, whether Andy died or she and Ted were lost here forever, there would be that. *I set it back on its true course. I did something good. One thing at least.*

As if responding to her train of thought, the flow of *sha* began to ease.

Had the ley done this to her? Had that tormented dragon-line of earthpower resonated with something inside her or knocked it loose? Or woken it up?

Didn't matter. Bollocks to Walter and his mystical hippy mumblings. This was real. It had come out of her flesh and was pooled in her cupped hands, and it was real. It wasn't *sha* – it was her pain. This was what had been inside her all along. Before, she'd let it out in her blood, and the only difference now was that the process had been somehow distilled. Refined.

She found a chamberpot under the bed and emptied her hands. The smoking black vitriol evaporated quickly once out of contact with her skin, leaving the glaze pitted and scorched, and she found that the need to cut herself had disappeared along with it. She put away her little first aid kit and slowly slid the craft-knife's blade back into its red plastic handle.

***

An acrid, ammonia-like stench jerked Andy out of sleep, and he twisted awake, sputtering. Through tears and the sudden shock of his eyes opening fully for the first time in nearly two days, it seemed for a moment that three shining figures stood over him. The central and tallest of them approached, saying 'We know that you can understand us. Do not be afraid.' As he blinked his eyes clear, the shape resolved into a perfectly normal-looking human woman, but even so, in their conversations over the next few days, he would always have that impression of brightness hidden beneath the surface of her skin.

She was flanked on one side by a beak-nosed man wearing a variety of amulets and arcane devices around his neck, and on the other by a second man who was clearly some kind of military commander, to judge from his tabard-style tunic and the sword at his side. His heavily-scarred forearms were crossed over a barrel chest, and every line of his body seemed to frown thunderously.

He tried to reply and suffered an apocalyptic sneezing attack which made his already dry throat feel like it had just been sandpapered. 'Can I...?' he swallowed. Grimaced. 'Water?'

The younger, dark-haired girl from before came with a cup. She helped him sit up to drink, and in the touch of her hand he became aware that *(Bruna her name is Bruna she is wiever-maiden to the Lady and dutiful it is an honour to be given the care of guests even though)* somehow he had hurt her. He couldn't imagine how. There was a defiance in the way she tended to him, as if daring him or readying herself for something painful. *What have I done now?*

All of this was driven out of his head when he tried to sit up and discovered the weight of the chirurgeon's devices attached to his body. Nurse Barton's face loomed in his memory, her scream and her mutilated hand, and he had a sudden horrible suspicion about what might have happened while he'd been unconscious and why Bruna was so wary of him. Alarmed, he started to pluck at the nearest device – a sun-rayed medallion gripping the skin above his heart chakra with dozens of tiny claws – and the chirurgeon jumped forward to stop him. 'You must not do this!' he admonished. 'It is perfectly safe. Please…'

'No,' he grunted, digging with his fingers. 'You don't understand what's going to happen if you leave these things in me.'

'You are safe here, trust me. Whatever attacked you in your realm is not here. But you are not yet fully…'

'It's not me, it's you lot who aren't safe.' The thing came half free, and a blue-white spark burnt his fingers.

'Andrew.' Lady Holda's voice was low but pitched with an authority which made him pause. The way she had pronounced his name had sounded more like *Indra*. 'You imperil yourself and my people with your actions. Please do not force me to treat you as a threat. It would grieve me to have to do so.'

'Dama,' the scarred warrior growled, 'he is already a threat. All three of them were, from the moment they arrived.'

'What my chirurgeon is trying to tell you,' she continued, as if he hadn't spoken, 'is that you are not yet fully restored to yourself. Your mind is still fragmented, and your memory is incomplete. You are not aware that your partial recovery has already caused… difficulty.'

As if simply saying it were enough to make it so, he caught the trailing ends of drifting memories: of fitting uncontrollably as the pieces of his consciousness tumbled together, his unfixed *ch'i* spasming in response, bright ribbons of energy arcing out into the room. He saw scorch-marks on the curtains and bedclothes and a bandage on Bruna's forearm. It hadn't been *Hello*, he realised now. It had been *Help me*.

'The augurs attached to your skin are providing you with the stability which you lack,' said the chirurgeon, readjusting the device. Andy felt faintly sick as he watched the little claws dig into his chest, but didn't interfere again. 'We do not know how this can be. It is as if you possess no bones and yet are still able to walk.'

'Never mind that,' snorted the warrior. 'Why don't we start with why your friends claim to not speak a word of our language, but you're happy to. Either they are lying or you are wyrd-touched. Which is it?'

Andy looked from one to the other in utter confusion. If he expected the Lady to intercede and rein in the man's belligerence, based on his first impression that she was the least bizarre of them and that the other two deferred to her, he was mistaken. She regarded him coolly, waiting for his reply, as if there were nothing untoward about interrogating half-conscious invalids. The only reason he knew his own name was because she'd used it a moment ago. 'I have no idea what you're talking about,' he protested. 'What friends? I'm here on my own.' *Aren't I?*

'As I said,' the chirurgeon entreated the Lady, 'it is too soon…'

There was a sudden commotion outside the room. Another female voice raised high in protest, demanding to be let in, using language as colourful as the fabrics surrounding him. Beyond the curtained doorway he could make out struggling movement as the guard *(they set a guard on me?)* attempted to prevent someone a lot smaller but extremely determined from getting in.

'That damned girl…' The soldier turned for the door.

'Iaran, wait,' commanded the Lady. 'Allow her in. It may be that her presence will hasten his recovery.'

The chirurgeon was just as unhappy with this as Iaran. 'Dama, it may also be that the sudden shock splinters his mind again, and with no hope of recovery this time.'

'Nevertheless,' was her sole reply.

The curtains parted, and Bex flew across the room without a glance to anyone, flinging her arms around Andy's neck. 'They wouldn't let me see you!' she gasped. 'Everybody suddenly started running around like headless chickens, and I could hear you calling out – things that didn't make any sense

– but they wouldn't let me in! Are you okay? Are you hurt?' Then she seemed to realise what she was doing – hugging him hard enough to make his eyes bulge – because she abruptly let go and stepped back apace. 'And what exactly have you been doing for the last two bloody days, anyway?'

He gave her a small, embarrassed smile. 'I'm sorry,' he said. 'I know I should know you, but…' He shrugged.

'No,' she whispered, stricken. 'Don't you dare.'

'I'm sure it will all come back to m…'

'Nonono-no *no* NO NO!' she screamed, and she was on him again, but this time she was pushing and punching and slapping him, with tears streaming down her cheeks, and the breath of her denial hot in his face. After everything else, to have got him back only to find this – how much more was she supposed to take?

Iaran peeled her off him, and the fight simply drained out of her, leaving her limp and sobbing. 'Dama,' he asked, holding the girl at arms' length with distaste, 'how much longer do you propose for this charade to continue?'

'Have a care of her, Captain,' the Lady answered him. 'She is out of her realm – confused, afraid. This is to be expected.' All the same, she was disappointed at the outcome, even making allowances for what manner of creatures they were and where they had come from.

She ordered the others to leave and sat alone with Andy while the augurs did their job.

'You must not blame him, either,' she said. 'He is a soldier. It is in his nature to suspect everyone and everything. You should understand that your kind are not unknown to us, and on those rare occasions where you have strayed into our world, you have acted with fear and aggression, so it is not surprising that he considers you to be little more than animals. Are you anything more? Will you be only what the tales of others have made you, or do you have the strength to be greater? Tell me now everything about yourself and how you came to be here.'

So he did, and he found that the gaps, where they came, filled themselves. By the time he'd told his tale, evening had fallen, and the last of the augurs had been removed, as if he'd made himself whole again in the telling.

He dressed, ate, and went in search of Bex.

***

He found her on the caral's roof deck, under a sky so ablaze with stars that for a moment it took his breath away. The great vehicle had stopped, having made good ground on the rest of the Nation but still unable to chance the road in darkness, and several of the smaller roof-sails were left unfurled as shelter against the biting night wind. Bex and Ted were sitting together in the lee of one of these, swathed in thick robes and playing cards with a pack which had presumably come out of her bottomless rucksack of odds and sods. A scattering of coins – some pre-decimal – sweets, and small, coloured stones lay in piles between them. It appeared that she was teaching him poker.

'Deal me in?' he said.

Her eyes, when she looked up at him, were guarded. 'Depends.'

'On what?'

'On whether or not you're completely batshit. On…' Her voice was suddenly thick, as if the words were fighting each other in her throat. When the battle was won, what emerged was little more than a whisper. 'On whether we're going home. Or not.'

'We are. We most definitely are.'

'Prove it,' she demanded tightly, fixing him with such intensity that he could see coils of it wrapping themselves about him like pythons. 'Prove to me that I'm not stuck here for the rest of my life. That our homes didn't get wiped out for nothing. That this is not all some kind of cosmic-sized fuck-up. I mean, I'm basically a pretty resourceful gal, and you know, if this is it, then this is it, and I'll find a way to get by – but not with you. I don't think I could stand being here with you like that: waiting for some kind of miracle. Hoping for… no. I'd rather just get on with getting on. So you want in, you damn well *prove* it to me.'

He thought of a dozen things to say, knowing that none of them would make any difference. Bex had heard every variation on the theme of empty promises in her time on the streets and, no doubt, long before that. Laura would have told him that in the end it was really only actions which carried weight, and she'd have been right. Even Clarke – fat, complacent git that he was – had a point with his pet mantra of 'there's no profit margin in window-shopping lads; a sale is a sale'. But these were, in the Lady Holda's words, nothing more than the tales that other people had made of him. After Holly End, he knew now not just who he was but *what* he was, and more importantly what he could do. There'd be time enough to explain it all, but right now he simply had to sell it.

Putting out his right hand, he *unfixed* it, and felt through the skins of the worlds which lay between their current realm and home (there were so many of them; had they really travelled so far?) until he found something which felt like it would do for proof.

Bex and Ted gaped in amazement as he withdrew his fist from the apparently empty air and opened it to reveal a cupped palmful of clean, white snow.

'Not even Barber can do that,' he said. 'We're going home, and we're going to put a stop to him. I swear.'

PART FOUR: TOWER

1

ON THE OUTER CIRCLE

Rosey set out in the dark of a midwinter morning to do battle against arcane forces beyond his comprehension, armed only with a homemade map, a thermos of tea, and his bus pass.

He'd sellotaped together the photocopied pages of Bex's Birmingham A-to-Z, working late into the night after an exhausting drive back from Aston-sub-Edge, though it wasn't the drive which had kept him awake so much as the mental shockwaves which kept bouncing from one wall of his skull to the other. Having seen the way the landscape had unfolded when she'd jammed that stake into the hollow of the missing Kiftsgate Stone, it was impossible for him to simply walk away from all of this. It occurred to him that whatever she'd been looking for wasn't likely to be found flicking piecemeal through its pages, so he'd cleared a space on his lounge floor, laid them out like a gigantic jigsaw puzzle and stood back.

And then he saw it: the markings that her missing friend Dodd had drawn – the ones that looked a bit like astrological symbols – formed a rough circle approximately four miles in radius around the city centre.

Moreover, they described a very particular route, one which he doubted would have been recognised by a homeless teenager whose life was geared around shortcuts and straight lines. It was the sort of slow, meandering route used by schoolchildren and pensioners, and occasionally by pensioned-off ex-policemen who couldn't drive anymore but needed to attend physio clinics and spinal scans every few months. It was, of all things, the legendary Number Eleven Outer Circle bus route.

He'd googled it to be certain. It was one of the city's oldest, having come into service in 1923, when the West Midlands was not much more than a loose collection of villages. It was apparently so picturesque that holiday-makers used to spend day-trips on it. At twenty-six miles in length, it was the longest urban bus route in Europe, taking just over two hours to complete. People who did so were called 'all-rounders' and one chap had even organised an 11-hour marathon on it in celebration. Poems had been written about it. It passed more than two hundred schools, forty pubs and six hospitals – not to mention the childhood homes of JRR Tolkien and WH Auden – and Rosey had absolutely no idea why any of this was significant. What had any of it got to do with ley lines? Why would Barber choose to map out the reconfigured topography of a fragmented magical landscape onto a *bus route*? Rosey suspected that it was nothing more perverse than the reason he'd chosen to heal his back: because it simply amused him to do so.

What mattered was that he do something with the knowledge.

Two and a half hours later, he was now officially an All-Rounder. He had also discovered with a weary lack of surprise that every point marked on Dodd's map marked a location which had something to do with the name 'Jerusalem'. Mostly they were construction sites owned by a development company called Jerusalem Industries, but there was also an Arabic 'Jerusalem Travel Agency', a 'New Jerusalem Christian Bookshop', and even a Jerry Salem Hair Salon.

'Okay, now you're just taking the piss,' he said when he saw that last one.

It's so deliciously perverse, he heard Barber say, as if in reply. So delicious that he had apparently spent god-only-knew how much money and pulled a lot of strings over a very long time to acquire these properties. The amount of forethought and planning that it implied – not to mention the resources and connections he must have – was staggering. Rosey spent his first orbit of the Outer Circle simply identifying these locations, and as the bus came back around to where he'd got on at Bearwood, he prepared to spend the rest of this short day investigating them in closer detail. He felt the familiar old satisfaction of seeing the pieces of somebody else's puzzle begin to fall into place. Barber had overreached himself; there was no hiding this kind of paper trail.

Someone sat down heavily next to him. Right next to him on an otherwise empty top deck. Every instinct in his body began screaming at once, but before he could do anything about it a gnarled hand (*almost a claw, really*, he thought, *will you look at that*) clamped down on his shoulder and shoved him back in his seat.

'Hello, policeman,' said Carling.

***

Andy sat on the caral's roof deck and explained everything.

'I know what Barber is planning,' he said simply. 'All of it. When he got into my head and tried to kill me, I got into *his*, because that's how it works. There's no such thing as a one-way connection. I think he knew that, but he was prepared to take the risk anyway, because he though he was strong enough to kill me. He had no idea that I'm unfixed and that his power couldn't even touch me.' He laughed a little. 'Come to that, neither did I.'

'Us being here isn't an accident. There are no such things as accidents or coincidences. There's only Pattern. We're here because I needed somewhere as safe and as far away as possible to rest and get myself together; I found this place in Barber's memories, and it was simple enough to ride the ley here.

'Yes,' he said, answering Bex's look of sudden surprise, 'Barber has been here before us. When he first escaped Holly End, he had no idea of the forces he was working with, and he simply got lost – went wandering in a lot of strange places before he found his way back again.

'The Dobunni, or at least the race of people that the Dobunni belong to, are already quite advanced in their knowledge of what they call the 'telluric sciences'. In our world, we started to get a basic idea when we cottoned on to electricity and magnetism, but since then we've dead-ended in our obsession with all things electrical, and it's really only part of a very big picture. Imagine a caveman finding a flute. He discovers that it's a hollow tube and makes an excellent blowgun, and from then on all he ever uses it for is hunting. It works fine, but sort of misses the point a bit, you know?'

'Actually,' interrupted Ted, 'a flute would be useless as a blowgun because all the holes would...'

'Ted?' said Bex sweetly.

'Yes?'

'Shut up, dear.'

'Yes. Right. Sorry.'

Andy continued. 'Barber was here for years, living with them, learning from them. At first it was purely for the purpose of getting home, but then, when he discovered the time dilation effects which operate between the worlds, he realised that he he a had a little bit more luxury to explore. A short six-month absence at home could afford him decades here in which to learn their science, and then return to put that knowledge into practice in a little experimental bubble of time which had hardly changed at all. How could he resist?

'And the Dobunni were only too happy to teach him. They were flattered, and I think amused. The caveman decides he wants to learn how to play the flute. So they taught him everything that he was capable of learning – I don't think it occurred to them for a second that he would turn any of it to destructive purposes. If you taught a skavag how to light a fire, you'd hardly imagine that it would be able to build an atomic bomb.'

'Yes, but we're not skavags,' Bex protested with an expression of distaste.

'We are to the Dobunni. You know we have seven energy chakras running down our bodies from crown to crotch? The sources of all our physical, mental and spiritual power? They have *twelve*.'

'Well whoop-de-doo for them.'

'Our world isn't on the surface of the Cosmic Onion. We're probably not even halfway up. There's an infinite number of worlds above and below us; places where even the Dobunni are like apes, and the skavags are like angels.

'The point being that whatever he learned here, it gave birth to an ambition much greater than just playing Cold War silly buggers. He'd never been particularly bothered about rescuing Holly End in the first place, mind you. He hadn't even wanted people there at all – but something about the experiments wouldn't work without the interaction of human beings. We know why now, of course.'

'We?' Bex looked at him suspiciously, but he was ploughing on without really listening to her.

'It's because earth-leys and acupuncture meridians are all part of the same system. We are the world writ small; it is us writ large, and not in some hippy bullshit way but in actual, measurable terms. The only difference between something like Stonehenge and the human heart chakra is one of scale, you see?'

'I see that you're getting a bit over-excited. Why don't you calm down a bit and tell us what Barber's big plan is.'

'But I can see it all!' Andy was grinning the kind of feverish, jouncing grin which she'd seen on the faces of crack-heads. His eyes were wide, and his pupils very dark. 'I can see everything! The Pattern! I understand how it all fits together!'

'*Andy!*' She used her voice like a slap, and with what seemed to be a great effort his attention returned to the here and now. 'Focus! What is he planning to do?'

'It's nearly finished.' His voice was hushed now, low and scared. 'He's been setting it up for nearly fifty years. The disappearances, the closures – they're just the finishing touches. The final adjustments. Calibration before the big switch-on.'

She wanted to really slap him this time, but something about his fear was infectious, and she stayed silent. She was suddenly very aware of the distant murmur of voices drifting up with woodsmoke from the campfires below – voices talking in a language which nobody in her world had ever heard before – and of the clear sky above, blazing with stars beneath which they were utterly insignificant. The prospects of either returning home or tackling Barber seemed absurd.

'Holly End was just a test,' continued Andy. 'A prototype, to see if the mechanism works. What he's got planned now is the real deal – it's an absolute killer, you might say. It's going to make what happened to Ted's home look like a dolls' tea party.

'I'm unfixed, okay? The *ch'i* meridians of my body aren't tied to their proper nerve clusters in the same way as everybody else. It's like, imagine the electrical wiring of a house, only the wires and plugs aren't fixed in the walls where they should be; they can be moved and reconnected and made to do weird stuff. I don't know why. In all probability, I should be dead. I don't know if it's what Barber intended when he... when I was a kid, or if it's just a crazy, random happenstance. Either way, it explains how I can open Narrows that have been closed and see auras and the thing with needles – and everything, basically.

'But I think it also makes it harder for me to *hang on*, so to speak, when things get stressful. There's not much to anchor me. So when that ley hit us it did more than just throw me physically, it also splattered my mind across dozens, maybe even hundreds of worlds. It's taken a long time to come back to myself, bit by bit, bringing back little snippets from all up and down the Cosmic Onion, and here's a really weird thing… by the way, what was the date when you found Holly End?'

'Why?'

'It'll make sense, trust me. What was the date?'

'The twentieth, I think.'

'Ted, what date was it in Holly End when she arrived?'

'December twentieth, too.'

'Same date, fifty years apart,' said Andy. 'Time in our world moves nine times faster than in yours, and it *just happens* to be exactly the same day?'

The boy whistled. 'Crumbs, that's a coincidence.'

'You're going to love this, then: as far as I can tell, everywhere, in every realm, at every possible level of the Cosmic Onion, or what our hosts call the 'Tellurean', right now, it is *exactly* the same day.'

'Yes,' protested Bex, 'but not everywhere has a December, do they? If these people have got twelve chakras, then they've probably got thirty-seven months or something.'

'I didn't say *date* – I said *day*.'

Bex's eyes suddenly widened. 'Oh my god!' She'd just realised what he was getting at.

'Yes.'

'The Winter Solstice!'

Ted was looking increasingly baffled. 'What's that got to do with the Professor?'

'He knows about it too. He's always known. Right from the moment he returned to Holly End after his travels with the Dobunni. They surely must have known about it long in advance: the Great Convocation. The first, and for all we know only time in all of the aeons of existence that the concentric layers of reality have aligned on one of the four great Gates of Life: the two solstices and equinoxes.

'The *ch'i* system of the cosmos is a circulatory system like that belonging to any living being. It ebbs and flows, like the tide, or breath, or a heartbeat. There's the moment of inflow, the moment of outflow, and the pause in between. The equinoxes are the pauses: spring, when life is just beginning to stir, and autumn, when it ceases, and ripeness turns to rot. The summer solstice is the absolute riot of heat and vitality, sex and drugs and rock-and-roll. Winter, on the other hand, Bex?'

She shuddered. 'You don't go into the Narrows at midwinter. You just don't. You could end up anywhere. And sometimes *things* come out. Walter once said that the midwinter solstice is like a cyclone in the Arctic ocean; it dredges up all kinds of black, frozen stuff from the bottom of the sea that'd be better off never seeing the light of day.'

'And this year it's midwinter everywhere,' Andy continued, 'in every world, all the solstices lining up, stacked up one on top of another like a huge, cosmic combination lock.'

'What does it open?' Ted was almost afraid to ask.

'The centre of everything. The absolute source of existence. The Navel of the World, the Great Void, the Throne of God. Our hosts call it the Omphalos. It's the place where all lines meet, and where all circles emerge.

There all the barrel-hoops are knit
There all the serpent-tails are bit
There all the gyres converge in one...'

Bex finished it for him: '*There all the planets drop in the sun.* Omphalos. Jesus. Do you think Walter knew?'

'I think he must have.'

'I still don't understand what that's got to do with the Professor,' protested Ted, who in any case was having great difficulty following what they were saying. He was tired, it was cold, and more importantly he'd been *winning*.

'Professor Barber,' said Andy, 'plans to take advantage of this alignment and punch a hole right down to the centre of existence, where he will inhabit and control the wellspring of creation itself. Very simply, he intends to make himself God.'

Incredibly, Bex started to giggle.

'Bex?' Ted was even more confused now. 'What's so funny?'

She couldn't answer. All she could do was press both fists against her mouth and apologise mutely to Andy with her eyes as irresistible waves of laughter crashed around inside her and leaked out from between her knuckles. 'I'm sorry!' she managed to gasp eventually. 'It's just… it's just…' she swallowed hard. 'I just got this mental image of him as the Great Onion God…' and she was off again, collapsed in the cushions, clutching herself and hooting. Somewhere in the middle of it he caught the phrase 'Lord of the Onion Rings'.

After a little while, she subsided, gasping for breath. 'I'm sorry,' she repeated, 'I couldn't help it. But just how mad does that sound? Even by our standards. He is insane, isn't he? He has to be. He couldn't possible do that, could he?'

Andy smiled mirthlessly. 'It doesn't matter. He believes he can, and he's going to kill thousands more people because of it. You haven't heard the half of it yet. 'Barber's problem has been in generating the amount of power needed to reach down that far. You know how big the stone circles are at places like Stonehenge and Carnac? Huge things, great earth-*ch'i* accumulators hundreds of yards across, built using massive granite pylons, some of them twenty tons apiece, the ritual focus for hundred of human souls – and even then only able to open a way through to the nearest realms, the ones where their 'spirit ancestors' lived. Even with the alignment of solstices working in Barber's favour, it's still a massive undertaking.

'Fortunately for him, when he returned from the Dobunni armed with everything he could learn, he found a nice big fully charged energy circle around Holly End, waiting for him.'

Ted sprang up in alarm. 'Then that means…!'

Andy held up a hand. 'Hold your horses, Tonto. It's too small. He pulled an entire Cotswold valley out of the world and it's *still* too small. Do you see the scale of the forces we're dealing with here? It's all just a matter of scale. He drains the life out of a single person to open or close a Narrow, like flicking a switch. He tries to kill me, but he can't, and desperate for more power, he drains the life out of Holly End – or at least he would have done, if you hadn't broken the stone.'

Ted sat back down, looking haunted. 'I remember,' he said. 'It was like he was, I don't know, calling it back in. That's the only way I can describe it.'

'Calling it back in,' mused Andy. 'Yes, that'd be a fair description. Like a big, psychic noose. Be that as it may, it's still too small. Too few souls. Good as a prototype, like I said, to test the principle and refine the mechanism, but just too small. Think bigger.'

'What's bigger than…' and Bex put her hands to her mouth again, but this time there was no laughter – just naked, shocked understanding. 'It's the closures, isn't it? He's going to turn the middle of Birmingham into another Holly End.' In her memory, she saw again a circle of death tightening across fields and hedgerows, draining the life out of everything it touched, and she tried to imagine it on a city-wide scale, washing over buildings and streets. *That*, she could believe. 'How big? How many people?'

'Roughly fifty square miles. Just over half a million souls. Enough life energy to punch down to the centre of everything and become the Winter King incarnate. Absolute winter, everywhere, forever.'

For long moments, it seemed as if the night itself had been shocked into silence. The sounds of the caral beneath them

– footfalls, shutters closing, murmured voices – seemed far away. By the outer watchfires, flames glinted on armour and the tips of javelins as the warband's sentries stood together in small groups, talking quietly. Alien constellations burned clear through an atmosphere devoid of any kind of pollution. Yet it seemed to Bex that she could see all of it – sky and earth, light and voices – overwhelmed by a blood-black tide of the same corrosion that was in her own soul, from one horizon to the other, in every world, with no hope of healing.

'It won't be winter,' she said, half to herself. 'It won't be anything that natural.' She shook herself. 'Right. So. Plan. Where do we go to put a stop to this? What's at the centre of this one? An Egyptian bloody pyramid?'

Andy told her.

She looked at him. 'You're kidding.'

'Nope.'

She blew out her cheeks in surprise. 'Well,' she said. 'Talk about having a twisted sense of humour.'

2

INTO THE CIRCLE

It sounded to Rosey more like *Ullo puhleezmun.*

Carling was all but buried in a thick coat, scarf, and hood, beneath which his eyes glittered. Despite the bulky clothing that hid his body, Rosey got the impression that there was something twisted and malformed about it. His strength, though, was prodigious.

'No need to run,' Carling said. *Nonee-durun.* 'Not here to hurt you. Far as I know, you're the only person who's tried to help me. *Person,* anyway.' He chuckled, a thick phlegmy sound. 'You stopped her killing me.'

A horrible suspicion made Rosey turn around and look back down the length of the bus. An elderly Indian woman sleeping, surrounded by Sainsbury's carrier bags, was their only other travelling companion – unless you counted the skavag squatting beside her, and the other one sniffing her shopping.

'Please,' Rosey begged, 'don't hurt anybody.'

Carling responded with a sound which might have been a laugh or a snort of derision. 'We don't do that any more.'

We?

'We'll kill, but we're not killers. Not for Barber, not anymore. Not for anyone. What he did to us – what he made us do – it was wrong. Sick. But we're better now.' *Beddanow.*

'Then why are you here?'

'Just got one question. The girl. Bex. Did she do it? Did she take out Barber's stone?'

'The honest truth is I don't know.' Rosey explained everything that had happened since the fall of Moon Grove, including Bex's disappearance into thin air on the road above Aston-sub-Edge. He spoke quickly, hoping to answer Carling's questions and get rid of him as soon as possible, and praying inwardly that the woman didn't wake up, or that the bus didn't stop for some innocent member of the public who fancied a ride up top. 'I don't know if she found the village,' he finished. 'I don't even know how we'd know if she'd done it or not.'

Carling made that guttural noise again which might have been a laugh. 'You know, for a policeman you're not very good at keeping track of people, are you?'

'Don't think it hasn't occurred to me.'

'Been watching you going round and round, all morning. We know what you're looking for. Piece of advice: don't.'

Rosey turned to face him squarely. Either he had wrapped the scarf particularly thickly, or there was something wrong with the lower half of his face. 'Tell me why I'm going to take your advice,' he replied sceptically.

Carling sighed, threw back his hood and started to unwind the scarf. 'We're not animals – not stupid. Barber never got that. We learned. We saw what was done, and we learned how to do it ourselves: how to steal life and how to give it back. I was dying – shit, I was *dead*, or as good as – and they gave themselves to me to bring me back. Not from kindness – they needed someone to lead them. Someone strong, to make sure nobody like Barber ever took advantage of them again. He pulled the strings, but I led the pack, you understand? Top dog. I had a right to expect it from them. So they fixed me up, gave me everything they could spare of themselves. Only…' he finished unwinding the scarf and grinned at Rosey, who shrank back involuntarily '…only it was a bit rough and ready, know what I mean?'

Rosey had never been a big fan of horror films, preferring good old-fashioned war movies over the strange and fantastical – it had all seemed a bit near the knuckle after rescuing baby Andy. But one he remembered, back when such things were called 'video nasties', was called *The Fly*, in which Jeff Goldblum managed to get his DNA mixed up with that of a common housefly. Typical rubbish. The monster at the end had been freakish enough but obviously a big puppet; it was the intermediate transformation stages which he remembered as being the most disturbing – when Goldblum was part human and part something else. All twitches and sweat and bits dropping off.

Carling was worse, probably because he was real and sitting next to him, in broad daylight, on a number eleven bus.

He was a mottled, badly-patched thing, hunched heavily within his coat and hoodie. Where the Fane had eroded him, the skavags had given him new flesh, but it sat ill at ease with the old: parts of him were leathery grey and lumpen, as if something were struggling to free itself from his human shape, and there were gaps where naked muscle and sinew worked. A twisted jawline crammed with too many teeth grinned at his evident shock.

'I know I'm pretty,' he said. 'The way I see it, this is what I always was – just now it's on the outside. You're going to take our advice, because we've got no reason to give it. You've got nothing we need and you're not a threat to us.

'Gates.' He tapped a gnarled finger at the map, which Rosey had tried unsuccessfully to hide between his knees once he'd realised who was sitting next to him. 'The Twelve Gates of Jerusalem. *Guarded* gates.'

'Guarded by what?'

'We won't go near them. When we were just me, we saw what came up for the poor buggers that got sacrificed. He laughed – laughed and said it was like going fishing.' Carling shuddered, and the skavags mewled their unease. 'Urdrog,' he growled and spat.

Urdrog?

'You think *we're* dangerous.' Carling wound the scarf back about his face and stood as the bus slowed towards it next stop. 'Policeman, you got no idea. You never have. Hell, it's your funeral.'

He clumped down the stairwell without another word, and when Rosey looked back for the skavags, they too had gone. He peered out of the window as the bus pulled away again, trying to catch one last glimpse, maybe to reassure himself that Carling had really gone, and thought he saw him – just another coat in the crowd.

He looked back at his map.

Skavags. Urdrog. The Twelve Gates of Jerusalem. *It's your funeral.* As if he could simply do that: let creatures like Carling wander freely in the parts of the city where people were weakest and most vulnerable. Might as well suggest he change the colour of his eyes. Rosey was no idiot; twenty years of unremarkable policing – with the one obvious exception – had taught him the virtue of being slow and deliberately careful. It was broad daylight; he was only going to inspect these places, and probably not even all of them, safely from the outside. If anything looked remotely dodgy, he'd be straight onto the real police.

He'd thought it all through very carefully.

***

At dawn the following day, Andy, Bex, Ted, Bruna and Edris rode out east and a little south, back up into the range of hills from which the caral had but lately descended. The day was clear but not particularly bright, with banks of cloud massing behind them and a biting north wind which promised snow before nightfall. Being unable to ride a horse, Andy clung behind the warrior, while Bex shared Bruna's mount. Ted had surprised everybody by climbing smoothly up into the saddle of an old roan mare and settling her with a few gentle clucks and pats on the neck, and in response to their questioning stares simply said, 'Farm boy,' as if they were all idiots.

Lady Holda had granted Andy and his companions an audience, despite the lateness of the hour, in the long chamber which comprised most of the caral's ground floor.

It served as both feasting hall and factory for the clan, whose history was told in brightly-worked tapestries hanging between many tall, narrow windows. At the room's heart, and occupying a good portion of it, four great looms were set in a square, powered by cogs and shafts which were linked to the wheels below and fed by bales and reels and skeins and bobbins of thread in every colour and texture imaginable; the whole being tended by wiever-maidens like the priestesses of an oracle. At one high end of the chamber Lady Holda took their audience while sitting amongst a group of her seamstresses on wide cushions, embellishing the plain cloth with gold thread and precious stones.

After considerable wrangling with Bex, Andy had agreed to simply express their gratitude for a hospitality which they could never hope to repay before taking their leave. He'd wanted to warn the Dobunni about the threat which Barber posed, but she was vehement that they say as little as possible. Even if they believed a single word, she argued, there was nothing they could do, and they'd most likely make things worse by insisting that Andy stay to explain himself before their king or high priest or whatever, and wasn't he supposed to be in a hurry?

So Andy, Bex and Ted took their leave of the Lady, who accepted their apologies graciously but nevertheless insisted on one final gift for them: the loan of horses for their journey, with her handmaiden Bruna to tend them and the warrior Edris to guard them.

'Yeah right,' Bex had muttered. 'She probably just wants to make sure we're *orf her lahnd*,' this last delivered in a thick yokel accent which made Ted scowl at her. She stuck her tongue out at him.

Things had been frosty between them ever since Ted had said goodbye to Hael. Andy had seen the two of them struggling over the language barrier and, realising that the new-found friends might never see each other again, offered to help. Rather than simply translating, which was what everybody had expected, he had placed his hand at the base of Ted's throat and made a series of odd swirling motions with his fingers, as if dialling an old-fashioned telephone. To his delight, Ted found that he and Hael could now understand each other perfectly. When Andy had offered the same thing to Bex, explaining that it was simply a minor adjustment of the *daath* chakra governing speech and communication, her reaction had been violently negative. Nobody, she insisted, was making any 'adjustments' to her, however minor.

Now, bouncing along uncomfortably behind Bruna as they picked their winding way up a thickly wooded escarpment, she called ahead to Andy: 'Where exactly is it that we're going, anyway?'

'I don't know,' he replied, and while she was hunting for precisely the right piece of abuse to hurl back at him, he added 'Which is to say, I've never been there, but I know it's up ahead.'

'What do you mean?'

'It's a lacuna.' Barber's word, she noted with unease. 'A thin place, where the skins of the world are close together, or the walls between them are weaker. Same thing. It's like a Narrow, just a lot older and deeper.'

'And you know this because?'

'Pins and needles, just here.' He placed a hand in the middle of his chest.

'Tell you what I can bloody feel,' she grumbled, shifting painfully. 'My arse. How can something be completely numb and in total agony at the same time?'

They reached a wider space in the zigzagging trail, and Ted urged his horse past hers. As he did so, he stuck out his tongue.

'Great comeback, farmer boy!' she retorted. Ted grinned and went on ahead.

Eventually, the slope evened out, and they found themselves at the edge of a wide upland which stretched as far as they could see, in swelling rises of russet moorgrass and black, winter-bare heather. Patches of unthawed snow clung in dips and northfacing hollows. During their climb, the clouds had overtaken them and slid past overhead like huge pieces of slate, seemingly near enough to touch.

Bex dropped from the saddle and landed gracefully on her back in a clump of heather, clutching her buttocks and swearing softly to herself.

Ted nudged Edris and pointed. 'Looks like we're stopping here for a bit.'

Edris frowned and cast a doubtful eye up at the clouds. 'Very well. But as brief as may be. Even without resting, we will be hard-pressed to reach the gate before this weather strikes us. I fear it will not be pretty.'

'Oh no she doesn't,' Andy declared and dismounted to stand over her. 'Come on, you.'

She squinted up at him. 'Five minutes. Just five. I'm knackered.'

He seemed to consider this. 'Fair enough – give you a hand up?' He reached down and helped her to her feet – but as her hand grasped his she felt a sudden wave of pins and needles sweep through her from feet to head. She gasped and staggered back, nearly falling again.

'Did you feel that?' she asked. Her hair seemed to be waving like sea anemones, and the pain in her back, buttocks and thighs had disappeared completely. 'What just happened?'

'What does it matter? Do you feel better?'

'Yes, but…'

'Well then. Come on. We have to get out of this weather.'

'No, wait.' She was staring at him suspiciously. 'Did you just do something to me?'

He sighed. Why did every conversation with her have to turn into an argument? 'Bex, I need you. Sorry if that sounds all Hallmark, but it's true. The plain fact is that I'm stronger with you than without you, and I'm going to need that if I'm going to deal with Barber. I'd love to have the luxury of time to fight with you over it, but I just don't. I'm done pissing around. I really am.'

'That doesn't give you the right to just reach into me and… and *adjust* me!'

'You're right. It doesn't. And if both of us get out of this alive, I'll buy you a big bunch of flowers and a puppy to show you how sorry I am. In the meantime, though? Try saving your hangups and your precious self-righteous anger for a time when the whole of creation isn't at stake, okay?' He turned away from her and remounted. To the rest of them he ordered: 'We do not rest and we do not stop until we reach that gate. Let's go.'

***

The first site Rosey chose was the only one labelled with more than those funny astrological-looking symbols; Dodd's name had been scribbled underneath in rounded, girlish handwriting which he assumed was Bex's. He guessed this meant that it was the last place she had seen her friend, and it seemed as good a place to start as any.

It turned out to be a construction site – or at least, one small, closed-off subdivision of the sprawling development around the new Queen Elizabeth Hospital complex in Harborne. A large wedge of semi-wooded brownfield land lying between the Worcester-Birmingham canal and Harborne Park Road had turned into acres of reinforced concrete, gravel dumps, portacabin villages and the I-beam skeletons of new buildings scratching at the sky. The core of the new hospital was complete, but Rosey knew that its own little suburbia of ancillary buildings would still take years to finish, if they ever were. The global recession had caused many small subcontractors to go to the wall, and despite the fact that even today, on Saturday, the main site was busy with cranes and concrete mixers, there were still areas like the one in front of him now which were padlocked and abandoned. Derelict before it was even finished, like a stillbirth.

If there were a 'gate' here, he failed to see it. If it was meant to be anything like the way Bex had disappeared then he couldn't understand how; there were no standing stones or empty gaps where they should have been. There weren't even any trees.

He did a circuit of the chainlink fence. All he could see was roughly poured concrete with the rusting ends of reinforcing struts sticking up out of it, and sheets of torn plastic flapping in the spaces between girders. It looked like it had been abandoned in a hurry and not that long ago: there were a few hardhats and tools lying around which no chippie would ever ordinarily leave behind, along with sodden clumps of paperwork. Other than that, nothing.

Then he saw the figure.

It was pale and emaciated, sitting cross-legged, with its back propped against an upright, either stoned or dead or simply just staring into space – and aside from being wrapped in shreds of plastic, it seemed to be entirely naked. Despite this, he couldn't tell if it was male or female, just that they were plainly starving to death and undoubtedly suffering from exposure.

'Hey!' he called. 'Are you okay there?'

The figure lifted its head slightly in his direction, but otherwise gave no sign of having heard him.

Old instinct and new caution warred within him. Everything that was humane in his temperament told him to get over that fence, get some clothes around that poor devil and call an ambulance – but he'd seen the world he thought he knew split open too many times in the last few days to trust anything. He settled for a compromise.

'I'm going to call for an ambulance, alright?' he called. He took out his mobile and dialled 999. If it were nothing more than a junky vagrant, he'd have done the right thing. If it were something more… well at least he hadn't been stupid enough to try to deal with it on his own.

The figure climbed painfully to its feet and began to stagger towards him. It clasped shreds of plastic tightly about itself, but Rosey could now see plainly that it was a young man. Or what was left of one. It paused and was seized with a spasm of tubercular coughing, which sounded like stones being stirred in a bucket, and said hoarsely: 'You called an ambulance.'

'You'll be alright, mate. Is it Dodd? They'll be here any second.'

The scarecrow which had once been Rodney Stokes made it as far as the chainlink fence and curled its fingers around the wire for support. This close, fresh horrors revealed themselves: the man appeared to have been tortured. Black burn-blisters punctuated his skin like a sadist's dot-to-dot puzzle, and there were at least two very deep stab wounds down the middle of his torso. That he was alive at all was a miracle. That he could *walk*…

'No point.' He coughed again, rattling and gluey.

'What do you mean, no…'

The spittle was black, and where it hit the wire, it fizzed like acid.

'I mean they won't be in time to save you,' said the Gatekeeper, and his flesh unravelled in dark streamers like some deep sea creature opening to feed.

3
URDROG

The *urdrog* were the oldest of all terrors. They came out of the frozen darkness at the beginning of time, as humanity fled before the ice and the circles of the world shrank about them with death on every side: by claw, by cold, and most of all by their own hand. Whether their own fears had created the urdrog or simply called them, none could say, certainly not the creatures themselves. They cared nothing for such questions, being as they were the purest embodiment of naked, predatory hunger. When the first cities rose and humanity began to lift itself out of superstition, riding the widening circles of the world out into the light of civilisation, the urdrog remained close to the centre of all things, in the uttermost depths of eternal winter. In the shadows of shadows.

Which is not to say that Man forgot them. They lurked in the lightless abysses of dreams and were worshipped with blood and fire as demons of one form or another by every race throughout the ages. Every so often, an unfortunate traveller's feet would lose him along forgotten roads worn down through the skins of the world; if he survived the lesser creatures like the skavags and their kin, he would certainly not escape the oldest of all terrors. The most he might hope for would be that the sight would drive him insane before he was killed.

Dodd's body was puppeted by a veined webwork of black sha, the death energy which was all that remained of his soul once Barber had plundered the rest of it to open a way for the thing which now emerged from inside him. Rosey watched it unfold from the boy, rooted immobile with shock.

He said it was like going fishing.

It was a bit like a wolf, but only in the sense that a Tyrannosaurus Rex is a bit like a budgerigar. He had an impression of too many eyes and *far* too many teeth, but these were the only features he could make out with any certainty, because the rest of it seemed blurred, as if his brain refused to acknowledge what his eyes were seeing, and when it howled the sound seemed to come from the middle of his own head.

Its claws shredded the chainlink like cobwebs.

It was funny really, thought Rosey. Here he'd been all these years trying to set the world to rights, and it had all been for nothing, because nothing could ever be right in a world with such things. He should have known that the moment he set foot inside the house on Tyler Road. He began to laugh as it drew itself up before him. Were those tails or tentacles? He was seized by a sudden appreciation of the absurdity of it all: his job, his marriage (such as it had been), his own kids, Andy, Bex… trying to make sense of any of it. The map – oh yes, especially the map! He laughed harder, tearing great chunks out of the map and cramming them into his mouth at the same time as tears rolled down his cheeks.

By the end, he was laughing so hard that he barely noticed when the urdrog began to eat him.

***

Bex was snapped out of her fugue state by the sound of Andy's screaming.

He fell from the back of Edris' horse, already convulsing before he hit the ground, and writhed amidst the twisted black stalks of heather, his fingers clawing at the sodden earth. His eyes were upturned, unseeing, and the sounds coming from his throat were of appalling, unremitting agony.

Order fell apart. The horses, spooked, reared and skittered sideways. Edris was able to bring Compa to hand with relative ease, but Bruna had to struggle to stop hers bolting off across the moor. Ted had been further ahead, but his mare was snorting and tossing her head, fighting his attempt to ride back.

Bex dismounted awkwardly, landing on her knees in the waterlogged moss, scrambling to reach Andy. Everybody seemed to be shouting at the same time. He was thrashing more wildly now, heels drumming up great gouts of black water, and scratching his arms and face badly on the vegetation. And screaming, screaming, screaming.

'What's wrong?' yelled Ted, badly scared. 'What's he doing?'

'Some evil possesses him,' Edris warned and unsheathed his sword.

'No!' Bex threw herself on the twisting figure, clutching the back of his head with both hands and burying his face in her shoulder as she tried to calm him, murmuring meaningless words and just holding him as the bucking subsided and his muffled screams became moans, and then whimpers, and finally silence, and they lay there like dying lovers.

***

'It was Penrose.' Andy's voice was hoarse, and his face was haggard. 'I felt him die.'

They'd moved to a slightly higher, less boggy rise of land, and Bruna was applying some kind of salve to his cuts.

Bex couldn't believe it. Penrose? 'How?'

Andy just shook his head, closing his eyes. 'Something terrible,' he whispered. 'Ancient, and – god – so *cold*. I don't know where or what happened. I suppose he must have been, I don't know…'

'Snooping.'

'Trying to help.'

'Same thing.'

'Of course Barber would have left the gates guarded, but what was that thing? Weren't skavags enough?' He laughed shortly. 'No, of course not. It's never enough. Why rule one world when you can rule them all? Why kill a village when you can kill an entire city? Jesus.'

'But I thought you knew what his plans are now?'

'I got a flash of the big picture, not the fine details. I was sort of being killed at the time; I wasn't concentrating too hard.'

Edris showed little sympathy. 'We shall all die if we do not find shelter before nightfall. If you are fit to ride, then we must do so at once.'

Bex helped him to his feet. Just before he remounted behind the Dobunni warrior, he turned back to her and said 'It ate him, Bex, while he was still alive. But it ate his mind first.'

***

Through veils of driving sleet, they saw the stone circle emerge. It was not the majestic Stonehenge-like edifice which Bex and Ted had expected. The stones were blunt nubs of weathered limestone, carved and pitted by the elements, and some were almost completely buried under thick tussocks of grass. They reminded her of the Kiftsgate stone. The ruins of several roundhouses stood a little way off, once inhabited by those who had looked after the gate; but they were not so long abandoned that they couldn't still provide shelter for travellers.

Ted and Bruna struggled to get a fire going in the lee of a wattle-and-daub wall, while the others inspected the stone circle cautiously from the outside.

'So there's a Narrow here?' Bex asked.

'A lacuna,' replied Andy, 'but yes.'

'Weird. It seems so open, I'm used to them being all tucked away and hidden.'

'Remember, the Narrows are just distorted fragments of one ley. This, on the other hand...' Andy was becoming restive and excitable again, his eyes darting everywhere as if either trying to take in everything at once or seeing things beyond her perception. '...this is a bruise in the flesh of the world. Inside, there the skins are so close they virtually overlap – these stones probably exist in dozens of worlds, including our own. Have you ever been to the Rollright Stones?'

She shook her head, shivering.

'This is them. An identical fixed point in parallel realities. Completely fantastic, isn't it?'

'But they're miles away from Birmingham! We'll never get back in time for the solstice!'

'Don't worry about it; we have all the time we need. This world is higher up than ours, not like Holly End; we could spend days here if we needed to and still get there in time. Like I said before, I can't do this on my own. I need you with me, and this is the nearest place thin enough to bring all of us through. Plus, I can make these things go wherever I want; you know that.'

'Bottom line: will it get us home?'

'Yes,' he said in tones of absolute certainty.

'Right then,' she nodded and went off to help the others.

All that remained of the roundhouses were circular stone walls about four feet high, faced on the inside with crumbling wattle and daub, and many jumbled rafters which had once supported the high, conical roofs. They were able to construct a flat-roofed semi-circular shelter which they waterproofed as best they could with some spare bedrolls – too low to stand up in, but with enough room for a fire. Despite his earlier reassurances, Andy chafed at the delay, but Edris was firm on the matter of seeing Bruna properly protected against the elements.

'It will soon be dark,' he said. 'Impossible to make the return journey, and death without shelter. Four of us will make short work of it, and then we may leave.'

Ted's eyes lit with excitement. 'You mean you're coming with us?'

'Indeed I am.'

'Topping!'

'Sorry, what do you mean 'us'?' Andy's scepticism was plain. 'There is no us. This is way too dangerous for kids. You're staying here with Bruna. We'll come back for you if everything goes okay and the world doesn't, you know, *end*.' He turned to Edris, and in more conciliatory tones said 'And I'm honoured, but that was never part of the arrangement. You were just supposed to escort us here, and you've done that. There's no need for you to come any further with us. Please, go back to your people.'

Edris' face was impassive in the gathering gloom. He had made little concession to the weather, and if he felt the cold didn't show it, despite the ice that had formed in his hair and moustache. Gold gleamed at his throat, and an unswerving resolve shone in his eye. Andy had a frightening sense of what it would be like to come up against this man in battle. 'As I understand it,' the Dobunni said, 'you go to fight a terrible evil which threatens not just your world but many others, my own included. To walk away from such a venture would be dishonourable in itself. To allow children and women to fight in my place...' he shook his head. 'It could not be borne.'

'It is true,' Bruna added. 'Edris is a warrior. This fate was woven for him.'

'But won't you get in trouble for not going back?' asked Ted.

'If I return, it will be with a glorious victory which honours my clan and my people.'

336

'And if we fail,' said Andy, 'there'll be nobody left alive to take him off their Christmas card list, anyway. Fair enough. You're in. Far be it from me to stand between a man with a big sword and his destiny. But you, Ted, are still staying here, and that's an order.'

'I'll follow you. You can't stop me.'

'Ted, please, listen. I'm responsible for you. I can't have that on my conscience. No offence, but I can't be watching out for you. Edris, please make him see sense.'

Edris looked across the flames of their small fire and saw Ted's eyes pleading silently with him. The boy had made a long journey uncomplaining, and if the stories about him were true, then he was both resourceful and brave. Edris himself had been prenticed to Iaran at much the same age. 'If there is to be fighting,' he said at length, 'then I will need a spear boy.'

'Yes! *Owl!*' Ted had leapt up in joy and cracked his head on a rafter.

'A *conscious* spear boy,' the big warrior added drily.

Andy admitted defeat. 'Fine then. Can we just go?'

Bruna watched them approach the stone circle. The sleety rain had diminished to a fine, drizzling mist which rendered them all but invisible after a few yards. She was gripped with the utter conviction that she would never see any of them again, and acting on an impulse which was most unlike her, she ran forward to the girl Bex – that strange, angry, funny creature – unfastening her wieve-maiden's brooch from her tunic.

'Here,' she said, pressing it into Bex's hand. 'Now wherever you go people will know that you have a clan. They will accord you respect.'

Bex laughed, grateful, after all, of Andy's 'adjustment', and that she could now understand her new friend. 'Somehow I doubt that. But thank you. Here…' she rummaged through her rucksack, and found a small cardboard packet. 'I know you're all into sewing and stuff.'

Bruna tried to refuse it, saying, 'This is a gift, not trade.'

'Honey, in my world everything's up for trade, know what I mean?'

Bruna relented. 'Then I will use it to make something beautiful, to honour you and your world.' Then it was Bruna's turn to be surprised as Bex crushed her in a sudden fierce hug.

'You get yourself a big warrior man and have lots of scary babies, okay?'

As they disappeared into the middle of the stone circle, Andy fell in beside Bex and said 'Did you just give her a motel sewing kit as a goodbye present?'

Bex sniffed at him. 'Might have done.'

'Cheapskate.'

'Just shut up and get us home, Dimension Boy.'

***

The Rollright Stones were little more than bleared shadows in the greater gloom. Andy led them on a curving route, skirting the centre of the circle, and hesitated for a moment, feeling for which gap would lead them home most quickly.

Beneath his feet, he felt the great slow song of the Omphalos, as of mills and factories labouring far underground, or the tumbling chambers of a lock the size of continents. He saw how the leys fed into it, and how the great rolling beat of its vast heart spread out in ripples which were the circles of the world. He saw them narrowing as they approached the centre, how very few of them were inhabited by anything even remotely human, and the countless worlds lying in between, which were barren of everything except nightmare. He saw how their energy was tapped, distorted and stolen by the needles of stone and concrete which humanity had been planting in the earth's flesh for tens of thousands of years, and how each individual was also a pinprick in this Pattern.

He could not see the centre. He suspected that to comprehend the Omphalos directly would be the same as possessing it, but what he could see was how very far away it was and the magnitude of the journey required to reach it. It could be done, there was no doubt about that, but it would be a journey measured in lifetimes. Barber was about to bludgeon his way through in a matter of hours.

He led them through the circle and out the other side.

Bex was surprised to find that the atmosphere lightened immediately and that they were following the line of a hedgerow which hadn't existed on the open moor. Looking back, she saw that the stones now seemed to be in a perfectly ordinary field bordered by trees, and there was even a small shed with brightly-lit windows where the roundhouses had been. It was her first glimpse of anything like normal civilisation for days, and she excitedly tried to draw their attention to it, but Andy pressed on urgently.

The hedgerow broadened and deepened, and he led them down, into the heart of it, with great, glossy holly-brakes overarching on either side so that the darkness enfolded them once more, despite the fact that outside it was almost full daylight. The vegetation became more tangled so that they had to fight their way through, and when they saw the first signs of rubbish and heard the blank white noise of city traffic, her heart leapt with the joy of homecoming.

Andy stumbled suddenly with a grunt, as if he'd tripped or crashed into some unseen obstacle.

'This is as far as we go,' he said, slightly dazed. 'No more Narrows into the city centre except the ones Barber has made – and they're guarded.' He shuddered, remembering the feeling of Penrose's death.

They had emerged from the undergrowth onto wasteland overlooking acres of sprawling construction site. Edris surveyed the scene with grim distaste. 'What is this place? Why do they tear at the earth so?'

'They're building a new hospital,' Bex explained.

The Dobunni warrior sniffed sceptically. 'How do your healers expect the sick to recover, living in such an open wound as this?'

'Don't ask me, mate,' she replied, 'I just work here.'

Their attention was soon drawn by the ambulance. It was parked several hundred yards away with its emergency lights dark and its back doors open, with a litter of medical equipment strewn across the ground. There was no sign of any paramedics, casualties, or even bystanders – but through a ragged hole torn in a chainlink fence, there was a telltale glimpse of paramedic green. And a lot of red.

'This is where Penrose died,' said Andy.

'I don't think he was the only one,' Bex whispered, trying not to look too closely and failing.

'We deal with the gates first. Just this one, just enough to screw up his network so he can't kill anybody. Whether that weakens him at all, I don't know. Whatever's guarding it is still there.'

The sound of police sirens rose in the distance.

'Whatever we're going to do,' said Bex, 'we'd better do it fast.'

Keeping as low as possible, they ran across the open ground and crouched alongside the ambulance. They could hear the CB radio crackling with the dispatcher's increasingly urgent pleas for a response – but from their new vantage point, they could see all too clearly that none of the crew would ever return that call.

Ted paled. Bex clapped both hands over her mouth to keep from screaming, or puking, or both. Even the normally stoic Edris paled at the wanton carnage before him. Andy, whose senses were wide open to the subtle energies in the vicinity, felt the backwash of terror and slaughter rebounding around him in waves. When the ambulance had disturbed the urdrog, its millennia-old hunger had been momentarily sated with

340

Penrose, and so it had simply played with them instead. There was nothing recognisably human in the abattoir it had left.

It was sitting in the middle of it all, watching them. It wore a human shape, but Andy could see instantly from its aura that…

'Jesus, DODD!' Bex shrieked and ran towards it.

4
HOLLY KING, OAK KING

'Bex, NO!' Andy grabbed for her, but the urdrog was appallingly quick, tearing at him with ice-black whiplashes of *sha*, forcing him to retreat instinctively into a protective shell even as it began to unfold itself. *It's wearing him like armour*, he thought, incredulous. *It's a creature of the deep; it can't survive at this level. It's wearing him like a fucking spacesuit. Barber, you bastard.*

Bex was yelling '*Dodd!*' at the top of her lungs and running, unable to see yet what he was. 'Get out! Get the fuck out of there!'

'Bex,' it smiled, shaking its head. 'You finally came to rescue me. Just a little too late, don't you think?'

She faltered, unsure. 'Uh…'

'You left me to die, bitch.' The sirens were a lot louder now, and Andy became aware of a radiant yellow glow intensifying just behind him. 'After everything I did for you. Everything I gave you. You ran away, and you let them put *this* inside of me.' The urdrog shrugged itself free from Dodd's shell and reared up over her tiny, stupefied figure. Jaws the size of rubbish skips drooled black vitriol, and a claw-tipped tentacle lashed down.

It was met by Edris' blade. With his other hand, he grabbed her by the scruff of her collar and flung her to one side, out of harm's way.

The Dobunni warrior was ablaze with light. The goldwork which adorned his body – the torc about his throat and the curvilinear bands on every part of every limb – was not just for decoration, Andy saw now, but each was an augur just like the chirurgeon's devices. They amplified his soul's energy, which was already substantially greater than anybody in this world, in burning lines of force which made it seem like there was a sun inside him leaking fire through fissures in his skin. Yet that was as nothing compared to the savage glee which burned in his face. This was what he was born for.

The urdrog was heavy and splay-limbed, with elbow-spurs curving up wickedly over its back, and the hackles which bristled from its steeply bunched shoulders were like a thicket of spears. Its eyes were set in multiple rows like a spider's but without the same alien blankness; these were roving, intent, and burned with intelligence. Behind the cage of its teeth writhed a host of tongues, each lined with more teeth in turn.

More crippling than the creature's physical attributes, however, was the overpowering terror which it generated. Daylight itself tried to shudder away from it, and from the howling void of its entry into the world, glacial blasts of wind ten-thousand years old tore at their clothes and minds. It stank of bodies piled high on the tundra under skies without hope of sunrise. It shrieked of running without hope of escape, of sobbing death under jaws whose hunger could never be satiated.

Andy, being unfixed, was able to evade the worst of this; the urdrog's malice slithered off him and was grounded, leaving frozen black scars on the concrete. Ted, brave though he was, lay curled in a foetal ball on the ground, the javelin that he had been given to care for discarded on the ground. Only Edris met it full on, burning it aside with the solar intensity of his own life energy as he ducked and parried and slashed.

'Go!' he roared. 'Destroy the gate! I will see to this abomination!' Despite his strength, he was being driven steadily back towards them, and for every wound he dealt he received half a dozen more. The creature gathered itself and bore down on him in a writhing tumult of darkness.

Andy dragged Bex to her feet. Defenceless, she'd caught the full force of the urdrog's psychic assault and now staggered, slack-jawed. Her hand was ice cold. Still, he hauled her past, towards the Narrow which the beast guarded, the gate that led directly to the centre of Barber's web. It hovered like heat-shimmer in a triangular gap between two crossed girders, and through it Andy could see the construction site on the other side superimposed with the gate's destination in the city centre.

Rebecca! the Urdrog raged in her head, and this time its voice was Shithead Dave's. *What do you think you're doing? You don't actually think you can stop this, do you? Get your arse back home right now and do not take another step nearer that gate, do you hear me, you silly little cunt! Do you hear me?!*

She heard.

A week ago she might have had the strength to tell that voice to go fuck itself, but she'd fought as hard as she could and run as far as it was possible to run, and it still hadn't been enough. She hadn't been able to save anybody, not really, and everything she'd done to avenge or atone for Dodd's death now turned out to be a sick joke. The notion that Andy might need her strength in some way was patently ridiculous. She heard what it said and knew it all to be true.

Andy felt the sag of her weight as she collapsed and turned to see that her aura had gone completely black – where he clutched her wrist, it crawled over his skin like worms.

'Bex, NO!'

For a moment he forgot everything. He forgot about Barber, about the Narrows, about gates and lacunae and Oak Kings and Holly Kings and the beating heart of the universe and every little piece of the insane weirdness that had overtaken his life since he'd met her; more than that, he forgot even the details of the mundane life that he had been fighting so desperately to regain: his flat, his job, his girlfriend. His entire world was the young woman lying at his feet, with her stricken eyes and her soul twisting like a pit of snakes trying to eat themselves. He wanted to reach into her, to take possession of her and burn out the darkness completely. And he could – she'd never forgive him, but he could fix that too. It would be so easy, given the luxury of just a little time.

But Edris was fighting with increased desperation to keep the urdrog at bay, and he was losing. Each wound that the creature inflicted was black with frostbite, and the augurs that empowered his flesh were damaged, some smashed completely, the brightness guttering from one part of his body to another, and the geometries of his aura were tattered like windswept constellations. The urdrog's jaws lashed down and enclosed his shield arm, crushing it, and he was driven to his knees with a broken cry, even as he stabbed at the head which was worrying at his mangled arm.

The creature suddenly reared back with howl of pain, a javelin buried deeply in one eye socket. Ted was on his feet, tottering but defiant.

'What are you waiting for?' he shouted at Andy. *'Go! GO!!'*

Andy paused only an instant longer to draw a burst of fresh strength from the earth before slinging Bex over his shoulders and leaping through the gate.

***

Barber stood on the roof of the Rotunda, a wide, circular platform nearly three hundred feet above Birmingham City centre. It comprised two levels: a lower, outer walkway, protected from the drop by a meter-high railing, surrounding the higher, topmost level which housed the building's lift machinery, air conditioning and other such service hardware. A little like a very wide, very flat top hat. From the centre of the top emerged the axle housing for a great metal boom which extended out to the building's circumference like a single clock hand, and from this was suspended its window cleaning and maintenance cradle. It was on top of this housing, barely a yard across, and unperturbed by the freezing easterly wind which had had touched nothing higher since the Ural Mountains in Russia, that Barber stood and looked down on the city whose death would furnish his passage to godhood.

He felt something like affection for it at the idea.

It might have been his imagination, but he fancied that he could also feel the building alive with energy even before he'd started. Like any form of power, it was generated from a conflict of opposites, and Brummies had a unique love-hate relationship with the Rotunda. It was both icon and eyesore, a property investor's folly whilst simultaneously the epitome of chic urban living, a visionary landmark and a concrete toilet roll. Ten people had died in it in 1974 when the IRA bombed the Mulberry Bush on the ground floor. It had been scheduled for demolition and then, when reprieved and refurbished, people had queued overnight for apartments which sold out in twenty minutes. He was standing where at one stage the designers had envisaged a large, flame-shaped sign which would have changed colour with the seasons and turned the building into a huge beacon. He was glad that it hadn't; sometimes you could push a metaphor too far.

Not that any of it would have made any difference. The necessary design elements had been well in hand even before the foundations had been laid in 1963 – it was amazing what could be done with a few well-placed bribes and the promise of government money to a city council desperate to reinvent itself in the bleak post-war decades.

The concrete core which served as the building's spine extended a good eighty feet further than anyone believed, deep into the sandstone ridge upon which the oldest parts of the city were built, and which in turn was the product of a geological fault line bisecting the whole city from southwest to north-east. Brummies. Their home was cut in two under their feet, and they didn't even know it. As fault lines went, it was a tiny thing – responsible for only three minor earthquakes in over a hundred years – but in geomantic terms, it represented a source of power which dwarfed anything that mankind had attempted to manipulate. Stonehenge, Nazca, the Pyramids – all were little more than scratches in the topsoil, pinpricks in the earth's skin. The Rotunda was plugged into its very bones, and Barber was plugged into the building. It was the only thing big enough to anchor him against the energies he would soon be commanding.

In the air below him, around the edge of the lower roof level, there shimmered twelve incandescent lacunae through which the *ch'i* of half a million souls would soon come streaming to him, powering his descent to the uttermost core of all reality: the Omphalos. And then – why, then the real work could begin.

Yes, an anchor was definitely needed when dealing with such absolutes. One slip – a moment's hesitation or the most minute miscalculation – could prove catastrophic.

There would be no miscalculation. It was unthinkable. This was the culmination of more than half a century's work – he'd long since lost track of exactly how long, having moved between different realms so often, and he couldn't even remember how old he was with any real accuracy. The reappearance of the Sumner boy at almost the last minute had shaken him a bit, he'd admit that, but he'd never been a real threat and was now either dead or hopelessly lost in the labyrinth of concentric worlds.

The policeman's death had been amusingly inevitable, given his stubborn insistence on making himself more significant than he had any right to be. His part had been played years ago, and he should have been content with that. Barber could feel that the urdrog which had dealt with Penrose remained agitated, but he wasn't unduly worried; it was to be expected that such guardians might draw attention to themselves. The local police would be dust and memories, along with the rest of the world, long before anybody had the faintest idea of what was happening.

Still. It was almost as if…

Then Andy and Bex fell through one of the lacunae and onto the Rotunda's lower roof.

5
THE OMPHALOS

'You surprise me, boy, and that's no mean feat.' Barber took in their travel-weary appearance and mud-splattered Dobunni cloaks. 'Although you appear to have had the more interesting time of it.'

'Save it,' Andy replied curtly, climbing to his feet. 'I'm not in the mood.'

'Indeed.' Barber scrutinised him narrowly. 'You've certainly – how can I say it – *deepened* since we last met. Why it seems like it was only yesterday.' He gave an ironic little laugh that made Andy want to burn the face off his skull.

'I haven't come to play games, you smug shit.'

'And why exactly is it that you have come, I wonder?' Barber's tone was still playful, but venom twitched underneath it like a cat's tail. 'For more answers to your pointless existence? Or to die properly like you failed to do last time? I warn you, I won't be so indulgent. Yesterday, you were a curiosity to me, a puzzle worth expending the energy on breaking apart to solve. Today, you're just not that interesting. If it's death you've come for, then you'll have to wait your turn, along with the rest of creation. Calling me names won't hasten the process.'

'Andy,' Bex whispered. She lay where she'd fallen, not bothering to get up. Her eyes were haunted. 'He's right. There's nothing we can do.'

Barber grinned viciously. 'Your little street slut seems to be all out of spunk. I rather fear the urdrog have that effect. It's a shame, though no doubt you'll be blaming me for the fact that you led her into its teeth.'

'Nope. Not at all. That one's on me. *So is this.*' And Andy struck at him with everything he had.

Barber might have closed and rechannelled the Narrows for his own purposes, but he could do nothing about the white-noise background roar of *ch'i* which emanated from all around: it was generated by the souls of the people living in the apartments below his feet, on the streets outside, and further into the city, the country, the entire world. It vibrated in the spaces between the atoms of the concrete around him and in the wood of Holda's caral, a thousand thousand worlds away. Her people called it wyrd; Laura's mother would have prayed to it as the Holy Spirit, and Barber had called it earth-ionosphere cavity resonances. Andy wasn't educated enough to give it a name, but he was unfixed, and he felt out as widely as possible to draw in as much as he could, as hard and as fast as he was able. He flung it in a raving blue-white blast of energy directly at the dark figure who laughed mockingly at him from above.

It never even reached him. Before it was halfway there, it splintered into a dozen weak streamers and was grounded harmlessly by the building's superstructure.

Three more times Andy hurled bolts of blue fire, with increasingly desperate ferocity, as Barber stood inviolate amidst a tempest of St Elmo's fire which crawled impotently about him and dissipated, leaving the air smelling scorched and Andy on his knees retching for breath.

'Well,' Barber commented, when the echoes had faded, and all that was left was the sound of ragged gasps and the indifferent wind singing in high-tension wires. 'That was imaginative, now wasn't it?'

'Barber,' he begged. 'Please. Don't do this.'

'NO!' Barber lashed back with sudden fury. 'You would have done well to beg before! You beg *nothing*, do you understand? *Nothing!'* With a savage sweep of one arm, he compelled Andy straight up into the air and held him suspended a dozen feet above the roof, as if examining an insect. Andy held his breath and waited for a killing stroke which never came.

'Neither will you provoke me with such tantrums,' Barber added coldly. 'You will die with everyone else at the appointed time.'

Midday crept closer, and the solstice was nearly upon them. Both men could feel its slow turning in worlds up and down the universe, the tumblers of a vast combination lock aligning with the inevitability of continental drift. Andy knew that if he looked with wide enough senses, he would be able to see, low down in the sky, an eastward-trailing arc of suns, each chasing the one before it to superimpose themselves on one another at the height of their journey. The *ch'i* energy of all creation trembled in its network of leys as it plunged towards crisis, a rollercoaster gathering speed at the bottom of the ride. The Narrowfolk were right to Lay Up at such a time. Sane people hid themselves away and prayed, in whatever form it took, for the roller coaster to continue upwards again, for light and life to return to the world, for the death of the Holly King. Only madmen stood up and actually opposed him. It was He that held Andy up to scrutiny, with eyes that promised everlasting winter.

'Then...' Andy struggled for breath against the vice-like force constricting his chest, 'then let me help you.'

'Andy, no!' Bex's voice was a hollow shell. She was sitting where he'd left her, propped against the lower roof's circumference rail, seemingly too weak to stand. Black tears were streaming down her cheeks and along her arms. It was a sight so profoundly and unexpectedly weird – even after everything so far – that he almost lost his resolve, because what could possibly be more important than answering her distress?

'You can't!' she begged. 'After everything he's done! After what you *said!* You can't do this – you can't *help* him!'

Barber's expression was amused and puzzled. 'Indeed, you can't possibly help me after all of this. Why?'

'Because you're about to cause the deaths of hundreds of thousands of innocent people, and it doesn't have to go that way. I can give you all the power you need without anybody having to die – you know I can; you've seen it. You've already proved that I can't hurt you – you would be in charge, you can direct the energy exactly how you like, just use me as a – as a *conduit.* Because I'm unfixed. It's how you made me.'

'You are nothing more than a failed experiment, boy. An aberration.'

'It doesn't matter – I am this because of what you did. What did you intend me for if not for this, or something like it? What better purpose can I serve now but to help fulfil your ambition?'

Bex was moaning softly, helplessly. He couldn't look at her.

Barber laughed in his face, and it was like being stabbed with icicles. 'And you think to sway me from my course just like that? The prodigal son returns to be reunited with his father at the time of his death? Please. There are no circles to be completed here and no Pattern to give meaning to this futile gesture. Oh yes, I know all about your anile philosophy, as if a grubby little suburban shop boy like you could ever come close to conceptualising the nature of the universe. There is no Pattern, no grain in the structure of the world. There never was one. There is only power. The coincidences which you set such store by were the power of your own unfixed nature manipulating reality around you. The only thing you have been following all these years has been yourself, like a dog mindlessly chasing its own tail. The people you wish to save are still doomed, ultimately.'

'Everybody is, ultimately. I can't do anything about that. I can't save the world – I understand that now. But if I can give a few of them one more day, or an hour, or whatever, that'll be enough for me.'

'You're absolutely certain of this. Of something. Finally. You will die knowing that you did what you could, hopeless though it was, and that will be enough for you.'

'Yes.'

'You're wrong. Dead wrong.'

'You'll never convince me of that. Think about it – what better way to destroy the world than by an act of hopeless self-sacrifice?'

This was met with glacial silence, and Andy knew that he had Barber then. Despite all his work over all those years, in the end he simply wasn't able to resist the delicious, black irony of it all.

At length Barber replied. 'So be it. But your arrogance in presuming to alter my plans, however marginally, will not go unpunished. I had intended to grant you the mercy of a swift death – you, and all the world. Now it will not be so. You will have your wish, and when I have obtained the Omphalos, you will remain by my side and watch in helpless despair as I unravel creation by slow degrees. The leys will die, and parents will watch as their children inherit a world incapable of sustaining them. In their desperation, they will unleash fire and plague on one another, and when the survivors emerge sobbing from the wreckage, they will find that chaos was nothing compared to what happens when the walls between the worlds themselves begin to fall and the urdrog come forth.

'But here, boy, I will allow your precious few thousand to remain protected and besieged, watching the world around them falling apart and knowing that it is all at their expense. What will they do, I wonder, as the world burns? Debauch themselves in guilt? Or try to follow your fine example and save others? What fun it will be for you to watch.

'At the last, these walls will fall too, and your special few will be devoured by the darkness, cursing your name for having inflicted this on them, and when it is just you and I alone in the void, the last thing you will do before I snuff out your soul will be to tell me whether you thought that was *enough* for you.'

Then the solstices converged, the suns shone as one at their height, and Bex hid her face as Barber used Andy to tear the life-energy out of the world.

He didn't require the use of needles. They were beyond such things now. Barber's meridian points burst into life all over his body, and from them lanced out thousands of glowing tendrils which found their counterparts in Andy's flesh and began to feed.

The energy drain was manageable at first, but it increased exponentially, threatening to tear the very fibres of his body apart. The seven multipetalled hubs of Barber's chakras spun faster and brighter as they became supercharged with plundered *ch'i*. The Rotunda, and its interconnected network of lethal gates whose creation had taken such a toll of years and lives, remained mercifully inert as Barber took all the energy he required through Andy instead, fashioned it anew, and directed it out again, straight at the low-hanging midwinter sun. At this time, as at no other, the circles of the world overlapped so closely that the barriers between them were whisper-thin, and Barber's stolen power began to burn through them one after another.

Gradually, the sun darkened. In the bright washed-out blue of the sky, a black hole irised open, as if the sun had become an enormous eye.

Andy struggled to meet the demands being placed on his system. When he'd been attacked by the dog and the skavags, his body had reacted instinctively, drawing a relatively tiny amount of energy from his immediate surroundings to deliver a single sharp retaliatory slap, and then afterwards to heal himself. At Holly End, he'd been on the receiving end and dumping into the earth the energy with which Barber had been trying to fry his brain. Even the bolts of raw earth-

ch'i which he'd thrown at Barber just now had been simple, short-lived exercises of power. This, however, was something entirely different. Although the amount of energy which Barber demanded of him – which half a million souls would have satisfied – was an infinitesimally small drain on the earth's resources – the question was whether or not a single human being could channel it all and survive. He felt stretched to the point of invisibility – a mannequin of molten glass with neon tubes for bones, sparks spitting from the marrow.

The hole in the sun quickly spread out to its full circumference, and then further, filling half the sky, and in another of those eye-watering twists of perspective, it wasn't far away in the heavens but right beside them: a wind-blown tunnel wide enough for a man to step into, had it been stable enough.

It twisted and whiplashed unpredictably as reality fought the power which was tearing it open, but in brief moments of calm, there could be glimpsed at its furthest end – the points where all parallel lines converged, and from which all concentric circles spread – the glint of something golden.

The Omphalos.

He couldn't see it clearly. He knew instinctively that to comprehend it fully would be the same as possessing it, or inhabiting it, but through the buffeting squalls of energy which wracked his body, he could hear it singing. It was the music that underlay the whine of blood in the ear, or rain on endless plains of grass, or the white noise of city traffic. It was wordless, mindless, not the voice of God or anything with a sentient purpose. It demanded and promised nothing. It didn't ask to be rescued or worshipped or obeyed or possessed; it didn't offer answers or healing or hope or love. It was nothing more or less than the song of all life, and the pulse of light at its centre was a human heartbeat. It made his every cell and nerve-ending thrill in resonant sympathy, and for the first time in as long as he could remember, he felt the glorious, expansive relief of having nothing expected of him. There was no destiny. Barber was right – there wasn't even any Pattern to follow or ignore. The uncertainties of his future were as irrelevant as the accidental circumstances of his past. There was only the glorious, singing Now, in which he was unfixed and free at last of considerations of what he was supposed to do next, because there was nothing and nobody to suppose anything about him except himself.

As revelations went, he was afraid that it was too little and too late, because Barber had stepped into the tunnel. He drove his copper staff into the threshold to anchor it and rammed Andy's power into the fluctuating portal to subdue its wild contortions. From the sweat pouring down his face and the set rigidity of his limbs, Andy saw that it was costing him an inhuman level of control.

A thin hope began to form in what little of his mind could still think coherently. Andy had felt a shadow of that monstrous arrogance on the moor, when he'd goosed Bex to her feet, knowing that it would offend her but not caring. If that had come to him through their connection at the Kiftsgate stone, what, he wondered, had been exchanged?

Less than a hope – little more than an uncertainty. He had almost no time to act because the pulse of the Omphalos was slowing to match Barber's heartbeat, and the umbilical tunnel through reality was steadying with each measured footstep which Barber took. He was already halfway there.

'Barber!' he shouted. 'You know what your problem is? You can't leave anything to chance! You had to know, and you had to get into my head to do it. You had to be *certain*, didn't you?'

Unable to spare him a fraction of his concentration, Barber continued steadily, half a dozen paces from the Omphalos, its light gilding his fingertips. Five paces.

'So here's that back at you: I know you're going to fail, and I'm going to enjoy watching it, you arrogant shit. You know how I know?'

Four paces. Three.

'Because you're not up to this! You never were!' Andy's voice was hoarse and ragged with desperation, trying to pluck at the tiny worm of uncertainty which he prayed that Barber had picked up from him in return. 'How could you ever think this would work? I mean really?' All the questions that he'd never been able to answer about himself. *What if you're unfixed too?'*

Two.

Barber hesitated. He frowned slightly.

For a fraction of a second he lost control over the energy flow, and the tunnel spasmed in violent reaction. The infinitely thin layers of reality which comprised its walls scissored together in every direction simultaneously, slicing him apart so suddenly and completely that it seemed like he'd simply exploded in a cloud of red mist.

The lacunae in the air around the Rotunda's roof winked out of existence, and the gates to which they had been linked imploded, shattering windows all down the building's length and creating in turn a scribbled chain-reaction as the suddenly untethered Narrows became free to find their original courses, like hundreds of miniature versions of the Ryknild Street ley. All over the city, there were stuttering power cuts and electrical surges, scores of minor road accidents as traffic lights went haywire, small earth-tremors localised on single streets or even individual houses, lights in the sky, random snow flurries, and eruptions of static electricity. Deep within the sandstone bed-rock of the Birmingham Fault, the Rotunda's concrete-sheathed copper core split along its length, propagating a series of seismic shocks which were detected as far away as Cardiff. They caused serious damage to most of New Street Station's platforms and subsequent chaos on the national rail network from London to Glasgow. Ripples spreading ever outward. However, none of this was as inexplicable as the appearance of an unpredicted solar eclipse over the city.

Ted saw it as he cradled Edris' body. The urdrog had been sucked back into the collapsing gate, but he couldn't move the big warrior, and he didn't know how to stop the lights in his torc and amulets from guttering towards extinction, so he simply held him and moaned, 'Please, oh please,' over and over again to the hole in the sky.

Laura Bishop saw it from her mother's conservatory as she sat with her lunch and the property lettings pages of the local paper open in front of her. It occurred to her to wonder whether Andy could see the eclipse from wherever he was – but she found, with a kind of guilty relief – that she didn't actually care.

Bruna watched it gleaming darkly between the stones of the Rollright Circle, and, unsure of what it portended, huddled closer to her fire.

A man in expensive Italian shoes wrapped his car around a lamppost when his hands-free exploded with a shriek of feedback and deafened him permanently on that side.

And when the lights went out in the Tap and Spile, Aston Stirchley the Third raised his pint of Bombardier to the sky in salute and simply said 'Get in there, my son.'

Meanwhile, the Omphalos hung in the centre of the black-hole sun: golden, singing, inviolate.

***

'Mine,' said Andy, reaching out his hand.

And after all, why not?

Didn't he deserve it, after everything he'd been through? After everything that had been done to him and to others on his behalf? Wasn't he morally obliged to make amends, to repair the damage now that the power to do so was within his reach?

He could find the scattered communities of Moon Grove and Holly End, bring them back together and find them new homes. He could repair the Narrows, and heal the wounds inflicted on the nature of his own world – *all* worlds. He didn't subscribe to the notion that such power was too much for a mere mortal to cope with. Absolute power corrupts absolutely? Why? Who was to decide what he did or did not deserve? He'd had nothing asked of him, been promised nothing, expected no reward, and earned no punishment. Everything he'd done had been motivated by necessity and the promptings of his own conscience, and if that had been enough to save the world, then it should be enough now.

The earth-*ch'i* continued to pour through him, but it was his to control now, and he knew better than to try and dominate it as Barber had done. He was unfixed; he would slide through the gaps and take by stealth what his creator could not by force.

Then Bex was in front of him – he cursed himself for having completely overlooked her – throwing a double handful of black vitriol in his face, and he went down, blinded and screaming.

'...never!...' she gasped, '...kill you first...' and fell where he lay writhing.

With his concentration broken, the earth-chi slipped from his control. The moment of the solstice passed, and the hole in the sun closed irrevocably, leaving them both stark on the empty rooftop, under the pale midwinter sun.

6

THE LAST GATE

Three days later, in the early evening of Christmas Eve, a perfectly ordinary terraced house in Ladywood was burgled in reverse.

Which is to say, the elfin young woman in multilayered clothes who let herself in easily through the back door didn't live there, but she didn't have to break any windows this time and wasn't there to steal anything.

In a very real sense she wasn't actually there at all. The couple arguing in the kitchen certainly didn't notice her as she squeezed between them, except possibly as a sudden draught of cold air or a flicker of shadow on the wall.

The teenaged boy in the living room – slumped on the sofa in his hoodie watching *Deal or No Deal* with sullen detachment (new DVD player, she noted. That was quick) didn't notice as she passed between him and the screen and rummaged in the untidy heap of DVD cases lying on the floor.

That done, she turned and spent a long moment considering him, listening to the argument coming from the kitchen. Something about where did *he* think the money was going to come from and why didn't *she* just trust him for once. The boy appeared as insensible to the shouting as he was to her presence. He was pale, his eyes dark with shadows and red-rimmed.

She went upstairs to find his room. No surprises here. The detritus of neglect: unwashed laundry, empty bottles, fag-ends, porn. The smell of a long-untended zoo cage. She left on his pillow the other thing which she'd brought with her, but as she opened the door to leave she found a tiny, solemn-faced girl on the landing, staring straight at her.

Bex smiled. She brought herself fully forward so that the girl could see her properly, crouched down, winked, and placed a finger to her lips: *shh*.

The girl copied her, *shh*, and gave a wan smile of her own.

Bex left the house.

There were two reasons why six-year old Millie Chadwick never got around to telling her mummy and daddy about the strange woman in the hall. First, the very next day her big brother Glenn disappeared and wasn't seen for a week, which caused all sorts of shouting and crying and policemen coming in and out, and in all of this nobody took much notice of little Millie (at least, less notice than was normally the case) – especially when Glenn came home again with a carrier bag of sweets and a battered A-to-Z, saying that he'd only just taken a shortcut down the high street and what was the fuss about?

The other reason was that she just plain forgot, in her own private excitement that Father Christmas had brought back her favourite Spongebob Squarepants DVD.

***

The meeting place was a narrow country lane hidden between high banks and overarched with a bare latticework of hazel and hawthorn. In the summer, this would be a green tunnel, strewn with white sprays of cow parsley. It was still too early in the new year for any sign of spring, but those with the senses for such things could feel the slow slackening of winter's torpor, like the pause of an in-drawn breath. Meanwhile, ash trees raised their black-budded antlers protectively over the sleeping hedgerows as the grey January sky sieved itself through them in a fine, clean rain.

The throaty growl of an old diesel engine built rapidly in the silence, and in the lane appeared a campervan exactly the same shade of orange as an old penguin paperback, except where it was mudspattered up the wheel arches. Its headlights were owlish in the half-light.

Behind it followed a motley retinue of similarly dishevelled vehicles: caravans, minibuses, ordinary cars with roof-racks piled high.

Rabbit John braked the camper to a halt and peered out through the windscreen. 'Well,' he said to the man sitting next to him, 'this is the place if you say it is, but I'm blowed if I can see anything.' He might have added something about useless Jerry headlights, but there was a tense expectancy in the van which hushed him without words.

'Don't worry,' Andy replied. 'It's here.' He turned to look over his shoulder. 'How's our patient doing?'

Edris lay full length on one of the camper's bunk beds, bandaged in a dozen places. He propped himself up on one elbow. 'I mend,' was all he replied.

'Eating us out of house and home, is how he's doing,' complained Kerrie the Kook, sitting beside him. 'The sooner we're shot of him, the better.'

Andy grinned. It wasn't surprising. The Dobunni warrior must be finding it hard to regain his strength in their comparatively lacklustre world. Kerrie, on the other hand, was as fit and cantankerous as ever, with little if any outward sign of the battles she had fought. He wished he could say the same for the rest of them.

He let himself out of the Shed and walked back to where the other members of their small convoy were stretching their legs. Bex ran up, clamped herself to him, and gazed up in mock adoration. 'When am I getting my van back?' she demanded.

'Soon,' he laughed and kissed her. 'One piece of unfinished business first.'

'We've got more than enough of those, alright.'

Looking at the collection of individuals milling around the vehicles, he couldn't help but agree. In the weeks of wandering since Barber's defeat, they'd collected a few refugees of the chaos – but precious few. Most of the Holly End villagers had been picked up by the police and subsumed into the existing welfare system – Ted included, once they'd found his parents and Sam living in a shabby, council-funded bed-and-breakfast. It had seemed a poor reward for everything they'd been through, but Andy supposed that at least they were together. Some, like Rabbit John, had taken one look at the modern world and decided to chance the open road instead. Many of the Narrowfolk from Moon Grove had dispersed amongst the other squats and shelters in the city, but again, there were a handful for whom the return to normality was impossible.

And here they were, following him, hoping that he could somehow make it right. Strangely, he found that the burden of responsibility didn't terrify him half as much as he'd thought it would.

Slow hoofbeats distantly in the road ahead, approaching.

What looked for all the world like an old-fashioned gypsy caravan with a thatched roof rounded the corner, driven by a tall woman in a hooded robe, and drawn by a pair of white horses whose tack flashed with horse-brasses. Its sloping sides and steep eaves were elaborately carved and coloured, and the thatching was fashioned into the shapes of wheels, stars, and prancing horses. It gleamed, untouched by the dirt of travel, and seemed more real than its surroundings.

Lady Holda drew her team to a halt and smiled down at the travellers. 'You have been busy, by all accounts,' she said.

'Just a bit,' agreed Andy. 'Sorry it took us so long to get to you. Time moves more slowly for us here.'

'It has been almost a year for my people; soon we will be

preparing to move on from our summer pastures. But time is a burden only to the idle, as they say, so have no fear. The hour was well kept.'

'Thank you, Lady.'

'I do have a pressing need for the member of my warband whom you keep, however.'

'Of course.'

Edris was helped out of the campervan but stood unaided before his mistress.

'Warrior,' she said to him, 'there will be a time and a place to praise your bravery fittingly. For now, the best gift I can give you is simply *home*.' She turned to Andy and Bex 'And what of you? Where is your home? It seems to me that this world offers little enough cheer to the needy – will you not come to live in mine? You would be accorded the respect which your actions have earned, and it would honour me greatly.'

Andy declined as graciously as he could. 'A lot of our friends are still missing,' he explained. 'I couldn't rest comfortably knowing that they were still stuck here somewhere, living hand to mouth.'

'I understand.'

They parted warmly, each returning in the direction that they had come.

But later that year, at the height of summer, a much larger – but still just as motley – collection of vehicles wound its slow way along that road and stopped in the same place. Because the circles of the world may be very wide, but they are still just circles, and on an island eventually even the most long-journeyed of travellers ends up retracing their footsteps.

There was an old wooden gate in the hedgerow which nobody had noticed before, for the simple reason that it hadn't been there until just now, and a bright field of yellow grass beyond, beneath a sky wider and bluer than even England on a June morning can boast. A young man got out and opened it, watching as the last of his people passed through, and then carefully closed it behind him.

Then the gate faded back into forgetfulness, and their tracks disappeared into the long summer grass.

ACKNOWLEDGMENTS

I am indebted to Nigel Pennick and Paul Devereux for 'Lines on the Landscape', Tom Graves for 'Needles of Stone', and of course Alfred Watkins for his immortal 'The Old Straight Track'. Thanks too must go to everybody who has ever been a member of Thethem, for teaching me that no plot survives an encounter with its characters, and Anna from Snowbooks for her patience while I fumbled through the process of getting this story out of the Narrows in my own head.

About the Author

James Brogden was born in Manchester in 1969 and teaches English and Media Studies at Bromsgrove School, in Worcestershire. He is also a regular contributor to the British Film Institute's annual Film and Media conferences, delivering workshops in online education, and is a qualified mountain expedition leader who enjoys exploring Britain's ancient and mythical landscapes. He lives in Bromsgrove with his wife, two daughters, and far too much Lego. *The Narrows* is his first novel.